T

I looked forward to this new foreign country as the train rattled
through France before stopping at the frontier where another
train on a different gauge lay waiting. It was boiling hot; people
went out on the platform to drink water from a fountain there.
Somewhere on the left lay the sea which I had seen sparkling
before the frontier tunnel. Now I was really alone, and excited,
and felt the lift of spirits which the south was always to give me.
My free new life lay waiting, I thought, and one day, I was
almost sure, happiness lay waiting for me too.

June Barraclough was born in Yorkshire. After completing a
BA (Hons) degree at Somerville College, Oxford, she went on
to study for a postgraduate certificate in education at the
University of London. June has written five novels and a
collection of writings. *Time Will Tell* reflects both her interest in
family history and her Yorkshire background. She has two
children and lives in Blackheath, London.

Time Will Tell

June Barraclough

Woman's Weekly Fiction

A Woman's Weekly Paperback
TIME WILL TELL

First published in Great Britain 1992
by Robert Hale Ltd
This edition published 1995
by Woman's Weekly
in association with Mandarin Paperbacks
an imprint of Reed Consumer Books Ltd
Michelin House, 81 Fulham Road, London SW3 6RB
and Auckland, Melbourne, Singapore and Toronto

Copyright © June Barraclough 1992
The author has asserted her moral rights

A CIP catalogue record for this title
is available from the British Library
ISBN 1 86056 025 3

Printed and bound by
HarperCollins Manufacturing, Glasgow

This book is sold subject to the condition that it shall not, by way of
trade or otherwise, be lent, resold, hired out, or otherwise circulated
without the publisher's prior consent in any form of binding or cover
other than that in which it is published and without a similar condition
being imposed on the subsequent purchaser.

Part One

1 Genesis

My best friend Susan Marriott was born like myself in the village of Eastcliff in Yorkshire in the mid-1930s. Lally Cecil, who came to live in Eastcliff when I was about ten was born in London, but her grandmother, Mrs Fortescue, lived in Eastcliff at The Laurels. Miriam Jacobs' family had come to the village a little before Lally did. Miriam's father was a jeweller in Leeds and they lived in an eighteenth-century house near what we called the Snicket. The boys, who later joined our group of friends, were all Eastcliffians born and bred: Nick Varley, and Tom Cooper, and Gabriel Benson – the son of Rector Benson of Sholey church to the north of our village.

My parents were Dick and Madeline Gibson who had been married at Eastcliff Congregational church where two years later I was christened Gillian Elizabeth. They were both teachers at a junior school in a nearby village. Although our village was only two or three miles away from small industrial towns it had, and has still, hundreds-of-years-old country lanes with pretty walks to woods where trees grow down the sides of narrow valleys watered by rushing brown becks, and farms with cows, and fields for hay-making. The older houses in the village are of stone, quarried in the delfs a mile or two away; some of them are 'Halls', built in the seventeenth century or earlier, with mullioned windows; and several of the tiniest cottages are also very old. There are also two or three grand eighteenth-century mansions where the most successful of the city mill-owners once lived, the grandest of them a ruin.

When the railway came to the village in 1855 over a splendid Victorian viaduct, straddling a broader valley, new houses were built for the middling classes, and in our own century other 'avenues' were built off the main roads that had once been turnpikes. These homes had back gardens that had once been orchards and none was far from our famous golf-links. Eastcliff was part of the ancient township of Lightholme which boasted an Elizabethan grammar school. One of its churches, now a ruin but still standing in my childhood, was where a chapelry belonging to the largest parish in England had stood for hundreds of years. It had a handsome rotunda and dome in a field of grassy graves, still used for burials. My parents' chapel looked like a church for it had a spire and dominated the view of the village from the distance. But the church that was even more of a landmark since it stood on a high ridge was where Gabriel's father was Rector. If you were travelling to Eastcliff by train you saw it high in the distance as you crossed the viaduct and as it was to your west it was often against the gold and pink clouds of a Pennine sunset.

We all played in the fields and woods and attended the long, low-built mock Gothic village school only a stone's throw away from most of our homes. It adjoined a field where sheep had once roamed and where we played cricket on long summer evenings, and had our Guy Fawkes bonfire in November. I remember that all the railings around the school and the churches were taken away in the war to be melted down, but the gardens and grounds and the field were always clean and tidy.

Like many old villages in the Riding ours was a hilltop one and the site of an ancient settlement. We were 400 feet above sea level and rather chilly in winter. The best place to get warm was the fire in the railway waiting-room. The station dealt efficiently with the punctually arriving steam trains from the city which you could hear chuffing along when you were in the school classrooms. If you were coming back from some treat in town you climbed steps to a wooden bridge and then walked down a slight incline on cobblestones to the road, passing under a wrought-iron arc with a lantern shining in its centre on winter nights, before you crossed the quiet but never entirely lonely road.

One row of shops catered for most of our needs. Susan's father, Mr Marriott, had the newsagent's and sweetshop. He was very hardworking. It was said he had started life in a 'back to back'.

I would call for Susan in the holidays or at weekends and we would explore one of the valleys or walk over to the woods or go to the public library. If it were winter we might be sledging on the slope of our 'Stray', a piece of common land dedicated to the dead of the Great War.

In the second war, 'our' war, a scatter of bombs fell one autumn on a ploughed field a mile away and just once or twice there had been shepherdings to a dank air-raid shelter dug hastily in the school field. My sister Rosemary and I found it exciting rather than frightening to be walking down our avenue in the moonlight, warm coats over our 'siren suits', and 'shelter boots' on our feet, pixie hoods on our heads.

My very respectable parents approved of my friend Susan, approved less perhaps of Nick Varley and Tom Cooper whose parents were in business – silk-spinning and wire-drawing – and almost as well off as Lally's grandmother or Miriam's successful father. *He* was a Socialist, but had more money than my own hard-working parents were ever likely to make. I had known Tom Cooper at the village school; Nick had gone away to a prep school at eight years old and returned to be educated in Eastcliff only when his father's profits suddenly plummeted. Then Nick went with the other two boys to the grammar school. We girls saw all three of them around the village, but did not take much notice of them till we were about sixteen, and by that time we ourselves had been five years at Greenfield Girls' High in a neighbouring town.

It had been at our last term at the village school before we went off to Greenfield that Lalage Cecil had joined us one summer morning just after the end of the war. She was led into our classroom by Mr Hammond, our headmaster, and we all looked up, glad of a diversion.

'You can sit by Susan,' said Mr Hammond, and Lalage was ushered into the empty half of a double desk, empty since one of the refugees from the Channel Islands had decided to return to Alderney. They never allowed me to sit next to Susan because I chattered too much.

3

We stole several glances in the new girl's direction as she sat there quietly. You could tell from the place the desk reached her body that she would be tall. Her clothes were very nice, a plaid skirt and fawn jumper and polished lace-up shoes, and she smelled of something like lavender. She wore her long, silvery-blonde hair down her back, not in plaits like girls with long hair did in those days. When I returned to my desk after going up to the waste-paper basket to sharpen my pencil, I saw the eyes in the new arrival's oval face when she looked up from the exercise book Miss Haythornthwaite had given her to do sums in. They were beautiful – green, like gooseberries. Truly green eyes were unusual, I thought. Lalage's complexion was like cream, with a few tiny freckles on the bridge of her nose, and her hands were the same colour, with pearly-looking nails, the flesh round them smooth, neither plump nor skinny. I thought Lalage was the most beautiful little girl I had ever seen and Susan agreed with me when we discussed it later.

At playtime Susan and I took her under our wing and Lalage consented to drink her milk sitting next to us on the low wall of the school field. She did not say much except to spell her name when asked, and then: 'But they always call me Lally,' she said. When she did speak she did not have the accent most of the other children had, but a sort of mixture of Scots and something else indefinable. I was always fascinated by accents. She replied in a clear voice when asked a question by Miss Haythornthwaite. I felt rather embarrassed, for Lalage spoke composedly as though she were having a private conversation with an adult with nobody else in the room. Other less charitable children might find this peculiar, might bully her. We learned later that she had come to live with her grandmother, Mrs Fortescue, at The Laurels for good, and that she had been intended for the local private school. But that school was undergoing extension and refurbishment and had broken up early, and Lally's grandmother had wanted her to meet other children straight away, so to our village school she had been sent.

That first day with us must have been a bit of an ordeal for Lally, but she did not seem too overcome. When I thought about it years later I considered she had shown a remarkable passivity, a quality perhaps acquired through the many

4

changes she had already had in her life. We pieced Lalage's early years together bit by bit for she never spoke of them much.

As I've already said, Lally accompanied me and Miriam and Susan to the High School for Girls in the town in the autumn. The 'eleven plus' had just been introduced, but I don't believe Lally had sat it; in those days you could still pay to go to the grammar school if you were not clever.

I have not said much about Miriam Jacobs. She was a strange girl, tall and bony, with dark brown hair which she swept back from her face and tied with a black velvet ribbon behind her ears. She had a cleft in her chin, a long neck, a wide brow and widely-spaced but deep-set eyes. I thought there was always a rather stony expression in those eyes, but she gave the appearance of being *very* clever – but not superficially quick in the way I was. When she had first come to the village school she had been bullied quite a lot, maybe on account of her unfriendly stare and loud, flat voice, but she appeared not to notice. She was a very serious-minded girl and I think she was also unaware of the rather lofty way she had of looking at people when she spoke to them. When actually taxed with standoffishness or swank she tried to compensate with a flurry of conversation, but I could tell she was not really interested in listening to others unless they happened to say something which connected with thoughts of her own. She did not know how to talk to people who did not enjoy listening to monologues. We made allowances, Susan and I, for she was interesting about things she had read – Greek myths and articles from the *National Geographic* and things about science and politics from magazines of her father's – different books from the ones I devoured. I thought that Miriam had a high opinion of herself. I suppose I was also quite self-confident too at that age – but I believed myself rather more popular than Miriam.

'Lalage-rhymed-with-allergy', we always called 'Lally', as she had asked us to, and whether Lally ever understood what Miriam was going on about nobody knew, for Lally hardly read at all. I taxed her with this once, rather bossily, and made her read *Little Women* which had been my own early Bible, and I'd grown up with it. Lally was to read a chapter a night and then report to the rest of us at the next meeting of the 'literary society' Susan and I had founded.

'It's quite a nice story,' Lally said in a puzzled kind of way. 'They are very lucky to have such a nice mother.'

Miriam said, '*I've* read *The Pickwick Papers* – have *you,* Gillian? It's mentioned as Jo's favourite reading.'

I confessed to reading only a few chapters of this masterpiece which at that time I did not find very funny.

Lally would rather play at Robin Hood or King Arthur, but we tired of that sort of game by the time we were eleven or so. Our literary society went on existing until we were about fourteen when we either went on writing secretly, like Susan, or stopped completely, or wrote as I did for wider consumption: reams of verse for the school magazine. Miriam scorned such a publication.

Our High School life in the late Forties was both boring and soothing, with enough small excitements to keep us reasonably contented, and we would also see a lot of each other at weekends. It was Miss Baker who first called us four 'The Quartet'. She was the music mistress, but her appellation was not because of any special prowess shown in her subject. I was in the choir; I had a loud voice, but not much sense of pitch. Susan could sing in tune but her soprano was weak. Lalage was musical and played the piano not at all badly, but by ear. Miriam was completely tone deaf, but said she was greatly interested in the theory of music and claimed to enjoy listening to things we had never heard of. Miss Baker probably named us The Quartet out of some ironic intention.

We spent a lot of time together as we went up the school. We had other friends, were not unpopular, but we knew each other very well having shared jokes and assumptions for years. In some ways however we were very discreet. As we moved into adolescence we didn't go in for confessions about our really intimate feelings. Just occasionally we might touch upon them, but would withdraw almost immediately, not wanting it to be thought that because we had 'confessed' to some small thing, others might be expected to follow suit. I was the one who was more open in these matters. I had a lot of nervous energy and was often liable to give my heart away to some actor or teacher, or even a character in a novel. Some people thought me superficial, I think, for I could accomplish a good deal without undue effort. Susan was much more methodical, a hard worker. *She* found it very difficult to talk about herself. When we went away to the coast on holiday with our families in summer, we all wrote long letters to each other in a rather nineteenth-century way, except for Lally, who only sent people postcards of things that had taken her fancy, with a message scrawled on the back in her curious backhand writing. Miriam's letters were quite different and I still have some of them. They seemed to continue a conversation the recipient could not remember having with her, probably one she was having with herself. I felt quite flattered to receive them in spite of finding her rather prickly. But Susan's letters were never about herself, rather about places she'd visited or people she'd seen or conversations she had overheard.

We did discuss each other though; I talked about Lally and Miriam to Susan, but not about Susan to the others. There were aspects of Lally that puzzled us. It wasn't just curiosity or a wish to pry. Susan said she was very vulnerable under her cool exterior and I imagined her at the centre of some mystery. But how could she possess a secret past? It was not, as it was with Miriam, that Lally's thought processes or opinions were intriguing, more as if her physical person – her beautiful face and her grace of movement and her glorious hair – somehow did not fit her personality. I puzzled over it, thinking that people and their bodies were one and the same. Sometimes Lally was a little distant, not from willed abstraction, but more as if she had gone inside herself to find something in her own mind and it could not connect with the outside world. She was always benevolent but could sometimes surprise us with a witty remark that seemed to come from another part of her. I felt the same about her as Susan did but we wondered if we were imagining this other self. I used to talk to Susan about such things, sitting up in her bedroom eating apples. Her family lived above and behind their shop opposite the station marshalling-yard, so the hiss of engines and the sharp melancholy sound of whistles was heard whenever a Marriott woke up at night.

Susan liked to visit me too. I lived in a neat semi which had a garden with lilac and rambler roses and a rustic fence. Lally

7

would sometimes come too and I'd be invited back to The Laurels, a large, square, stone-built 'mansion'. (No one could remember ever seeing any laurel bushes there.) I thought my own home more comfortable, though my mother was given to long bouts of spring-cleaning fever when the dining-room furniture would be robed under dust-sheeted shrouds and my friends and I would escape to the other downstairs room where there would be a leaping fire, or up to my rather chilly bedroom. My mother had to fit housework round her teaching duties and was never other than busy.

Sometimes Miriam would tell us to call round at her house. We were never invited 'to tea' as other mothers put it, but wandered into a vast kitchen if we felt hungry. The maid, Ellen, who was about ninety – otherwise she'd have been doing something more remunerative – would make a pot of tea and cut lots of slices of bread and Marmite. In front of the kitchen side of the house was a courtyard where there had once been stabling for horses. There were big old trees between that yard and the gardens that sloped down to a wall that had the Snicket on the other side. It was not as big a house as The Laurels, but I liked it better. I was rather in awe of Mr Jacobs, who shouted a lot, though we knew he was only being boisterous, not cross. He was an odd sort of jeweller to read so much. Books were piled in what Miriam called the library. She occasionally allowed us in there and we saw glass-covered cases with cloths over them like ones in museums. Under the cloth and the glass, on velvet and satin material, there were samples of uncut stones, lumps of amethyst and amber, beryl and chrysophase. Miriam was not much interested in them but we thought it was an Aladdin's cave. Miriam knew all the names for the stones, but said: 'I'm glad I'm not a boy. Father would have wanted me to go into the business and nothing bores me more.' We felt sorry for Mr Jacobs, who was so keen on his jewel collection.

'I hope there's a boy cousin who'll carry it all on one day,' I said to Susan later.

Miriam had two sisters, twins, Ruth and Rachel, who were as unlike her as it was possible to be for they favoured their mother in looks, being small and rather plump and round-faced. They were principally interested in dolls. Miriam's mother, Naomi, was a feminine sort of person, though she did not seem to do much housework. She cooked when Ellen had a day off, but there was not much you could do, she said, with turnips and snoek. In spite of that she put all sorts of foreign spices into whatever she baked, and the guests enjoyed the product. She knew her Miriam was clever, but never nagged her about her homework. Miriam was allowed a good deal of freedom, but she never showed much affection to her mother.

Susan was usually tongue-tied when she visited Miriam. I know she liked to observe others and amuse herself later writing secret reports on them, which grew into short stories, for she told me and swore me to secrecy. She knew she must 'cut her coat according to her cloth', as *her* mother was always pointing out, so she never confided any ambitions to anyone but me. Even in that last term at the old village school, when I had passed round descriptions of classmates, Susan had never showed us hers. I had given all my friends fancy adjectives: 'Lalage the Fairest of All' and 'Miriam the Wondrous', 'Susan the Exquisite'. I'd await pleasurable reactions and felt very disappointed if the recipients of these missives were not thrilled. At Greenfield High I had no more time to pen such things in lessons, though I always had a book on my knee for when I was bored. In this way I got through the whole of Dorothy L Sayers during science lessons.

One day – it must have been when we were about fourteen, before we got to know Nick and Tom and Gabriel again – Mrs Fortescue invited us all to tea at The Laurels. Afterwards, making polite conversation, we got talking about another of the large houses in the village, a house called The Holm, and the next day we decided to explore it. It was a school half-term and we had nothing much else to do, no money to go shopping – not that there was much in the shops – and a disinclination to spend all our time revising for the end of term exams.

The Holm was a house built during the Regency and there was a Palladian influence which we thought just 'pretty'. It had a ruined pergola and green shutters, and there was a shallow lake in the grounds near an old summer-house. Rain-pocked statues were stuck in the earth round the lake, imitations of classical deities – Pallas-Athena and Aphrodite and Hera. It

9

was smaller but more welcoming than the other, larger, abandoned mansion.

Lally stared when she saw the statues. She was still an enigma to us all, so graceful and so beautiful to look at, but always with something we couldn't quite pin down. That afternoon she said, 'They didn't live *here*, those statue people – why don't they have statues of old English people?'

'We were all painted with woad and dancing round cave fires when Aphrodite was going strong,' I answered.

'But they could have made people like peasants, or even kings,' said Lally. 'There were girls like us here once, a long time ago.' It was unusual for Lalage to voice her thoughts.

'We're not peasants,' said Miriam.

'No – but village girls – and ladies. I hear them talking,' she said.

We went off to explore The Holm.

'What do you think she means – hear them talking?' I said to Susan.

Lally was somewhere round the other side of the house and Miriam had climbed over the wall to the field beyond.

'Can't *you* imagine long-ago-people still somehow here?' replied Susan.

'Yes, I know what you mean – not ghosts though! What do you think Lally imagines? She's not an imaginative person, is she? She was never interested in ghosts when we explored the haunted house.'

'There must be hidden depths,' Susan said. Susan often tried to tell me what she thought the village had been like at different periods of its history. History was her favourite subject and she liked to muse on the past and on people who might have lived in the village. But we wouldn't have expected Lalage to do so. With Susan it was more a sort of study. We'd go to a local Hall that was now a museum and look at the old kitchens and stand in the big solar parlour and Susan would wonder aloud what it had been like to live there two or three hundred years ago or more, and look frightfully interested in bellows and warming-pans. She said she wouldn't mind staying in Eastcliff all her life. Already she'd been to meetings of the Antiquarian Society with Miss Dalby, our history mistress, for a treat, to see lantern slides and to listen to a talk

10

by a very old man who was an expert on the first Yorkshire poll tax. Susan had been thrilled. I couldn't see the attraction at the time. Perhaps I've made Susan sound too good to be true, but she was a really nice, quiet girl who didn't talk to other people much, only to me. I know some people thought she was a bit prim and proper but she wasn't – she was shy – until you got her on to history.

We walked round to the front of The Holm and looked at the old stables on the way. During the war the house had been used to house those difficult evacuees whom even the most long-suffering village families simply could not take, but now it was all shut up, though still romantic-looking. 'Too expensive to run,' I said, impressed by the place with its air of faded grandeur. Nothing could have made a greater contrast with my house or Susan's own untidy terraced house behind the shop than these almost-ruins. The house and grounds were beautiful. Miriam though was not impressed by it. As she lived in a Georgian house herself I suppose she did not set so much store by old houses. She never liked to be seen sharing the same reactions as other people.

'I was exploring,' she said when we all met again later. 'There's lots more interesting things over the wall.'

'What sort of things?'

'Oh, some farm workers haymaking,' she said. 'And a carthorse.'

Sometimes I used to think that Miriam was just as much a mystery in her own way as Lally was, though she did not carry around with her that almost intangible air of physical remoteness that surrounded Lalage. In looks Miriam and Lalage were still growing up opposites, Miriam dark and even a little ugly, and Lally fair and beautiful. When Miriam condescended to articulate her thoughts she still made the rest of us feel ignorant. She became animated, reeling out information about stars, and minerals, or strange tribes, jumping from one to another and frowning the while.

'What sort of people do you imagine, Lally, as having lived here?' we asked her when we were on our way back home, and Miriam had gone a different way, saying she wanted a longer walk.

'Not people who lived in *that* house,' she said, and then

11

paused. 'I think I once imagined a girl who lived in the village,' she said after a silence. 'She was unhappy.' Susan said nothing and I looked at Lally closely. 'I might have dreamed it. Do you think people who were unhappy can haunt places?'

'I don't know why ghosts should always be unhappy ones,' said Susan.

'Have you really seen a ghost?' I asked.

'Oh, no, no – it's just pretending,' Lally said hurriedly. 'Like you two – you make up stories.' She looked half fearful, half sly.

'I haven't much time nowadays for that sort of thing,' I said. 'You ought to write about it,' I added.

'No, I wouldn't want to *write* about them – I just like thinking about them,' said Lally. 'They don't come when I make an effort.'

'Sometimes before I fall asleep I think I "see" people, or hear them – Miriam says it's something to do with your brain – between being conscious and unconscious,' I offered after a pause.

'Oh, do you, Gillian?' She brightened up. 'What sort of people?'

'I don't know – if I've been listening to someone in the evening, say, just one person and they've been talking a long time, like a friend of my parents or someone, I can hear a sort of echo of their voice when I go to bed. It's not like a ghost or an imaginary person, I don't think.' I was trying to cheer her up, for Lally had looked rather frightened.

'I expect great writers like Shakespeare heard and saw things all the time,' added Susan sagely.

The subject of imaginary persons did not come up again for some time, although I suppose Susan went on thinking about the people who lived long ago in the village, but in a rational sort of way – how they dressed, what they ate, things like that.

My friends interested me more than history. I thought they were all exceptionally talented and would be outstandingly successful: Lally because she was so beautiful and Miriam because she was clever and ambitious. Miriam and I were planning to go to university, and exams would be important for Susan too if she succeeded in getting the job she coveted as a reporter on the local newspaper when she left school. She said her parents would not want her to go away to college even if she got a scholarship. They did not want Susan to waste her time. She said she didn't mind about not going away, it was enough that they accepted she would do the sort of work she wanted locally. I often used to wonder what Susan would have been like with different parents but she seemed to love her own, though she was unwilling to startle them. When I visited the shop she said they always remarked afterwards about me: 'She's so easy to talk to.' They did not realize that they hardly did any talking since I did it all. I knew I talked too much, often out of nervousness. They wouldn't have wanted their own daughter a chatterbox.

Teachers scolded Lally because they knew she was lazy, and praised Susan and myself. As for Miriam, they did not understand her at all. Not that we did either, but we were willing to support her when she annoyed others. She would not really need a scholarship to university, but I would.

Miriam was hopeless at games, even at tennis, which was at least a fairly civilized game, but came into her own in the swimming bath, though even there she was no match for Lally, who swam seemingly effortlessly. Lalage's long legs helped her to play tennis too and she was a good player. She was a 'physical' sort of person. As for Susan, she did everything doggedly and escaped censure when we had to play hockey, whilst I hated it and made little effort.

When we were fifteen or so we had the newfangled 'O' Levels to study for, eight or nine subjects with an obligatory pass in a certain five to get 'matric', the minimum university entrance. Lally scraped along, never seeming to give her full mind to school work. Susan worked because she enjoyed it and because it was an escape from her parents' shop. She liked organizing and ordering knowledge, though she always pretended to groan at the homework. I worked too, off and on, but I still disliked science and geometry. Miriam also worked only when she felt like it, rather despising the conventions of school. We joined her in this as time went on. Concepts important to me, like happiness and unhappiness, seemed not to belong to Miriam's scale of values. As for Lally – nobody ever knew what she was thinking about, if anything. She never mentioned those vague, imaginary girls again.

*

After 'O' Levels, and once the lower sixth exams were over, Miriam was going to depart to some posh boarding-establishment to prepare for Oxford or Cambridge. Her father insisted, which I thought was rather strange for a Socialist. Lally would most likely leave too and go off to London where her glamorous father lived. We'd all heard from Lally that he'd remarried. Our ways would part for a time, we knew, but we all felt we would go on seeing each other once the boring part of life was over.

My parents were not glamorous or exciting, but they took for granted I would go away to university and give them the kudos of having brought forth a clever daughter. I was prone to passionate enthusiasms and I expect they hoped I might harness them to academic work. They thought Susan very 'steady', and trusted her judgment, whilst they had reservations about Miriam and her parents. I would not have minded having the Jacobs as parents, but as I had not, I decided it was more fun to strike out for myself. I looked forward to the time when I thought my 'real' life would begin.

The Boys' Grammar School was that Elizabethan foundation in Lightholme. If we arrived home from school a little earlier than usual we'd see the youths coming out of their own venerable building. The boys wore grey flannels and navy blue blazers and red and blue quartered caps. The littlest ones would run and jump like demented grasshoppers, but the older boys, the sixth-formers, would follow later, either swaggering or skulking, according to temperament. The summer after our 'O' levels we got to know the boys again, Gabriel Benson and Tom Cooper and Nick Varley. They were all in their upper sixth. Since we'd passed our humbler exam the year before, we were not quite so hard-worked, though the year after that Susan and I would have our noses to the grindstone again.

Tom Cooper went round a lot with Nick, and Gabriel Benson would sometimes join them and they would chat about their school work to us when we met after school. Sometimes they seemed surprised that *we* knew about quadratic equations or Latin declensions. Nick, or occasionally

14

Tom, would talk, one brilliantly, the other rather ponderously, whilst Gabriel would smile and say little, though when he did it was always in my opinion both simple and original.

Tom Cooper was exceptionally attractive, had the sort of good looks that seemed wasted on what appeared otherwise to be quite an ordinary boy, if one went by the conversation rather than the face – and until you heard him play the piano or violin. He had a way of staring unwaveringly at whoever he was talking to – probably from shyness. Nick was not so immediately handsome in the way Tom was, but he had the *je ne sais quoi* which attracts the female sex, even when he was only seventeen or eighteen. He was very fair, not tall, had an aquiline nose and very hooded eyes. He was not as kind as Tom could be when he made the effort, or as Gabriel, who was unvaryingly benevolent. Nick always gave the impression that some steel coil was about to spring up out of him and knock you over. He was not generally liked, but people thought he must be 'interesting' because he was so clever. He talked about architecture or astronomy and seemed much more knowledgeable and much more scornful in his judgments than the rest of us, except for Miriam. Gabriel did not often agree with him, but did not argue for long. Often he seemed to annoy Nick, who called him Old Mystic, or The Angel Gabriel. We girls called Nick Old Nick, and Tom we christened Tom-Tom.

Tom lived for music but showed interest in more ordinary things like games and films too. He said to me shortly after we had all begun to meet again and were walking home in the same direction: 'I think Lalage Cecil looks like Ingrid Bergman, don't you?' I didn't think so, but it was Tom's way of saying he found her attractive, so I agreed. He often used to look at Lally as though she were a piece of precious china. But most of our time together with the boys we just chaffed each other and chatted desultorily. Occasionally there would be two or three different conversations going. We were not their 'girl-friends', for we were all a bit high and mighty about such goings on, but were rather flattered that older boys should seem to like to talk to us. As for the boys, perhaps they regarded us as the only passable examples of young womanhood handy in the village, but might have preferred something rather more exciting. Nick gave that impression certainly, as though he might be holding on in case as we grew up our charms might become more apparent.

I never knew what the boys were thinking. They were mysteries: handsome musical Tom; Nick with his sharp brain; and kind, 'deep' Gabriel; all different, all worth getting to know. It was Gabriel whom I really liked best and I know Susan did too. Young girls were supposed to prefer cads, according to a novel I'd read, but we didn't. I liked him because I thought he was a really good person, and virtue has enormous attractions. You were 'safe' with Gabriel, Susan said, but I don't think either of us really thought we might be seduced by any of them. Gabriel made us feel safe somehow in another way, I think. But although I liked him best, I didn't find he made my heart beat faster.

In the winter we met once or twice at Tom Cooper's to listen to records. His mother spent most days of clement weather playing golf on the local links. When it was inclement she spent her time drinking with friends in the clubhouse, so Tom fended for himself.

In the summer of 1952 after the boys had sat their 'A' Levels and before Lally and Miriam went away, we began to meet more regularly on the Stray after school.

There were swings for children tucked in one corner, and the gardens of houses sloped down on all sides to the broad open stretch of grassland. On the north and south sides were roads with buses and cars – not many of the latter at that time. At the top the path forked and ended in rockeries and a small granite obelisk with a plaque to say why the land had been brought. There were other paths of white-flecked stone that led across the Stray to meet in the centre at an orange, four-sided shelter where sat old men, or women with prams.

One afternoon we'd all met for half an hour or so on our way home. Susan and I heard Gabriel whistling before we saw his tall, lean body topped by wavy brown hair, walking along behind the trees that shaded the rockery path. He always carried a few books under his arm, never wore the school cap and did not bother with a satchel. He was usually just ahead of the other two, making his way home to Pear Trees, an ugly

16

house under the railway bridge. The Bensons had no rectory near their own church, if there had been one it would have been a shorter walk home for Gabriel since the school lay north of Lightholme at the top of a hill, half way to Sholey. I was always pleased to see Gabriel, though I was already aware he was the sort of boy whom a literary girl might idealize, liking to think there was a Giles Winterborne or a Diggory Venn lurking underneath. (Thomas Hardy was my favourite novelist.) He probably wasn't as clever as Nick or as good looking as Tom but I felt he was more imaginative, and Susan agreed.

We walked over to the swings and I sat down rather self-consciously on one, swinging a little to and fro. Miriam as usual had wandered away and was sitting fiddling with her sandal strap on the low wall that was the boundary to someone's long back garden. Susan sat down on the grass by Lalage and Nick, who were on one of the benches meant for mothers and fathers to occupy as they watched small offspring enjoy themselves. We all remembered those swings from a long way back. Sometimes little boys had got little girls on the larger see-saw that was suspended by steel ropes, called the 'rant' in local parlance, and pushed it higher and higher till they squealed for mercy. Not boys like Nick or Gabriel – rougher boys known in village school days.

Tom was leaning against the helter-skelter saying something about a concert he'd been to the Saturday before, given by the Hallé orchestra. When he started on music no one could stop him except Nick who would ask some esoteric question and pretend that Bartok was the only composer worth listening to, apart from Bach. But Miriam was listening to him holding forth and she slipped down from the wall to hear better. Nick was saying something to Lalage about living abroad. 'It would be cheaper, and my father wants to set up a business in Alsace – there's no hope for the old business over here.'

The textile manufacture on which most of the region had always depended was now being obliged to draw in its horns even further. Some mills had already closed or been taken over by larger combines.

'Would you go then?' I asked, overhearing him. Lalage had said nothing.

17

'Oh – I'll be off soon to Oxford anyway – but it would be nice for holidays, wouldn't it?'

'Marvellous!' I replied. The others looked a bit doubtful.

We had all been 'abroad' now at least once, Susan and I on a school trip to Burgundy, and Lalage on a visit to Paris with her father and stepmother. Miriam's family had taken their children to Italy. Nick had often spoken of his adventures in Savoy the summer before. To *live* in Europe would be wonderful, I thought. Nick too was mad about France and seemed to despise poor drab little England. He had hinted at dark secrets into which he had been initiated the summer before, not saying so in so many words but giving us to understand he knew a thing or two. I thought the classic 'older woman', whom I knew about from the French novels I used to read instead of doing my homework, might have seduced him, not the other way round. If anyone had 'done it' it would have been Nick. Should we all be flattered when Nick condescended to talk to us? He must find us rather naïve, I thought. He seemed not especially happy at home. We knew that at school they had marked him down early for Cambridge or Oxford. He was a whizz at maths and had a fantastic memory. He was *so* different from Gabriel, and I don't imagine that Gabriel took much interest in Nick's adventures, for any chasing Gabriel did would be more likely to be of butterflies or rare birds.

Susan had told me once that years before when she had fallen down one playtime in the school field, Gabriel had comforted her and taken her into Miss Ackroyd to have the knee bathed. It was highly unusual for a boy to comfort a girl and she had never forgotten it, for usually little boys carried on their strange antics and peculiar fighting games with each other and hardly noticed girls, except to tease them. Gabriel *was* different.

I turned my thoughts to Lally.

'It's Lalage's birthday tomorrow,' I said, and Nick said: 'Is it really? How old will you be, mademoiselle?'

'Seventeen,' said Lalage.

'Ah, youth, how it flies!' said Nick. Gabriel came up then and sat on the grass. 'Tom,' shouted Nick, 'tell them about that idea you had.'

Tom shrugged his shoulders and came over to the others, and even Miriam sat down beside Lalage and Nick.

'You know – the old ruined abbey,' said Nick.

'What old ruined abbey? Oh, you mean The Holm,' said Tom.

'He thought we might camp there in the grounds – take our work there and a gramophone; play tennis on the old court,' said Nick. 'You could all come along – we could rig up a stove or something.'

'You mean you want us to come and cook for you?' I enquired, trying to sound indignant. I was a strong feminist.

'Oh, *I* can cook quite well,' said Nick, squashing me nicely.

I immediately had a picture of us all camping out there, living a sort of idyll away from families, pitching tents on the long lawns and cooking on primuses. We might take books to read and have space, and talk. Our parents wouldn't let their daughters stay there at night, even if the boys' parents did.

'*I* only meant – play tennis there – and listen to the gramophone,' said Tom.

'Brahms or modern jazz, I expect,' said Nick. 'Anyway, if you care to come along when we've got it sorted out. . . .' He gave me a mock bow and we all laughed.

'We could put a play on there,' I suggested. 'A sort of pageant.'

'Festival of Lightholme and Eastcliff?' said Nick. 'Personally I'd rather play tennis.'

'Yes, that would be nice,' said Lalage.

I felt suitably crushed once more.

When the Quartet was with the boys it did not talk much about people. That was the first thing I had noticed when I used to ponder the differences between boys and girls. Tom and Nick would talk about *things* – games, or the work they were doing, or their exams, and even sometimes about politics and religion or the books they were reading; and Gabriel would talk about some wild flower or bird he was searching for. But we girls seemed to spend most of our time now discussing teachers, parents – and ourselves. We discussed the boys too, naturally, and wondered aloud what they were really like and which of them we liked best. Susan said that boys *did* talk about girls

19

because her brother Jimmy had often had mates round when he lived at home and she'd heard them guffawing over girls and listened to their discussion on 'vital statistics'. But boys didn't go in for long and earnest analysis of character the way we did. Did Nick and Tom and Gabriel appraise our figures as Jim Marriott and his friends had used to do? Jimmy was away at that time doing his National Service, but Susan said it was not the sort of thing she could talk to him about. When he was home on leave he spent his time roaring about on a motor-bike, unlike our new friends. I asked the girls the day after that particular meeting on the Stray whom among them they liked best and whom they 'fancied', making it quite clear there was a difference. '*I* still like Gabriel best,' I said. 'I mean as a person. He's kind and –' I searched for a word and came out with 'honourable'. Perhaps it was the wrong word, but he inspired confidence.

Susan looked at me quickly, but said nothing.

'You mean if you were on the moors in a thunderstorm he would give you his mac?' offered Lally.

'Well, not quite –'

'You mean you're not in love with him,' said Miriam rather maliciously.

'He's just *nice*. What about you, Lally?' I enquired. Once I got the bit between my teeth I could never resist shaking a subject to death. I knew that, but it didn't stop me.

'What?'

'Whom do you like – or fancy most – *you* heard. Come on. Nick, or Gabriel, or Tom?'

Lalage paused for some time, obviously giving the matter her mature consideration. Then: 'Well, it depends on the way the boy feels, doesn't it?' she said.

'Heavens! You *are* naïve!' I said.

'She's not – girls are expected to wait and see who likes them before they decide,' said Miriam ironically.

'How disgusting,' I said. 'But Lalage hasn't answered my question – come on, Lally, admit you fancy Nick Varley – "fancy" I mean. Not *like* him best.'

Lally looked puzzled.

Miriam, who obviously regarded this sort of talk as rather childish, eventually said, '*I* think Tom is the most sensible – the most manly. He's what my mother calls husband material.'

I was surprised. 'Tom? You haven't mentioned his Adonis-like profile – I can't see him married.'

'Oh, I can,' Susan said quickly, for Miriam was looking away again, lost in deep thought. 'She means he's ordinary – except for the music – and ordinary men make the best husbands.'

'I wasn't thinking yet – of husbands,' I pursued. 'I meant, you know, as a *lover*.'

Susan smiled. I know I did go a little too far sometimes but I only voiced what the others thought.

Miriam said, 'I can't see Gabriel or Nick married.'

'Lally still hasn't told us whom she fancies,' I said. 'And neither have you, Susan. Come on. Who's to be your choice for Young Lochinvar?'

'Who's *yours*?' asked Miriam.

'Nick, of course,' I said idly. 'He's going to be a real heart-breaker that boy.'

'I think he's a bit arrogant,' said Susan, unusually. 'Though he's awfully clever – probably he'll be famous, I shouldn't wonder.'

'Nick stares at you,' ventured Lally quietly.

'At *you*, you mean, or at everyone?' asked Miriam.

'At everyone, I suppose.'

'Tom looks at *you*,' I said. I added hurriedly, 'At all of us perhaps – he's very good-looking, isn't he?' They all laughed. Lalage looked serious, but said no more.

I was to remember that conversation, especially when to round it off – which I was fond of doing – I pronounced, 'Gabriel may be an ideal sort of saint, I think, and Tom somebody's husband, but Nick will go far.'

It was much harder to understand boys than girls. Even girls who went to coeducational schools seemed to have the same difficulty. I didn't understand them, thought of Nick partly the same way I thought of Miriam, whom I rather admired in spite of her prickliness. It was the boys' minds I felt I wanted to understand. How could I ever know men as well as I knew Susan, for example? How did you get to know young men as people? And how could you ever love men if you didn't understand them? 'Fancying' was different.

21

I did not think that either I or my friends really wanted to pair off, in spite of these theoretical conversations. Susan asked me later whether I thought one might both like and 'fancy' the same person for, unlike me, she didn't want to make a distinction. She felt that when you grew up the two things came together, and that if you loved someone you liked, then you would want him to want you. Whether anyone would ever fall in love with her was a possibility she said she didn't waste much time thinking about.

Before the summer term ended and when there were still months of more summer lying ahead with long, light evenings, we all began to meet at The Holm. True to his word Nick had reconnoitred the old tennis courts. There was one grass court, which was completely overgrown, but there was also a hard court and he had fixed up a net. We didn't tell anyone where we were going, for so long as we girls were all together parents didn't worry. Staying out at night in winter would have been a different matter. We felt rather emancipated. I thought that these what you might have called group meetings would help us all to know how to talk to the opposite sex. I suppose I would have preferred males a little older and more experienced, for I did not find even Nick all that erotically attractive, whatever I'd said to the others. No, if there were any shivers down my back at the age of sixteen or seventeen they were for the general mystery of people, and if the people were masculine, so much the better. But it was not different in kind from talking to Miriam. I didn't really want to 'get off' with a boy: I might later, with a man, but I wanted to find out what boys thought about. To us girls sex was not a real preoccupation: love was. I wasn't sure if boys were *really* different. Love was far more interesting and more mysterious than what I can remember referring to rather loftily as the 'merely physical'. I hoped someone might love me one day, did not think it would be anyone I knew. I was pretty sure I could fall in love – after all I'd been in love with so many things already – an actor, a line of music – but I couldn't connect these heady feelings of elation or melancholy or glory with anything so sordid as sex. What was called 'fancying' was more to do with the mystery of what men might want from you, not with any powerful physical need of your own.

I knew that there was life beyond Eastcliff and school and family and I was determined that I was going to seize upon this life as soon as possible. I did not expect to meet anybody exciting or come up against overwhelming passion whilst I lived in the village with my parents.

In the war Mother had taught in Father's place. Teaching was not a reserved occupation for men, and my father was called up. Unlike the other young women teachers, Mother had not laid down her tools when he returned but decided to go on and work for a pension. She was much happier when she was out of the house, though trying to keep up with the standards she thought my father deserved was another matter – thus the constant spring-cleaning. My sister Rosemary was totally unlike clumsy me and seemed to want to be a ballet dancer. They did not encourage these ambitions. I thought Rosemary ought to go to a ballet school or stage school like Lally's cousins, but I gathered that teaching, or if one was not quite up to that, nursing, was to be our fate.

We were not encouraged very much to care about our appearance, Rosemary and I, beyond being neat and tidy and well turned out. As I grew into adolescence I had spent time staring into my dressing-table mirror wondering whether I could ever be a beauty. I used to wonder whether I would prefer to look like Lalage. Curiously enough I thought not. I had rather nice golden brown hair, but a sallow skin, which I was pleased to call 'olive'. Once, when we were all in the city we had had our 'Polyphotos' taken, and exchanged our second-best likeness with each other. Susan looked rather palely out of her picture, her brown eyes and brown fringe the notable features. I looked purposefully big-eyed and soulful; Miriam looked shaggy. She was short-sighted and had taken off her glasses. Contact lenses had not yet been invented – or if they had, had not yet been marketed in our town. But we had now all left our spotty stage. Lalage had never had spots, and needed no specs and her hair had not darkened. No wonder Tom Cooper thought she looked like a film star! On *her* photo she looked ravishing.

Dior's 'New Look' was still influencing village fashion. Skirts were still long and so it was only when we had to change for hockey or athletics, and later for tennis, that we had been able to see each other's, and even our own, nether limbs. Lally's long, slim legs and trim ankles, legs as smooth as the skin on her face, were admirable.

That summer of The Holm we were not exactly grown up – we were not allowed to be that until we were twenty-one in those days – but we were not children any more. Even Eastcliff acknowledged that.

The boys were amazed when, on the first evening we played tennis with them there that summer of our emancipation, Lally proved herself a real champion. We were rather proud of her for she was a talented natural player. Susan especially looked rather pleased when Lally beat Nick Varley in a singles match he'd challenged her to. The expression on Nick's face was a picture. It was probably a fluke, for not many girls however good can beat young men of the same age; perhaps Nick was tired after his exams. Even so, it was a triumph. Afterwards we all sat around on the edge of the court and drank the lemonade we'd bought at Susan's shop, the long evening shadows stealing over us. The court was a bit uneven, but Nick and Tom had tidied it up. I wished we could use the other court at the side of the house, the grass one. We could all have enrolled at the village tennis club, but it was more fun at The Holm.

The house, with its green shutters and lacy rusted pergola and the long, long lawn that led out from the path, was like a dream house. Someone must have kept it going to a certain extent or the lawn would have been a wilderness. Nick said that the building society in the town owned it and were going to do it up for a future purchaser, but that they hadn't got round to the tennis court yet.

'Do you think they'll mind?' asked Susan. 'I mean, it is trespassing, isn't it?'

'If anyone comes we just say we thought it belonged to nobody,' said Nick. 'We're not doing any harm. There's nothing in the house to damage, I went in last week after we'd cleared the court. Only a few old sofas and kitchen cabinets and a few moth-eaten furnishings upstairs. The evacuees made plenty of mess.'

'It's a pity to let it go like this,' I said. 'At this rate it'll soon be as bad as The Nest.' That was the grandest mansion where small-arms had been stored in the war.

'I expect someone'll buy it soon,' said Gabriel.

'They ought to build on the land,' Miriam said. 'There's heaps of people without homes. A new council estate would be a good idea.'

'You mean pull it all down! That would be terrible. It's a little Palladian gem, you know,' I said, quoting from a book I'd just read.

Miriam gave a snort of disgust. She disapproved of my Cult of Beauty.

To mollify both of us Susan said, 'There's a lot of land elsewhere – all those fields on the other side of the main road and in Lightholme behind the library. Someone ought to restore this.'

'Just think if you had the money what a wonderful place it would be for a property developer,' said Nick. 'You could make a fortune!'

'Not up here – you might if there was a shortage of land because of bomb damage,' said Miriam.

Neither Lally nor Tom had yet spoken. Lally was lying with her head cushioned on her arms. Gabriel was peering at a moth he'd caught in his hand and Tom was looking at Lally when he thought no one else was. I found Tom a bit of a bore but then he looked up and said, 'There's a piano, you know – in there,' he pointed with his head.

'Give us a waltz, then,' said Nick. Tom hesitated. 'Go on,' said Nick.

Susan said, 'There's nowhere to dance – do you think they danced on the terraces?' There was a terrace as broad as a main road on three sides of the house with a pair of modern French windows at the back. Someone had once begun to bring the place up to date and then lost heart – or the war had come. We all got up and drifted round to look. Tom was already in the room behind the window and we sat on the wall that had been built up to the house, dividing one part of the terrace from the back quarters. Nick lit a cigarette and I naturally accepted one from him. Lally sat smiling, playing a tune on her racquet strings. Then Miriam went in Tom's direction to explore further. We heard a twangy, rushy sound emanate from the instrument and we all stopped whatever we were doing for a moment.

'It's *Valse Triste*,' said Susan to Gabriel who had let the moth go free. From behind the windows where Miriam was still standing, Tom's music came out. The shadows were lengthening and Susan and I smiled at each other, perfectly happy, though the music was so sad. Nick was looking now at Lally and Gabriel was looking at Nick, and the music went on and on and on and, for a few moments, we felt time had stopped.

That was the first visit and there was that indefinable something in the air; Gabriel with his moth, and the desultory conversation, and Tom producing such lovely music from a rickety old piano; Nick looked all burnished in the evening sun; Miriam at the threshold saying nothing; Lally head down, and Susan and I just smiling. I didn't even want to talk. Such moments are rare and the spell was soon broken when we crowded in to the piano and Tom played some jazz, and the evening ended with us all making our various ways home on foot or on bicycles. We played tennis there many times after that, but that first evening is the one I remember best.

Sometime during the next week or two Nick did beat Lally at tennis. Miriam brought a chess set and played with Gabriel once or twice, and I talked to everybody at some time or another, even to Tom.

We met there almost every evening till term finished at the end of July, and it seemed after only a few evenings that we owned the place and also that we all knew each other much better. Usually we arrived about the same time, after tea, and before we could be claimed for any parental idea of how to spend a July evening. We had no more homework or revision for the time being and our parents were happy for us to 'get a bit of fresh air' after the exams. We used to take our tennis racquets very ostentatiously under our arms – quite unnecessarily so because we did play tennis. My mother thought we were playing on the old Sunday school courts and I didn't disabuse her. Susan often took coffee in a thermos. The primus stove envisaged by Nick had not proved workable, so we would drink coffee, which in those days was quite a luxury.

26

Susan obtained it from the grocer in exchange for something as difficult to get hold of in her own shop.

How innocent it seemed. A group of friends, sixteen, seventeen, eighteen years old playing tennis, chatting – occasionally smoking. That was something most young people did then as a badge of grownupness. Except Miriam, who claimed it was bad for you and Gabriel who preferred to spend his money on other things. Not that any of us had much money. It was before the days when grammar school pupils did jobs as a matter of course at weekends or in the holidays. All any of us had done was to act as postmen in the Christmas season.

One of those evenings it had rained and we decided to stay in the house. The thunder came after we'd arrived, and then a sudden downpour. Tom got to the piano and Nick, for effect, lit two candles which he found in the kitchens. The electricity and gas had both been turned off and there was only a trickle of water from the taps. We sat around singing whatever Tom decided to play. He could improvise anything, but we ended up singing hymns, and songs from the war, an incongruous mixture; *Now the Day is Over* mixed up with *Roll Out the Barrel*, which had similar tunes, as Miriam pointed out.

Then Miriam said, 'Lally can play the piano too, you know,' and Lally was conscripted to sit by the side of Tom on another upturned tea-chest, which they'd found in the dark hall, to play by ear. They played well together. Tom had a vast repertoire and if Lally didn't know a tune he played it through and then off they went.

'*Home Sweet Home*,' said Nick, who could not play the piano. He began to sing in a rather reedy tenor. Lally turned round and stared at him.

'It's a very sad song,' she said.

'Well, let Tom play something more cheerful,' he replied.

Miriam was trying to read a book in the light of the candle, but now and again she'd look across at Tom and smile in a knowing sort of way. When the rain stopped and the light came into the room again we were in the middle of *The Foggy foggy dew* except for Miriam. It was odd, I could almost imagine that the house was no longer unused, but that we were some Victorian or Edwardian house-party amusing itself after supper. Susan echoed all our thoughts.

'Do you think houses can become *désaffectées*?' she asked. 'Like that French word for churches that have been deconsecrated?' We had had our French exam some weeks before and that word had figured in the long lists of vocabulary given us to learn. It was Gabriel who answered her with a question.

'Which household gods do you think consecrated this house?'

'Lares et Penates,' said Nick.

'When I was little, Susan and I used to imagine there was a god in the tree at the end of the school field and take it sacrifices of All Bran on a little dish,' I said. 'Tree spirits. Which primitive peoples believed in *them*?'

'Once we gave it a piece of chocolate,' said Susan. 'What a waste – it had gone in the morning!'

'Well, Greeks for one,' said Gabriel, answering my question.

'Come on, Lally, you haven't sung your favourite,' said Tom, impatient with all this reminiscing. As the light came back into the room she sang of the *lily-white boys*. The line made me shiver. I looked at Tom and Nick and at Gabriel lurking in the shadow. Lily-white boys were they? And what were we girls?

'I'm going to explore upstairs,' said Nick. 'Who will accompany me? I want to see what it's like up in the attics.'

'If you find any ghosts, let me know,' I said. 'I have to go home.'

Gabriel and Susan said it was time for them to go too, so we left the others to explore the rest of the house. I thought, Miriam's not going to let her precious Tom out of her sight – especially if Lally lingers in the gloaming.

I wanted to leave because I'd had enough of them all for the evening and wanted to finish reading an especially enthralling novel. Now the exams were over Susan and I were making up for lost time reading all the novels we could lay our hands on, stories by people like Mary Webb and Rosamond Lehmann. All these writers seemed to have got love and sex nicely sorted out, though it didn't seem to make them any happier. Nick had been rude about my novel-reading. He never teased Susan for

28

some reason. He said all my favourite novels, beginning with *Jane Eyre*, were only 'storms in feminine teacups'. Miriam had grinned her agreement. All I could think of was that he had got the phrase from somewhere. I didn't care what he thought. I really enjoyed reading more than anything else in my life, wanted to understand states of mind and ideas I came across in books. Life itself sometimes seemed fairly simple, compared with novels. But if there were something in real life I wanted to do, to feel, would I be able to go ahead and do it like people in novels? The one thing I felt sure about was that life was awfully unfair to women.

Miriam said I was just a 'machine for reading novels' like Le Corbusier's house that was a 'machine for living in'. I thought that Miriam wasn't much better and was probably also thinking of herself, except *she* didn't read novels, and preferred biography and politics. We were all now projecting ourselves ahead into our future but Susan was the only one whose present would glide imperceptibly into it. We read books about the destructive effect of passion, Susan and I, and I for one was beginning to dream of it; we discussed 'character' at school in English lessons and wondered if our own characters were our destinies.

My father had once told me that if you had taught children for thirty years you could fairly well predict their lives and, like Miss Marple, compare similar individuals. He always knew which children in his classes would have brushes with the law. It was rather depressing for he was always right.

On that thundery night when we left Nick and Tom, Miriam and Lally at The Holm there was a row when I returned because my father had found some cigarettes in my room. He disapproved of my smoking, which naturally made me even more determined to smoke. I shouted at him and he at me. I could see that it was a waste of money, but it was my money. I'd saved it from birthdays and pocket money and my small earnings as a postman. It all seemed so petty. Fortunately he had no idea that we were meeting the boys at The Holm or the fat would have been in the fire. Yet it was so innocent, I thought. I knew that I was safe in a crowd and that my father would imagine far worse things than were ever likely to happen to me. I was nearly seventeen but still treated as a child by him. I felt that people like my father, so conventional and respectable, deserved a little excitement in their dull lives, but I was not going to provide it for them in Eastcliff. I really had no idea what the 'neighbours thought' about anything except that the neighbours were far less respectable than my parents imagined. Money worries and his profession and the war and his own upbringing seemed to have quelled anything primitive in my father, Mr Gibson. It was about this time I began referring to him mentally as 'Mr Gibson'. He never drank, hardly had time to finish the newspaper, hardly ever went out, except to visit like-minded friends. Yet he was a very good teacher, had real insight into children – so long as they were not his own. Mother was different. She had once wanted to go to art school and enjoyed going round museums and galleries when we were small. She was much less authoritarian than her husband. She was also obsequious towards her 'betters', which infuriated me. 'She's a real lady,' was one of her constant remarks. It was once made of Mrs Fortescue and I wondered what she would have made of her if she had known her better. On the other hand social inferiors were despised by both my parents. They were baffled by the way some people ruined their lives. There were tight-lipped silences in our house rather than wife-beatings or drunkenness, and an atmosphere of disapproval if the code laid down were transgressed. Who had laid down that code? Funnily enough, both Mother and Father wanted me to be ordinary, but could not explain what they meant. Josephine Cooper, Tom's sister, was cited as an example. I pointed out that Josephine was practically a half-wit. Yet I liked the way Tom and Josephine's parents lived, for they were easy-going, unlike us. The Coopers thought life was to be enjoyed, liked playing golf and doing not too difficult crossword puzzles and reading thrillers. Mr Cooper grew roses and had even named a pink rose he had created after his wife. It was called Aimée Cooper. (Aimée was not actually her name, which was Betty.) Mr Gibson thought the naming pretentious. He was a puritan; it was the thing I most disliked about him. Even at Christmas he would always be sober. Not that I wanted him drunk, but a touch of unbuttonedness would not have come amiss. Lally's grandmother or Miriam's parents would not mind if bottles of beer were opened or friends toasted in sherry. It was so unfair, I thought. Yet Miriam did not take advantage of her parents' liberality. She was a bit of a health freak, never even *tried* smoking, and would go running across the Stray in the early morning, which was unheard of. Neither did she eat sweets, a failing which was common to our sugar-starved palates. And she was now a vegetarian! Miriam would do what she wanted, would never bother about public opinion.

I often wondered which of us would marry first, and decided it would be Lally. She was so good-looking and the sort of girl boys also *liked*, though Tom especially treated her with a certain amount of awe. My parents hoped I would wed someone respectable, but not just yet. The same rules would not apply to Lally. Mr Gibson was quite genuine when he said that he would rather Rosemary or I married a plumber, his example of a humble small businessman, than go to the dogs, meaning go around with a raffish crowd and become 'fancy' in our way of life. Money was not his criterion of value. His greatest fear was that Rosemary – not so much myself because I always had my head in a book – would one day commit the unforgiveable sin, worse than any other in his eyes, and become pregnant before marriage. Not sleeping around or having a love affair – that would have been beyond his comprehension – but simply 'going too far' with the fiancé or steady boy-friend before the wedding. The fact that Rosemary had no steady boy-friend did not affect his fears for her future. I managed sometimes to conceal my opinions and bent my will to one end, that of escaping for good and all from his limited social perspective. I was fond of both my parents, did not wish to hurt their feelings, but unless I dissimulated, that was what I so easily did. When I thought of Susan's father, who was –most unusually – a free thinker; or Miriam's, who was a beacon of enlightenment, I thought they had it easier than I did at home. But I did not really like Mr Jacobs's rather smug socialism nor Susan's father's taking it for granted his clever daughter would always be there to help him in some way or other. People chose their progressive diets, I thought: some have a blind spot about feminism, others about religion. All in all, so long as my parents could not stop me doing what I wanted and living the way I wanted to live, I was prepared to tolerate a good deal of their company. Rosemary was of a gentler temper than I and would therefore satisfy them better. I had gone on hoping that my sister would become a dancer, and encouraged her in her ambitions. But little by little I realized that it did not mean as much to Rosemary as I had thought and that she was prepared to relinquish that ambition for something more easily achieved. Rosemary never went to The Holm with us, nor did Tom's sister Josephine. Gabriel's sister, Christina, was ten years older, married and lived in Scotland, and Nick had only a younger brother, still in short trousers, whilst Ruth and Rachel Jacobs were also too young. The Holm was a haven just for the seven of us and nobody else knew about our visits there.

The day after the evening it had thundered was a Saturday and I met Miriam by accident in the library. 'Did you stay long?' I asked.

'The others went, but Tom played me some Bach,' she said. 'It's quite ridiculous that his father expects him to go into business. Tom really must go to study music in Manchester or London.'

'Haven't his teachers spoken to his parents then?'

'Oh, you know men teachers – too lazy to bother. Besides they all think there's "brass" in business and wouldn't dare suggest there was a better way of making it.'

If Miriam's determination was enough, Tom Cooper would soon be studying at the Royal Academy of Music. How well did his parents know Miriam? I didn't put it past her marching up to tell them what Tom should do. He wasn't half so ambitious as Miriam was on his behalf.

Miriam heard a week later that she was going, at her father's wish, for a year to a boarding-school in the south. She was predictably furious.

Susan and I had a year to go before we left the High School, and Lally was still undecided what to do. But in the autumn Lally's father arranged for her to leave school and go to live with him and her new stepmother in London.

'They want me to learn to type,' she said.

In this way, by October we were to be scattered, for Tom and Gabriel went off to do their National Service for eighteen

32

months, and Nick got down to some hard work, his eye on an Open Scholarship. By the following spring builders were hard at work demolishing part of the old house in which we had spent a magic summer.

Lally had lain listening in the darkness to the sound of aircraft. It was all right, Nanny Partington was in the next room so she need not be afraid of them even if they dropped bombs. Nanny was quite nice, but she was only there because Mummy had gone away. Please God let Mummy come back. Perhaps if she went to sleep she would see Mummy in a dream. Nanny Partington said Mummy could not come back because she was ill and needed looking after in a nursing home. A nursing home was a house full of nurses in blue uniforms and caps on their heads with red crosses like the uniform she had in her acting box. The nursing home where Mummy was in bed was a long way away, they said, away from bombs, so she need not worry about Mummy being bombed. It seemed ages ago that Mummy had gone away. She did not like to think about that time when Daddy had come home wearing his brown uniform with the hat with a gold badge. Before that too there were nasty things that she couldn't remember though she knew they were nasty. But when Daddy had come home that time he had been cross and had shouted at Mummy and thrown a bottle across the room. She had wanted to say 'Don't be cross with my Mummy.' But Mummy had been cross too. Mummy had gone on shouting, so Daddy had put her to bed and she had woken in the night and heard Mummy crying. She had got up and gone into the big bedroom and the light was on and Mummy had said: 'You love me, don't you, baby?' and Daddy had stopped her running over to Mummy and had taken her back to her own bed. She had sobbed herself to sleep again. It was all her fault. She had not looked after Mummy properly when Daddy was away. She did love Mummy. It was funny when Mummy gave her chocolate instead of a proper tea and dinner. Nanny Partington gave her proper dinner as well as tea, and porridge for breakfast. But she still wanted Mummy to come back from the nursing home. If she were very, very good she would come back. After Mummy had gone away Granny had come to look after her at first because Daddy had had to go away again to fight. Granny and Daddy whispered a lot together and one time she had hidden behind the black-out curtains when they were talking and Granny had said: 'She was incapable of looking after a baby.' 'I thought it would steady her,' Daddy had said. Which baby did they mean? Mummy didn't have a baby. She could hear him quite clearly and that was what he had said. Mummy had not been steady. She had often used to say: 'You're nice and steady on your feet, go and fetch me my little parcel from the grocer's.' And so she had gone all the way down the road by herself to the shop on the corner where they kept the heavy parcel wrapped up in brown paper, and put it in her basket, and walked home with it because she was steady on her feet. Mummy hadn't liked long walks outside. It was not her fault if she was not steady on her feet.

Granny and Daddy had not seen her hiding behind the curtains that time, listening, and after that Daddy had gone away again to fight in the war and Nanny Partington had come to look after her and Granny had gone home.

Oh, she did wish they would let her see Mummy. She could tell the nurses how to make Mummy happy. It was quite easy if they went to a shop if there was one near the nursing home and got Mummy her parcel of medicine. But perhaps they would have even better medicine there? She had asked Nanny to write to Mummy, but Nanny had said that Mummy would not be able to answer her letter just yet and they must be patient. Mummy would think she had forgotten her! Mummy would write to her soon and Nanny would read it to her. Long, long ago, when Mummy went away once before, she had sent her a postcard with a picture of a pretty lady dancing. Every day now she waited for the postman, but he had only brought her a picture of an Easter chicken from Granny.

Nanny Partington said Granny was looking after Grandpa because he was old. Once, she and Mummy had lived together in a little house near a field with a cow, and Mummy had shouted a lot and been cross with her and then taken her on a train to see Granny for a holiday. She would like to have stayed with Granny, and Granny said: 'Leave the child with me.' But she had clung and clung to Mummy so they had left and gone away on another train in the dark and that was how they had come to this house near the grocer's. And then, she could not remember all that had happened but Mummy said: 'You love me, don't you, you love your naughty Mummy?' which made her laugh and Mummy had laughed till she cried again. It was all mixed up with Mummy lying asleep, but not in bed and the telephone ringing and ringing. That had happened a lot and one day she had felt so hungry in spite of the chocolates that one day she had taken some money out of Mummy's purse and run out of the front door when Mummy was asleep. It opened on to the pavement and she had run down the pavement to the grocer's because she knew they had biscuits on the counter and she had bought two biscuits and the shop lady was nice. But when she got back it had been the time when Daddy had just come back and he was standing at the door with his brown uniform on and when he saw her he shouted: 'Where have you been?' She had been so surprised to see Daddy that she did not know what to say so she went on eating the biscuit and followed him into the house and they went into the room with the long sofa where Mummy used to sleep and where she had been asleep when she took the money for the biscuits. But Mummy was not asleep. She was standing in front of the fireplace and she had taken her clothes off. Daddy was being very cross with Mummy and he made her fetch Mummy's dressing-gown and then he said: 'Go to your bedroom and I'll bring you some more nice biscuits and a glass of milk. I have to talk to Mummy.' But Mummy laughed and shouted: 'She doesn't like milk.' It was not true. She did like milk but she had had only water to drink in this house. In the bedroom she could hear Daddy talking to Mummy and then Mummy screaming and screaming and she stuffed her hands in her ears and found her teddy bear and cuddled him. Why was Daddy so nasty to Mummy? It was ages before he brought the milk and she said: 'I want my Mummy.' And that time Daddy said: 'A doctor will come to make her better. I am sorry. I did not know she was so ill.' She had not known Mummy was ill.

'Does she have a pain in her tummy?' she asked him. And she asked Daddy if Mummy and she could go away to stay with Granny because they had a nice dog and Granny wanted them to stay, she knew she did. But Daddy said: 'Your Grandpa is ill and Granny has to look after him now and I have to go away. She will come to see you but I am sending for a very, very nice lady to come to stay and look after you. She was my nurse when I was a little boy.' 'But I'm not ill!' she cried. 'Where is my Mummy?' she shouted. 'Has she put her clothes on?' And it was the next morning that Daddy had got cross with Mummy again and thrown the bottle across the room into the fireplace and they had shouted again and Mummy had screamed and screamed. But then the doctor came and Daddy came into her bedroom at night and it was dark and he said: 'Mummy is ready to go now – to be looked after – and you can kiss her goodbye.'

'I have put a picture of the child in your case,' he said to Mummy and Mummy let her kiss her but then she pushed her away, and so she said: 'She wants her magic drink to make her better.' And Daddy said there were no magic drinks but they would make her better in the nursing home. And Mummy just said 'Goodbye,' again and the lady next door came in because Mummy was in a taxi with the doctor and Daddy, but then Daddy came back soon after and then Granny left Grandpa for a few days and stayed with them. And Granny and Daddy had whispered again and Daddy said: 'It's not my fault, it's hers.' And she had thought he meant her. Then he said: 'She could have managed to look after herself but I won't have my child put at risk.' Granny said: 'She's my child. She shouldn't have married.' Then Granny went back home in Scotland and Nanny Partington came and took her to live in another house and Daddy went away again.

Soon she nearly could not remember what Mummy had been like at all. Mummy was just something that seemed to fill an empty space in her head.

It was when Nanny Partington was still there that they told her that Mummy had gone to Heaven. A long, long time after. But she remembered that Mummy had not wanted to go to the nursing home. She had gone because of her, because she was a baby and had made Mummy ill. But it was Daddy who had sent

*Mummy there. And the nursing home had sent her to Heaven.
Daddy did not come back either though Nanny Partington said:
'After the war you can go with your Daddy.' She stopped asking
to write to Mummy in Heaven. She felt angry with her now for
going to Heaven and angry with Daddy for sending her away in
the first place and miserable because it was her fault. Every
night she lay thinking about those days in the funny house with
the shop down the road and Daddy in his uniform. What had
she done wrong to lose Mummy? She had tried to look after her.
Mummy had gone to Heaven because she had not been good
enough to keep her and it was no good any more being very,
very good because she could not come back. Nobody ever came
back from Heaven, Nanny said.*

*When the war ended she went back to the Granny with the
dog to live until she was grown up. Now she remembered
Mummy only when she was asleep and they were not nice
dreams, though she dreamed them less at Granny's. Daddy
went back to London and then he had to go abroad a lot on
business. She liked living with Granny. Later she began to
wonder how they knew that Mummy was really in Heaven.
When Granny talked of her it made her feel that Mummy was
somehow still alive.*

Just once Lally almost dared to ask her 'Is my mother really
dead?' but she did not, perhaps sensing that the old woman's
daughter and her mother had been somehow rather different
people.

During the following year I often saw The Holm from the
outside when I went down the road past the church, but now it
looked more ordinary with a FOR SALE notice on a pole at
the front of the drive.

It was Coronation year and only Susan and I and Nick were

37

left in Eastcliff, but we hardly ever saw Nick who was busy with his Oxford entrance before he went abroad. Gabriel wrote to Susan to tell her he had decided to read medicine in Edinburgh when he was released from the army. As for Tom, his exploits at Catterick were retailed to us by his mother. I felt it was unfair that girls were excused National Service.

In the summer Miriam came back from her boarding-school and waited for her results as Susan and I were doing. 'I've decided not to try for Oxbridge,' she said. 'I shall go to London instead.' Her political beliefs, which had been dogmatic enough before, seemed to have hardened after exposure to the suavities of the south of England.

'I expect she'll persuade Tom to go to the Royal Academy of Music there,' I said to Susan, for I was sure that was the real reason for her decision.

One August Saturday we got our 'A' Level results and met to compare them. Fortunately we'd all done rather well, especially Susan whose grade on her special history paper was outstanding. But she was still determined not to go to university. 'I want to study because I enjoy it,' she said. 'I can combine it with a job on the *Calderbrigg Gazette* if they'll take me.'

I was sure they would. They did, gave her a newfangled traineeship.

Miriam had also done very well, having specialized in the political side of history and in economics. Odd that both she and Susan should have done the same subject and yet be so different. I was sure though that my friend Susan was planning some other secret apprenticeship – to writing perhaps. As for me, I got results that pleased Mr Gibson extremely – especially in French. I stayed on at school an extra term to sit the Cambridge entrance. I had also found a new mentor, a writer whom I always called 'Simone de. . . .'

Susan enrolled for two evenings a week to study typing and shorthand, as the work on the *Gazette* was not turning out too time-consuming as yet. Susan laughed a bit at my feminism for she knew what a romantic I was. I agreed that squaring Eros with feminism might be rather difficult. I took to wearing yellow stockings and a pair of dark sunglasses, and smoked Gauloises. At my interview for Newnham I did not however wear the stockings, though I did smoke the Gauloises. It was a cold frosty weekend and I enjoyed every minute of it, in love already with the place and the people. I don't know what I'd have done if they'd rejected me, but they did not.

Before Christmas Miriam returned from her first university term and she and Susan and I went to an opera in Woolsford and afterwards sat rather daringly in a pub and drank sherry.

'The times are narrow,' declared Miriam. 'You'd never think there'd been a war not so very long ago. We've got to get Labour back – not that they're real Socialists, only the next best thing at present.'

'I didn't see much difference up here when they were in power,' I said. 'England was just as narrow.' I had decided that I preferred France to my own country and after Christmas I went there to work. It was a happy period of my life, teaching English in a lycée in Bourges – but nothing to do with this story. When I returned in the summer Susan told me that Lally had recently visited her grandmother.

'She's got a job and moved away from her father. And she's going to be a model!' According to Susan, Lally had looked well, very smart and stylish. After learning secretarial skills she'd met the brother of a fellow learner who had a friend in an advertising agency who knew some firm who wanted the right girl to advertise tennis racquets. Lally had gone just for a laugh and a photographer had done pictures for a new promotion at the agency where the friend's brother worked. 'He told her she could earn over a thousand a year, could be taken on by a photographic agency, wouldn't need a modelling course if they liked her!' said Susan. I thought, a thousand a year! Young men who earned over a thousand a year in Eastcliff were already successful businessmen. Lucky Lally.

'They liked her tennis picture,' Susan went on. 'She was taken on the agency's books as a sort of freelance – and left her typing job.' Susan had had the impression that Lally was well on the way to success.

'Nobody up here ever saw the possibility of Lally's face,' I said. 'She had to go to London for things to happen.'

'She said that when they want you for a photo you don't have to bother to be a "real person" which she finds an effort –you can hide behind the face. Those were her very words.'

We pondered this. ' "I can think what I like and just be the sort of person they want me to be on the surface", she said.'

I felt that Lally was a more complicated creature than we had imagined. What lurked *behind* the face? Susan was fascinated by Lally, I could see.

'A model has to be good at doing things quickly – packing an overnight bag, getting her face right, being patient – sort of mindless things, I suppose,' I said. 'Lally'd be good at that.'

'I expect the friend's brother and the agency fell in love with her,' said Susan. We knew that Lally was not conceited and guessed that it was rather unusual to begin the way she had, but she might be in the process of being groomed for stardom. 'She's wearing her hair differently, in a sort of helmet, short like a boy,' Susan continued. I'd read about the urchin cut. This must be it. 'And she's seen Tom once or twice in London and said she'd also heard from Nick,' said Susan.

'Nobody wrote to *me*,' I said. I already felt I no longer quite belonged with the old gang.

I was doing some temporary office work as I waited to go up to Cambridge, and disliked it. 'Lally'll most likely make a fortune,' I said. 'Think how hard *we* work – three pounds a week for forty-four hours.'

Susan told me more about her job in the poky office in Calderbrigg, pasting up items for the *Gazette*, making cups of tea for the editor and typing letters. Soon she'd be out reporting, doing the weddings to begin with if she was lucky. You had to start somewhere and next year she hoped they'd honour their promise and send her to head office on the larger paper in the city where they might give her more interesting work. 'I enjoyed the tours of the printing works, watching the typesetters and the compositors – all those old founts and antiquated metals,' she said. Susan appreciated people who were good at their jobs. She didn't seem to regret her decision to stay in Eastcliff.

'I expect you'll be editing *The Times* one day,' I said.

'More likely writing up bits of local history,' she replied, but there was a gleam in her eye. She'd dreamed up a series on local halls, she explained, and was biding her time. No one wanted a 'slip of a girl' to have too many ideas in her head at first, but she was getting some training.

40

Our conversation turned to clothes. I was coveting a dark blue slipper satin evening dress to take up to Cambridge. 'There'd be nothing you'd need a new dress like that for in Eastcliff,' said Susan. There was nowhere *she* wanted to go. She spent most Saturday afternoons in the big old library in the city, reading and mulling over and copying things from old local histories, what she called her 'primary sources'. She looked really animated. 'The librarian seems to find it odd that a girl like me wants to spend her free time amongst his books. But he's quite amiable, gets me out old nineteenth-century directories from his special cupboard. He says I'm a survival from the days of the self-educated.' I didn't envy her, was all agog for Cambridge.

I loved Newnham, liked Cambridge, though I found it hard to do much work in the midst of the social whirl. I wrote to Susan occasionally telling her about parties and dances and men.

People are not so dedicated to work or study as you are, I wrote. *At university most people find work the thing they have to fit into enjoying themselves.*

She wrote back to me in her familiar, neat, rounded hand.

I know I should be more sociable, she admitted, *but there's not much going on here I really want to join.*

I thought what a pity she couldn't have the good time I was certainly having. It would be more fun for her if Gabriel were in Eastcliff, but he was now in Scotland beginning his medical studies.

I never heard from Nick who had started his second year in Oxford when I started my first term in Cambridge. Tom Cooper decided – what a surprise – to go to London for his music studies and I heard in some roundabout way that Miriam was already a figure in the student world there. Whether for political activity or something else was not clear.

The year when I was in love with a French actor, Gérard someone – I had his photograph in a silver frame in my Newnham room – I was also falling in love with a different man every few weeks. But I kept the actor safe in his frame to outlast them all – never tested, always inaccessible – or accessible – depending on the way you looked at it.

41

The terms flew by for me as I went on meeting new people and then dropping them and meeting other new people. I was enjoying myself, rushing about, writing essays in the small hours – but sometimes I thought of Susan writing her long descriptions of weddings. My mother sent me the Calderbrigg *Gazette* and there I read of 'primrose, champagne and turquoise-coloured outfits' which were 'gone away in' and numerous 'costly presents' delineated: sideboards, toasters, drink-trolleys, coffee percolators, water jugs. It didn't sound like Susan, and I laughed over them in the vac with her. Mr Bell at the library was growing quite embarrassing, she said. He disconcerted her by suddenly popping up at her side or staring at her fixedly when she went to him for information or elucidation. She hoped he was not going to become really tiresome or her visits to the library would have to be curtailed. She knew he was a bachelor. How did other girls manage? She wished she could freeze him off with an icy glance, but he was a man and rather useful.

Lally never wrote to me at all so I assumed all was going well. I had a letter from Miriam though. I think it was when I was in my second year. Tom had started a jazz band in which he played piano. They had seen Nick once at a concert with a girl they didn't know. *Did you see Lally's photo in the* Illustrated? *She was the model for new cocktail dresses. What a waste of cash*, Miriam wrote. *Tom gives me news of Eastcliff – my parents never know what's going on. They have great hopes for Tom at the Academy, you know. He is too modest to tell anyone he won a prize for composition. He's also writing for a musical paper which should keep him going financially in the future.*

Miriam would sort Tom out, I thought.

Wouldn't it be fun if this year we could all be home for Christmas? she added. This was not Miriam's usual tone. Singing *Auld Lang Syne* round the Christmas tree was the sort of proceeding Miriam would satirize.

When I was home for the vacations I'd realize how things were changing even in Eastcliff. There were vast tracts of desolate land a little further south where mills had once stood – I saw them from the train on the way home. Far Eastern competition was really biting and small family firms disappearing. The whole of the Riding seemed to be in a state of advanced decomposition, yet there were still woods and fields and houses, and the walks people made when they imagined they were miles from industry. But I was glad to have escaped. They were even building new houses in Lightholme.

I wished *I* could earn a thousand a year. I often wondered how Lally was getting on, seemingly set for success in the world; in a world I could not help regarding as trivial, the local bridesmaids and their finery on a higher plane as it were, the plane afforded by money and style. There was a girl I used to see in Cambridge who looked a bit like her. Men used to swarm round her like bees round a honeypot. That was probably happening to Lally too, I thought. One day soon we should at last be 'grown up'. This was a term I had always found odd. Could you go on growing 'up' or did you stop the way your height did? I sometimes wondered if people became more like their parents. It would be disturbing if they did. Perhaps my mother had once wanted to live in a different way, had ambitions?

But I wasn't concerned about my parents when I was in Cambridge. I'd often go days without thinking of home. It was only Susan's letters that brought it all back to me.

Every Christmas vacation I became a postman, a job I loved. I remember one winter evening I visited Susan after work, since my mother was indulging in a bout of pre-Christmas cleaning.

'Last term went by so fast. Cambridge will be over before I know where I'm going,' I said. Susan waited for any revelations I had to make and handed me a tangerine.

'It's come up to expectations then, on the whole?' she asked. I ranged round her small bedroom picking up books and putting them down again absent-mindedly.

'You *are* nice and snug here. Do your parents bother you? Mine do. All the time – "Gillian, shouldn't you be studying. Gillian you must go and see your Grandma" – and I only arrived back on Saturday! How do you get on with yours?' I said complainingly.

'I help out in the shop a bit in the evening or on Sunday mornings for an hour or two – some people still won't come into the shop on a Sunday, not even for a bag of sweets, you know. Even now rationing's finished!'

43

'Are the swings still chained up on Sundays?'

'I think so, but I haven't walked there for ages. I usually walk home under the bridge and in winter I'm glad to get back and don't linger.'

'It's another world up here,' I said. 'Honestly, I like to think of everything going on the same and you still here. How's the office?'

'It *is* changing even here,' said Susan. 'Lots of people have television now. It was the Coronation that made them all want it. The office is much the same though. I'm always busy so time doesn't drag. I've been reporting on ladies' luncheon clubs and even a fashion show now and then – not Lally's sort though. So long as I get my evenings and Saturday and Sunday afternoons free, I'm quite happy.'

'Don't you feel – well, wasted?' I asked her. 'I mean, I'm sure you're happy – you *look* happy – but don't the folk get you down?' Susan handed me another tangerine.

'Sometimes,' she admitted. 'Mr Bell is still a nuisance. Perhaps I could pass him on to you?' I laughed, and sucked the sweep pulp.

'Have you heard from Gabriel? Nick's promised to come over to see me from Oxford one Saturday next term. It's a difficult journey. I don't suppose he'll ever come.'

'Yes, I hear from Gabriel now and then. He likes Scotland and he enjoys his work.'

'Not become a Buddhist yet? – or a Catholic?'

'No – I don't think so.'

'I always thought he'd make a good Buddhist. Or perhaps a Quaker. Is he coming home for Christmas?'

'For a few days, Canon Benson said. Then he's to stay in Scotland with his sister.' The Rev George had just been made a Canon and the village had been surprised.

'I can never imagine Gabriel having anything so ordinary as a sister. Have you seen Miriam?'

'I don't think she's back yet. Mrs Cooper says Tom's back next Saturday.'

'Miriam's got her claws into him,' I said uncharitably. 'He seems to spend most of his time playing jazz and composing.'

'Well, *she* has to be working too, some of the time.'

'I used to have the impression that he rather liked Lally –

44

but no one could be a match for Miriam if she decided she wanted him.'

'Lally must have lots of beaux. What about you? Is everyone hopping into bed with everyone else?' Susan imagined that I, once the courtesies were over, was just longing to tell her about my latest man – or more usually my latest unrequited passion.

'Cambridge is rather chaste on the whole. Some of the women are terribly proper and dowdy. They give the impression of an invisible chaperone and they go to lectures a lot. I'd rather read the book the lecturer wrote, it's such a waste of a morning. But I've met some lovely people – I told you –'

'Oh, yes – Sebastian, wasn't it?'

'That was *ages* ago! Others since then. The trouble is there aren't enough women undergraduates to go round – nice for us, but it means you get landed with a shoal of men you have to disentangle yourself from – takes all term just when you've met somebody you really like. Then the term's finished. It's a funny way to live, but quite interesting, I suppose. I wish I could study the way you do. It's so distracting in Cambridge, such a disconnected way of life with things going on in different places on different levels. Clubs and things – college parties. *Lots* of parties. Too many really.'

'But you must do pretty well what you want?'

'Who does? I don't know what I really want, that's my trouble,' I said. 'I can be quite happy sitting doing my essay or reading in the college library – but then people break into your life and you think, what did I come here for? People, or work? Some girls have a full social life in London so don't really need Cambridge, but for us provincials . . . it all gets rather hectic. Doesn't bring out the best in me. I try to manage everything – work, people, love, talk. One girl went down last year – she couldn't cope. But the alternative is to sit alone working, and you could do that anywhere. Like *you* do. Depends a lot on whether you've a good supervisor.'

'It sounds overpowering.'

'Doing what one wants . . . *I* don't know, men don't seem to find that difficult. But if you can't have the person you want – I mean if you're in love with someone and he isn't with you, there's nothing you can do about it, is there? Except wait for it to pass and for someone else to replace him. . . . Being free to go to bed with people if you want doesn't solve *that* little problem.' I had realized that it was not only conventions that got in the way of the 'free' life.

'Sometimes I'd like to live like a man, I think,' I went on when Susan said nothing, though she was looking thoughtful. She always listened carefully to me. 'Men nearly always have what they want because women are so bloody pleased to be asked,' I said. 'Just think – if you could do just what you wanted with no consequences – travel without worrying about being raped, go to bed with nice men without worrying about pregnancy, drink with no hangover, fall in love and not be rejected. Men get away with more, don't they? I bet Nick does what he wants. Even Gabriel – *he* doesn't worry over what his father and mother think, because nothing would ever shock them. Men are much freer, Susan.'

'But Miriam always does what she wants too, doesn't she?' said Susan. 'And I expect the Bensons would be upset if Gabriel left the church.'

'At least he'd have the courage to.'

'Has your father been getting at you again?' asked Susan.

'Not really – he just assumes I'll come back home to teach one day. Do they all ask *you* if you've got anyone special?'

'Well, as I'm here most of the time they'd know if I had, I expect!' Susan replied mildly.

'Then they would ask you when you were going to get married!'

'You'll be free one day, Gillian. You'll go abroad or something when you know what you want to do.' She was very comforting. It *was* usually my father who got on my nerves. Mr Gibson was perfectly pleasant and polite to my friends, but the things he said behind their backs were not always complimentary. The outward expression of young romance enraged him. Any of his old pupils who dared to call on him hand in hand expecting congratulations were treated to a contemptuous glare and enquiries about their financial position. For a man so keen on Christian marriage, which he must be as he so hated the idea of pre-marital sex, or any other sort of sex, you'd think he would welcome the conventional couples, but no, even their timid courtships disgusted him. No wonder I was a rebel. Yet because of the way I had been brought up I was always aware of the effect I might have upon others, and that I might offend them. When we were still at the grammar and travelled to town on the bus it had been Miriam not I who had talked in a penetrating voice, to which the other passengers listened, transfixed. 'It's so embarrassing,' I had once confessed to Susan who was usually on an earlier bus. 'Why must she talk about God or the Labour Party in such a loud voice?'

'She hasn't any tact and she doesn't know the meaning of embarrassment,' Susan had replied. 'She was brought up to say what she thinks.' I was surprised that Susan could say that, that she had even noticed. Perhaps Miriam was not really sure what she thought either, had never really been.

'I don't want to be an actress any longer,' I said now, changing the subject. 'I've seen such good acting in Cambridge – some real stars. I'd never be in that league.'

'You could be an interpreter,' Susan suggested. 'You're good at speaking all those foreign languages.'

'There's not much opportunity for that at present,' I grumbled. 'Is that the time! Mr Gibson will be locking up. I'd better go.' I felt rather depressed, always the effect of Eastcliff after a day or two.

I walked over to the small mirror on Susan's chest of drawers. 'I look terrible,' I said. Susan offered no comment, just shook her head and offered me another tangerine. 'No – I really must be off. Oh well, perhaps another twenty minutes.'

'Do you still write?' Susan asked me then.

'I try, but I only ever seem to write about myself and that's no good. I bore me.' I lit a cigarette. Susan did not smoke.

'It's nice here with you,' I said. 'I've got one or two really good friends in Newnham – you'd like them, Susan. I wish you'd come down for a weekend. Women are much nicer than men, don't you feel?'

'Some, I suppose – I think it's hard just to be friends with a man.'

Was she thinking of Gabriel and hoping he had not found some seductive girl in Edinburgh with an accent like Mr Bell's? 'I like talking to men,' I said. 'About books and ideas. But most men do that with their men friends – don't want girls for that! It's the women who go on together about their psyches and their problems. You have to be careful not to give too much of yourself away or you get saddled with the wrong sort of woman friend – a clinger who "admires" you and wants to hang on to your skirt when you're invited to a party.'

Anyone would imagine that I had become a ruthless social butterfly, but Susan guessed that this was not the case. She knew I was rather soft-hearted in fact and didn't like seeing people miserable.

'You can already see the embryo teachers and the embryo civil servants and the embryo housewives – even the embryo nuns. They tell me I'm ambitious – I wish I knew for what.'

'Just ambitious to be the Gillian Gibson that fate meant you to be.'

'I don't have to act a part with you, Susan – though sometimes it can be fun pretending to be different people,' I said as I was finally leaving.

I wondered later if most people acted a part with others, and whether Susan's self-sufficient attitude was an act. But Susan was always so honest. I had always been a bit of a chameleon. I hoped the animal would one day find a habitat that matched its colouring without further need for adaptation.

Miriam arrived back in Eastcliff the day before Christmas Eve. It had begun to snow and I had been trudging round outlying farms with my heavy mailbag, enjoying myself, feeling useful and a little self-important. I was just passing the station entrance on my way home when I saw the Jacobs' car parked near the footbridge, with Miriam followed by Tom Cooper carrying suitcases advancing towards it. She waved to me across the road. Tom was saying 'goodbyes' and 'See you tomorrows' and helping Mr Jacobs stow Miriam's luggage in the boot.

'Happy Christmas,' I said. 'Are you staying the whole of the vac up here?'

'No,' said Miriam. 'Lots of meetings and rehearsals in the New Year – and Tom has to get back to work. We thought we'd manage a few days at least.'

48

'Gabriel's here! I saw him on my rounds this morning – I do hope Lally comes home too,' I said when I had crossed the road.

'Yes, she is coming,' said Tom.

'I'll give you a ring when I've got organized,' said Miriam to Tom, and folded herself into the car. Mr Jacobs drove away with Miriam waving vigorously. Tom remained standing, looking rather lost, holding his case.

'Well, must push off and see the parents. Gillian, come round to my house to sing carols tomorrow – about eight o'clock. Will you ask the others?'

'Thanks. I will. You're looking very well, Tom Cooper.'

'So are you, Gillian Gibson. Very healthy.' I felt my cheeks glowing.

'I think I'll be a postman when I've left Cambridge,' I said. He laughed, then turned to go up Braemar Road with its tall Victorian terraces and a few detached houses. I went home for a quick bite of lunch. There was no one else at home, but a fire was banked up and it was cosy in the snow light and the firelight as I ate the apple pie Mother had left for me. In the afternoon I walked back to Lightholme to the Post Office, past Christmas trees in people's windows. There was a feeling of anticipation in the air to which I could add with my delivery of Christmas cards. Only Nick and Lally missing so far, I thought – and something to look forward to at Tom's. It was to be the last Christmas we were all together in Eastcliff though I did not know that then.

Nick collected me in his car. Susan was already sitting on the back seat. It was a big new car. A good year for Mr Varley I supposed.

We crunched down to The Laurels at the end of its drive about half a mile away. Lally was waiting in wellingtons in the hall, her hair bundled into a white wool scarf. She had arrived only that afternoon.

'Gillian *and* Susan! How lovely! Hello, Nick. What bliss, the car, I was just too weary to tramp to Tom's in my wellies. So you didn't give home a miss this year, Nick?'

'I didn't come last year. The parents are pleased, I think.'

There were few people out in the dark. Those who intended

49

going to the midnight service at Sholey would be toasting by their coal fires trying to absorb enough heat to get them through the service in the church whose heating was often defective. Over the fields we saw, on the nearer hills, lines of crystal lights that belonged to gas lamps. Now the air seemed colder.

'Gabriel will be helping his father,' said Susan.

'Old Mystic,' said Nick reminiscently. 'He must be used to the frozen north by now.'

'Miriam's taking her test next month,' he said later as they drove to the Coopers. 'Hope she'll pass this time.'

'I never knew she'd failed it!' I exclaimed.

'Miriam wouldn't tell if she'd failed something, would she? I happened to meet the retired police sergeant who was my driving examiner in town last year. He told me.' We laughed.

Soon we arrived at the Coopers' old terrace house. The moon was up now, the clouds had parted and the wind had died down. There was snow on the roofs but the black branches of the trees that lined Braemar Road dropped another soft cargo of snow from time to time on the pavement.

Every window of Tom's house was blazing out light and a piano could be heard as we stood before the broad door. Mrs Cooper appeared in a green chiffon dress, holding a glass. 'Nicholas! And Lally! Hello Susan. And Gillian! Haven't seen you for ages. Come along in all of you.'

There was the pleasant smell of cigars wafting through the hall and the sound of laughter from behind a door with velvet curtains hung on large hooks. Tom came out of another door at the end of the long hall. We found Miriam already sitting comfortably beside a glowing fire drinking coffee. That must have been an after supper drink, I thought. She's probably been here all afternoon. Tom was bustling about with glasses and trays. He seemed taller now than I remembered – and even more handsome in his still boyish way, his wavy hair flopping over his forehead in best conductor fashion.

'Drinks first – have a fag. Eat up these bits of things, will you?'

I looked round the large room. It had a window embrasure still uncurtained, and outside there was a long lawn, like a white apron with black ribbons. Tom put the lights out leaving only those on the Christmas tree, a real fir tree hung with green, silver and gold baubles that shone in the firelight.

'Lally, you're looking marvellous. Glad you didn't stay with your father in London for Christmas,' I heard Tom say quietly.

'He's gone to Paris with Claire. Doesn't like Christmas.' She sat down carefully on a high-backed chair. He looked at her for a moment then roused himself.

'Mulled wine,' he announced. 'Miriam made it.'

Nick lay back in an armchair and took a proffered cigar. He was looking quite handsome too. I began to gabble away to cover any nervousness I felt at this reunion. Only Gabriel still to come. Susan looked rather pink and excited, but perhaps it was the spicy drink. Lally stared into the fire, elegant ankles crossed. She was wearing a high-necked gold sweater made of silk stuff and in the lobes of her ears swung tiny gold rings. I thought, if I were a man I'd fall in love with her.

There was a grand piano at the side of the room furthest from the fire, and a music stand. How many such gatherings these high-ceilinged Victorian rooms had seen, Christmas after Christmas, year after year, drawn together on this eve of Christmas when to be excluded was only not to have a home, a tree, a fire, a family. The old crew were together again – except for one.

Just as the second round of glasses were being filled and Tom was being urged to move to the piano, the door was opened quietly and Gabriel Benson slid in, a smile on his lips. Susan turned in his direction. Gabriel smiled at each of us in turn, took the glass he was proffered, tasted it, put it down again absent-mindedly and came up to the fire to warm his long hands. 'I helped clean the church this afternoon. Short of ironing his cassock I think father's ready for Christmas. When I left he was tucking into a good meal.'

'I thought you had to starve for Communion,' I said.

'He took Communion in the early morning. This is an extra for his curate.'

'We could all go to the midnight service,' I suggested. 'If Nick would bring us back.' I thought that Gabriel looked at me a little sceptically.

'This is *our* carol service,' said Miriam sternly.

51

Tom lit two candles in the brackets on the wall behind the piano, then sat down and began to play a medley of old carols, some we had not heard before, some familiar from our earliest years. I realized he was parodying various composers as he plaited strands of *Adeste Fideles* and *God Rest ye Merry Gentlemen* and the good old Yorkshire *Christians Awake* along with others less well known, making them into fugues, then *Ländlers*, and even a romantic waltz.

I though we all looked good. I was wearing my best navy-blue taffeta skirt and a velvet top and long, dangly earrings. The velvet top was rather large for me but I thought I looked passable. Susan had fluffed out her soft brown hair and wore a topaz-coloured blouse with a cameo brooch at the collar and a straight brown skirt she'd told me she'd picked up in the last C & A sales, a good fit for her narrow hips. Only Miriam had not dressed up, was wearing her usual black jumper and black slacks, but even Miriam had wound beads of a dull amber colour round her neck and a black velvet ribbon held back the severe style of her hair. She was looking fondly and rather proprietorially at Tom as he sat and spun his harmonies and counterpoints. Half-way through she got up to refill our glasses. The house gave out a feeling of relaxation. My mother might have been like Mrs Cooper if she'd married a different man I thought. A woman's happiness seemed bound up with whom she married. If that were the case, I thought, better not to marry at all, it was too much of a gamble. Perhaps no one else had ever asked Mother? Living within their income and keeping up appearances took up all my parents' energy. *I* would not be like that when I married. My parents did not exactly disapprove of Tom's parents, but always hinted that it was said that Mrs Cooper was sometimes a little too merry at the golf club. What was 'a little too merry'? I often wondered.

Tom's sister Josephine pushed the door open and stood blinking. Behind her was the latest boy-friend, rumoured this time to be a steady. Everyone said hello, but Tom went on playing and after a moment's apparent irresolution Josephine gestured her young man out again with a toss of her well-permed head. Nick said, 'Young love,' and Lally smiled. Then Miriam got up again, smoothing the rump of her trousers, and fetched from the top of the grand piano a neatly typed pile of

52

papers which she distributed. Obviously her own work. What efficiency!

'Do we have to stand up?' murmured Nick. 'I'm too comfortable to sing.'

'You can't sing sitting down,' said Miriam severely. We all struggled up to our feet and straggled up to the piano, emptying the remains of the now tepid wine down our throats.

'It's in the correct order,' said Miriam. 'We checked it this afternoon. We had a similar recital at college when Tom came to conduct.' Lally looked at her sharply, but said nothing. I thought, how tedious, she is making sure we all know she and Tom spend all their time together. He did not seem to mind.

'If I stand next to you, you can keep me in tune, Susan,' said Gabriel.

Susan looked pleased to be singled out. Nick moved up to Lally. 'Same here,' he muttered.

I felt a little left out till Susan moved a little nearer to me.

Tom started on *Once in Royal David's* City after saying, 'This is for you, Lally. First three verses for you then everyone join in.' She had a soft, high voice with a pure tone, though her speaking voice seemed recently to have become lower. It sounded like a choirboy, which was doubtless the effect Tom wanted. She sang obediently without emphasis. The chorus was rather ragged, not up to Tom's usual standards. We all tried harder. The three men sang *We Three Kings* followed by *Good King Wenceslas* with Susan as page and Gabriel as king. I was then allowed to sing *This Endris Night*, which I loved, even if I was never quite in tune.

'We sound rather well,' said the usually cynical Nick. 'I'll sing you *The Kings*, if you like.'

'We've sung that,' I said.

'No, not the Kings of Orient – Cornelius's kings *from Persian lands afar*.'

'It's not on our list,' said Miriam, but Tom was already launching into the slow chorale.

'Old Mystic can sing the second verse,' Nick said. 'I'm sure *he* knows it. And you can all join in the end, if you want.'

His own voice had improved, I thought and found myself rather moved. Strange what men's voices could do to you, even singing Christian carols. Like choristers' voices affected

Mother, who always wiped a tear from her eyes at an especially poignant high voice. But Nick's voice was no longer so reedy; it had grown deeper, stronger, a man's voice now. You could almost be in love with a voice, I thought. How exciting men could be – and mysterious, even ones you thought you knew quite well. Gabriel too, who did not need to look at the words, but sang in a dreamy baritone of shining stars and royal gifts. It was the desire, the promise of intimacy rather than intimacy itself, that excited me. I did want men to be different from me.

At *Offer my Heart* I was not too exalted to see how Lally was also staring across at the men. They seemed invigorated, taking charge.

Afterwards we each chose our favourite from Miriam's sheets. I chose *Of the Father's Love Begotten*, first heard in the Minster at York on a snowy night and then in one of the Cambridge colleges the week before; Miriam chose *Stille Nacht* in German with Susan improvising a second harmony; Tom *While Shepherds Watched* as an antidote to all the medieval carols he usually preferred. 'The barrack-room favourite,' murmured Nick, but did not sing the barrack-room words for once. Gabriel's turn was *Personent Hodie*, with its thumping bass chords, Lally's *In the Bleak Mid-winter*, and Susan's *Angels from the Realms of Glory*. It was not so long ago that we had sung like this at school, but that time seemed to belong to a different century now, from the standpoint of nineteen or twenty. Josephine and her suitor crept into the room and settled on the sofa with a bottle to listen.

Mrs Cooper brought in a large Christmas cake saying, 'I didn't make it myself I'm afraid.'

'Do *you* want to come to father's service tonight?' Gabriel asked Susan. 'I could bring you back in the boneshaker. Come with Gillian.' I was pleased. I didn't want the evening to end – but then I never wanted evenings to end.

'I'll bring you both back,' Gabriel said. 'Would *you* like to come, Old Nick?'

Nick said no, he was expected to wait up for his grand-parents who were to arrive later that night. Lally too had promised to help her grandmother with their guests – her

54

Uncle Hugh and his three aspiring ballerina daughters, now fledged on to stage and able to stay only for Christmas Day.

'Imogen's the pantomime fairy in Birmingham on Boxing Day,' she explained. 'She says it's better than "resting".'

Tom and Miriam obviously had their own plans. Tom sometimes played the organ in the town church – but not this year, apparently. After mince pies and coffee the party broke up. Nick dropped me and Susan in on our parents to explain our sudden conversion to Christianity and then whisked us up with Gabriel to Sholey before driving Lally back to The Laurels.

When we arrived at almost midnight I was surprised to find the church full to capacity. It was a plain, beautiful church, restored about a hundred and forty years before with none of the late mid-Victorian excrescences. Wreaths of holly and white chrysanthemums decorated the pulpit and windows, the latter of plain glass. The pews were high but comfortable. Mrs Benson was in the front one, looking vaguely benign as usual, and occasionally tucking in a stray hair from her wispy bun under her felt hat. Susan and I did not join her but let Gabriel go to his mother in the family pew. We squeezed in at the back, with the mulled-wine-feeling still in our veins, and concentrated upon looking sober. I was thinking about love, as the Collect for Christmas was read. I shut my eyes and tried to restrain my wandering daydreams. I was not sure whether it was Nick or Gabriel with whom I would like to be in some foreign city, driven away from 'all this', to some exotic paradise. Tomorrow, the dull proper family Christmas after the Eve, when for one night mystery was traditionally allowed to reign supreme – an exciting, erotic night which should have no anticlimax.

It had been friendly and heart-warming to have the old gang together again. Would we all go away separately for ever and never come back again? After the service, which filled me with nostalgia for a belief I had never quite abandoned, I felt I must fight against another sort of nostalgia that was already creeping over me as Gabriel whisked us back under the moon, the wheels of his old car scrunching over long-fallen snow. It had grown colder, the rain had moved away and we would have a reasonably white Christmas, even if no more snow fell.

Back to the family. Back to ordinary life, I thought crossly. I wished every day could be lived as a festival, as a gift, as a sort of Christmas.

Happiness came from such ordinary things as friends and conversation and music, but Christmas was not ordinary. I had noticed how happy Susan looked when Gabriel was there. I wondered if one day Gabriel Benson would stand with her at some High Altar and pledge himself to her. I was sure Susan dreamed of it already.

I remember one particular afternoon at the end of the vacation when I was alone in the house. The firelight was flickering over the old familiar objects, Mother's sewing basket on its low table by the side of the fire, the brass coal scuttle and the iron poker, the brass candlesticks on the mantelpiece. By the window Mr Gibson's bookcase with its pre-war Pelicans, and the sideboard on which stood a bowl of apples and oranges. In the corner the wireless from which I remembered as a very small child hearing the man I thought was called Mr Chamberpot telling us we were at war. There were several photographs in silver frames and a few unframed snaps tucked into the oblong mirror over the fireplace; plants on the window-sill that ran round one whole side of the room, a table runner embroidered by Rosemary on the solid oak table; Mr Gibson's big chair and Mother's smaller one, and the four dining-room chairs round the table; the rust coloured carpet and the curtains of a similar shade. All very peaceful, all very homely. I remember feeling how glad I would be to be back in college and yet a little guilty that I was glad. I was sure that my life would not any longer be spent in Eastcliff. Even so, Eastcliff had set the scene for all our adult lives.

2 *Exodus*

I left Cambridge after three years, having been in love many times, or at least ennobling my frequent infatuations with the name of love. I'd never fallen in love with the men who wanted me, and it had taken some time to realize that I too might enjoy myself without paying for the enjoyment with heady misery or heady elation. For me, love was 'romantic' only when it was unrequited and usually I'd fallen for men I'd met abroad. But there had been at the end of my time in the Fen city a man called Robin Carpenter who was tender rather than greedy, which was a change. I liked him too, but just before I went down for the last time I realized that he was not ready to commit himself to anything more lasting. The May Balls had come and gone and the second part of the Tripos was only an edgy memory which I was putting off thinking about until nearer the day of reckoning. I was aware that I would probably achieve a reasonable Second Class without having over-exerted myself. With a little of the effort expended upon work which had gone into my feelings, I might even have aimed for a First, but I had not made that effort. Susan would have done, I found myself thinking. My last summer term, my last term in Cambridge, would be over in a day or two.

'Is Robin coming round this afternoon, because if he is would you mind asking me for tea later on so that I can bring Laurence with me?' asked my best Newnham friend Jessica Coleman, a plump young woman who was still inviting men round whom she had met in an alcoholic haze at parties and then discovering they bored her.

'No, he's got his mother and sister up for a few days. Anyway, I suppose the less we see of each other now the better. He'll be off to his job in Finland for the British Council soon and I've decided – or rather *he* has – that we shan't go on.'

'Oh dear, I thought he was so nice,' said Jessica. Robin had been known by me for only four months but already seemed a fixture – almost a 'fiancé', I thought rather guiltily.

'Yes, well, he *is* nice, but Finland calls, and his career – and I don't want to go to Finland – not that he's ever asked me to –

unless it was something both of us wanted to go on with. And he says he can't feel as much for me as I obviously do for him. Same old story.'

'I felt he was as fond of you as you were of him,' said Jessica rather tactlessly, emptying the dregs of her cup of Nescafé in the sink.

'He probably *was* – but he's still looking for his ideal woman, and I'm not it. But if you want to freeze off your Laurence you can both come round to my room for tea. Tell him you forgot that you had a pressing engagement with me. I'll ask someone else – Andrew or Richard – both if you like.' These two were the sort of men who could always be asked round at short notice. They were amiable, had no designs on me, and I liked them, without experiencing other more awkward feelings which so often came between me and a beautiful friendship.

'No, don't bother, it's my own silly fault. I just have to tell him I don't want to go on seeing him in London. Trouble is he's so thick-skinned.'

Jessica had often confided in me how she wished she could be 'lust free'. Lust was apt to come upon her after only one drink, but she was a cheerful girl – and not a great drinker. Perhaps it was just a zest for life? 'No, it's just Mother Nature,' said Jessica.

I had suffered from Robin Carpenter's decision more than I would admit, but I no longer wet my pillow with tears, as I had done for several beloveds met abroad, especially a young French Canadian. I had always feared Robin would say what he had so predictably said. I did not at the bottom of my heart really believe that anyone could fall in love with me – for they did not know the *real* me! If they did I feared they might be even more reluctant to commit themselves.

Sometimes I would think about my romantic passions and be amazed that there seemed to have been so many people to whom I had for a time given my heart – or thought I had. 'The changing tenants in the House of Love' some book I had once read had called such people, implying that as the feelings of a person like myself were always unrequited they shifted to others. My house of love seemed to have had many rooms, but also to be in a constant state of ill repair. There had been

beautiful Sebastian who turned out to prefer choirboys. He
had been followed by Rupert, a public school *homme moyen
sensuel* who had at least taken me to a lot of pubs. Then Max,
one of my passionate holiday attachments, and Jean-Pierre
from Montreal (Yes, that really was his name!). Jean-Pierre's
eventual cooling off had been followed by Constantine, a
naturalized Greek with old-fashioned manners and a terror of
marriage. Then, just before Robin, Cedric, who belied his
name that seemed to belong to a Victorian melodrama, and
who was quite ordinary and actually read the same books as I
did and with whom I could talk for hours. But Cedric had not
been keen on other sorts of commitment, and so had been
followed by Robin who was very keen on kissing and other
practices, but easily distracted afterwards, returning into his
shell. What was the matter with them? – or was it with me?
Perhaps the proverbial older man would be my next destiny?
In the meantime there was a living to earn, or soon would be.
The grant had already run out and I had an overdraft. There
was always Eastcliff – but Eastcliff precluded the Robins and
Cedrics and also any freedom of manoeuvre in other ways and
I was determined not to return home till I had a permanent
room and a permanent job in London. Meanwhile I had
applied for and to my amazement had been accepted for a
temporary job teaching English in Spain for two months in the
summer.

I found most Englishmen a little childish compared with
women. I had long ago realized that a pattern seemed to exist
in my relations with the opposite sex, but this time, for once, it
had initially been Robin who had done the pursuing – and then
tired before the race was over.

I sat down and tried to think about packing, as opposed to
actually doing it. All the non-essential items could be stuffed
in my old trunk to be conveyed to London and then stored at
Jessica's. I was hoping that by the end of September there
would be some further work in Spain for another month. It
was cheaper to live in Spain, everyone said. I wished it were
France rather than Spain, for my Spanish was only just
adequate. First though I had to work for the money for my fare
and Jessica had offered me a bed for two weeks or so in
Hampstead. I intended finding a job in a coffee bar. The

Instituto de Idiomas would pay me enough to keep me fed for eight weeks in Barcelona and my fare back to London.

I cast an eye at my wardrobe and bookshelves. Strange to think that come October someone else would be living here, someone else would be writing a diary, studying, boiling a kettle for coffee in the old-fashioned kitchen and one day being visited by some man she thought she loved. I must concentrate upon my packing. I looked round my room, at the one-bar electric fire which stood in front of a big Victorian fireplace. How nice it would have been to have had a coal fire. There was no central heating and one bar had not been adequate in winter in Cambridge, which was a cold place. I gazed at the wardrobe, which was large and old-fashioned but roomy. There was a lot of space still in there for I did not have many clothes. Then a small table where library books were still piled; two bookcases, one belonging to me, the other to the college; a divan bed with my own folkweave bedspread that I had chosen three years ago for myself; a clutter of cups and plates, another table, this time an originally octagonal one whose legs had been shortened to make a coffee table. Books in and on all the cases and everywhere else. Still some books at home in Eastcliff too – I must get them back sometime. My Gauguin and Matisse prints were on the wall and two shabby armchairs completed the picture. The photograph of Gérard the actor was still in its frame on the low table. I would have to sort out the bookcase and the funny table to send to London along with my trunk. It seemed a pity to try to sell it. I had sold my christening spoons, purloined from home – but they were mine; and I would take along the textbooks I did not intend to reread and sell them at Heffers.

I decided to start on the masses of files and papers that were strewn on every available surface and on the floor. Among them was information about the ninety-seven jobs I had so far applied for – in copy-writing, in the Civil Service (to please Mr Gibson), in publishing (but my typing was not good enough), training to be a manager in a large bookshop (but they wanted a man), in the BBC (but that was impossible unless you were 'good with machinery' and could start as a studio manager), in a translation bureau (but they wanted someone with an interest in technical language). . . . Most of the jobs I fancied needed secretarial qualifications – I ought to have learned in the vacation in the classes where Susan had learned. But my friends and I had been snobbish about typing. I was now trying to teach myself to type, hence the small twenties typewriter I stubbed my feet against, as it stood in the middle of the room buried under files. I could type very rapidly but inaccurately with the wrong fingers. It seemed to be the story of my life so far. Bad typing, fluent French, a vast reading of novels, and a little experience in amateur acting were definitely not enough to equip one for Life, never mind a job in London with enough money to pay for a bed-sitting room. The year before, I had gone to London on a dry run, had decamped with a few tins of spaghetti and a few pounds to seek employment, selling first hats, then candy-floss for the six weeks of the Easter vacation. But I had been forced to retreat when the tins of spaghetti were finished (heated in a crooked pan over a gas-burner) and the pounds had all gone for two weeks' rent in advance for a room in a very curious hotel in Bayswater. Nothing I knew seemed to be useful for earning money, except what I had learned and might teach others. I should have done like Susan and begun work immediately. But no, I couldn't have stayed at home – and Susan had missed all the excitements of university, of meeting new people all the time, of freedom.

What was I to do in Spain though, except teach? The tentacles were closing round me already. Learning more Spanish would add only to the same problems – my unsuitability for anything but teaching. I'd rather work in a shop, or be a postman, or even a skivvy – except they were so poorly paid. They could all be experience. But work like that, though it gave you time to yourself after work, was physically exhausting. All I wanted was a humble salary which would pay for a room, however awful, in London, enough food to keep me going and some leisure time. No wonder most girls were going home for a rest whilst they waited for openings. Just think, if I'd accepted my first suitor, whom I'd never taken seriously but who had clearly been prepared to marry me eventually, there would now be no problem. No wonder that 'nice' girls got engaged to be married so they did not have to sell their christening spoons or work in snack bars. What did men do? They took not very interesting jobs, but jobs with prospects that would eventually pay well. There were not so many of these for women and most needed further training.

As I finally bestirred myself to fold clothes and sort papers, I decided to apply at another translation bureau in London, hoping that by October I'd be able to offer three languages instead of two. For the present there was Jessica's offer of lodging but I couldn't expect them to put me up after I returned from Spain. If only I had just enough cash to clear a month's rent in Kensington bed-sitter-land, but I had none. Going abroad was the only answer for the summer, just as it had been for all those impecunious characters in nineteenth-century novels who landed up in Boulogne as it was cheaper.

When I had a little more experience I could write short stories about penniless female graduates of ancient universities! I'd already written quite a few stories like this; the London débâcle of the year before had provided many vignettes of the strange folk I'd met in Joe Lyons or at bus stops. Evidence of these earlier attempts was now in my hands as I sorted and threw away. I should have concentrated either on my degree work or on writing. Instead, as usual, I had tried to do everything and was the mistress of nothing. I piled up the photographs and the programmes of plays where I'd had a small part – failed actress too. Cambridge already seemed the past, unconnected with me really, after all was said and done. I'd remember it more for the men I'd met and loved there, even though they too had never measured up to my great ideal. But I was still optimistic. Everyone went through a patch like this on leaving. I had been told to expect it. Like Mr Micawber I felt that Something Would Turn Up.

Only one week later Jessica and I were in London. Cambridge, as well as being the past, seemed also to belong to another world. I had both not wanted term to finish and yet had been impatient for it to finish. I'd always known that it would end one day but had imagined myself both older and wiser by then. I regretted my regular grant; inadequate though it had been, it had given me a certain financial independence from my parents. Later, I knew I would regret the settled termly existence, but for the time being it was exciting to have to live by your wits. I certainly did regret the time I'd wasted but it turned out that, as I had predicted for myself, I was awarded an Upper Second degree. The news arrived at the Colemans' breakfast-table during my first week in Hampstead. The next day I was to start on Haverstock Hill at a coffee-bar, where frothy *cappuccinos* were dispensed to the duffel-coated young.

The rest of the day of the results of the Tripos was spent receiving telephone calls from women friends who wanted to know how Jessica and I had fared. Jessica had done no work to speak of and scraped a Lower Second, but as she was already booked for a posh secretarial course nearby this did not matter. Others congratulated me and gabbled their news of holidays to come and autumn activities. Most were to stay in, or come to, London for training as housing managers or hospital almoners or teachers or librarians or secretaries. One, Mary Rivers, announced her engagement to her Cambridge steady. How infinitely depressing, I thought, and thought I did not envy her. Jessica was more philosophical. 'She's happy. It wouldn't suit you or me, but there you are.' I did not expect to hear from dear, but ultimately unsatisfactory, Robin till he was safely arrived in Helsinki. I was clearly not the marrying sort. They said men always knew. Neither was I the waitress sort either, I rediscovered after an hour or two at the espresso machine the next day. Still, there was Barcelona to look forward to. After a few days I wrote home. I had always been a good correspondent and knew what to leave out and what to emphasize in my letters to Mother and Mr Gibson. This time I emphasized the job I'd found and the work in Spain – which would be 'good experience'. For what I was not sure, but Mr Gibson would assume I meant for teaching. I always timed my letters judiciously, and was by now a practised hand at not exactly telling lies but smoothing over the truth – which was that I was short of money. Jessica's parents appeared pleased their daughter had 'such a good friend'. I wished I could be more honest with my father. I: seemed to me that he forced me so to accommodate myself to his expectations, when I spoke to him or wrote home, that I found myself transposing not only my own situation or my own opinions but the world in general, into terms he could understand. Even in matters of religion and politics, since my

63

own outlook was so different from his, it was up to me to make an intellectual leap and interpret it for him in *his* terms. Naturally he would never do the same for me, nor take my attitudes seriously. I was his daughter and therefore must take his world and beliefs as the true ones. Mine were an aberration until I 'grew up'. I wanted nothing more than for him to accept me as grown up – and the best way was by earning my living. It would be wonderful to have had an objective adult in whom to confide now and then, but I had never confided in anyone in Eastcliff except Susan. Susan certainly had an adult sort of life, even though she lived at home.

I had survived my knocks and bruisings alone. My father might moan about my absence from home but would, I knew, be secretly relieved that I could take care of myself, for he was a busy man. Well, so long as I could go on keeping him moderately happy whilst able to live my own life, fall in love and out and wander around London in my free time. . . . Once I got a good job and some cash I would be all right. And my respectable degree should also please them, though Mr Gibson might think I ought to have got a First.

'*You* can stay with *me* when I am rich,' I said to Jessica who laughed and said with no malice: 'That'll be the day.' The household reminded me just a little of Miriam's, whose parents were also magnanimous. Miriam had digs not far away in NW1 and I had tried to telephone her but 'They're away,' was the only answer. So too apparently was Lally. London was nowhere to be at the height of the summer, even if it were not too oppressively hot and dusty, yet I scarcely noticed the weather. The physical labour made me so tired that I had a bath and went to bed with a book when I got back to the Colemans'.

I was waiting for an interview at the Olympia translation bureau when a letter from Mr Gibson arrived. He informed me that Nick Varley according to his father who had stopped for a paper in the Marriotts' shop at the same time as himself, was researching abroad after his 'brilliant First' of the previous summer. He'd have to do his military service later. I wondered how Gabriel was getting on. Susan would know. I felt a little lonely when I thought of Susan, for there had been no one in Cambridge quite as close as Susan had been to me. But Susan would not run away, she'd always be there; that was the nice thing about her. My mother had recently said in a letter that Susan was doing well, but had not elaborated, and it had been some time since I had heard from her.

I gathered myself together in the next week or two and was not displeased to get off finally to Spain, along with a case which contained my one or two decent dresses, my journal, a book by Ortega y Gasset as a bow to Spain, a mound of make-up and an umbrella, (the rain in Spain?). The rest of my possessions I left at the Colemans'. At least I'd be safe for two months. I looked forward to this new foreign country as the train rattled through France before stopping at the frontier where another train on a different gauge lay waiting. It was boiling hot; people went out on the platform to drink water from a fountain there. Somewhere on the left lay the sea which I had seen sparkling before the frontier tunnel. Now I was really alone, and excited, and felt the lift of spirits which the south was always to give me. My free new life lay waiting, I thought, and one day, I was almost sure, happiness lay waiting for me too.

I walked daily up and down the Ramblas in the heat of the Catalan sun. I had a room in a small pensión just off the Barrio Gótico, and after my morning classes between the hours of 10 a.m. and 2 p.m., I would go for a sherry in one of the cool little *bodegas* that abounded there. Nothing happened then until four o'clock, and I had now learned to spin out a *cerveza* and a plate of tasty bits and pieces in the Plaza Real for my lunch. There was that smell of drains and garlic, and something else at first indefinable that I had smelt for the first time on my arrival in Barcelona. Down from the bottom of the Ramblas, where was situated the Instituto, and then turning as if to go to the French station, by the empty hugeness of the church of Santa Maria del Mar – sacked by the Reds in the Civil War – I had seen broad grey pavements where heaps of melons awaited the market traders, or perhaps for export. They lay, plump, green, occasionally yellow, like severed heads, in gigantic piles. I thought their scent pervaded the rest of the city, with occasionally a fishy smell too.

I had loved this city on sight, amazed that it should be so big, so lively, so *there*, with its purposeful inhabitants. Somehow I had imagined it would be smaller, more provincial, but it exuded the feel of a capital. Neither was it, I was always being told, really Spanish. The Catalans were not Spanish, they were Catalans, speaking Catalan, using Castilian only when forced to speak to foreigners or Madrileños. This could have been unfortunate, because I did not speak any Catalan. The Spanish I had acquired in England was useful only for reading newspapers and books. Catalan was prohibited as a written language and on the radio, but the Catalans were talkative and I discovered many of them also spoke French, which was a relief. Books of a political or anti-religious nature which the Generalissimo did not wish his subjects to read could always be obtained in French, and there were newspapers in French too.

The Rambla de Flores was a riot of blooms: bouquets of red, orange, yellow, purple flowers festooned the stalls, and further down there was the bird market with birds of similar colours. The female human inhabitants were also dressed in colours of emerald, and egg-yolk yellow, blues and reds, colours which seemed of a different dye than in England. But if you tired of sun and colour all you had to do was to turn in at any point of the upper Ramblas to find yourself in the old Gothic quarter with its cool, dark buildings, large and small, set in their cobbled squares. I had not yet ventured further north of the centre of the city than the Paseo de Gracia whose elegant shops took my breath away. They seemed to belong to a sort of more spacious Paris with their wide pavements patterned with the shadows of leaves from the lime and plane trees. There was even an underground station, which also surprised me, and always crowds of people. I was visited by a strange feeling: what had all these people been doing when I was growing up in a nothern English village? How could they be there only a thousand or so miles away and be so different, taking their own ways for granted? What made the mothers dress their children so exquisitely in starched cotton dresses of pure white, with white silk ribbons in their hair? There were children everywhere and even the poorest seemed to be clean and starched. I had seen them in the municipal park dancing tangos in the open air at some wedding feast and observed them as they strolled hand in hand with older people down the Ramblas at all hours and ate large meals at midnight *en famille*.

Sometimes I turned down Santa Ana or Santa Lucia towards the old quarter when the feeling of the too muchness of people and activity overwhelmed me. What could I teach people of such grace and liveliness that they did not already know? The English language was all I had. They could teach me far more, teach me happiness and grace and style. Their tiniest actions were endowed with chic. If you bought a postcard it was ceremoniously wrapped up and handed to you in coloured paper tied in a little bow. I wanted to belong here in this great southern city even if it had a Fascist dictator and was full of the resentment of a vanquished people. The Middle Ages seemed to brood here still. I had not thought I liked Catholicism, but here it seemed a natural part of life, which appeared easier and more pleasant than life in London. But working hours were long; people often had two or three jobs to keep going, and women especially were overworked. Yet the cafés, the street life, the restaurants (into the best of which I naturally hadn't the money to penetrate) all seemed to be full of lively, happy people. Was it the Mediterranean climate that caused their apparent joy in life?

I tried to absorb something of the history of Spain and of this province, traced Moorish words in the Castilian language, learned what had happened here only less than twenty years before – but Barcelona was bigger than all this history. It seemed so successful, so sure of itself, a mixture of tradition and the very up-to-date. Women and girls looked just as chic, or even more so, than in Paris. And then you came across the dancing of *Sardanas*, at noon in the old squares, to the melancholy cadences of pipes, dignified folk dances that were far removed from revivalist Morris dances or fake olde-worldiness. I was urged by my students to visit the Sagrada Familia, the unfinished church that winked in the sun, in the distance, seemingly made out of barley sugar, and Gaudí's other monument, the house of fantastic design; urged to go to the Pueblo Español to see the remains of some 1920s exhibition, and to the park of Montjuich – but so far I had resisted these temptations. The square mile or so around the

Ramblas and the Gothic quarter down to the sea where loomed the great, ugly monument to Columbus was enough for me to assimilate. I had not yet even walked along what the inhabitants called the Diagonal and the Paralelo, the wide streets built and called after Generalissimo Francisco Franco and José Antonio Primo de Rivera. It had been enough to wander down the Ramblas to eat my *tapas*, to sit in the summer night late at the *pensión* supper, to penetrate the gloom of Santa Maria del Mar or the Catedrál, to see the old shops like medieval workshops, to watch the people circulating in the Plaza de Cataluña. I had seen only the exterior of the provincial governor's old palace – the Disputacion, and glimpsed through an open door the Archives of the Crown of Aragon with its courtyard where the sun glinted on a splashy fountain, but I had been down to the port beyond the Colón monument to see the boats leave daily for Palma de Mallorca, Minorca and Ibiza. Occasionally I saw an English tourist or two, not many, on their way to the Balearics. I had been told that the *Franceses* and the *Ingleses* and the *Alemanos* were now beginning to invade the villages on the Costa Brava. Tourism on a grand scale was beginning, was indeed the reason why so many people wanted to learn English. It was a pity that I had not yet learned to speak Catalan. It was not too difficult to read, for it resembled Provençal, the literary language of French Languedoc, which I knew about. The people were first cousins, or even closer, of the French Catalans. Their kingdom had once included Perpignan, was in some ways as remote from Paris as it was from Madrid or Seville. The Barcelonese were perfectly capable of speaking Castilian to visitors if necessary, but it would have been better if I could have spoken Catalan and shown them on whose side I was. Yet even ordinary Spanish words at table were invested with glamour. How different were *mantequilla* and *melocotones* from butter or peaches – so romantic! How I loved it all, the sun, the buildings, the smells, the people. I would have liked to stay in Catalonia for ever; I found it all so entrancing. It seemed to correspond to the extrovert, happier side of myself that loved talking and touching and gesticulating and laughing and singing and flirting. But I was careful not to flirt with my students. One drawback of Barcelona was the apparent tendency of young men to whistle through their teeth at girls, usually from behind pillars. I had not wanted to find my solitary walks or café-sitting obstructed by importunate males, so I had used that umbrella, which for some reason I had packed, as a sunshade, and was careful to look, I thought, slightly eccentric, and always to carry a book and a *cuaderno* so that people would leave me alone at café tables or in the street. It would be nice however to have a young man of one's own to walk with occasionally. I had not dared to walk alone in the notorious Barrio Chino where I had been told prostitutes for the busy port would hang out of windows shouting at sailors, and I had noticed that Catalan women did not stroll anywhere alone. Usually the strollers were young couples or mothers with children, or on Sunday, family parties, and occasionally women students arm in arm. Even here it was more fun being a man.

When I went into churches I was careful to drape a long-sleeved cotton cardigan over my arms, having also been told that women could not enter churches bare-armed, never mind in trousers. They said that on the beaches of Barcelona even the bathing costumes of women must be covered. No bikinis allowed. Well, if the Pope wanted good Catholics to behave thus I was not going to offend him. I cultivated my pure scholarly look wherever I went alone.

My English classes were held in a run-down building which had a warren of little rooms not far from the port. The teaching groups were rather large and as the classes were not cheap, people wanted value for their money. I found I was, to my surprise and chagrin, a born teacher, enjoyed preparing topics and going through points of English grammar and vocabulary and giving many tests. I had had a little practice before, in Bourges. But the proficiency of my intermediate classes was not yet great enough for any interesting topics to be discussed, though occasionally I would speak daringly for a few minutes about politics – or on English writers and life in England, before asking the students questions in English on what I had been saying. Most of the class were men, and mostly over twenty-five, already possessing a degree or business experience. I found I was not very well up in English exports or business methods and resolved to try to find a book in one of the many delicious bookshops which might enlighten me. Spanish or Catalan was theoretically not allowed to be spoken at all in the English classes. The directors of the Instituto favoured a quasi-Berlitz method of learning, but I managed to learn quite a lot from my students of the Spanish equivalents for my English ideas. They must have found me amusing for they laughed a lot. But fancy my fiancé (hastily invented) allowing me to travel alone !

It was one morning after a particularly sticky lesson when I had felt particularly inadequate, having attempted to explain the English educational system, that I decided to look for a better textbook than the official one they all had to use. I went down Via Layetana and turned in towards the Barrio Gótico where I remembered seeing a second-hand bookshop in a narrow street that led back to the Ramblas. I was looking at some of the 1920s paperbacks, rather flimsy stock, and at some translations from French poets of the Nineties, wondering what cultural life here had been like in the Golden Age of Symbolism long before Franco, for the Spanish often seemed to follow French fashions in writing and literary cliques. Suddenly I heard a man's voice exclaim, 'Gillian Gibson!' and I turned, surprised. The bookshop blinds were down and it was dark after the glare of the sun, so at first I could not see the owner of the voice, who was standing in the doorway. He came up and I saw it was Nicholas Varley. Surprise made me drop my book and stare at him. He was sunburnt, was wearing a linen suit, looked relaxed, his fair hair bleached pale gold.

'What are *you* doing here?' he went on.

He seemed abrupt, almost rude.

'Teaching English for a time – and you?' I answered politely.

'It's my thesis,' he explained. Of course, he *would* be writing a thesis as he'd got a First the year before. 'It wouldn't interest you – economic theories of the Twenties, but I think the Generalissimo's hidden most of the original papers – or burnt them.'

There was a portrait of the Generalissimo in almost every restaurant and café, usually hidden away I had noticed in some back room. But the saucepan-hatted Guardia Civil were omnipresent and I half looked out of the door in case Nick were about to say something disrespectful about him. A moment later I realized that they wouldn't speak English – but Nick was the sort of person who said things in a loud voice openly that were better said in a whisper or not at all. A bit like Miriam.

'Come for a drink – where are you living?' I explained and he told me he was renting a flat for a few weeks, owned by a Spanish professor, a contact from Oxford, who was away for the summer. I put my intended purchase down, could not concentrate, and we walked out of the shop towards a *bodega*, which Nick seemed to know, down a short flight of hidden away steps. It was cool after the glaring sun in the square.

'I thought you were intending to do Russian at Cambridge – you haven't done your military service yet, have you?'

'Putting it off for as long as possible – I'll have to get it over with when I've finished my thesis next year – it's a confounded nuisance.'

I noticed, as we sat on two upturned barrels in the cellar, with a handful of Catalan businessmen and two English tourists, that Nick had a slight drawl. At first he affected an amused manner. How long was it since I'd seen him? Must have been that Christmas when we sang carols at Tom's. He'd never made it over to Cambridge needless to say.

Over a thin glass of deliciously cold, extremely dry sherry, I told him what I was doing, and my impression of the place. Nick had apparently been in Catalonia the year before for a week or two and was now putting the finishing touches to the Spanish section of his thesis. My knowledge of what had happened here before the Civil War was hazy, but Nick filled me in effortlessly and then sat looking at me with a faint smile on his handsome, chiselled face.

'You look well,' he said finally. 'And what are *you* going to do now you've got a degree?'

I must have looked gloomy then. Somehow Barcelona had banished all worries about what I would in fact do, once returned, and I didn't want to spoil my stay thinking about it. I had enjoyed being alone with no ties and no plans, just observing and drinking the place in. 'What about *you*? Are you hoping to stay in Oxford? Is that what another degree is for?'

71

'God, no – I had the chance to have two years on a post-graduate scholarship they gave me whilst I made up my mind. I think either I shall go to the States – or join the Diplomatic. I really want to be a financial adviser to governments.' I tried to look suitably impressed. Economics was a subject I felt extremely ignorant about. Nick seemed to have all the advantages, especially when on our second glass he said he'd managed to acquire some Catalan.

He looked at his watch. 'I'm due at the Archives at four – what about meeting tonight for a meal when you've finished your classes? Have you been to any good restaurants? The Cortijo? The Sacha? Or would you like to eat seafood or sample special Catalan delicacies?'

My money was barely enough for one square meal a day and I thought Nick must know this. I replied, 'I haven't the cash to go to posh restaurants, but . . .'

'Oh, I've plenty,' he said. 'What about meeting on Santa Monica? I know a good one there.' He had obviously decided not to waste his money on taking me to one of the fashionable open-air restaurants but why should he? I wondered if I might borrow from him to be paid back one day in England. 'We can have a gossip about all the old gang,' he said. 'Keep me up to date with Miriam's fame and Tom's etc., etc.'

'Oh, is she famous?' I asked.

'Sort of going-to-be, I think. Tom too.'

He piloted me across another paved square and left me with the prospect of seeing him again at eight o'clock for an aperitif and then a good meal. I felt a little dazed. Usually one glass of that sherry was enough. It was very strong and I'd drunk two.

I stayed indoors that afternoon wishing I had the money to buy a decent dress. Although the people in the city always looked smart and chic it was not a dressed-up sort of smartness. I had a sun-dress with a piece of the same material which I could tie round my shoulders, a dress I had bought with the last of my money before I left Cambridge, a green and orange dress with patterned squares. There was a laundry and a *plancha* place where they would do it for me in an hour or two – that was one of the wonders of the place – and I was there as soon as it reopened after the siesta. They promised to have it ready by

7.30 and as my class that day finished at 7 I could return and change and walk over to Santa Monica which was only about ten minutes away from my *pensión*. I washed my hair and put on my best earrings – a present from Rosemary for my twenty-first birthday, long, dangly, marcasite things. I swept my hair back in a French pleat and applied a liberal amount of eau de Cologne de Tabu. I didn't want Nick to think I was some naïve little provincial creature even if I was poverty-stricken.

But when he came up to me outside the café on Santa Monica he said, 'You *do* look good – sun suits you. You look quite Spanish, Gillian – I shall call you Juliana.' And I was pleased. Perhaps he was not quite so sophisticated as he liked to pretend and it was nice to talk English for a change and not to have to explain everything you said over and over again or consult a dictionary. He looked more handsome too than formerly, with his hair burned blond and his eyes brighter than I remembered. We sat down for a beer and some *tapas* first.

'I went to the *zarzuela* last night,' he began. 'Sort of music-hall at the Liceo – it's very *fin de siècle* the culture here, isn't it?' I knew exactly what he meant, had thought the very thing myself and for a time we discussed the Nineties and the theatre until he got on to the politics of Spain in the early part of the century. He did not show off as he had sometimes used to, but did seem knowledgeable. How did men always seem to acquire a large amount of esoteric knowledge? Still, I wasn't exactly a moron myself and surprised him with several quotations in my best Spanish.

'*You* don't need to speak the language – how did you get so far with it?' I said.

'Oh, I like learning languages – it's a hobby of mine.'

Somehow he got on to religion and then to Oxford and Cambridge and it was only by the time the second *cerveza* was being sipped that we turned to mutual friends.

'Susan's doing very well, Mother says,' I offered, ever loyal to my best friend.

'Yes, my father saw her in the village, said she'd been offered a byline of her own on the Saturday edition of the *Gazette* – the big one, not the Calderbrigg one – that's quite something – I wonder why she never wanted to go away,' he mused. 'She's clever, isn't she?'

73

'I'm beginning to see why,' I said: 'It's all very well getting a liberal education – but for what? I don't want to be a glorified typist or to teach little girls, but what else can I do?'

'Have you ever thought of taking a further degree?' he suggested.

'No, I'm not a scholar. I want to earn my living. I wish now I'd trained like Susan for journalism.'

'It's not too late is it?'

'I've got to earn my bread and butter away from home. They don't pay trainees much. Tell me more about Miriam then – and Tom.'

'Remember that play she was telling us about that Christmas? Well, she wrote another – a sort of satire, I think, something quite new about young people, and about the Jewish past, all mixed up with the future of England. It was put on in some Marxist outfit – and was a success among the *cognoscenti*, I'm told by Tom. Anyway, some little theatre wants to put it on! She's touched a nerve, I think – she always was an odd girl, wasn't she? Tom's apparently quite besotted and together they're going to burst upon a grateful public. He gives concerts already where he mixes the popular and the classical for youthful audiences. Not averse to a bit of rock 'n roll either, old Tom. *And* he writes for a musical paper – who'd have thought it?' Nick seemed both surprised and a little aggrieved. 'It seems they're going to get married,' he added. I gaped. 'She always intended that, didn't she? They're going to be the Socialist couple *par excellence* appealing to New Left audiences and collaring some critics' corners too. What about you? Don't you want to get married? I thought all girls did?' he went on.

'Oh – no – not yet anyway.' I was not going to pour out my disappointment over Robin to Nick Varley who was looking at me in a kindly but slightly superior way. 'Lally's the one who I thought would marry young,' I said after a pause. 'Have you seen her recently? How's the modelling world?'

'Didn't you see her in the mags? She was all over the place in the spring. I saw her once or twice in London. Haven't seen her for some time. I believe some mogul was after her.'

I digested this.

'And Gabriel?' he enquired as I crunched up the last of the delicious fried fishy bits that went with a beer in Barcelona.

'Susan says he works very hard but it'll be another two or three years before he qualifies.'

'At least he's got his military service over and done with,' said Nick. Then, 'Come on, the night is young, let's go to that Catalan restaurant. You'll never have eaten paella so good.'

He took my arm as we walked down the Ramblas on the other side from the old quarter. The crowds were thick and the air was warm, the trees green in the lamps that had only just been lit. It was about ten o'clock and all Barcelona was now going out to dinner. I began to say that I was sorry I couldn't pay my share, but he silenced me. 'It's nice to have a woman to go out with,' he said. 'Too much poring over those treaties and economic records and statistics make Nick a dull boy.'

I began to hum a Spanish song as we walked along.

'What's that? You're always hearing that tune here. Is it an old one?'

'Ancient – it's a tango your parents probably danced to,' I said and gave him the words.

'It's a very civilized place, isn't it, Barcelona?' he said as we sat down at a table laid with a creamy starched cloth. A large buffet at the back of the restaurant was piled with peaches and melons in ice and there was a profusion of flowers. I sighed with contentment. I *did* enjoy the good things of life. I had never exactly been showered with them, and England in spite of winning the war still seemed dull and starved of good things unless you were rich, although things had begun to improve a little. One's pounds here were favourably exchanged for pesetas and there seemed to be plenty of Catalans who also had enough money to eat well and enjoy themselves in spite of the Generalissimo. His portrait was more in evidence in this smart restaurant. The people seemed older than the ones who walked in the Ramblas, married couples, the women usually in black silk and piled with jewels, and there was the smell of cigars and perfume. I felt suddenly very happy. We ordered some Castellribas wine with our paella and some Valdepeñas with the cheese afterwards and hoped we had done the right thing. Nick smoked a cigar and I smoked Spanish cigarettes.

I was not drunk, just comfortably merry, when Nick said, 'I can make coffee back at my place – will you come back?'

He probably meant for more than coffee, I realized, and

then I thought, well, why not? He's attractive and he knows me well and I know him quite well, but not too well to make him out of bounds. I used to think him very fanciable once. Perhaps I still do. But I guessed that there would have been an endless procession of young women in Nick's bed. He exuded the old *savoir vivre* which would now extend to knowing about women. I could feel that in my bones and it was a relief after some of the rather less stylish approaches I'd suffered in Cambridge. It might even allow me to forget Robin Carpenter, or at least put him where he belonged – in the past. But I didn't think I could ever be in love with Nick Varley somehow. He *might* mean just coffee, but he now was smiling again and he said, 'You look very pensive.' He was the sort of man who noticed you and although he was most likely rather selfish, at least he made an effort. Without thinking: 'Have you ever been in love?' I asked him as I took out another cigarette. I loved the smell of the smoke they made.

'Oh, hundreds of times,' he said lightly.

'No – I mean really in love – I'd like to know what men mean by that?'

'So would I. Girls are always in love – it's their nature –some girls anyway.'

'Not Miriam?' I offered.

'Oh, not Miriam – no, she wouldn't waste her valuable time.'

'Isn't she in love with Tom then?'

'I don't know. You understand women better than I do, I expect. She loves him – I'm sure. And he thinks she's wonderful. She'll make something out of Tom, mark my words. Those two are suited to marriage. They'll probably have a brace of kids before you can say Jack Robinson.'

'But you said they were going to be successful.'

'Having children and being successful are not mutually exclusive activities, Juliana.'

'They usually are for women.'

'Well, actually I never thought of Miriam as a woman. I was never attracted to her.' How arrogant could you be!

'I always thought Tom really liked Lally best, you know,' I said.

'I believe he did, but I don't think he got anywhere. Miriam would see to that. And Tom liked to please Miriam. Why? Do you think Lally fancied him?'

'I don't know. Perhaps. She was always a mystery. But so are most people, don't you find?'

'I don't find you mysterious,' he said in reply. 'Very attractive and nice but not a mystery.'

'The tragedy of my life,' I said lightly.

'How did you find Cambridge for masculine talent? I never seemed to find the Oxford women all that enticing – too frumpish most of them – apart from a few nurses and a few debby types.'

Really, the cheek of him, but I played his game.

'I expect they were terrified of you,' I said.

He took the bait. 'Well, I didn't spend all my time mooning over women like some men did – I worked quite hard, you know.'

'Oh, I thought it all came effortlessly?'

'Glad to give you that impression.'

We were out of the restaurant now, still exchanging *badinage*, had crossed to the central promenade of the Ramblas under the plane trees where the strollers in their hundreds paraded day and night, chatting and sometimes making remarks upon other strollers. On each side was a one way road where the trams swung along purposefully and noisily, up and down, up and down.

'Shall we sit and watch for a bit? We can have our coffee at another café,' suggested Nick. I was still just nicely intoxicated, enough to feel very happy and carefree, not enough to act in a way I might regret later.

Was he having second thoughts about me? As we walked slowly along I had been thinking I'd like to go to bed with him. I don't think I'm drunk, just a bit tight. I want to enjoy myself without being in love with someone. I feel Nick has often done that. He's civilized, though I never can guess what he's thinking about. I'm sure he knows I'm not a virgin from all I've said, though perhaps he thinks I've had more experience than I really have? Previous episodes of love-making had been episodic, off and on – not in fact wildly exciting when I came to think about it. If it were wildly exciting with Nick, would I then fall in love with him? I hoped not. Men usually wanted to make love with a willing girl and I decided I was certainly willing. Everything was conspiring to make me feel excited – the warm night air, the colourful crowds, the feeling of being freed from the bonds of England, limbs uncramped from the Protestant conscience, happy, relaxed. Would I feel that dizzy, swoony, melting feeling if he kissed me or would it be a disappointment as it had so often been in Cambridge?

As we walked along in the thick crowds I felt his arm upon mine, not tentative but firm. Nick Varley was the sort of young man who knew what he wanted.

'I don't mind. We could perhaps have a cup of coffee now. There's such a lot to see here, isn't there? I love it.'

When we sat down, a little further in the direction of the port, having now crossed the tram tracks on the other side of the road, I gave a big, big sigh.

'Weight of the world?' he enquired.

'Weight of the world slipping off,' I replied.

Then Nick began to talk a bit more about why he was here in Catalonia, what his researches were about. He seemed to have seen a lot more of the place already than I had and waxed knowledgeable about the Consistorial and the archives of the city which he'd sampled in various buildings whose interior yards, shaded by palm trees or orange trees, fountains splashing in the centre, led up Baroque staircases to long, cool galleries. This was a side of Nick I had never seen before. When he was younger he had been a bit of a show off but now he spoke out of genuine enthusiasm. When I thought about it, I had been more interested, if I were honest, in the modern city and the way the people were, than in exploring Gothic and Renaissance and Baroque buildings. I was lamentably ignorant – *I* would not have known it was a magnolia tree in some courtyard he had visited. *I* would not have known that the theatre of the Liceo which I'd passed every day in the tram when I went to the language institute was in fact an 1890s survival, a mixture of club and theatre. Nick had been inside, described the red velvet boxes and the mouldings. But it was true it was a lot easier to explore if you were a man. Women did not have an entrée to public places. He had eaten also at famous restaurants – money helped here, naturally. I felt small and ignorant, as I described to him the things that had impressed me, and I thought, I probably notice the wrong things: like the red earth of Catalonia seen from the train; the sensation of being in the middle of a huge and glittering city dwarfed by splendour and a history I could only guess at. Nick was telling me a bit about that history and I listened and tried to fit it into my preconceptions of both him and Spain. Apparently he was taking the model of Catalonia – whose old Counts were also Kings of Aragon and ruled Languedoc, Sicily, Sardinia, Naples and Malta at some time (when exactly I wasn't quite sure) and who had had the earliest parliamentary constitution in Europe as an economic idea that might serve as a model one day for the concept of a united Europe. He was speaking of old trade routes, old laws. The Catalans had looked across the Mediterranean and had once held Athens itself for eighty years. I grasped then that this was all of six hundred years ago. What had all this to do with what Nick called 'planned European economy'? He grinned and for the first time looked young and a little uncertain.

'Oh, it's only a small part of my economic history thesis – I'm not a historian. I'm really concerned with widening national boundaries. One day Europe will have the same currency, be governed from a centre . . . I wanted background and it was a good idea to spend my money here, don't you think?'

I realized he was no Marxist. Why had I ever thought he was? He seemed as interested in the magnificent monasteries and in the cultural history of the place as in politics.

'You seem interested,' he said, sounding a bit surprised.

'I always lap up information,' I replied. 'I'm a culture vulture.'

'I have the feeling that most women are not interested in ideas,' he said in a lordly way. Well, perhaps most of the women he was likely to have gone out with, or to bed with, I thought.

But I was not pretending an interest for flirtatious reasons: I knew myself for a serious-minded girl – conscious of my own laziness too. 'I'm interested in Provence,' I ventured. 'All that poetry – I bought a book of Catalan poems – I suppose they only allow it to be printed because it's ancient stuff.'

'Have you been to Montjuich yet to see the Romanesque frescoes?' he asked sternly.

'No, I don't have much time in the day when I'm teaching – it's shut at night.'

'You *must* go there. The Catalans were great scientists too and some of them were also more than a bit mystical – anyway they quarrelled with the Popes.'

I had a vague idea that the golden age of Catalan literature was also in the thirteenth and fourteenth centuries and said this to him.

'Quite right – but I don't know much about that,' he admitted. 'I'm interested more in the architecture. They borrowed from everywhere. The magpies of the Middle Ages, these Catalans.'

'They don't like the rest of Spain. They always say "you're not in Spain – you are in Catalonia",' I said, draining my black, bitter coffee.

'Can you understand the *spoken* lingo? I can't,' Nick admitted.

'I do speak Spanish but I can't understand what they say here – it's not too difficult to read though.'

'I need it really to understand their old political ideals and their separate economic development,' he mused. 'Sorry, am I boring you now?'

'No, of course you're not.'

As we were speaking and I was beginning to think that he only wanted to discuss these concepts which, although interesting, were not to me at the present time, quite as interesting as the proximity of his sunburnt arms and gold hair burnt blond; the life of the place was surging around us after midnight in an even more lively fashion than earlier in the evening. There was a spring in the step, a feeling that life was good and worth living, a noisy cacophony of horns from motors and shouts of stallholders under the plane trees that were lit up bright viridian against the dark blue night sky. People now stood around in groups chatting or sat on seats under trees in the pedestrian middle of the Ramblas; others were still walking up and down along the wide pavements and as they passed looking at those who were seated there. I could not have been sitting at a café table alone. It was acceptable and approved of to sit with a young man. Nick would have sat in such a place alone and probably estimated the girls who passed, for I saw him often looking at women, openly appraising them. Yet I too liked to look at people.

'Let's walk to my place – if you want to come?' he said.

I looked at him and as I did so he leant across the table and covered my hand with his larger one. I shall abandon myself to whatever he wants with me, I thought. But I must be up in the morning for the ten o'clock lesson! I must get *some* sleep!

'I must be up for the ten o'clock lesson,' I said aloud.

'Don't worry – I start my own researches in the Barrio Gótico at half past nine,' he said.

We got up and walked back up the Ramblas now, past the flower stalls and the parrots in cages and the newspaper kiosks and the Loteria Nacional stands, and the bootblacks. Nick led the way and I followed, pleased for once not to have to decide where I was going.

'Have you noticed no one wears hats here?' said my guide.

'I hadn't thought about it – but it's true, I haven't seen anyone with a hat on, not even a sun-hat.'

'Older men do sometimes wear panamas,' he said. 'But the girls show off their hair- they're attractive, aren't they?'

'Yes,' I said. I spoke quite impersonally.

Both men and women looked full of energy. 'They never seem to go to bed,' I said. 'They're full of beans – no wonder they were good business men and revolutionaries.' I thought, they're ambitious people, industrious. Like Nick. 'Do you want to be rich?' I asked. It seemed now we could talk of anything.

'Of course – don't you?'

'No, not really – I don't think so – I'm not good with money.'

'That's because you've never had any,' he answered. 'Business is in my bloodstream. I like these people. Father once did business with Barcelona before their war.'

'Look, there's the church of Belén,' I said, pointing across the road. 'It means Bethlehem, you know.'

'No, I didn't know.'

'I'd like to stay here for years,' I sighed. 'All these buildings to see and the paintings and the places around. . . .' We crossed over to the pavement.

'Yes, we must go to the Tibidabo – and to Montserrat,' he said. 'There's time.'

I thought, we can go on seeing each other for a week or two. Good.

We went down a street now on the other side of the top of the Ramblas and towards the Plaza de Cataluña. Then we crossed the square and turned left towards the university.

'It's not far,' he said as we went across the Diagonal and down another street and then left again. This was a quieter quarter, full of tall nineteenth-century houses. It reminded me again of Paris and I said so. For answer he pointed to the name of the street above us, Calle de Paris. How strange.

He was taking his keys out of the pocket of his linen jacket. 'The watchman is there all night in the entrance hall. I'm on the third floor. There's a lift. I've the run of the flat till September.'

How well Nick looks after himself, I thought. Just like him to have the run of some splendid flat in the centre of a great city. He nodded to the *sereno* and we took the lift.

The large double doors opposite the lift on the third floor reminded me again of France where I had been so happy for six months before going up to Cambridge – but when we entered the spacious flat I saw that the floors were all marble. The rooms were high-ceilinged, the outer balcony doors as yet not completely closed together so that the sounds of the city came faintly through till Nick shut them.

'We're just off the Diagonal,' he said as though I didn't know. 'I'll make some more coffee – unless you'd prefer a mineral water.'

'Yes please – I'm thirsty with all that wine,' I said and went off to find the bathroom. When I returned he had brought a silver tray and two glasses and a bottle of *agua*.

'The maid doesn't sleep in – she comes in the morning around nine,' he explained. 'Shall I show you the rest of the flat?'

I sat down rather uncertainly. Obviously he didn't want to go to bed with me. I must have been mad. The effect of the drink was fading and I was glad. Maybe it had too with Nick and now he was regretting his quixotic proposal.

'Drink up,' he said. 'Then we can go to bed!' So he'd waited till we both felt more sober. He was certainly original. No fumblings or looking covertly at me to gauge my reaction.

A little later he did not kiss me either, but took my hand and together we went into a large, clean-smelling room with a small light in a corner. Everything tidy, no evidence of adolescent muddle or squalor. He took off his shirt, folded it on to a chair and said, 'Now it's your turn, Gillian Gibson. You needn't stay if you don't want.'

For answer I unbuttoned my orange and green sun-dress and took off my bra. The air was still warm. It did not seem like Nick when we fell gently on the bed together, but some foreign prince or unknown but kind stranger who then made love to me delicately and lengthily as though he were tasting some particularly delicious dish. I enjoyed it.

When I awoke he was not there but I heard sounds from the bathroom. I had slept deeply and satisfyingly and got up to look for another glass of water.

'Good morning,' he said as I joined him in a vast old-fashioned kitchen with a refrigerator and large oven, and a stove with a pipe going up to the ceiling. He smiled at me. 'Hot water and comb laid on,' he said. 'Breakfast in the dining-room.' Over the coffee and bread he said, 'Are you always so passionate?' and looked at me over the rim of his coffee cup.

'Am I?'

'You must know you are. It was good, wasn't it?'

I laughed and he took my hand and kissed my wrist, looking up at me mischievously.

Yes, it had been good. I realized with a start of surprise that I was not the slightest bit in love with him, though I would be happy to repeat the exercise.

'It's a happy chance we're both here together,' he said. 'No, stay on your side of the table. I've got to get off to work – so have you. I'm frightfully randy in the morning, you know – keep off!'

I had booked for the first two weeks at my *pensión* on Via Layetana. I had been uncertain how long I could afford it.

'You can come here when you like,' he said. 'So long as I'm not working. This evening? Better keep your own room on though.'

'I shall be quite busy myself,' I found myself replying. 'But I

83

should like to see places with you – the Tibidabo, you said? And Montserrat?'

'We'll go there one weekend. I'll give you a ring or call in at siesta time this afternoon to see if you'd like to come back here.'

'I owe you a dinner,' I said, laughing.

'Don't worry about that, *ma fille*. OK then? See you this afternoon,' he said as we went down to the lift. It was another *sereno* behind the desk this time. The sun was already burning down as we went out of the dark entrance hall. He took my arm. 'It was lovely,' he said. 'I'd like to repeat it. Would you?'

For answer I took his hand and squeezed it. 'Perhaps I would,' I said.

'What I like about you, Juliana,' he said a few days later as we went up the funicular of the Tibidabo to view the city from the steep mountainside that overlooked it, 'is that you don't cling – or pretend.'

'What don't I pretend?'

'Oh, that you love me or some such nonsense. Most girls are so peculiar – act as if they had no bodies or that if they have them, somehow they don't quite belong to them.'

'Lots of people would call what we do, *love*, wouldn't they?' I said, turning to look at him.

He put his arm round my neck, a gesture I'd seen lots of men here do to their girls. 'I don't own you and you don't own me,' he said. 'Most girls want to be owned.'

'But men don't, usually,' I said. 'They might *sometimes* though – even you.'

'Why even me? I'm not unusual, you know – I just enjoy sex. I'm honest about it, am I not?'

'So am I.' I was about to say, but I might love you if you loved me. Why was it different with Nick? Usually at this stage – or even less far along the road, I'd have been eating my heart out. With Nick there was more of a balance. I thought, it's because the sex came first. Anything could grow out of that – or nothing. He had brought me to great enjoyment but the pleasure didn't seem to be connected to him especially, it was a private thing which I had not exactly used him for but agreed to exchange.

84

Walking back alone that first morning and afterwards when the experience had been repeated, I felt a little as if I had found myself again, as though I had been unfaithful to the place. I wanted then to go alone to some of the other delights of Barcelona, to walk alone, be my own person who was not dependent upon anyone else for other pleasures. So I went by myself again to Santa Maria del Mar, to know that I was still the same person, that my individuality had not been leached away by Nick's urgent love-making, which could be both tender and imperious. And I found the same self alone and was happy to find it. Yet walking back from the church I had had several young men approach me or whistle at me from behind the usual pillars as though they knew that I had risen from some man's bed. It annoyed me. Why could I not walk alone where I wanted without let or hindrance and men's annoying me?

But I liked Nick making love to me, it was an experience, one in which I was willing, for once, not to call the tune – so long as I reserved part of myself for when I was alone. It was a paradox: I could enjoy love-making, or sex to give it the name which others might give it, could even enjoy not having to initiate it or worry about it, so long as I was not *in love* and he was not *in love*. But if my emotions were involved I would stop noticing the rest of the world, the observation of which I so enjoyed when I was alone. These feelings called love had always led to misery and then to a determined effort to uproot them when they were not requited, or even to suffering alone. Once they had gone away, the rest of life seemed more delightful. There must be something wrong with me, I was musing as the funicular approached the top of the little mountain. The view when we got out and walked to the belvedere was breathtaking, although spoilt by the excrescences of modern buildings: funfairs and a general feeling of being on Blackpool South Shore. Nick said he could see a faint blue on the horizon over the distantly sparkling sea that was Mallorca, but I could not. Behind us in the distance was the jagged outline of the mountains of Montserrat and below us the whole city of Barcelona that swept down from where we were to the sea and harbour and the docks. Patches of yellowy green showed the public parks, and the Gothic quarter was only one brownish part of the whole with its towers and spires pricking up from it. The Tibidabo was steep; it made me quite giddy to look down from its top. Nick was talking about a meal at the restaurant. It was Saturday; I had taught all morning and also felt rather hungry. But we lingered for a moment, looking now again at the mountains behind and to the west with the dark green forests on their distant sides and the vineyards and farms.

At lunch Nick bought a bottle of Penedes wine, adding this to the repertoire we had already enjoyed: Castellribas, Valdepeñas, Sangre de Toro. We ate on a terrace, the sun sneaking under the awning. When we were not in bed I felt he was, if not exactly a stranger, once more the old Nick of my adolescence.

'What makes Nick tick?' I asked as I sipped the wine.

'You don't really want to know, do you?'

'I know you're an ambitious bastard,' I said, emboldened. 'But also a bit of a mystery. Is it wrong to want to understand the mystery?'

'In mystery there is attraction.' He smiled.

'Am *I* a bit more of a mystery to you now then?'

'Oh, perhaps a little more! Not as much as some people I've known – but, yes. . . .' He paused. 'Don't be too much of a mystery, Juliana. It's best!' He was so enormously self-possessed. Had he made me so too? I hoped so. It might be that you only became so through a sort of osmotic contact with people who always had been or had learned to be. Before Spain I had begun to grow my shell, just a little, thin beginning, when Robin had defected to Finland. I wondered where he was now, but did not seem able greatly to care. I was fickle.

'I'd like to walk into the mountains,' he said. 'And make love under a haystack or some stream.'

'I didn't know you were so romantic – how do you know *I* would? I'd prefer a bed.' I was thinking of our large bed in the Calle de Paris flat where during the afternoon siesta the light came through little chinks and threw an eau-de-nil light on the white sheets and the marble floor.

'I said make love in the abstract – I was speaking impersonally,' he said. What a beast he was.

86

'Well, I could do that too – quite impersonally,' I replied. 'With some garlic-chewing peasant.'

'Could you really? Would you?'

'No, I don't suppose so. You know what happens to girls who do things like that? They get raped or murdered. *You* could just indulge yourself, but think of the girl.'

'Essentially you're a feminist, aren't you? I don't think you need a man so long as you can get what you want.'

'I expect I need people as much as most people, more perhaps, so I'm learning to do without – or bounce back when the next one gives me up.'

'You make yourself sound like a bad habit.'

'Well, that's what I was taught sex was – a bad habit.'

'I've known women who were far worse than you,' he said. I looked questioningly. 'I mean, who needed a man, couldn't do without one – or said they couldn't. How can a man please a woman who takes you like a drug or, if she's displeased with you like an especially nasty dose of medicine, and then won't let you go when you and she have drained everything out of a relationship.'

'Goodness! I expect most girls could be like that though. Mostly they want to get wed,' I said.

'Oh, for children and security – it's nothing to do with pleasure.'

'Well, the race has to be carried on somehow, unless you want to argue the game's not worth the candle? And women are often left alone with babies anyway.' I stared down at my hands.

'Don't worry about that. I promise you – you won't get pregnant by me!'

'I hope not. It's a worry – men are so lucky.'

'Come off it, men are left feeling guilty too, unless they're complete shits.'

'It's not nice hurting people if they love you,' I said, 'though why *I* should worry, I don't know – I've more often been on the receiving end.'

'Still, you're learning not to be. I may have done you some good, sexy Juliana.'

'I don't think you mean that!'

'Of course I mean it. But some big, strong man comes along

87

one day, even to sexy girls, and they give him their heart or whatever it is women give.'

'So might you – one day. With a big, strong woman.'

'That's possible,' he agreed. 'But it's much nicer like this, isn't it?'

And I had to agree that so far, in the experience of my admittedly not very long life, it was. There would be no regrets when Nick or I left this beautiful city, alone.

Nick stopped my mouth with probing kisses if I ever talked in bed before he made love to me. Talking was for afterwards. Yet thoughts sometimes came even when we were as physically close as two people could be and he was groaning with pleasure. What right had I to enjoy this game whilst half the world was starving, whilst children were born unwanted and then ill-treated, when money was the magic sesame to so much? Why should I be privileged when the life – even of most of the pushing, surging crowds down on the Ramblas – was so hard? Even though they seemed to enjoy that life more than the English working classes. I felt glad to be different from my usual self, and free, even if it was all built on sand and in a few weeks I'd be back in grimy old London earning my baked beans on toast, but my Protestant conscience couldn't help the questions. By mutual consent Nicholas and I agreed we would not continue this affair in England. Nick spoke of it first.

'I don't want it to be spoilt. It's been a little idyll,' he said. 'Don't let's allow the world in. You have to find out what you really want – it isn't me, I know that.'

'And you?' I asked.

We were both smoking Spanish cigarettes a few days after our trip up the funicular. The next day we were to go to Montserrat.

'I don't want to get too fond of you,' he said.

I saw that what I had imagined as 'free' love was not free, even for Nick. He made love to me with only a part of himself. Some other part was far away. I felt more jealous of this than of any future entanglements he might have. Other women would find him the same. He liked to be alone just as I did and the time we spent together in bed at siesta time, the best time to make love according to Nick, was never too long for us to find anything less than perfect, punctuated as it was by my morning's teaching and my later evening classes before we might meet once more for a meal or to wander round the place. Once or twice I stayed all night with him again, but never felt I must be there when he was busy. I was busy too, toiling over my conversations with the aspirant mercantile classes of Barcelona. Still, we managed a good deal of rather thrillingly unpredictable intimacy and I found the beginnings of quite a talent for giving pleasure. The only way to learn a new language, I thought, would be to take a lover. But then one's verbal attempts might be a trifle limited. At the end of the second week after our meeting, I announced to Nick that the curse had arrived. It was a relief to me, though he had continually reassured me that I would not get pregnant by him. The curse did not stop his siesta antics however, though he said, 'I won't if you don't want.' He was attentive to my own physical feelings too. Strange that a young man who was so wary of any emotional commitment was such a good lover. I said something of the sort to him, but he laughed and said I was too much of a puritan to think I could have a lot of fun without paying for it with the agonies of romantic love. He seemed to have all that side of life nicely filleted. I knew he would not do for ever, but decided I would play his own variations. The very fact of our being there together in this place for a limited time helped me to envisage it as a time cut out of ordinary life. I was still not in love with him, if those words meant the old feelings of rapture and misery I had suffered so often, yet the habit of his constant interest in my body combined with his own never flagging desire, at the hours and times we chose to exploit it, might become a drug. Or it might become a bore, I thought. I did not want to be with him all the time and could not imagine feeling possessive about him. He let me feel free.

Nick told me more about his work and his ideas and I was a ready listener. Just once or twice he would allude to other women in his life since he was apparently one of those men who start young. 'I always thought you'd been seduced by an older woman,' I said. 'Years ago, when you went to France at first, do you remember?'

He laughed, but did not disagree. 'Well, you have to start somehow.'

One afternoon, after we had spent a longer time than usual lying together on the high, old-fashioned bed with the warm air seeping through the window and the faint sounds of traffic seemingly far away, he said in a strange voice after falling asleep for a time, 'I don't think I can really love *anybody*, Juliana.' There was a vulnerability behind his technique and his almost obsessive desire, but I did not want to pierce through it. Some day a woman who loved him might do so; it would not be me. So it was my turn to say I thought there were too many words said about love. What bodies did and felt must have something to do with being in love – but you could have one without the other. 'You make me feel happy,' I said, and it was true. But I knew that there might be something behind all that, though also part of it, that led people not to be able to do without each other. 'But that sort of love doesn't last either,' I murmured following the train of my own thoughts. What had Anna Karenina and Emma Bovary been but victims of Eros? Was it not better to do without all that and still enjoy an almost impersonal passion?

'Women always want more,' he said. 'Oh, companionship, security, a kind husband.'

'I know, but I don't think they always go hand in hand with – this.'

Both he and I seemed to have split somehow in our emotions between the ideally romantic and the tenderly lustful.

'You're not as greedy as I am,' he said later. 'But we're alike, you and I.'

One Sunday afternoon we took the bus to Montserrat. I shall never forget that day. The strange needle-like pinnacles of the towering mountains seemed like phallic symbols and made me shiver. The Black Virgin in her chapel seemed to have little to do with the place. The female and the male principles they were, the strange little black Madonna dressed in her ceremonial robes, and the jagged mountains outside. You could forget the monastery and the tourist shops. It was a pilgrimage, I felt, and understood why newly-married couples came there to worship at both shrines and called their girl-children after the place and the woman. The woman's face was black on account of the hundreds of years of candles burned near her. Her dazzling robes made her into the Queen of Heaven but I wished we could see the statue as she was underneath them. Postcards showing this were on sale and gave me a curious feeling of aesthetic joy. It was said to have been carved by Saint Luke himself and was unlike any statue I had ever seen before, primitive, its head out of proportion with the body.

Nick was reading the guidebook. 'Only virgins without sin are allowed to clothe the statue,' he quoted. I remembered the phrase *quedarse per vestir sants*, the Catalan expression for a spinster who is unlikely to find a husband – 'to remain ready to clothe saints.' How mixed up with each other sex and religion were. Well, I was not such a spinster, though I doubted I would ever find a husband. But the Virgin was also a mother.

I was sure that such worship had existed long before Christianity arrived on Catalan shores, before the statues of virgins had become like mannequins with their richly decorated robes, carried high above the heads of crowds on saints' days. I had seen such a procession in Barcelona along with the giant-sized replicas of the Counts of Aragon swaying above the people. It had made me feel a little frightened.

'They've made the Virgin into a model for clothes,' I said to Nick. 'She ought to be the patron of models and mannequins.'

'It says here the best dressed is the Mother of God of Mercy – the Virgin of Mercy,' he said, reading again from the guidebook.

He had seemed rather preoccupied that day when we had visited the shrine but cheered up when we had eaten another copious meal before returning. 'What can I do to repay all these lunches and suppers?' I asked him.

'Well, I'd have eaten them myself anyway and it's not so much fun eating alone.' He loved his food as he loved sherry and the table wines of the district. Although he was not a large man I thought his appetites were large.

He was more cheerful the week after that when we went round the whole of the Barrio Gótico, guidebooks in hand. We saw Romanesque and Gothic and Renaissance and Baroque, and Nick was in his element. The Episcopal Palace, the Canonry, the Casa Consistorial – my second visit and I got more from it this time. The patios and inner stairways merge in my mind – orange trees, gargoyles, fountains, coloured tiles, galleries. Nick took me with him too to the Biblioteca de Catalunya and on the way I showed him some of the smaller streets which were my favourites with their overfresh smell of medieval plumbing. Together we walked round the Cathedral cloisters with its palms and aloes, though the geese that the guidebook promised seemed to be absent. I introduced him to Santa Maria del Mar and he seemed as awed as I was. But I went alone to Montjuich one Sunday when he was busy writing up his notes, and was glad I had done so. The great frescoes taken from little chapels and churches in the Pyrenees all assembled in room after room – wonderful Romanesque illustrations of hell and heaven and earth, with the tortures of the damned, and it seemed of secular enemies too, impressed me more than anything else in Barcelona itself though I could not have said why.

We went together to the Pueblo Español – the Spanish Village, the week after that. Such a visit was more fun with a companion. Some places one must see alone, others accompanied – it was strange I always knew which.

The day came when Nick announced he had done all he could in Barcelona. I was to stay on there until the end of the month.

'We'll see each other if we're ever in Yorkshire at the same time,' he said. 'Soon I'll have to go off on my Russian course in any case.'

I knew that the affair would be over without any bad feeling on either side and told him as much. 'I knew it was only for a few weeks, Nick,' I said. 'It's a good thing you're going – you don't want me falling in love with you, do you?'

He did not say anything at first, but when we were out for our last supper together he said, 'It's been lovely, Juliana – I shan't ever forget it. We'll always be friends, won't we?'

'I suppose so – I'll miss our siestas,' I replied with a lump in my throat. 'But it has to be over – I hate loose ends. If I thought you were going to want me like that again in England I'd feel sort of unable to enjoy myself with anybody else.' I knew he would not have the same compunction, even though now he was looking rather miserable.

*

'Do write to me sometimes – I'll let you know where I am,' he said as I saw him off at the French station. He gave me a most chaste kiss and then leapt on to the train which was late setting off, the only one that day. I waved as it puffed away. No promises. All over. I could not help that lump in the throat, but I knew it was sentiment, not love. In a way it was a relief to have the last week or two alone. I was glad I had had Nick, whatever it had all meant, did not believe I would regret it. We were physically in tune. I felt older, somehow.

When I returned to my little routines I felt the city welcoming me back again as a whole person. Now I could rationally extract as much as possible from the rest of my stay, visit one of my student's families and be an English young lady with no secrets. I felt independent. Nick had done me good – or something had. He sent me a card from Paris and this made me a little sad, but I knew I would get over it. Nick Varley would be part of my sentimental education as long as I lived. But now he was most likely enjoying himself with some other young woman – he was not the faithful type. Neither was I, I decided. The summer of siestas it had been. Nick wouldn't forget me. I was quite certain about that. Neither had made the other unhappy and that was to me a small miracle. I had survived and was ready to survive any new love in future with a feeling of self-confidence. Somebody had really wanted me; somebody had thought me exciting and passionate. Somebody had also said I was rather intelligent too.

In the big world there had been all summer the reverberations of the previous year's Suez crisis. I had gleaned what news I could from the French papers, but it all seemed so remote. I met a few Americans in the cafés who talked, and I listened to them. But by the end of September my bags were packed ready to descend upon London once more. I finished long letters to my family. Odd not to mention seeing Nick, but I was taking no chances. To Jessica and Susan I said nothing either. This affair was something I was going to keep to myself. For once in my life I'd done what I wanted and it seemed there was no retribution.

Part Two

1 Chronicles

I was sitting with Miriam at a table in a peculiar wind-blown café, part of the South Bank complex thrown up by the Festival of Britain and now definitely run down. Strange how you remember silly little details: there were 'fancies' coloured shocking-pink under plastic domes on the counter, and I remarked on their colour to Miriam who was blowing on some greasy-looking coffee. My summer in Barcelona had sharpened my criticism of my native land and I had been waxing enthusiastic to my old friend about Catalonia, though I had not mentioned Nicholas Varley.

It was November and there was an end of pier feeling about the grey South Bank though the interior decor of the café where we were seated was almost as pink as its iced cakes.

I was feeling slightly depressed. Even Eastcliff seemed tempting: to stride across fields, walk in soggy woods. I'd promised my parents to go home for Christmas, when I had a day or two's leave from the Olympia Translation Bureau where I worked in a stuffy office near Victoria station – which was perhaps the nearest it could get to abroad. I was already suffering from a yawning boredom, unusual for me. But the Olympia was necessary if I were to keep going financially; apart from selling dog-collars at Selfridges, the only other job on offer.

When I thought of Nick I found it hard to visualize his face exactly; it became the face of the Nick I'd known in Eastcliff when we were seventeen and before we both went away to start our lives. There was something about that younger face

95

of which I had not quite approved, and absent from the face which had lain next to mine on the pillow in the greenish light of those Catalan afternoons. Something a little pursed up about the mouth maybe, or the ears too neatly tucked away – or the eyes a little too hooded, the jawline too firm. He had been more relaxed in Spain. Whatever it was, I decided not to let it worry me. Whether we met again or not didn't seem to matter. Someone else would be appreciating his *gourmet* sex – I was rather proud of this phrase which had come to me in the middle of the night and made me laugh. Not *gourmand* sex, like so many young men.

There wasn't much to laugh about in my London life, I thought, but I was not going to confess that to Miriam. The wind was slapping the dirty grey waves of the Thames against the struts of the railway bridge; it was chilly outside and the café was almost empty – nobody but me seemed to know about it, it was always deserted.

Miriam told me she was busy writing for a Socialist paper and her play was going into rehearsal at a small 'committed' theatre. I remembered that Nick had said she'd be issuing her manifesto any day now from the coffee bar in Soho where she spent so much of her time.

She was looking awfully bright-eyed and healthy, had grown a little fatter, so that she appeared less forbidding. She'd pulled down some of her dark wavy hair over her brow, taking away from that austere high forehead, and although I'd always thought her rather ugly I saw now that she had good cheekbones and her eyes seemed deeper and darker. But she hadn't lost her brusque way of talking.

I knew I envied Miriam but was unsure how much of her busyness was just Miriam and how much was part of the process of becoming famous. Miriam had to be asked about her impending marriage. I could not pretend not to know.

'In spring,' said Miriam shortly. 'How did you know?'

'Oh, it was all round the village – Mother told me,' I lied.

Miriam, not apparently wishing to discuss anything more personal, talked politics. Her friends seemed to include both the New Left and the older people who had protested against Suez the year before, those who had left the Communist Party over Hungary; those who were beginning to speak against the nuclear bomb; those who were 'angry' and those who wanted to change the class system, wanted England to wake up and take politics seriously. As usual I could not quite make up my mind whether to join in, couldn't decide whether a political answer would be the right one, never mind *this* political answer, when there were so many other answers. The Conservative Party seemed to have been in power for ever, and probably would be for years with their Never Had It So Good.

I listened to Miriam, tried to look intelligent and tried not to annoy her with half-baked wishy-washy political attitudes. When she took a breath I searched for something to discuss that would make her feel her friend was not too irredeemably frivolous. It was odd how people like Miriam always did make me feel frivolous when in reality I agonized over ideas. Miriam did not agonize, went straight for the jugular.

'Have you seen Lally?' I asked when I had lit a cigarette and we were finishing our coffee by the window, that looked out blearily on to the water.

'She was in Earls Court,' said Miriam, drinking her coffee without apparently noticing what it tasted like. 'She was ill in the summer – went home for a bit, but she's back. I saw her last week.'

'What was the matter with her?'

'I'm not sure – you know Lally – some man trouble I expect.'

'But she's doing awfully well in her work, isn't she?'

'Well, if you can call that work,' said Miriam.

Why was she so hard on her? Was Tom still a little attracted to the lovely Lally, as I had always suspected he might have been?

'I must ring her up – perhaps I've not got the right number – do give it to me,' I said. Miriam complied, looking faintly abstracted. Then, 'You must come and see my play,' she said. 'It's on in three weeks at the Citizens.'

'Thanks, I will.'

'You see, Gillian, it's not just a question of being furious over the Suez madness – this country has never tried *real* Socialism. Osborne's play was reactionary rubbish. There's plenty to be angry about in reality.'

I thought, there always has been and always will be, and said something about the opposition in Spain.

97

'What are the Catalans like?' asked Miriam. I told her but still did not mention I'd met Nick Varley in Barcelona.

'One day I hope the province will be self-governing,' I said.

She said she knew lots of older Socialists who had fought in the International Brigade.

'Why does England have to be so *awful*, Miriam? Honestly I'd vote for any party that could give us a bit of style,' I said.

'I can see you're pro-European.'

'Why? Is that not what you approve of? Is it unsocialist?'

'Well, I agree a Socialist Europe would be wonderful, but that would have to include Eastern Europe.'

'Some hope,' I said thinking of what had recently happened in Hungary, which had in fact enraged me more than Suez.

'Hungary drove a lot of Communists out of the Party,' she said. 'They're all with us now. You should come to our meetings, Gillian – you know Fabianism's finished. We need a radical new mixture for our new socialism – *and* a party everyone can join, not just educated people *or* workers, but both.'

Then Miriam lectured me on the class system which I thought richly ironic.

'You're a rebel, Gillian,' I heard her say. 'Not a revolutionary.'

It was true. She could be quite perceptive.

'There are quite a lot of fashionable people with us,' Miriam went on, watching me sucking sugar from my spoon that had been left at the bottom of my cup. 'I mean culturally – more like your idea of continental Socialists. Writers have joined – and some painters. And of course Tom is there as a link between the old folk music and the new stuff like skiffle – he's a high opinion of all that though he's classically trained.' She went on to tell me all that Tom was doing, her cheeks flushing with pride.

I resolved to go to the coffee bar in Carlisle Street and see for myself what they were talking about when I had a minute free from my wage-earning. If Miriam talked of culture perhaps we could meet on this ground? Culture was, I felt confusedly, to do with the way men and women interpreted the world – or the different worlds they lived in, and interested me more than dogma.

'I must go,' she said, getting up. I thought, she looks like a Valkyrie – but a dark one.

'So must I,' I said, stubbing out my half-smoked cigarette and carefully blowing on it and pinching it before putting it back in its packet for later consumption.

'Tell Lally about the wedding in spring if you see her,' was Miriam's parting shot as we said goodbye after crossing Hungerford Bridge.

She was going with Tom to look at a flat near Great Ormond Street that was said to need very little key money, for they wanted a place of their own together. Miriam had managed to secure a temporary part-time lectureship in the new science of sociology at one of the London colleges, and this, combined with a small private income she'd inherited from her grandmother plus her earnings from journalism – and even perhaps theatre receipts – together with what Tom was already making from his musical journalism and recitals – would be enough to manage on for the time being. I had also gathered that she thought Tom would soon be appearing on television! What a compulsive worker Miriam had turned out to be. I guessed she was well on the way to making Tom one too, though I found it hard to envisage his enjoying political meetings. Miriam was a shining example of an ambitious person who knew that fame must be worked for. I remember thinking that she was old for her age and that she actually *looked* older than me.

Miriam always started me arguing with myself. I wished *I* had clear convictions and acted upon them, but I could never quite bring myself to join anything except perhaps a society for romantic sceptics. I'd thought Tom Cooper was like me in that but he'd apparently fitted himself quite neatly into Miriam's scheme of things.

I managed to reach Lally at the third attempt at the end of the month and we fixed a meeting for the beginning of November.

'I'm back for just a few weeks now at Dad's flat,' Lally explained. 'I was ill in the summer and they're seeing I have enough to eat and get to bed early. But I'm fine now – I'm going to get a flat of my own in World's End in the New Year.'

I duly went on a rainy evening to Westminster to Denis and Clare Cecil's flat. It was off Victoria Street, not far from my own work, and was on the third floor of a venerable block of mansion flats, the sort of place Members of Parliament use for a *pied à terre* if they are fairly rich. Mr Cecil must be doing rather well for himself I thought, though I was vague as to what his business was and Lally had never enlightened me – perhaps she was equally vague. I went up in a lift and rang a bell outside the thick oaken entrance door. It was opened by a small, pretty woman who must be the second Mrs Cecil. The door led into a central dining-hall which was separated from a sitting-room by folding doors. Lally came out from a little room which she was using as a bed-sitting room.

'Gillian – how lovely! It's ages – how are you?' She seemed taller and thinner. Her cheeks were rouged and her lipstick of the brightest post-box red. 'I wanted you to meet Daddy, but he's out at the moment. Let's sit here – it's more comfortable.' The room was most impressive. There was a large Chinese screen and several tall oriental vases – had Mr Cecil travelled in China then? – and many well-polished nests of tables. I perched on the edge of an armchair upholstered in dark blue velvet and Lally sat on a sofa opposite. There were other armchairs with rather chintzy patterns, for the room was large; the carpet too was Chinese, a lovely blue. 'Clare's just bought that,' said Lally pointing upwards at one of the portraits on the wall. They were all framed in heavy gilt. On every available surface there were flower arrangements – red roses, baskets of carnations and an enormous bower of bliss about five feet high and as wide, filled with gladioli, roses, carnations and other summery-looking flowers. Everything shone with the soft glow of well-beeswaxed surfaces. Lally saw me looking at the flowers.

'The ancestors are not real,' she explained, 'but the flowers are. It was Clare's birthday the other day and her friends in America sent all this.' Clare came into the room just as Lally was saying these words.

'Aren't they lovely?' she said. 'I was evacuated to the States in the war and they always remember.'

I thought, she doesn't look much older than Lally and me! She must be in her early thirties if she married Mr Cecil at twenty, say, at the end of the war when Lally was about ten. . . .

'I'll make some more coffee,' offered the subject of my calculations.

'Let me help,' said Lally and followed her stepmother into a small kitchen.

Clare stayed with us for a drink of quite delicious coffee, certainly not coffee of the snack-bar variety, then went off on her own devices. She was very well dressed, had that look of band-box perfection I could never achieve in a million years.

I still felt a little shy. What could we talk about? I could not barge in after so long with an inquisitive enquiry about Lally's health. But Lally now seemed to know how to conduct conversations.

'You saw Miriam then?' she said stretching out her long legs and holding her cup and saucer together in the air.

'Yes, I hadn't seen her for absolutely ages – they've begun to rehearse her play and it's going on at this little theatre in January.'

'I must ask my cousins if they know anything about it,' said Lally. 'All three are still actresses, you know.' Somehow I did not think they would be actresses of the sort who would appear in a play by Miriam.

'And what about you?' I asked as I finished my coffee and refused any more.

Lally lit a cigarette and then said, 'Oh, I'm sorry, do you smoke, Gillian? I get so selfish nowadays lighting up without asking other people.' She handed me a fancy box of Passing Cloud, a brand I had never seen before, never mind smoked, but I took one and lit it with the onyx lighter before us on the table.

'I'm OK,' said Lally shortly. 'I'm going into this little flat after Christmas.'

'You've a lot of work then?'

'Heaps – but it's rather boring. What about you?'

She seemed reluctant to talk about her modelling career so I obliged by telling Lally what I was supposed to be doing at the Olympia agency. Lally looked puzzled.

'I thought you'd teach,' she said artlessly.

I grimaced. 'I may be reduced to that,' I said with a sigh. 'I get frightfully bored at the Olympia – in my office I actually watch the hands of the clock go round. It's a big wall clock with

101

Rawsons of Leeds printed at the bottom. It reminds me of school.'

Lally laughed. 'You look well,' she said. 'I like your fringe – it suits you.'

I was never sure about hairstyles and it was usually more through luck than management that I was able to pass muster. Lally's hair was cropped short and more silvery than ever. She was still as beautiful as ever too, though there were, when she stood against the light, rather deep shadows under her eyes which I did not remember seeing before.

We began to talk of Susan, and Lally said how kind Susan had been when she had gone north in the summer when she had been 'feeling rather low'.

'Have you read her articles? Gran sends me them now and again. She thinks Susan is wonderful.'

'She's doing awfully well,' I said. 'It makes me wonder whether I need have gone away at all – what I'm doing now is so deadly.'

'She works terribly hard,' said Lally. 'Do you think she'll marry Gabriel?'

I was a little taken aback. What did Lally know that I did not about my best friend. 'Why? They're not –' I searched for the word – 'courting' didn't seem quite right; 'serious' sounded like a grandmother's enquiry.

'In love,' supplied Lally. 'I don't know. But I'm sure Susan is very fond of him. When I was ill at Gran's she talked about him a lot.'

'Gabriel is a very *good* person, I think,' I said. 'But I don't really feel I know him any more. And people change. . . .'

Lally got up and looked out of the window and then she turned to look at me. 'What about you? Tell me all – how are you getting along?' She must mean in the love department. I didn't want to talk about Nick to Lally either. I realized I wanted to keep my summer to myself, didn't want to spoil memories by talking about him.

'I'm fine,' I said. 'Not enough cash but keeping fairly healthy would sum me up, I think. I see a few friends from Cambridge. I don't think I shall stay in my present job. For most openings into something more interesting you need a secretarial training – but then you can get stuck as a secretary.'

'I can guess,' said Lally sympathetically. 'Though I quite like typing away. Modelling doesn't last for ever.'

'But you're making such a great success of it. The pictures I've seen of you in the papers! Swathed in furs in one magazine I saw. Do they ever let you walk away with the stuff you're advertising?'

'Not likely. The travel's a bit of a bore. I nearly gave it all up last year. The fur picture was taken ages ago. Furs don't go out of fashion.' Lally sat down again and composed her features into a smile, crossed her legs and lit another cigarette.

'Where exactly will you move when you leave here?'

'I'm buying this little flat in what you might call Kensington. It's convenient for the airport bus when I have to hop on a plane at London Airport – you must come when I'm settled in.'

I thought she must be making a reasonable amount of cash if she could afford a small flat in Kensington. Yet she hadn't a car. I changed the subject.

'What do you think about Tom and Miriam's getting married next year? Were you surprised?'

'I'm awfully glad,' said Lally. 'Miriam does such a lot for Tom.'

'And Miriam and her play – everything seems to happen to some people.'

'She's very ambitious,' admitted Lally. 'I don't think she approves of me.'

'Oh, she's such a puritan about money and clothes and work,' I said. 'You know,' I added rather rashly, 'I always thought that Tom, in spite of all this Miriam worship – always rather liked *you* best.'

Lally blushed. 'Oh, no, Gillian. I mean he used to like me, I think, and I liked him – but, you know, he always *admired* Miriam.'

Lally interested me, but I thought it would now be too intimate a question to ask her whether she thought Tom was in love with Miriam Jacobs. 'I think liking people's important,' was all I said and the conversation then passed to clothes, about which Lally seemed to know a good deal.

I had put on my best black suede shoes, my only decent pair, and a long, full skirt, because I did not want Lally to think I was too deprived of taste, only that I had no money to indulge it. I felt a bit of a fraud. I quite liked nice clothes but mainly on other people. I liked bright colours and berets and waistcoats and boots and lots of old-style jewellery. Lally's little silk blouse of a stone colour and the shoes of dark blue suede, fine nylons, and her simple A-line wool skirt proclaimed a person who spent a long time thinking what suited her.

But after I had left and walked to the underground I thought there had been something missing in her that used to be there. Was it a sparkle or an unselfconsciousness or what? I wished I could have seen Mr Cecil but he had not returned when I left.

Although I was fond of Lally and even a little grudgingly admiring of Miriam, it was Susan with whom I could feel most myself. I might want to confess to Susan about Nick but it was not the sort of thing you could really broach in a letter, so I put it off.

When I should be translating some mind-bendingly boring technical article about aeroplanes or lawn mowers from the French I found myself day-dreaming or actually falling asleep. Not that I did not try hard to do my best at the Olympia, but it was not my *métier*. I found it humbling to know how much I did *not* know about things in the world, and about French, in which I was supposed to be an expert. It was all very well deciding inner life mattered most – and maybe the way I was living was not right for me – but one had to work to live. I was still friendly with Jessica Coleman and we often went to the theatre together, once to a recital of genuine flamenco dancing. 'A wonderful escape from thinking', was how I felt about that sort of rhythm. Afterwards we had coffee at the Partisan and Jessica said she thought I was a serious-minded person who ought to write.

'What *about*?' I asked. 'I can't write about people like myself – it would be too boring.'

'Make it up then,' suggested Jessica.

A mutual acquaintance from Cambridge had had a novel accepted, said Jessica. This depressed me even more. 'Pretend *you* are someone else,' advised Jessica. 'I see lots of writers and they are rather ordinary, mousy people. All they do is open up their imaginations and find the right style.'

'It's good coffee, isn't it?' I said, changing the subject. 'You see that man near the stairs? Isn't he –'

'Aaron Wildberg,' interrupted Jessica and giggled. 'Will your friend come here today, do you think – Marian wasn't it?'

'Miriam – no, she's busy rehearsing her play.'

'She must be over the moon to have a play accepted at her age.'

'Yes, but she's very political you see – she never believed in art for art's sake.'

'Art for *my* sake,' said Jessica and made a silly face. I found her company refreshing.

I despaired off and on about my job, my clothes sense, my lack of money, my general lack of talent and more particular lack of a man with whom I might feel both natural and close. I wished I were simple, like Lally, or amusing like Jessica, or unworldly as I imagined Susan to be, or successful like Miriam and Tom, or self-confident like Nick. But apart from the office I spent my happiest times alone reading, or occasionally visiting the Academy Cinema, or just walking round London. There was so much of the past to explore in galleries, bookshops and museums and the past took my mind off myself. I made one or two new friends, but as often went out alone; even dined alone in Soho one evening to show I was independent. I got some rum looks from waiters. When Edwige Feuillère came to London in *La Dame Aux Camélias* I waited at the stage-door afterwards to pay homage. Yet I seemed to have no purpose. Watching the clock-hand go round at the Olympia was no way to spend my days. Finding a lover might not be the right thing either before I understood what I wanted to be or do. I cheered up when I visited the theatre or the concert or listened to Gigli on my new record player or read a novel or wandered round the Tate or took the 24 bus across London to Kenwood. Why should I imagine that someone might exist in the world who would understand me, never mind save me from myself? I had been happy with Nick Varley for that short Spanish summer because I did not feel possessive about him; he had both appreciated me and made me feel free. But was that what people call love?

It was Mr Gibson's bequest to me, I thought, that I should be satisfied at a deeper level only with a paragon; a man with similar enthusiasms to myself who would be both passionate and virtuous, a man with inner resources; a man who would be

105

content with my existence but allow me to be independent also. Life was so much easier if you forgot all this hankering and just lived from day to day.

I puzzled over the attitude of young men towards the idea of babies. Girls in books spoke of 'giving him a child', yet all the young men I knew would have run a mile at the idea of such an offering. I must know the wrong sort – or the books were dishonest. I rather liked babies, in the abstract, but feminism and love, feminism and babies assorted ill, I thought.

I struggled to fit together all the ideas I read about, but did not succeed. There was no one idea or person or thing I could wholeheartedly believe in, though I was quickly aroused to some defensive reaction when I read or heard some opinion I disagreed with. I read novels by young men in quirky modern styles. How utterly self-confident such writing seemed, typically male, written by those who had had no self doubts – or seemed never to have had any. . . .

I went home for a rather insipid Christmas. Rosemary, now at a teachers' training college, was unusually silent, and neither Lally nor Nick came home – or I did not see the latter if he had. Tom and Miriam came for only two days which they spent with their families. Susan was disappointed too, for Gabriel had had to stay in Scotland; he was needed to help out on the wards of a teaching hospital. She was the only person left in Eastcliff with whom I could enjoy a conversation. She hadn't changed much but she looked very competent in her navy-blue costume and her hair neatly tied back.

'It seems he's been training for a hundred years,' she said, uncharacteristically depressed. 'And there are still two more years to go. Somehow I can't believe he'll ever be finished.'

'At least he'll have a proper job at the end of it all,' I comforted her. We spent the whole of the day after Boxing Day on a long walk away from the village. I had forgotten how invigorating it could be tramping along in the cold air. We walked up beyond Wynteredge to the Heights where there was a wonderful view of Eastcliff and Lightholme and miles beyond under great skies, the sound of the wind always in our ears.

Susan told me about Lally's illness. Apparently she had

suddenly come back to The Laurels in the early summer – thin, pale, almost silent, not hungry, sleeping little and often with tears running down her cheeks. Her grandmother had been terribly worried, had called in her doctor and immediately telephoned Susan to ask her to come round. As soon as she could, Susan, who was now working in the city and going there on the train every day, dashed down to see what she could do. The doctor had been that afternoon and had just said Lally had been overworking, but Mrs Fortescue had clutched Susan in the kitchen and said she was sure it was a nervous breakdown. 'I didn't really know what that was,' Susan said, as we rested for a moment on a stile and looked over the fields and the drystone walls. 'But I was shocked when I saw her. It just didn't seem like Lally at all. I hadn't seen her for about a year but I was so worried I telephoned Gabriel when I got back. I hadn't been able to get much out of her – I think her grandmother thought she'd tell *me* what the matter was. I explained it all to Gabriel on the telephone. I said it seemed to me it was more than overwork.'

'What did he say?'

Susan started walking up the grassy slope and it was some time before she answered me as I toiled along behind her. 'He was very kind. He rang me back and said that as he couldn't see her he couldn't really diagnose what the matter was but he thought it sounded like a depression.'

'Well, she does sound to have been depressed.'

'Yes, but it was more than just feeling miserable: she looked physically ill. Gabriel says that depression is a clinical illness, just as real as chicken pox. He told me about the symptoms and they sounded just like Lally's.'

'But what was she depressed *about*? I mean, doesn't something start if off?' We stopped by a drystone wall to get our breath again before tramping up a hill that led to an old house and crossroads.

'Not always, he said – but *I* thought something had. It came out later bit by bit. "Man trouble" she called it.'

'But that wouldn't give you a nervous breakdown, would it? – a depression? Or is it the same thing?'

'Apparently there was a man she was in love with and he'd left her. I couldn't get many details.'

'Had he jilted her? I mean had she thought he was going to marry her?'

'I think so. I'd thought Lally of all people would know how to manage men, wouldn't you? But perhaps she's just a romantic at heart and quite conventional, and took it for granted he was going to marry her? She struggled along and then began to feel dreadful. Not just sad, she said, but as though she'd stopped living.'

'I've certainly suffered from unrequited love,' I said, 'but it's never made me as ill as that.'

'You see, I don't think Lally has all that much imagination, Gill. She kept saying it had made her feel unworthy.'

'What rubbish! Honestly – *men*!' I said indignantly.

'Yes, I know. But she really did feel that.'

'It doesn't sound like her. She seemed all right when I saw her last month – I told you.'

'Yes, thank God. I just hope she's fallen for someone else – someone worthy of *her*. She's an awfully nice girl but we've never really known her well, have we? I mean ever since we were little.'

'I suppose not – I always thought she was quite simple at heart. Come on, let's go to the top before it rains.' The sky was a silvery pewter now.

Eventually Susan said, 'I think she *is* simple, but because of that she suffers. I mean if it were you – or even me –'

'We'd be miserable and unhappy and think we'd never get over it, but we've got other things to think about, haven't we? Is that smug?'

We tramped along side by side. The air felt good in my lungs. 'Lally's got her work,' I said.

'She doesn't seem to take it all that seriously. But as soon as her agency noticed her exquisite face was being too much affected they told her to take a holiday.'

'She probably needed one anyway,' I said. 'How long was she here?'

'She stayed three weeks. Her agency kept ringing up and Mrs F was quite fierce. Anyway, she gradually seemed to come round. It was almost as though someone had hit her on the head, I thought.'

'As physical as that?'

'Yes – and she kept saying, "It's all my fault. It's all my fault", till honestly I got a bit fed up because she wouldn't say *what* was her fault. I felt completely useless. I went up every evening and at the weekend and Gabriel rang again – he says the Americans are working on something to counteract this sort of depression, but he wanted to know if she was eating properly. When I told him she was, he seemed relieved.'

'She cheered up in the end then?'

'Yes, she'd begun to eat and the doc gave her some sleeping pills, though she said she didn't want to get dependent on them. She went back to her father's in September.' We stopped again by another stile. Now you could see woods stretching out in the near distance and hear the hum of traffic from the opposite direction.

'She seemed a bit thinner when I saw her but she didn't volunteer any information. She didn't talk much about herself – she never does.'

'I think she *needs* to talk to people. I promised Mrs F I'd do what I could but I can't leave my work up here.'

'Of course not, but couldn't her father have done something?'

'Lally seems reluctant to trouble him. What's the step-mother like?'

'Awfully young looking and fashionable. She seemed quite nice. I didn't see Mr Cecil.' I was thinking – how far away the problems of people seem up here.

Susan jumped down from the stile.

'She looked just diminished,' she said . 'It was awful – but Gabriel did see her just before she left when he had a week's holiday. I don't know what she told him because they walked for a bit in the garden and I talked to Mrs F, but she did seem better after that. Gabriel thinks she's very vulnerable – he always has done. I remember I used to think so too. One thing she did tell me – she hadn't had the curse for months. I thought that was odd. I mean she hasn't been pregnant or anything – the doctor did ask her that, Mrs F said.'

'Can you die of a broken heart?' I said as we began to walk over the field.

'Well, according to you she's better now. Gabriel did say to me that certain people were predisposed to this illness. He was so kind.' Susan looked in the distance and paused for a moment.

It was not the time for me to ask her what she felt about him. It seemed quite obvious to me. That unrequited love could lead to real illness was a new idea though. I'd suffered from it emotionally so many times myself! I supposed I must just be tougher than poor old Lally as I'd never broken down.

'Men!' I said again. 'They shouldn't be let loose.' Susan laughed and then we talked about her new job with the *Gazette* group as we walked along. Susan now had her own byline on Saturdays and apparently she was allowed to write about practically anything she wanted. The editor, Lachlan Anderson, had needed someone who could turn out a regular column on subjects of interest to the erstwhile readers of one Dudley Simpson who was about to retire, and Susan had put in for the job. She had had a six month stint on the mother *Gazette* in the city and had learned how to sub, but there was no direct ladder to a post as sub editor there. I listened to all this with interest.

'You knew about my pieces in the *Calderbrigg Gazette?*' she said. 'On the histories of some local farms and Halls? I was surprised when Mr Anderson offered me the six month contract – which he's now turned into a yearly one – to write my own byline for the group. It'll be syndicated throughout the North!' She didn't sound triumphant, rather surprised.

'Don't you ever want to go to Fleet Street?' I asked.

'No,' she replied. 'I like the paper up here. It's so Yorkshire, and so am I.'

'Sturdy individualism they call it,' I said. I thought Susan rather impressive – she didn't ever seem to have wanted to follow fashion. It didn't seem to bother her that she didn't want to.

'I don't want to work for anyone else – Anderson is an eccentric. Anyway it's very hard for women to find work on national papers unless they want to specialize in women's subjects you know – jams and wombs – or stay on as reporters.'

'How much will they pay for the articles?' I couldn't help asking.

'It's two guineas a time – that's on top of what they pay me, now I've graduated from the traineeship. I've more time now I'm back in Calderbrigg to concentrate on my own writing.' She looked at me rather shyly.

'What *are* you writing – short stories? It must be hard to work all day on a paper and then work when you get back!'

'Oh, I don't suppose what I write for myself will ever be published. Keep it a secret, Gill – I've begun a historical novel – it's hard going. If I ever finish it you can read it!'

'Does the research overlap a bit with your things for the antiquarians?'

'Yes, all grist to the mill. There was such a lot I couldn't use for them or for the *Gazette*.'

'You've always wanted to write, really, haven't you?'

'I suppose so – but it's quite different from journalism – my sort anyway.'

'I suppose you find ideas for your stories when you report about people's lives – things like that?'

'Sometimes. Facts are *stranger* than fiction.' She went on talking about her job. It was unusual for her to tell me anything about her personal ambitions. 'Old Anderson is a bit of a tyrant but he wants me to give the woman's view in my Saturday column – provides a bit of a contrast with the other feature writers who are all men.' She laughed. 'It's the women who encourage the men to buy the *Gazette*. The men read the sports page mostly and the women read more of the other stuff – the human interest. I don't think I'm really very good at human interest – I prefer places and buildings, but I have learned how to convince myself.'

'What sort of things have you written so far?'

'Oh, family outings – where-to-take-the-kids sort of things –then I can smuggle in art galleries and museums and old houses! And *View from a Farmer's Wife* – that was a hard nut to crack. He wanted folk remedies too and that was interesting – herbal remedies. And I'm doing bookshops in the Riding and the history of seaside holidays. *You* name it!'

'It sounds a lot more interesting than what I'm doing,' I said. 'I get awfully fed up with translating. I think sometimes I'd even rather teach, you know.' I hadn't confessed this to anyone else. It just slipped out.

'Why not?' she said. 'You were always good with people

and you like talking. It would scare me stiff. I mean I like children but I don't want to spend more time with them than necessary.'

'Wouldn't you like some, one day?' I asked.

'If they were my own I suppose it would be different,' she said.

She told me about her colleagues on the city paper – Jim and Ernie they were called – and how ambitious they were to work on television. I was surprised that occasionally she'd go for a drink with them to the Great Northern bar. Somehow I'd never imagined Susan with that sort of social life, but she seemed to enjoy it.

'You learn more about people when they've had a pint or two,' she said.

'*You* don't drink beer, do you? I can't imagine it.'

'My usual tipple is vermouth and fizzy lemonade,' she answered. 'I'll never be a serious drinker.'

We came home over the other side of Wynteredge in the direction of Priestley, both silent now. You could see the old house at the turn of the lane and its sloping garden enclosed behind drystone walls at the back. I loved that place, always had. I was thinking over all she had told me. It seemed a satisfying sort of life she'd made for herself and I was intrigued by the historical novel. We stopped and looked over the wall at the old place. There seemed to be nobody living there now. I tried to bring myself to tell Susan about Nick and me in Spain but just couldn't.

Back at the shop Susan fished out the cuttings of her articles amassed by Mrs Marriott and lent them to me. They were impressive, but depressed me when I thought how little *I* had done.

When I got back to London our conversation seemed a long way from Miriam's play which was being put on at the Citizens Theatre, in a part of London I had never visited before, a rather grim area. I was accompanied by Robert Scott, a young man whom I seemed to have acquired after a party. He was undemanding company and the sort of person who might last six months if I were careful not to seem too keen about him, except in bed, where all young men liked you to appear keen. If you played their game, I thought, you could enjoy yourself reasonably enough, provided you never let the tiniest sprig of feeling – as opposed to what the young men called sex – grow on your mutual plant. Rum friends I had, he said in the interval of the play.

It was rather puzzling, I had to admit. I felt myself reeling from the assault of Miriam's ideas and the recognition that I profoundly disagreed with them, but was not able to explain why. Not to Robert anyway. The play was about a girl from an upper class German family who had been so affected by the war that she had decided to lock herself in her room as expiation for the sins of others. One by one her friends came to her door to speak to her, tell her why life was worth living and how they could all help to make a world where there was no more war, no more injustice or suffering. I could not believe in the reasons they gave for the continuance of life if all they could offer was political action, but they convinced the heroine who joined the workers in a new party. In the last act she was seen writing a blueprint for society which came down from the ceiling in the shape of a giant screen, rather like the ones that had used to descend at pantomimes with the words of songs written on them for the audience to sing. The evening ended in the singing of the *Internationale*.

I wrote to Miriam with my congratulations the next day.

After two weeks her play was transferred to the Sloane Palace amidst rave reviews. But it did not last long there. I was sorry. It was exciting that Miriam had got so far and I did not begrudge her her success. More fame was however round the corner, for in April Tom Cooper and Miriam Jacobs were married at the Registry Office nearest to Eastcliff. It was a very quiet ceremony, no fuss about the actual wedding. But a few days after the marriage there took place the Aldermaston march for nuclear disarmament. Miriam was one of the leading lights on this committee too and she and Tom were among the leaders of the procession. They were on their honeymoon and so the press had a field day. *Honeymoon playwright and musician husband camp out for CND* was one headline. Another was: *We think peace is even more important than our love*, which somehow did not sound quite like Miriam. There were photographs of them with others, in sleeping bags, camping in church halls, and marching with rucksacks like some Thirties' youth hostellers. Typically I had *almost* decided to go on the march but I could not quite bring myself to believe that it was the right thing to do. I admired those who did, was on their side, but the spectre of Uncle Joe Stalin and what happened to people who imagined their own virtue was proof of the wickedness of others stopped me from throwing my energies into the campaign. Robert, who still seemed interested in me, was paradoxically one of the reasons I had almost supported CND for he was so obtusely Conservative in his politics that he roused my radicalism.

After Easter I began to consider leaving my job. I had not given the matter really serious consideration before, being too concerned to try to pay off my debts, but the two hands of the wall clock began to exert an hypnotic effect upon me. I could not spend the rest of my life watching it. I would go mad. I was not a very good translator when there was nothing to translate that needed any imagination, only technical language and logic. I sat hour after hour fighting yawns, allowing myself one trip per hour to the ladies and thinking that anything would be better than this. What could I do that was both feasible and something at which I would not fail?

I decided when I was spending a weekend in Oxford with Robert. He was not short of money and had booked a double room at the Randolph. It was to be our last time together, for he had decided to take a job in the States. He went out to see his old tutor to have a manly chat and I was glad of the peace of the large, comfortable room and the vast bathroom with its thick, fluffy towels. Robert worked in advertising so was well able to afford such luxuries though I did wonder once or twice whether I had sold my body for a well-sprung bed and a good meal. But he found me attractive. . . .

After my bath I wandered around the top floor of the old building and listened to the cooing of pigeons amid the high roof-tops, with the sun beating down through a glass skylight. It suddenly came to me that I was actually thinking seriously about teaching, had in fact been thinking about it for some weeks. It had not stopped me from applying for other jobs but it had been at the back of my mind that if none of them materialized, or on further consideration were unsuitable, I could always try it. I sat down abruptly in a deep chintzy chair placed at the top of the landing for dowagers to rest their weary bottoms. What in God's name was I thinking of? The one profession I'd sworn never to enter. But I *was* qualified to enter it, no doubt about that, and I'd already had some practical experience of it in Spain. I didn't expect it would give a direction to my life but I might be doing something socially useful for a change.

A few weeks later I was being interviewed for a place on a course for intending graduate teachers. If they wanted me I could leave the agency and teach for a few months before the course started in the October. 'Going on supply' they called it. At least it would show me whether I was really suited for the work. It might be quite fun to meet small children in Bethnal Green who would not yet, I hoped, have been infected with the virus of delinquency. Teaching would pay about the same amount of money as the Olympia, but I would have far more holidays and shorter hours, even if they were spent in preparation, as I well knew they should be, for Mr Gibson had spent hours marking books and preparing work. I would probably not teach small children after my diploma, or whatever it was called, but might as well begin there. A week later I received a reply to my application and interview. Rather quick! They must be very short of future pedagogues. Yes, they would put my name on their lists and meanwhile I must apply for a grant.

I gave in my notice immediately and nobody seemed either surprised or interested. I sweated out my last four weeks and at the same time said goodbye to Robert, who went off to the States. He had never asked me to accompany him and I did not mind too much. We had really had only one thing in common. I might soon begin to wonder whether I had imagined him!

Roman Lane Primary School was a surprise and not an entirely unpleasant one. I worked there for six weeks and was too exhausted to do anything but fall into bed after returning to my digs and preparing a meal, then my work for the next day's lessons. In a curious way it was fun, certainly not boring. As I was the daughter of two teachers I was not a complete greenhorn, though I soon realized that Cockney sparrows were different from Yorkshire tykes.

When the children's teacher returned from hospital I was sent to a secondary modern school in the same area, which was not as pleasant. I was supposed to teach French to adolescents of both sexes, but spent most of my time trying to keep order and wondering whether I ought to ignore or to punish rude personal remarks. I sympathized with many of the children who were just dying to leave school, but as I wished neither to be a sergeant-major nor a social worker, I decided I would rather teach in a grammar school, and applied to the university to do that post-graduate diploma in the autumn. If I was finding that teaching was less boring than work at the Olympia Translation Bureau, I learned from her letters that Susan had almost finished her novel and that Lachlan Anderson had so approved of Susan's feature articles that she had been deputed to cover further historical aspects of Yorkshire life. She had spent a wonderful day at the university listening to the tape-recordings of some old people whose dialect words and turns of speech were now fast disappearing. She loved these perks of her job, said you could scarcely call it work. I really envied her.

Gabriel had been home for a short holiday and was intending to do his practical year at Leeds. There was no disguising Susan's joy at the thought that he would be in Yorkshire the following autumn. What she had not been able to tell me face to face was evident in the words she wrote to me. *We went to Betty's Café*, she wrote. *Remember? We had tea and crumpets and honey and talked for ages. He was reminding me about Tom's carol service that Christmas – doesn't it seem ages ago? We even talked about The Holm. Did you see it when you were here at Christmas? It's going to be a private nursing home. Gabriel talked to me a bit about his parents – he thinks his father's a saint. Gabriel's not sure now whether he really wants to be a GP. He's more interested in mental illness, I think – and in some sort of social work. We went on a long walk and then went over to Sholey where his parents were at Evensong. I told him about my heroine who is betrayed by her lover and he asked if it was based on Lally. Do you know, I hadn't really thought of that! He said again he* *thinks Lally is a very vulnerable sort of girl. His father told him that her mother, Ginny Fortescue, had been a bit wild, and had died, he thought, in a nursing home when Lally was only five or six. He didn't know the details. Did Lally ever talk to you about her mother? Mrs Fortescue never said anything to me, but perhaps that was why she was worried when Lally was ill last summer. His father more or less hinted that it was a tragedy. Gabriel highly approves of your teaching – he's got such a social conscience – it must be inherited. He says he's no longer a Christian believer, but I think he's very religious. He sends his love. He says Nick was up here for a day or two, according to his mother who saw him in the Post Office.* The letter ended with Susan's saying she hoped to have a short holiday later in the year walking in the Northern Dales with Gabriel.*

Any of these models could be the Face of the Future ran the caption in the woman's magazine that I was reading at the hairdresser's. Tom and Miriam, ensconced in their own flat in Belside Park, were giving a party that evening to celebrate their wedding, as that had been only a family affair, and I had decided I must do something about my hair. The girls at Roman Lane Sec Mod where I was in my last week of teaching, would be surprised on the Monday.

I hated hairdressers except that some of them gave you the chance to read the sort of magazines I wouldn't have been seen dead buying at that time. I stared at Lally Cecil's face on the page. There seemed to be shadows round the eyes but perhaps that was the effect of the new eye-shadow some girls were wearing. Lally was very photogenic; she stood out from the other faces like a light in a dark room. The others were pretty; Lally was beautiful. I turned to the writing underneath. *After the gamine look, will it be the Ice Maiden or the English Rose?* it asked. I read on. Lally was meant to be the Ice Maiden, I supposed. English roses were plumper, photographed in soft focus. I had noticed a certain fashion creeping in which equated women with flowers or past elegance and had them photographed on Victorian *chaise longues*. But Lally too was elegant. Would she be at the Coopers' party? It was strange to think of them as the Coopers even if Miriam was to keep her maiden name for her plays. I hoped I might meet a nice man

117

there but did not think it very likely. Miriam's friends – and Miriam's would be Tom's too – would be either political or musical, and of all men I found musicians the hardest to get to know and could never stop myself arguing with the political ones. Both lots seemed to live in worlds of their own. Still, there might be a few Hungarians who were said to be flirtatious and sexy. Serious love was not for the moment I had decided.

I read on under the dryer. They had probably ruined my hair. I'd meant only to have it cut, not curled, and hoped the waves would soon disappear if they were too awful.

Lally Cecil it said, *is the toast of all those who prefer mystery to the 'natural' look fashionable at present.* I wondered, if the others had the natural look, what did most women have? *She may well be the Face of the Sixties. She is popular with those young men who have stopped being angry and it's rumoured she is secretly engaged to an Austrian baron. Miss Cecil is tipped to be chosen for the new British Film,* Water Lily, *but screen tests had not yet finished at the time of writing.*

Lally an actress. This was new. She couldn't act for toffee, wouldn't even want to act. This must be what you did if you had a beautiful face – become a starlet. Lally was not the starlet type. I did hope that she would be at the party and then I might discover how much of all this was sheer fantasy on the part of the writer. What strange worlds Lally must mix in. It had been six months since I had seen her and since then Lally had been away whenever I had telephoned. Could she really have changed in those six months? Of course not. This sort of rubbish was what they always wrote about models – or mannequins as older people still called them.

I sighed and tried to manoeuvre my head from under the dryer and look round, but the girls were busy and I would have to wait my turn. Where did the fabulous Lally have her hair done? *I* was suffering at a small establishment in Pimlico since I was now resident in Lower Belgravia in Jessica's flat which we shared with a friend of Jessica called Philippa.

Would Nick be at the party? I had wanted to ask Miriam, but dared not. Since Robert had gone to the States I had not met any young man with whom I might feel comfortable, never mind love. Teaching in the East End rather cramped your style and if men knew you were a teacher that seemed to put them off, unless they also taught. I fished out my *New Statesman* from a carrier bag and read some book reviews. The weekly had predictably damned Miriam's play with faint praise in January. They were never satisfied. If they agreed with the political stance, they didn't like the style, and vice versa. As I read on I found my mind wandering. 'Why are you having your hair done?' I imagined Miriam asking me, 'if not to attract a man?' No, it's for myself, I almost said aloud. And what leg was Miriam left to stand on, she who had carefully manoeuvred Tom-Tom into marriage after years of making herself indispensable to him? But marriage wouldn't soften Miriam; there was most likely another political play waiting in her head. The first had made her quite famous, if not for very long, and Miriam would not give up. I had once thought of smuggling myself into Miriam's sociology lectures, but had decided that it would only make her cross.

I must tell Susan about the article on Lally the Ice Maiden – perhaps Mrs Fortescue had clipped it out for Susan to read? Susan was quite thick with the old woman. My mother had sent me another of Susan's articles, thinking it would interest me, and I had read it only the day before. It had been about the colours of childhood, different from her other writing, and it made me wonder whether Susan was going to be a real writer one day rather than a journalist. She had a good visual memory and a capacity for detailed observation. I laughed over the things Susan had remembered: the colours of almost twenty years before at the beginning of the war, when we'd only been tiny children – 'modish mustard' and 'dusky pink', the 'apple green' of our school uniforms, the 'powder blue' and the 'pillar-box red' of our poster paints. I'd shared all that childhood with Susan, and those schooldays, even remembered the beige stockings we'd worn and the brown velvet collars of our Sunday best coats. Where had Susan got the description of party cloaks from? I was sure she'd never had one. It was probably Lally who had owned a green velvet cloak and silver shoes.

I now felt my ears burning, not metaphorically but literally, and managed to extricate myself from under the drier and to wave at one of the girls who was back-combing a large beehive

119

hairstyle. I must insist they didn't style my own hair into one of those. My thirteen-year-old pupils spent all their dinner hours at school back-combing each other's enormous confections. One day even these girls would have memories of colours and styles and forgotten crazes. Now I was no longer a child – or even at present a student – but one of them, an adult. I couldn't quite believe it. My own childhood was beginning to be marooned somewhere in my mind along with the sight of bluebell woods and strange half-forgotten things like the harmonium at Sunday School and the dried up lake at The Holm. For a moment I had a sharp more-than-memory of a sunny evening at The Holm. I was becoming nostalgic at only twenty-three!

Miriam was greeting people at the door of the basement flat in Belsize Gardens. The door was open and led on to a small paved area where someone had placed a tub with, as yet, nothing growing in it. Miriam looked solid and rather worried. Behind her Tom was taking coats and placing them on neat pegs in the square hall behind the kitchen. Beyond that was a largish room where food had been laid out and there was also a good-sized bedroom with twin beds. How odd. I discovered this when I explored a little after a trip to the bathroom. I had looked at my strangely waved hair with its turned up ends in Miriam's bedroom mirror, and groaned.

Miriam was in her element. I had half expected a rather *vie de Bohème* atmosphere, but no, that was not the Cooper style at all. They looked as though they had been married for years, and Tom called her darling. Miriam had acquired a curious sort of pronunciation. Her voice was still flat but it was some time before I realized that this was Miriam's Yorkshire voice exaggerated for London consumption, perhaps to claim proletarian origins. I wouldn't have thought Miriam capable of that, so possibly it was unconscious. She was making a great thing of her northernness though, I could tell. It must be in fashion. 'This is Gillian Gibson, a friend of ours from back home,' said Miriam to a young man as she introduced us. 'And this is Jonathan Lamb who writes about jazz!' The young man and I eyed each other. The room was filling up – lots of young men, not many women. That was a change.

'Have I met you at the Cellar?' asked Jonathan.

'No, I'm sure not,' I said.

'Lovely people.'

'I've known both Tom and Miriam for years,' I said. What else could I talk about? I was not well enough up in jazz, preferred flamenco, knew nothing of skiffle beyond what the girls at school talked about, and anyway they preferred Cliff Richard and Tommy Steele. He wouldn't want to talk about Gigli!

'Were you at college with Tom?' I asked.

'No – I'm self-taught,' he replied. Then, 'Tell me,' he said, looking over my shoulder, 'who is that gorgeous blonde coming in?'

'That,' I said with a quick look behind me, 'is the famous model Lalage Cecil. I've known *her* for ages too.'

'Oh, the famous model,' he said, noting no irony. 'You knew her too? Please introduce me, will you?'

Well really! I thought – is the whole evening to be like this? But, 'Follow me,' I said. 'Lally – hello!'

Lally with a man on each side of her was looking blank but then her face became wreathed in smiles. 'Gillian! I wondered whether you'd be here – we must have a gossip.'

'We will,' I promised. 'But here is Jonathan Lamb who wants to meet you.' There was a tiny flicker of amusement in Lally's eye, I thought, before Lally shook hands solemnly with the young man who turned his full attention upon her. I left them to it.

'Is Nick coming?' I asked Tom, who was busy uncorking bottles.

'Gillian, did we thank you for the wine glasses? They *are* nice. We've only just brought everything down from Yorkshire.' I had my glass refilled. 'No, he's busy on his course; they don't let them out for much leave. Susan was asked too, you know, but she couldn't come.'

'I don't think she'll ever come to London,' I said. 'I wish she would. But Gabriel's going to finish his practical work in Leeds next year.'

'Good Old Mystic,' sighed Tom.

'Well, how do you like being married?' I asked, as he was for a moment relaxed and pouring a glass of wine out for himself.

'Very much!' he answered. 'But we're both so busy! What are *you* doing now?'

'Learning how to teach Cockneys to speak French.'

Just then Miriam signalled her husband from the other side of the room.

'Sorry,' murmured Tom. 'Have to greet Magnus.' And he was off. That would be Magnus Bottomley, I thought, the man who edited the paper Tom wrote for. It was clear that Tom would run a mile to fetch Miriam's slippers. Had he seen Lally yet?

I felt rather lonely amongst these three old friends and their friends. Usually I enjoyed parties. It must be because I had not so far done anything. Not got wed. Not had my picture in the papers. Not written a play. Not been offered a contract on television – I heard a couple behind me obviously talking about Tom's. There didn't seem to be many of Miriam's political friends here yet. I wished Nick were coming. He was so much nicer than anyone else in the room. Well, not nicer, just more interested in *me*. But he would probably not be interested in me now, would have passed on to fresher fields. I had had a card from him at Christmas sent to my Eastcliff address. It had been a rather unsuitable photograph of Edith Piaf, not at all Christmassy. He had written: *La Vie en Rose – Love from Nick!*

I wandered into the hall and found myself talking to a fat man whom I thought I had once seen in the Partisan or on a photograph of the Aldermaston march. I soon found myself arguing politics with him. After a bit he said, 'Let's talk about something else. I always find myself talking shop.' But I had not been to any of the plays he mentioned, nor seen the film he then discussed. So we talked books and the man looked quite interested in my remarks until Lally came up. She looked glowing, almost ethereal, though thin.

'This is Lally,' I said to the fat man. 'I'm sorry I didn't catch your name.'

'Fairbairn,' said the man to Lally. 'Do you read as much as your friend?'

'I don't think so,' said Lally. 'Gillian and Miriam were always the bookworms.'

So we told the fat man about our mutual school days and he

laughed a lot. Whatever had been wrong with Lally the year before was obviously right now, I thought. The man in question must have come back to her. That was the only explanation I could think of unless Lally had another, newer, conquest. Wherever Lally stood, men soon joined her, and made a little group round her. A large posse of young men had just arrived and spread into the courtyard outside. Some rock and roll was put on the turntable and then Miriam was sending Tom round with trays of small warm sausages. I talked to a thin man who played the classical guitar and to a television producer and even to one Hungarian who said he was off to Canada any minute. They were probably *all* famous; the party was a success – Tom and Miriam each in their own orbit and occasionally giving each other a fresh impetus as they gently collided. I did not have the promised chat with Lally, for Lally had to leave early on account of an engagement she said. She even worked on Sunday mornings.

I wrote to Susan about the party. *Miriam is writing a book about 'commitment'. I nearly asked if it was about marriage, but I thought they would think me too frivolous. You'll be much more interested I'm sure to hear that Lally was there looking marvellous and that she was the focus for male attention. I noticed that although the men always wanted to be introduced to her they never seemed to have much more to say to her, just hovered and stared and fidgeted. She's not really a sexy person, doesn't flirt or look suggestive or even talk very much. I've decided she's just an ordinary, nice, athletic girl who happens to have a marvellous face and body.*

It was all very tidy and organized, I went on. *Miriam is very competent. There was a modern-looking kitchen with a big refrigerator. I expect Mr Jacobs bought them some of their furniture too, Swedish-looking, teak I think, and curtains with geometric patterns. A piano of course, but not much room for it, squashed in the main room. Things will clearly run like clockwork in the Cooper household; her articles and plays will be written, her lectures given, marches for nuclear disarmament attended, but the housework will also be done and cakes will be baked. Well, perhaps not cakes, but good wholesome food.*

I thought, Miriam is talented and admirable and confident;

she most likely has enemies because of this. I was not one of them, but saw how others might find her infuriating. Tom obviously didn't. Never having made youthful mistakes Miriam would obviously succeed in marriage too. Miriam lacked romance, wouldn't flirt, but neither would Susan or Lally. *I* was the one who did that. I hadn't though with Nick. If I'd made a beeline for him earlier might I have caught him in marriage as Miriam had Tom? I considered this, pen in hand, still trying to finish my letter to Susan. Some people seemed not to have to make mistakes. Susan seemed to know what she wanted; Lally might also know, athough what it was I had no idea. And Miriam; there was just one little flaw in Miriam, apart from her lack of romance, and I had noticed it when I had seen the famous play. She had absolutely no sense of humour. I had never seen her laugh as opposed to smile. I looked through my letter to Susan and added: *I miss Yorkshire sometimes, which I never thought I would. It's certainly preferable to the East End and that's my fate till the end of term. Then I'm off to France. The course starts in October, so I hope I'll be able to have a good year's reading of all the books I've been meaning to read for years –* War and Peace *to begin with. Have you read it? I expect you have. Lots of Love, Gillian.*

I had earned enough to pay my fare to Paris from a strange job I found advertised, looking after the offspring of American diplomats, and had rather enjoyed it. Later in Paris, sitting in the library at the top of the tall International Hotel on the 'Boul Mich' I felt happier than I had for some time. Jessica had come across with me to France and we liked doing the same things and didn't get on each other's nerves. Yet something in me could not seem to help living either in the past or the future, never in the present. Was that another legacy from Mr Gibson? When I returned to London I'd make another effort to take life as it came, stop looking for the impossible. But the very effort was an example of my inability to live without introspection or the need to control.

One day in the early summer of 1959 I was sitting in Russell Square. It was pleasantly warm and I had intended reading some notes for my forthcoming examination on the theory and practice of education, which were in a folder on my knee, but the air was too beguiling and my mood too vague for work. I'd do the work that evening when I returned to Pimlico. I was rather unexpectedly enjoying my studies if truth were told and would be sorry to have to get down to actual teaching in the autumn. Nobody took the examination very seriously and I did not dare to confess to fellow students that I was quite caught up in some nineteenth-century thinkers, especially Matthew Arnold, since his ideas corresponded to new interests of my own. If any other students were interested in such things I had not so far come across them in the large, fawn-coloured building where we were based. It was fashionable then as now to sneer at such studies and I suppose that if they are done badly it is worse than their not being done at all, but my hero *had*, after all, been an Inspector of Schools – in a vastly different England.

The leaves were hanging quite still on the plane trees; it was one of those days when you feel suspended, floaty, rather happy, a little drunk with nothing more than youth and sun. I can remember feeling often like that.

I shut my eyes and leaned my head back, letting the sun gild my brow like some burnished Roman empress. It was not hot, just pleasantly warm. I could hear bees buzzing and there was the faint scent of grass that had just been mown. The squares and the streets of London were always clean and tidy and safe. I had a large bag of library books next to me on my bench. I always took out too many. When I say that I was enjoying my studies I must qualify this unexpected enthusiasm, for I did not agree with my mentors for the most part, who seemed to me to live in cloud-cuckoo-land. It was all very well talking and lecturing about the beauty of learning or the order of the acquisition of concepts, but what was the good of knowing all about these rather interesting topics if you could never put your knowledge into practice because of the unwillingness of so many young Londoners to acquire knowledge? Teachers were too busy quelling riots to teach according to these no doubt fascinating insights into the way minds worked. I had been quite lucky; I had my time in Roman Way behind me, so was under no illusions, and I had also been doing my teaching practice in a convent which would have made the most obdurate conservative a little disquieted. No noise, no insubordination at Jesus and Mary – which was soothing, except that not much more of what I considered education went on there than it did in dockland or the wilds of Tottenham. But I had enjoyed going to lectures, disagreeing with people, and writing essays. It was not what I called work. I had nearly finished my year off. In September I would have to start teaching seriously and such social conscience as I had, dictated a grammar school in the East End. There might be *someone* there who wanted to learn French?

The sun drove thoughts of work away for a few moments as I sat basking in it. Soon I would have to rouse myself and find some lunch in one of the university canteens. I got so awfully hungry by about half past twelve because I never had time or inclination for breakfast. The sunlight made me feel that something nice ought to happen. I might meet some wonderful person or be invited to some splendid party. There seemed to be no Sebastians or Cedrics or even Robins in London University. There had been a nice young man whom I'd met at a poetry reading – but it turned out he took me out only because (he said) I looked a little like the actress Claire Bloom, with whom he was obsessed, though she had never heard of him. I could not honestly see any resemblance myself; he just saw her everywhere.

There had been one or two attempts on my virtue which I had successfully resisted. One from an army officer on leave at one of Jessica's parties, but he had pink sweaty hands and a stiff bearing and was obviously terrified of girls. The other was a rather unpleasant man whose balcony was near ours, and into whose room Jessica's cat had leapt on her way from our balcony in search of adventures. I had apologized and asked him in for a cup of coffee, but he had mistaken my intentions.

I got up and was striding purposefully across the square when I saw a man running over in my direction from the Hotel Russell side. Then at the shout 'Juliana', I stopped in amazement. I had certainly not expected to see Nick again – well certainly not here in Bloomsbury. The answer to a prayer I thought as I waited for him to come up.

'I saw you – I was sure it was you with purple stockings!'

He was looking quite pleased to see me. Two years it had been since our time in Catalonia. I had thought of him off and on with pleasure and affection but life seemed to have got in the way of any nostalgia I might have entertained.

'What are *you* doing here?' I asked, holding my bag of books against my chest. I didn't know how to react really. He stood there for a few moments getting his breath, looking at me with a smile on his face. 'Thanks for your Christmas card,' I said finally. 'Shouldn't you be in Cambridge?'

'Research,' he said. 'I'm finished soon in Cambridge anyway – what are *you* doing here?'

I told him and we walked along the pavement and through into Malet Street.

'Would you like some lunch?' he asked. 'I've to go to Dillons on Store Street – but we could meet – what about Bertorelli's?'

'I'm supposed to be having my lunch in the canteen,' I said. 'And I must take these things back to my locker – I can't carry them round all afternoon.'

'Meet you at Bertorelli's at 1.15?' he said. 'If you want to, that is?'

I looked at him seriously and couldn't help feeling that lift of the spirits, that light-heartedness I'd felt with him before.

'You've cut your hair,' he said.

'1.15,' I said.

He touched my arm, was gone, and as soon as I lost sight of him I thought it must have been a mirage.

I went quickly into the college and waited for a lift. There were a few girls waiting and a man I'd seen before who seemed to work somewhere in the building. The whole place felt different; I didn't belong there, that was my immediate reaction. How silly could one be? Nick had not written nor tried to get in touch with me, apart from Christmas. Still, he was a friend, whatever else he had been. I had thought he looked older.

The tall man next to me made way for me politely in the lift and we creaked upwards. He smiled at me – I must have been smiling myself.

Half an hour later and I'd done my best with lipstick and comb and powder and lashings of Chanel No 5 which I always carried in my bag and considered a permissible extravagance. I was not dressed for lunch anywhere, but Bertorelli's was not too smart and I thought I would pass muster. Why was I bothering anyway? I ought to be like Miriam who never dressed up for men. People often say in novels, 'When I saw him again everything was just as it had been.' This was not true for me. He did seem older, but perhaps that is not the right word. One might have said worried, if one had not known that worry was claimed by Nick to be something he never did. We ordered fish, and drank some dry white wine as we waited for it. Very politely he asked me about my work at the Institute.

'I enjoy the theory,' I said. 'But that's the trouble. It seems to have made me more reluctant to do the actual teaching for which the theory is meant to provide a frame.' I told him about my teaching practice and made him laugh.

'I can't see you in a convent,' he said.

'Twenty-four and never been kissed,' I said. 'Oh, it's all been quite pleasant – better than snack bars or Selfridges – it's a second best though.'

'But what do you really want to do – be?' he asked as the fish arrived. He was showing more interest in my life, it seemed to me, than he had ever done before. We had not yet alluded to Barcelona. I could not say, 'I want to write,' because that was what people said who never put pen to paper or finger to typewriter, so I said, 'I'd quite like to do another degree now but there are no grants – proper post-graduate work – not this phoney stuff I'm doing.'

'You'll be better off earning your living,' he said avuncularly. 'There are lots of girls in Cambridge who are vaguely doing post-graduate work but most never finish.' I supposed he must have met lots of new women, placed as he was in the Fen city, even as a conscript in the army on a Russian course.

'How's your Russian?' I asked him.

He neatly scraped the spine of his sole free of flesh and placed it as neatly on his plate. He took a sip of wine and poured more for us both. I was always a slow eater and somehow this time I felt awkward, could not marshal my thoughts. I concentrated on the fish as he replied, 'I'm finished soon with it all – still it may come in useful.'

'Is it a very difficult language?'

'Quite, but you know I like learning languages.'

128

'What are you going to do then after you leave your National Service?'

'Well, I got my post-graduate qualification – the one I was in Spain to do – and I'm going to the States in the new year, to Harvard; more study, but also the possibility of work over there. I'm sure the Democrats will be in next time. There's a new idea they call a think tank.'

I laughed. It seemed a silly word though I could just see Nick swimming round a green tank with fearsome fins.

'I shall do some work on the economic implications of nuclear power for the Democrats, I hope. I'm pretty sure of a job once *they're* back.'

It sounded very impressive. 'What about though, exactly?' I asked. 'I nearly went to Aldermaston again this year.'

'Nearly,' he laughed. 'You haven't changed, Juliana.'

So I told him about Miriam and he never told me any more about the think tank. I'd asked only out of politeness anyway. I found economic theories extremely difficult to understand.

Whilst we were on the zabaglione, which was my favourite pudding, I told him about Gabriel who was going to do his last year in Leeds, and about Susan's column in the *Gazette*, and about the rumours that Tom was going to write a 'People's' opera.

'Miriam's expecting a baby,' I said, and I don't know why I felt rather shy saying that, but I did.

'Good for her,' he said. 'Good for Tom too, I suppose.'

'I haven't seen Lally for ages. I saw her in the autumn two years ago. Susan told me she'd been ill that summer – but then later she was at one of Miriam's parties surrounded by a host of men. Sometimes I feel it must be almost harder to be so beautiful than to be ordinary. People expect so much of beauty.'

'Oh, I saw her modelling some dresses in a posh mag,' he said.

Nick told me he was to be released in September from his Service and might come to London then to sort out things at the embassy. It seemed a long time ahead. I was enjoying our talk now. 'I'll look you up,' he said, 'before I go to the States. I can't stay tonight – have to be back at the grindstone.'

I thought, does he mean he would have liked us to sleep

together again? I couldn't be sure. He would never let it appear that he took a woman for granted, but neither would he ever risk rejection I saw now.

'In four months I'll be teaching,' I said. 'In the East End again.'

'Glutton for punishment,' he said, wiping his chiselled lips on a snowy napkin. 'It's been lovely seeing you, Juliana. But I'm afraid I shall have to go.' I insisted this time on sharing the bill. I felt rather unreal as we went out and he hailed a taxi to Liverpool Street. I went back to Pimlico feeling unsettled. It was only when I arrived in the flat that I realized I'd left my books behind in my locker.

I had no money to go abroad that summer. Thoughts of Nick would occasionally come in and out of my head but he never wrote or telephoned. I realized that if he had not seen me in the square he would not have contacted me. I tried to reconstruct his face again behind my eyes – something I always found difficult with people's faces. I tried to imagine an Italian film star whose looks I'd admired that summer, transferring the dark curls to Nick's blond straightness. Nose and mouth were similar, I thought.

On my last foray to Bloomsbury to clear my locker and take books back to the university library I went into the canteen of the adjoining Institute, another part of the spider's web of the university. I staggered to a table with one hand carrying a tray and the other grasping a carrier-bag and just about managed to make it. I was still clumsy, had never managed to co-ordinate my hands and eyes and balance. A man who was sitting there at the table rescued my tray from me and smiled when I finally sat down. I thought he looked vaguely familiar as someone whom I'd seen round and about the place since my time there.

'Isn't your term ended?' he said. 'You're at the education place, aren't you?'

Then I remembered. He was the man who had stepped back for me to enter the lift that morning Nick had invited me out to lunch, and then smiled at me.

'Yes,' I answered. 'I've just been to the library.'

'I thought I'd seen you in the building,' he went on. 'Arthur Noble.'

130

It was unusual for people to introduce themselves by name in the student world but he looked older than most of the students.

'Where are *you* then?' I asked. I thought he looked rather like a bank clerk in a navy-blue suit and with horn-rimmed glasses. But apparently he was a post-graduate in his final term studying some aspect of history – social history anyway – at first I had thought he must have read English for he was talking about dialect and traditions.

'You ought to meet a friend of mine,' I said. 'She stayed at home in Yorkshire to write on the local rag, but history is her passion.'

He asked me what I had been doing and seemed really interested. I was so used to people groaning if I mentioned my hero Matthew Arnold or looking at me disbelievingly if I said I enjoyed trying to analyse the values of humanism, bourgeois or not. They always made me feel I was a bore. Nick had listened, but that was probably politeness, I thought.

Arthur Noble ('Yes, it's a terrible surname to bear,' he said) took me out for a drink at the university pub and it seemed to be full of the sort of people I hadn't come across myself in the purlieus of the place. We stayed till closing-time – I really enjoyed talking to him. His thesis was nearly finished, just had to be rechecked and bound, and he'd applied for lecturing jobs. He was a graduate of London University too – the college just across the road. We exchanged addresses and he said, 'We must meet when I'm back in autumn before I go to Leicester, or wherever they want me.' He didn't say where he was going in the summer before that.

Myself, I found a job coaching more children, this time of the nobility, for their Common Entrance, and when I wasn't doing that I was reading detective stories in the interval between trying to prepare work for the coming term. I'd had my interview and been accepted on a probationary year. It was a county grammar school just out of the East End proper and I'd liked what I'd seen of it, though naturally I hadn't yet met any of my future pupils. I wasn't exactly looking forward to it, but I was resigned.

I'd been to see Miriam and her new baby, Jake. They'd already moved into a much larger flat and were saving up for a proper house. Miriam seemed to have everything under control. I could never have imagined her with a baby, but I found it hard to imagine *anybody* with a baby. By the time I saw him he was a big, lusty, black-haired child who yelled a lot. She was feeding him herself but didn't whilst I was there. I didn't stay too long in case I inhibited her. Tom was still working on this popular opera of his, she told me, and she was writing a column now for a weekly. No more plays for the time being but she hoped to continue with her part-time lecturing. 'It's all a matter of organization,' she kept saying, and I believed her. She looked rather fondly at the baby and said, 'You should try it one day.' We talked a bit about Susan – she seemed quite interested in Susan. She said she had not seen Lally for ages. 'Gabriel ought to do psychiatric work,' she said. She did not mention Nick, so neither did I.

I looked forward to seeing *him* again, I can't deny. I found I couldn't live without an adult version of the tooth fairy who will reward you from time to time. I had to have my little treats – an ice cream or a new novel from the Great Smith Street library. I didn'y mind working, even with the offspring of the Hon Camilla Somebody in whose luscious house in South Kensington I sat at a large mahogany table in the basement with two little boys and tried to drum some French and Latin into their sleek heads. But I did not find that work – any kind of work – involved me completely. Why wasn't *I* studying dialects or Victorian novels, or even continuing with the problems of educational theory? Because I hadn't concentrated enough in the Fen city that was why.

Once I began to teach at the county grammar school I found I was in real need of a tooth fairy, or an everyday angel who would reward me for my hard work. I did work hard. At the end of the day of six or seven lessons I needed some little perk. Usually it was a bag of boiled sweets or a glass of sherry when I returned to the flat.

When Nick telephoned at the beginning of October it was on a rainy Friday evening.

'I'm outside an hotel on Bloomsbury Square,' he announced. 'The point is, do you want to spend the weekend with me in it?' He waited whilst I gathered my wits. 'I'm only staying till Monday morning,' he added. What a cheek he had, I thought.

'Why don't you come here?' I said, giving myself time to think. I knew he wouldn't do that. Nick liked to do things in style.

'No,' he said. 'You come here. We can have a nice time.' I disloyally wondered if there was anyone else he'd asked first and been refused. 'I'm off to Harvard on January first,' he went on as he waited for my reply. What could I lose? Except perhaps the memory of Barcelona which was sealed up in me as a good time, not to be had again. I was aware of not wanting to fall in love with Nick Varley. I had not been in love with him before, but I detected slight indications that I might do just that and it would be most unsuitable and also, I thought, annoy him. It was all to be an above board exchange of pleasure.

'All right,' I said finally.

'Don't sound so grudging,' he said. 'I'll go in and order a double room then for two nights. Meet me outside Holborn tube in an hour, can you? We'll go in together for the sake of respectability.' He told me the name of the hotel and rang off. I ran round the flat collecting a few necessities. Jessica was out so I left a note. I had work to do over the weekend and had also planned a visit to the library but that could all wait, I supposed. Did he want me or would anyone do? No, that was an ignoble thought. I wanted him, didn't I? This was the tooth fairy *par excellence*.

When we finally arrived in the cosy room that looked out over Bloomsbury Square, things seemed simpler – at first at least. He sent for a bottle of champagne and then sat on a seat in the window alcove looking at me.

'Is it a quizzical look?' I asked.

'An admiring one, Juliana.'

I didn't quite know how to be. How could one snuggle up to a man not seen for two years until our fortuitous meeting in the square? He hadn't bothered to get in touch but then neither had I. Had he expected me to?

'Tell me of your amorous adventures – since the one with me,' he said, after the champagne had arrived with two long-stemmed glasses on a tray. I decided, as I usually did, that the

best thing to be was to try to be honest and straightforward –
well, as honest as I could afford to be.

'Oh, I've had a few flutters in the dovecote,' I answered as
the cold, sparkly stuff went down. 'But everyone is always
going off to the States.'

'A pity,' he said. 'I don't want competition over there.'

'What about you?' I asked boldly.

'You know me,' he said. 'Never say no – unless they fall in
love with me.'

'Don't you ever want to fall in love?'

'I didn't say unless *I* was in love – I said unless *they* fall in
love.'

I pondered this for a moment. Who had ever fallen in love
with me? Not Jean-Pierre, though I thought he had. Not
Sebastian, or Robin. Only the people I didn't seem to want,
though I couldn't at that moment recall any particular one.
Did I operate on the same principle? 'Someone has to start it
off,' I suggested as he poured me another glass.

'Why? Start *what* off? If it's any good it must be mutual.'

Was he teasing me or did he really look serious for once?
'Even so,' I said. 'Things don't happen at the same time for the
same people, do they?'

'I am told they do – sometimes.'

'Well, wanting can be mutual.'

'Do you want me, Juliana?'

'I don't know,' I said. 'I certainly don't want to fall in love
with you.'

'What's love anyway?' he asked after a pause in which we
eyed each other rather warily. I said nothing.

'Isn't it always just a desire for mutual pleasure?' he went
on.

'There is that,' I said. 'But that needn't be love. There is
something more romantic – something.' I groped for words.
Why was he asking me all this?

'Either infatuation, or a desire for a soul mate,' he said.

'You might actually find a soul mate. And infatuation is
usually for the unattainable. There are *other* sorts of love.'
Miriam and Tom I was thinking. They didn't seem infatuated
with each other; they were friends; they probably, I hoped,
gave each other pleasure. They loved each other.

134

'Mutual dependence,' he said.

'Well, it's better than a one-sided dependence.'

I thought, he doesn't look happy. I know I can make him happy – for a time – like he made me happy in Catalonia.

'It's all words, isn't it?' I said. 'It just depends what people want – and want from each other.'

'That's not usually the same thing.' He put his glass down and sat on the arm of the chair I was sitting in. 'Champagne always makes me randy,' he said.

'I know, – that's why you order it. It makes me carefree too –I've been rather care-worn recently – too much work – a dull girl.'

I thought, he wants to be thought wicked, I don't know why, but he does. There was none of this before. Some of his aplomb seemed to have deserted him.

'Old Nick,' I said. 'Wicked Nick. Naughty Nick. Clever Nick.'

He bent his head and nuzzled my neck. 'I'm not a bad man – as the man said as he gunned down the barmaid,' he said.

'Aren't you?' I answered. 'I thought you liked being bad.'

'I like being what *you* call wicked. Let's get undressed,' he said.

I opened the door and turned the Do No Disturb notice outwards. Nick drew the curtains on the rain and cloudscape. It was getting dark. 'We can eat downstairs – afterwards,' he said.

He was fierce and a bit uncontrolled, different from before. I had the sudden thought, I suppose after thinking about Tom and Miriam and their baby, that babies could be conceived within minutes of meeting a stranger. Yet Nick was not a stranger, though he felt like one. That's why they said rape was animal. A little animal from an animal act. Yet he wasn't raping me. I was quite willing. You need never even to have spoken, I thought, to a stranger. Just this, and then all the knowledge of the world could be found one day in the embryonic head that resulted. A blob that could turn into a human being. I didn't want a baby from Nick. He would be appalled. Probably appalled too at the thoughts going round my head when I was supposed to be enjoying myself. He fell asleep, but I did not. How nice it would be to be in bed with a man you loved, who loved you too. I probably wouldn't ever see Nick again after Sunday and here I was as near to him as two human beings can be. He woke up then, just as I was just deciding to fall asleep, but I was not tired, so we made love again, if you could call it that. Afterwards we went down to a supper I was not especially hungry for.

His mood changed once we had had a little walk in the rain and had returned to the room where the champagne bottle had not yet been removed. I felt easier with him now, but regretful when I thought of two years before. What I wanted, needed, was someone to love me. Yet he said, when we were back in bed and talking quietly with the sound of the rain against the pane, 'There are not many women who leave one alone. You do, don't you? You don't make me feel guilty.'

'Did you get my Christmas card?' I said.

'Did you like mine? When I was in Paris I thought of you, you know. But then back home there were other girls – *you* know.' I did know.

'It's all right, I knew there would be, and anyway I wanted to keep that time separate – it was lovely.'

'I wish I could be in love with you,' he said. 'But I told you I can't love – not for long anyway – and certainly not for ever.'

'Whoever loves for ever?' I asked.

'I'm told that people can *feel* they will. Whether they do or not is not the point.'

'They settle down,' I said. 'However they begin. Some men do too.'

'Women are all so different,' he said.

'The connoisseur speaks.'

'Are men too – different?' he said, looking at me sharply.

'Some are silent and concentrated – if you mean what I think you do. And some groan and gasp and shout. Some think about nothing else and others have other things they'd rather think about.'

'Yes, some women writhe and heave and others shut their eyes and look as though it's all a terrible effort.'

'Well, it can be – we're not so lucky as you – need more – manipulation.'

'But really, they are all the same in the end,' he said. 'They all want to love you and want you to love them for ever. Do

136

some women love for ever do you think? Are they turned on only by the one man?'

'Some, I suppose.' I was not used to this sort of talk from Nick. He'd never wanted to compare notes.

'Perhaps some have been in love with you. How unwise,' I said a little maliciously.

'Oh, yes – and I have thought I have been too, you know – we have to learn. All that syrupy forever-and-ever stuff. . . .'

'But haven't you *ever* felt that? I spent most of my adolescence falling in love – though it was usually with men I didn't know very well. Like being under a spell. It's sad to think the magic goes if you have what you want.'

'Maybe we shall both find it doesn't one day, with someone.'

'But I shouldn't want never to have felt it,' I said. 'Except it's hard to imagine it as a mutual thing.'

'I expect you'll marry one day – most people do, don't they? And I shall marry when I can con myself into believing a feeling will last – desire never to fail and all that. But she'll have to be bloody unapproachable first. Difficult.' I wondered whether all this came from some childhood resentment, some buried unhappiness. As though echoing my thoughts he said, 'I didn't have a very rosy idea of marriage with my father and mother. They were always having rows. Father was baffled by mother's moods and then made her worse because he was baffled. He bought her all she wanted – he made a lot of money, and spent a lot – but she was still miserable. I think she's just a difficult person and he was unimaginative. But he used to get so angry with her and with me. She always said he got his own way but had never understood her. I can't imagine their sex life. It all rebounded on me. I was happy when they sent me away to school. They bored me. She, I thought, was stupid and he was a bully. She won't ever be satisfied but I think they get on a bit better now. He has it off on his business trips, I expect. Women seem to lose interest in that sort of thing. Most of them do, I think. I just *hate* marriage!'

'Well, they are in their fifties, aren't they? I think babies get women down – and domesticity – and the menopause. *I* don't know. It's a minefield.'

He laughed. I could usually make him laugh.

137

Later that night he made love to me again and afterwards he said, 'Women *are* different you know. Some want it more – or their bodies do – some find it hard to feel pleasure. Others, I don't know why . . . find it easier.'

He was silent – head under hands folded behind.

'I knew one woman who came like a bird,' he said. 'Just as if she were flying – straight away – and only with me she said. No little local difficulty at all!'

I was silent now, envying this paragon.

'It was just like lighting up a room – whoosh – straight away the lights went on.'

He seemed in a strange mood. I thought, men are different too, with different women.

'Lucky her,' I said.

'Came like a bird.' It was an unusual thing for Nick to say and I pondered it when in the morning – Sunday morning – we could hear all the bells from the City borne on the wind – we got up and dressed. I looked at him thinking how men all look different. Some have the backs of their thighs like hairy buttresses; some are smooth-skinned, brown.

'The northern races are supposed to be hairy,' I said. 'But you are not.'

'*You* are. You see, I noticed!'

'I hope in the right places,' I said. 'Except for legs and they can be shaved.' He had few hairs on his chest either. In fact he did not look at all like a he-man.

We spent Sunday exploring my favourite place, the National Portrait Gallery. It had stopped raining. I didn't really want to go back to that hotel to more soul-searching. I wished he would come up and have a cup of tea at the flat. Besides I wanted to do some things of my own, hated getting behind-hand. But if he did, we should go back to the hotel afterwards and I'd feel that out-of-time feeling which I found I particularly did not want to feel just then. I wanted the comforts of my routine. Yet I also wanted to understand him better.

'We could get the 24 bus,' I said. 'It's only five or ten minutes to Pimlico.'

'You go if you want,' he said. 'I know I haven't been very good company, Juliana.'

I hesitated for a moment. As usual I decided to compromise. 'Let's go to a place I know for supper,' I suggested. 'Then I *will* go back to the flat – there are things I haven't done for work tomorrow. And you need a good night's sleep,' I added, aware that I did too.

'All right – you win,' he said.

We went to a Polish restaurant I loved on Grosvenor Gardens and afterwards we sat in a bar on Victoria Station. Nick talked about his work a bit, no more about his emotional problems, whatever they were, and I was glad. I felt inadequate and I was fond of him and he would not want me fonder. What did we talk about?

Stupidity was evil, Nick said. There was nothing wrong with snobbery – about the right things, Nick said. Most men wanted to have their cake and eat it, Nick said. And intellectual men were the worst, he said.

I was thinking, I respect his brains but I don't know whether I trust his judgment. A bit like I used to feel about Miriam.

Nick wanted his own way. Nick was selfish and yet Nick was also kind. Nick was a good lover when someone wanted the same thing he did – pleasurable sex. Clever, sexy, soon to be successful Nick Varley, wreaking emotional havoc right, left and centre, I guessed.

We said goodbye outside the station; he didn't want to see my flat.

I did not see him for almost twenty years.

Afterwards I thought how stupid I'd been not to go back to the hotel with him. But I received a postcard from Yorkshire where he was staying at home for a time in which he thanked me 'for Saturday'. If I had wondered whether I was going to find myself in love with Nick after all these years I now knew what the answer was. The desire for his love-making, which had been quite intense when I was with him, seemed to have fizzled out. Yet I *liked* him better. I wondered often about him and what he would do with his life. If I had played my cards better would I have married him eventually? There was always the possibility. He liked me and he knew that like most women, whatever I said, I probably did want to get wed, eventually. And I did not seem to annoy him.

I spent much of my time travelling to work and back,

teaching adolescents, preparing work, marking work, reading, just as the rest of the staff did. They were a devoted lot, most of them unmarried, the last wave, I suppose, of the spinster teachers from before the war. They lived for the school, worked wonders with the girls, many of whom were bright with that Cockney sharpness, but not very keen on hard work. The Jeans and Joyces, Marys and Margarets of my childhood had gone. A few Gillians had arrived – I had been the only one when I was at school – but now every other girl seemed to be called Susan and the rest were Janet, Carol, Jacqueline and Patricia. Surprisingly I managed after a few weeks to distinguish them all.

Would I spend the rest of my life in Ham-by-Bow? Marriage did not preclude work, as I knew full well from my mother. It was a tiring sort of life and we deserved the holidays. There was the promise of my taking groups of older girls to Paris and to Germany – no Spain, alas – the next year and the year after. But I needed more intellectual stimulus. I decided to write a little book – more for myself than for publication, a sort of diary of teaching with quotations from the educational theorists, to point up the gulf between theory and practice. I thought it could be amusing. In the meantime there was the day-to-day grind to get through but I was young and enthusiastic and ever hopeful of life bringing me some more nice surprises.

I went home for Christmas again as usual. As usual I wished we could celebrate in a more jovial way. Rosemary was moping round the house and I suspected some love problem, but did not enquire. She was always rather secretive, unlike me, but had seemed to be enjoying her second year teaching at an infants' school in the next county. As usual I escaped to Susan's as soon as I decently could. This time I told her I had seen Nick, but she did not seem very interested. Gabriel came over whilst I was there and it was a pleasure to see him again. Now *he* was the sort of man one might envisage for a soul mate. But there was no physical attraction between us. I had always thought him tall but he must have shot up in youth and then stopped for he was not a very tall man now and was thinner than I remembered. He had only two days off from the teaching hospital where he was now in his final year. 'Never ask a doctor for a diagnosis,' he said, 'till you are sure he's had at least a week in bed. We exist in a permanent state of sleeplessness.' He talked about a new sort of medicine too, a cure for both mind and body together. 'But with all the advances in antibiotics they won't bother – so many of the illnesses GPs see are the result of unhappiness or something wrong with the mind – which is part of the body, not a ghostly halo hanging over it.'

Later, Susan told me that he had not yet sorted out all his thoughts. She believed he would eventually decide to be a psychiatric social worker. 'Some people would say if he did social work it would be a waste of all the years he's spent doing medicine, but a qualified doctor with Gabriel's interests would be the right person for so many problems.' She saw him as a pioneer, I could see.

We went to see Susan's grandmother later that evening and in the way of the old she talked about the old days in the village.

'Aye, so many of the folk now are incomers,' she said, as we sat and munched her home-made Christmas cake. 'I mind yon Mrs Fortescue when she first came – just married they were –Willy Fortescue and her. He was from Huddersfield way, they said. Made a pile in the war, that was the first war, mind, very la-di-da he was but that were just the way he'd been brought up. It were fifty year ago or more when they had that Ginny.'

I pricked up my ears. Lally's mother had always been a mystery to us all.

'They said she died of drink you know and she only a young lass. But she was always a bit wild.'

'Yes, you remember Lally, her daughter who we were at school with?'

'Oh, aye,' said Mrs Sharp. But I could see she was more interested in the past than what might be happening now.

I wondered how far her memory could be trusted and said so to Susan on our way back.

'I never heard she died of drink,' Susan said. 'I don't expect, if she did, that Mrs Fortescue would tell me. But I had the impression she was a difficult person. Mrs Fortescue always calls her Ginny. Sometimes she used to mix up Lally and Ginny to me.'

'I don't think Lally drinks much,' I said. 'Whenever I've seen her she always seems to be drinking orange juice.'

'No, I'm sure Lally doesn't drink too much. Can you inherit alcoholism in any case? Gabriel would know. Yet I don't think Grandma *is* right, it's probably village gossip.'

'Has she ever said anything else about Lally's mother?' I asked Susan.

'No, but she knows all the people in the village from way back. She once said Mr Varley was a skirt chaser. She thinks Mrs V is "jumped up". Funny how people like Grandma are. Old money is la-di-da and new money is somehow immoral.' We laughed.

I took some of Susan's latest *Gazette* cuttings home. I had to ask rather hard for them because Susan never alluded much now to her work. But as I left the shop she said, 'I've nearly finished another novel – I wasn't going to tell you, only Gabriel knows about it.'

'Can I read it? I asked.

'When it's finished – if you want – next time you come home.'

But as it happened it was some time before I went north again and by that time many other things had happened.

I thought a lot about Susan and Gabriel when I was back in London. They seemed not just 200 miles away, but themselves somehow marooned in the past. I read all Susan's clippings. She must have done a good deal of research, for there were bits about superstitions and the survivals of the Old Religion and she'd visited the Standing Stones on the North Yorkshire moors for another piece. I was amused when I read about girls who used to look for their future husbands in the shapes left by candle wax round the blown-out candle. Girls were always wanting something to happen. What did married ladies look for? How many children they would have, I supposed, or whether they would live long enough to see their children grow up. Were Gabriel's ideas about the-mind-in-the-body connected to these old ways and beliefs? Now that we were all so rational there was a gap to be filled. Even people who had believed in Christianity had also once looked to magic. Was psychiatry anything but a sort of sympathetic magic? I'd ask him one day.

I thought he'd seemed, as well as tired, as though he were searching for something in which to believe. It was easy to see that Susan believed in *him*.

Back in London I went to see Miriam again. She was just pregnant with her second child, who would be born only eighteen months after Jake. The little boy was about a year old and an active sort of child. Tom was there too that time; they'd just moved again into a Victorian house in Kentish Town and they were papering and painting, or at least Miriam was. I don't know how she found the energy or time. The opera was finished and they were hopeful of an American backer. I didn't talk about Eastcliff to Miriam. I didn't think she was interested in mulling over people and the past. She was always talking about the future. I supposed babies must make one more interested in that, linking you to something new.

And then the bombshell fell. I was on holiday. It was Easter and I was planning to go abroad for a month to Paris with a group from school in the summer term. When the telephone rang I'd been expecting my contact in Montmartre, Madame Poirçon, to ring, so at first I didn't recognize the voice which said, 'May I speak to Gillian Gibson?'

'Yes, it's me here. Who's that?'

'It's Lally, Gillian. Can you come to see me please?'

I thought she sounded a bit odd but I said, 'When? I don't think I've got your new address.'

'No, I'm in hospital, they told me I could have visitors.'

'Lally! What's the matter then? Are you ill?'

I thought perhaps she'd been in a road accident or something. I didn't think at first what sort of hospital. All she said was, 'They say I'm a lot better. Can you come this afternoon?'

I wondered why it was me she was telephoning, but Susan and Gabriel were naturally in Eastcliff.

'I didn't want to bother Miriam,' she said.

'Of course I'll come, but where are you? What's the matter?'

She gave me the name of the hospital in south London and it

143

was then I realized. But if she were well enough to ring me up, surely she couldn't be 'mad' or whatever name they gave it? I promised to come and she rang off.

The hospital was pleasant-looking, not what I'd expected, at the end of a tedious journey by rail and then a walk. It was a cold day for Easter time. I enquired downstairs and they sent me up to a large, open ward on the second floor looking out over trees at the back.

'Miss Cecil is resting,' they said. 'Just go in.' It seemed to be open house all round. There were women in dressing-gowns, and one or two dressed, all sitting or lying on divans or in armchairs. But it was very quiet and the room was so large I couldn't find Lally at first.

It was all rather haphazard; there didn't seem to be any nurses around. Perhaps this was just the ward where you recovered or waited to go home? Then I saw Lally lying on a bed in the far corner and went up to her. There was a chair by the bedside. No other visitor for her. I stood there for a moment. Her eyes were shut. She didn't look capable of telephoning anyone.

'Lally,' I said and she opened her eyes. 'How are you?' I asked for want of something to say. A silly question. She would surely not be in the Walmsley Hospital if she were well.

She sat up slowly. 'Thank you for coming, Gillian.'

'What can I do to help?' I asked her and sat down on the visitor's chair.

'It's nice of you to come,' she said again.

'What happened?' I said finally as she said nothing more but lay propped up against a cushion. I fussed a bit pulling it up behind her. I hadn't seen her since that party at Miriam's. Miriam must have seen her more recently. I tried to remember if Miriam had said anything the last time I'd been to see them.

'I'll get up,' said Lally. 'They like us to walk round.' She swung her legs slowly over the edge of the bed and then stayed like that as though she were suddenly paralysed.

'How long have you been here?' I asked then. 'Does your father know? And Clare?'

'Oh, yes, they've been twice,' she replied, looking up then. 'The doctor said I ought to have visitors and I couldn't think of anyone I'd like to see except you.' I was flattered but what

144

could I do or say? I'd have to know more. I tried to remember what Susan had told me about that time Lally had been ill at The Laurels – how long ago was it? – nearly three years.

Lally got slowly on to her feet. 'Let's sit over there,' she said. She dragged herself across to the window and I followed. 'They'll bring tea soon,' she said.

'All on the National Health,' I remarked.

We both sat down. Then she began to cry. Great tears gushed out of her eyes and rolled down her cheeks silently. 'Sorry,' she said. 'When it starts I can't stop.' The tears didn't seem to be the result of a sudden access of grief, more like a tap being turned on casually and left on because someone had lost the strength to turn it off.

I offered her a Kleenex. 'Do you want to talk about it?' I asked.

'I'm a lot better,' she whispered as the tears ran down. I said nothing, just offered another Kleenex. Then they wheeled a tea trolley round which gave me the chance to ask her if she wanted sugar, and to thank the orderly, and for Lally to blow her nose.

She had her hands in her lap and made no effort to take the proffered tea-cup. Her fingers were limp, like the pink stems of a dead cyclamen, but I saw she was wearing her mother's ring, the one her grandmother had given her that Miriam had said was unlucky. 'What a lovely ring,' I said and she looked up and took the cup of tea.

'Dad said Gran took it off my mother before they cremated her,' she said. I thought this was an unfortunate subject and wished I hadn't mentioned it but I couldn't think what to say. I made an effort again, plunged in.

'Why are you here, Lally? You didn't tell me. I thought of ringing your father but decided not to.'

'I had another breakdown,' she said and looked at me with a far away look. Then she refocused.

'When?' I asked.

'I think it was about three weeks ago. I can't really remember. Dad brought my address book and I found your number. That was yesterday.'

What exactly did a breakdown mean? She did look thin and pale but otherwise herself. No make-up, I saw. That would make a difference.

145

'They gave me electric shocks,' she said, 'at the other hospital. Then I came here and they'll let me go home soon, I think.'

'Isn't there such a thing as a convalescent home?' I asked. I couldn't see her recovering in that smart flat of her father's in Westminster.

'I want to go to Gran's,' she said. 'But it's selfish, I know. Dad's looking for a little nursing home, I think.'

'When did you stop work?' I asked.

'I haven't worked since New Year,' she said. I was horrified. That was four months ago. She must have been really bad. 'I tried to kill myself,' she said, quite matter-of-factly.

'Why?' I asked baldly, out of shock.

'I can't really remember,' she replied, but she had a shifty look as she said it.

'Was it a man?' I asked. 'They're not worth it.' Even as I said it I thought it must be worth it for Lally. I had never loved anyone enough to feel that about them – never wanted to kill myself when they left me.

'No, everything got on top of me,' she said. She took her tea, calmer now, and drank it thirstily. 'I'm always thirsty,' she said. 'It's the drugs they give you, I think.'

'Do you want to tell me about it?' I said. I didn't know whether you were supposed to ask people for the details. But after all, she'd asked me to come to see her.

She frowned and for a moment she looked like the old Lally. The drink had put a little pink into her cheeks.

'If I talk much I begin to cry,' she said.

'Then don't,' I said hastily. I couldn't bear the sight of those tears. It made one feel so impotent. What was the good of words anyway?

'They make me talk to a lady who comes round,' she said. 'But they're awfully busy. And they don't understand. I'm so wretched, Gillian. I'm no good, you see.'

'Of course you are! You must have been hurt by something to be miserable like this but it's not your fault, whatever it was.'

She looked out of the window. Then she looked directly at me. 'They say I'm depressed – I am a depressive because of my mother,' she stated flatly. 'Dad says Mother was one and I've

146

inherited it.' I was uncertain whether you could inherit depression just as Susan and I had not thought you could inherit alcoholism, and I said so. 'You think it's just a let out then? They're just being kind to me saying that?' she pounced.

'I don't know enough about it. You've never talked about your mother.'

'I can't really remember her,' she said. 'I know she was unhappy.'

'Perhaps she made you feel guilty,' I suggested. 'So you feel it's your fault – whatever happened. She probably made you feel a bit depressed and then – afterwards, when you grew up it came back?' It sounded plausible to me. But what did I know about psychology? They shouldn't let visitors like me into hospitals like this in case they put their foot in it, I thought. There must be a man at the bottom of it all. But it was ages since her first illness. She must have known heaps of men since then, if that party had been anything to go by. Perhaps that was the problem. We were silent for a time drinking our tea. I can see the scene unwind now like an old film. . . .

'Tell me something nice,' said Lally, brushing back a strand of hair. 'I'm really a *lot* better, you know.' I wanted to ask whether it had been an overdose of sleeping pills, barbiturates or something. I'd read of many such cases in the papers. But evidently she didn't want to say any more about it.

I tried to think of something nice.

'Susan's writing another book,' I said. Then I remembered the last was about a girl who was jilted. I veered away from that subject and tried to think of something else. I told her about my pupils and about my planned trip to Paris. 'I can't believe I am not one of them, that I'm not a pupil any longer but a teacher. I keep thinking I shall wake up and be back at Greenfield with you and the others.' She said nothing, just looked fixedly ahead at me now, so I went on about the happy times we had in Eastcliff trying to make her remember good times. About the time we were all young and played tennis at The Holm. Then I thought, maybe she wouldn't want to be reminded of the happier part so I changed tack and talked about my sister and Josephine Cooper who was married and about Miriam's Jake, and Tom's opera. I told her about Gabriel. 'Gabriel could help you, I think,' I said.

'He's just the sort of person who would know how to make you better.'

Then I saw the tears pouring down her face again, silently, and I'd been talking for about an hour.

'Sorry, sorry, I can't help it,' she said. So I got her another Kleenex.

Perhaps it was a good sign that you could cry, but these tears unlike the ones I shed when I was miserable didn't seem to purge. I wanted to say that nothing was worth being so unhappy for, but this wasn't ordinary unhappiness. Was she really mentally ill as they call it? She was certainly not mad though people had not yet stopped saying that people who tried to kill themselves were out of their minds. I wished I could find out more about the man trouble, *if* it were that, but it couldn't be just that. There must have been another reason. Had there been something terrible in her childhood, long ago? It was no good telling people in Lally's state just to grin and bear it or pull themselves together. It was exactly as though she were bleeding inside. I wished there could be an elastoplast I could stick over it all. I looked around and saw the other women who were mostly now lying on their beds with their eyes shut.

'I have to take my pills soon,' Lally said. I took this as a hint I'd been there long enough.

'I wish I could go to sleep and not wake up,' she said. This was no good. Had I made her worse?

'You are so attractive, so successful,' I said. 'That counts for something, doesn't it?' But it was like talking to a person who doesn't understand your language.

'No,' she said, after a long pause. But she'd stopped crying again.

'Well, I suppose we all feel failures inside,' I said. 'I know I do – often.'

She tried to smile. I could see the effort in her eyes. I felt unworthily irritated, impatient. I would not be a good nurse. I'd tried my best. There is nothing more tiring than sitting with a depressed person and saying the same things over and over again.

I stayed three hours with Lally Cecil. Perhaps she looked a little less woebegone when I left but that was the result of the pills they brought round.

'You must talk to someone about it all,' I said. 'Write to Gabriel – or go and see him if your father sends you north.'

'I have to see the therapist again tomorrow,' Lally whispered.

When I went away the staff nurse who had been out of sight in a lobby said, 'We shan't keep her in much longer.' There was apparently a great pressure on beds. So many depressed people, some worse than depressed.

'What treatment is there really?' I asked.

'We give them pills and send them home. Some come back.'

But Lally never wanted to be a burden on her father I thought as I went out into the blessed air of the everyday world. That might be partly the trouble. Would she ever work again? I caught myself thinking as I looked up at the handsome building. Lally was not at the window to wave goodbye. I felt so relieved to escape that I was ashamed of myself.

I couldn't stop thinking about her attempted suicide when I got home. That a person like Lally had felt she had nothing to live for was inconceivable. At least *I* could not imagine it. When I arrived home the full horror of it struck me. It had seemed rather commonplace if not very acceptable when I had been actually in the Walmsley to think that the ward was full of people who had attempted suicide, however half-heartedly. Now it seemed monstrous and unbelievable. I had to talk to someone. I didn't want to telephone Mr Cecil as I had never met him, but I supposed I ought eventually, to see what else I could do for poor Lally. But I did want to ring up Susan who had known far more about Lally, I thought, than I ever had. Gabriel too. I was sure he would be able to help her. What else were old friends for? I didn't want to worry Miriam – she had her hands full, and perhaps there was a little proprietorial feeling about her relations with Lally. She would probably refer me to Freud or something. I had a cup of tea and then at half past six when I calculated Susan should be home from work I rang the shop number. But perhaps Mrs Fortescue already knew about it and had told her? Susan would have written to me though, if that were the case, I decided.

It was her father who answered. 'I'll fetch her,' he said. 'She's just had her tea.' I imagined the little shop and the village and the buses going up and down the hill. I wished we were all children again and were playing in the village before Lally had gone to London where I was sure it had all started, whatever 'it' was.

'Susan, it's about Lally. I've just been to see her – she's in hospital. She said she'd tried to kill herself. Did you know?'

'Oh, God!' said Susan. 'How is she?'

'They say she'll be out soon. Her father's going to look for a convalescent home. Don't you think she ought to try to get back to work? Will you ask Gabriel? I know he can't see her, but he might have some ideas.' Susan listened as I told her all I knew. 'She said she'd inherited depression from her mother – somebody's been probing I think. She was in a very low state – if she's recovering I don't know what she must have been like before.'

'I'll find out if her grandmother knows anything about it, but I don't want to frighten her if she doesn't. She hasn't been well.'

We left it at that. Susan said she would ask Gabriel's advice again and would write to me.

I didn't hear anything further for some time except a card from Susan to say that Lally had been released. Mrs Fortescue had heard about it only when Lally was out of the hospital once more and had said she was going back to work. Gabriel was not sure that she ought to do that but as none of us knew exactly why she'd done the deed we were not in a position to suggest anything. And we supposed it was not really our business except that three years ago Lally had asked both Susan and Gabriel for help – and this time had asked to see me. Finally, when I returned from my month in Paris, which I much enjoyed – the French really seemed to like learning English, certainly more than the majority of my English pupils liked learning French – I rang Mr Cecil. It was Clare who answered and she sounded a bit cross. 'They say she's all right now though she's still under the doctor. She should have written to you. It was kind of you to visit her. She told us you had.'

'Is she back at work then – and in her flat?' Somehow I'd wanted to speak to someone else before I tried to contact Lally once more. And I knew how elusive she was, always on some assignment abroad modelling shorts in the desert or evening dresses in winter palaces. I thanked Clare for the information and rang Lally's number straight away. It struck me that I had for a long time stopped trying to contact her till now. I had always let her do the ringing up. I should have been more willing to arrange something. I waited as the phone rang. I felt nervous. How do you speak to someone who, the last time you saw them, was in what used to be called and still was by some insensitive folk, a loony bin? But the phone rang and rang and nobody replied. I had visions of Lally slumped in a bathroom with cut wrists but I was sure her father or Clare must be keeping an eye on her. She was probably out of town and there was no way of contacting her unless I rang her agency and that might have seemed a bit officious.

School broke up and it was high summer. I'd had a letter from Susan and she had communicated the latest news to Gabriel. *Gabriel says she needs unconditional love,* she wrote. Don't we all – don't we all? I thought to myself. Gabriel had now only one final year as registrar to do in Leeds. Susan had other news too. Her novel had been accepted! I was sworn to secrecy as she was using another name – her mother's maiden name of Sharp. *Jane Sharp* was to be the author. Jane was Susan's other at that time very old-fashioned, unfashionable name, and the book was to be called *Alys of Northwaite. Historical–seventeenth century* she wrote. She went on then to write about Gabriel who seemed much on her mind. It was a long letter for Susan, who did not go in for the lengthy letters I wrote to her, when I had the time. Gabriel, with whom I saw Susan was much in love – I had seen it at Christmas and now it was even clearer – was still undecided what to do with his life when his final year was over. *He talks a lot about 'meaning'* she wrote – *I think he has the need to put his own meaning where the religious explanation used to be. Otherwise he says he's tempted to a sort of nihilism which he can't bear.* She rarely wrote of such things to me. I hoped *he* was not suicidal too. But I was sure he was not. He was too unselfconscious. It was the world that was worrying him, not himself. There seemed nothing more to say about Lally. I would try to telephone her again soon. If I wrote she would feel the need to write back and I knew how she hated writing letters. Yet if I could get no answer I'd have to do that.

In August Miriam had a daughter, a little prematurely, but they were both fine after a stay in hospital. They announced it this time on a special card. *Miriam and Tom Cooper are pleased to announce the birth of their daughter Naomi Miriam* it said. I put it up on the mantelpiece. At least someone was happy. I had another month before I had to go back to school, and luxuriated in leisure, not even wanting to go abroad. The month in Paris had been like a holiday.

I had another letter too, and at first I couldn't think who it was from, postmarked Nottingham. I knew nobody in Nottingham and did not recognize the hand either.

Dear Gillian it said. *I'm sorry I did not contact you before. I meant to but my mother was very ill and died in spring. . . .* I looked over the page – *Arthur Noble*. Good Heavens, I'd almost forgotten him and the long chat we'd had in the pub. He went on: I *often think of Gower Street and the conversation with you and hope when I do visit London again I may look you up? This post is only temporary – for two years – it's pleasant, especially when I do not have to commute from the wilds of Middlesex but can be near my work and the library and the shops. I do look forward to hearing from you if you can spare the time to drop a line. How is your new job? I hope they are not all stupid and xenophobic as you said they were in the convent?*

Well! I could hardly remember what Arthur Noble had looked like but he seemed to remember all I had said to him. I *had* hoped he might write the year before because I had liked him, but had forgotten him with the pressure of work in London.

I went out, rather cheered to think someone had been thinking about me. I took the bus to Soho for some exotic vegetables then walked up to Charlotte Street where I'd lunched with Nick that day. I'd heard nothing further from him but had not expected to. He must now be raving it up in Harvard or on some hot beach with some cool, tall American girl, the sort he liked.

I walked back down through Dean Street. I still liked wandering about London. What was the point of living there if one could not occasionally sample its more interesting locales?

When I had first come to London I'd gone with Jessica to the Mandrake Club where people drank out of licensing hours, but I'd stopped doing such things. I was getting less interested in the Bohemian life, I supposed. I was just coming back up to Greek Street when I saw Tom Cooper on the other side of the road. This was an area near large theatres where musicals were often performed and so I wondered if the opera were now on its way to the public. I rushed across to him to congratulate him on the new baby. I felt too that he ought to know about Lally. He turned, surprised, but beamed when he saw me. I gave him the obligatory congratulations and then asked about the opera.

'On in the autumn,' he said. 'Can't stop now – just on my way to my agents. Lovely to see you.'

So I never told him. I still thought he had once been in love with Lally Cecil years ago. I'd tell Miriam about Lally when I next saw her. I made a good meal of aubergines and mushrooms and onions and tomatoes from the market that evening and thought about all our various fortunes – Gabriel with his *wanting to find a benevolent principle in the universe* as Susan had written, Lally with her miseries, Miriam and Tom with their babies, me with my just about bearable work, Susan with a novel actually being published at Christmas – and Nick far away. Then I thought about Arthur Noble and sat down, replete, to answer his letter.

A few weeks later and Arthur Noble and I were now regularly exchanging letters, though I had not yet set eyes on him again. I used him rather as a safety valve I think. He was lecturing on Victorian history and the realities under the respectable surface of Victorian England. I wondered whether our own times were any less hypocritical, wrote to him of my thoughts about the possible reform of the abortion law and the treatment meted out to suicides, who had so recently still been criminals. If they did not succeed in their attempts the logical punishment would be death by hanging, I thought – the most appropriate way for moralists to score a point. I wasn't sure about those who did succeed. It was still a taboo subject, as was homosexuality, in spite of the Wolfenden Report and the Street Offences Act which had only swept things under the

153

carpet. Arthur agreed with me about these things. I wrote on other matters too, for what Susan told me about Gabriel had caught up my own preoccupations. 'Evil need not triumph even without God,' she had quoted Gabriel as saying. 'He believes in virtue and an objective morality.' Did I? What were my indignations over public attitudes but the result of my thinking that so much that was regarded as sinful was not? But what was evil, what, goodness? I did not write to Arthur Noble then about more intimate things, the strange hinterland of the mind in dreams or in those states of half-consciousness that had always intrigued me, when I would wake up sure that a poem or a story would arise eventually if I tried to remember my thoughts clearly enough and shaped them. But I never could and never did.

At Christmas I was back in Eastcliff once more and in the New Year I was to see Arthur again in the flesh as he had a conference to attend. I looked forward to this. Lally was not at The Laurels with the old lady where I had half hoped she would be, just for once. Mrs Fortescue who was still not well did however invite Susan and me and Gabriel on the day after Boxing Day to take a glass of sherry with her and it was there in her cold drawing-room as we sat making polite conversation that she made a few remarks about her daughter. I feel that even then her mind had begun to wander a little or perhaps it was that she had so few people to talk to and was lonely. I thought at first she might be mixing up Lally and Ginny. None of us had mentioned Lally's last breakdown and did not intend to do so unless the old lady did first. Gabriel was sitting next to her looking sympathetic and saying she must get more help in the house and Susan was looking quite at home there.

'Ginny used to have these breakdowns,' she said with no preamble, turning to Gabriel whom she already treated as a doctor. 'Nobody knew why. She used to be hysterical and make scenes . . . Lally was neglected, you know. I think my daughter suspected that Denis – her husband – had had an affair with an actress friend of my son Hugh's.' We all looked suitably shocked and interested and embarrassed at the same time. We knew we should not be hearing this. 'Lally isn't Ginny,' she said and looked at us one by one. 'Not a bit. You will look after her won't you when I'm gone?'

We cleared our throats and mumbled of course and, don't worry, she'll be all right.

'I wish she'd come for Christmas,' went on Mrs Fortescue. 'She's not in London, you know. Denis got her to a little rest home in York – you didn't know?'

Oh God, I thought, she must have tried again.

'No, dear,' said the old woman as if reading my thoughts. 'She's a lot better but she says she's had enough of that work she was doing. I'm surprised she hasn't told you. They're going to find her a little secretarial job in York when she's got her strength up. . . . Now will you have another glass? Susan, do take the decanter around.'

I felt that if we were ever to discover the mystery of Lally and her mother it would be now, but the old lady must have thought she'd said enough and the talk passed to Susan's book. I had already had an advance copy and was full of admiration. She'd written about our village, thinly disguised, as it had been three hundred years before at the time of the Civil War and it was the sort of book you couldn't put down even if you hadn't much interest in those times. I suppose we Eastcliffians were more interested in it than the ordinary reader because we recognized the place and were delighted to find out what it had really been like. She described the lanes and the houses and the work and the churches. Her characters were lifelike. I realized I'd never be able to write anything as good as that. She wrote with much detail in a style perfectly suited to the subject matter without sounding fustian. It had not been reviewed, but I was overjoyed for Jane Sharp who was also Susan J Marriott of the Saturday *Gazette*. Gabriel was thrilled too by what she had done. I wondered when they would marry, for I was sure they would.

In the New Year I saw Arthur, talked to Arthur, but did not go to bed with Arthur, not then anyway, but another chapter of my life had quite clearly begun.

Part Three

1   Lamentations

Some time in the spring of 1961 Mrs Fortescue fell ill again and
Lally went over from York where she had her mysterious little
job and looked after her. She had always been very fond of her
grandmother; it probably did her good to have to tend another
person, and the old lady recovered. I decided that Lally had
escaped something or someone in London and would not
return there, but I could not help feeling that when Mrs
Fortescue did die it would hit Lally hard and there was always
the possibility of another breakdown. Everything seemed
however to be going well for the time being. I had other things
to think about.

Whilst Arthur Noble had been at his conference, ironically
in Bloomsbury which gave me a pang or two, I met him for one
of the sessions and we went out together for a meal. We found
we enjoyed talking to each other as much as we enjoyed
writing to each other. The next day he had to go back to
Nottingham and I had to start back at school and it was all
rather a rush. I had wanted him to come and see me in the flat,
but there was not the time for that. When we said goodbye
after our supper he suggested we might meet again when he
came down to London again a few weeks later and said he
would like to take me out again. He was rather shy and seemed
to think that a man had to take a woman out to the theatre or
to a meal to establish his credentials. I knew that if he came to
the flat I would feel awkward, wondering whether he really
wanted something else, which might happen inevitably if he
stayed with me. Or he might *not* want it, and that would be

157

that. He wasn't like Nick or some of the other men I'd known who would assume that bed was the aim and purpose, but neither was Arthur a lump of puritanical ice. He wanted us to get to know each other as friends, and that was refreshing. I didn't find him difficult to talk to, though we didn't have much time during our meeting in the New Year. This time I did not want a too impetuous flight into intimacy. I had a feeling he might be important to me and didn't want to spoil it. I don't suppose all this was obvious to me at first but as the year went on and we told each other more about ourselves, mostly in letters, which Arthur, unlike most men obviously enjoyed writing, I knew I was right. I lent him Susan's novel and he said he read it with relish and that pleased me. He would meet Susan one day in Yorkshire, but I didn't want to take him home too prematurely. I waited.

I suppose I must describe Arthur. It's easier if I imagine him in a certain place at a certain time. On his second visit to London that year I'd had an invitation to the Coopers so I asked Miriam if I could take a friend. They still entertained, but I imagined rather more selectively. Tom's opera was to be on later in the year and I'd asked for tickets ahead of time. It wasn't the sort of thing I thought Arthur would really enjoy but *I* wanted to see it – or rather hear it.

Arthur was not the sort of person who shone in company but neither was he the sort to make a fool of himself. He was quiet and listened to people and I could see Miriam approved of him. I don't know why I should have cared about Miriam's opinion since I'd never trusted it, but it pleased me that she obviously took him seriously. I felt at this time that I hardly knew him in the flesh.

It was a sort of buffet dinner with an odd assortment of guests. There was a fat American who must be the backer, and several of Tom's friends, musicians or composers, and the music critic of the paper Miriam wrote for. No other of her friends except for me. I felt honoured. Miriam had everything under control and must have slaved all day over the food. She disappeared at one point to feed the infant. I was the only person who went up to see the children. Arthur was sitting politely on a piece of Scandinavian furniture listening to the critic and occasionally asking sensible questions. I can see him now. He wasn't wearing the normal sports jacket and cords but a dark grey suit, and looked neat and tidy. He never drank much, though he had a good appetite and consumed large quantities of food without seeming to notice. Neither did he talk much about his own work. They probably thought he was a fellow teacher.

I had tiptoed into the nursery and was looking at Jake asleep. Naomi was in a crib and she stirred a little. I didn't want to incur Miriam's wrath; she had enough to do without guests disturbing her infants and I was just creeping out again thinking what a lot Miriam had taken on when I met Arthur on the landing.

'Shh,' I said. 'I was just peeping at the babies.' I wasn't the kind of woman who usually swoons over babies and I felt he would think me sentimental. But he said, 'Are they asleep?'

'The boy is – the baby's stirring a little.'

We stood at the half-open door with the night-light dimly shining. He put his arm round me – he'd never done even that before and then he kissed me very firmly after taking off the horn-rimmed specs. It was a pleasant kiss. Then he put the specs back on and without saying anything smiled and went in search of the bathroom. I went downstairs again and they were all talking about *The Three Musketeers*, which was the name of Tom's opera. Arthur reappeared and asked some intelligent questions about how they were going to get the period flavour into the action which was set in Harlem in the last decade. I took another glass of wine and thought about the kiss. Arthur was across the room deep in a listening pose; tall, short-sighted, dark, the glasses occasionally flashing in the electric light. He looked efficient and sober, rather like a higher civil servant. But he was a don if not an Oxbridge one, though he did not smoke a pipe which most of them did at that time. Arthur declined a cigar, but he did take a glass of whisky before he came up to me again. I was thinking that though he was not a fashionable person, he never looked unsure of himself. If you knew him better you could see that he often reserved judgment.

Tom was promising that everyone would have a complimentary ticket so I thought that was a good time to fix another of Arthur's visits. He did not go home with me after the

Coopers' party. I wondered if I had not given him enough encouragement. Did I *want* to encourage him? He was so unlike any of the men I'd known before. Not exactly elusive, but busy in his own life. For all I knew he might have some girl stowed away in Nottingham. I thought, I'll wait till summer and see how I feel. He intrigued me and although I did not always agree with him he never seemed to take that personally as so many men would have done, but was ready with logical arguments – and also ready to listen to mine. I still felt a bit on my best behaviour with him and maybe that did not auger well, I thought. But most of that spring and summer I was busy at work and so was Arthur, who was overworked – or was too conscientious. I compared him with Gabriel, thought he was more like Gabriel than anyone else, even if Gabriel's sort of intensity and saint-like attributes were missing.

Arthur knew a lot about classical music rather than butterflies. His tastes were not too orthodox. I told him about my childhood and about my friends and background which was not too different from his, though he hailed from that indeterminate county called Middlesex. I thought – he comes from Middlesex, maybe he's a bit lukewarm about sex too? He confessed he was trying for a permanent post in another university, didn't like uncertainty in career matters, wanted to settle down for good in some history department. Not many departments at that time were concerned with his own special interests.

I heard from Susan, who'd visited Lally in York. *She sends you her love,* she wrote, *and often says how nice it was of you to visit her last year. She doesn't seem too bad at present, though some spark seems to have gone out. Difficult to explain. She had a long talk with Gabriel. He doesn't tell me all of her confidences but from what he lets slip I think Lally must have been a bit off beam last year. I still feel there's something she's not telling any of us. I found out a bit more about her mother by the way from Mrs Fortescue, who is getting frailer. I worry how Lally will manage when her grandmother dies. She says little about her father. You remember my grandma said that 'Ginny' was wild? Well, Mrs Fortescue began to talk about her the other day when I went down to see if I could do any of her shopping for her. Lally's job in York is in the office of a nursing home. I*

160

can't help feeling it had been suggested in case she ever needed treatment again – sad. Anyway Mrs F said again apropos of nothing: 'You know, my granddaughter was neglected at the beginning of the war when Denis was called up. I was worried about my husband at the time or I'd have made more effort to get Ginny and the child to stay here – as they very well could have done. But Ginny was cross with me – I can't remember why. My daughter was a difficult person, Susan,' she said. 'Denis didn't really know what to do with her. She should never have had children. She drank too much you know – I think she could have been cured but. . . .' Then she stopped and left that tack. I sat there listening to every word. Then she said, 'It would never have happened if they'd let her come to me afterwards.' But she didn't explain after what and I couldn't ask her because if she is once stopped she forgets what she's been saying. 'Denis came back for a bit,' she said. 'And then he got that old Nanny of his to look after the child.' I ventured a 'Then she came to you?' after a moment, but she looked up and said, 'The child didn't come to me till she was ten.' She often calls Lally 'the child' as though she still hasn't grown up or isn't the same person as the adult granddaughter.

I wondered whether being with a sick mother could account for Lally's problems, or there is something she's inherited. Gabriel says you don't inherit any trait as clearly as this. But it could have made her worried or guilty, couldn't it? Except we don't know how or why Ginny died or if it was from drink. Lally never says anything about it, but do you remember when we were about fourteen that time we were exploring The Holm and she said she heard a girl who had once lived in the village and was unhappy. Don't you think that must have been the memory of her mother? If so there's always been something in Lally that could have led to depression. It's probably some quite simple process. She was just the wrong person for whatever happened to her, may have inherited her mother's instability. I know it was never apparent to us but maybe it just went underground?

I went to Grandma's again today and she was in a talkative mood. Actually she must be older than Mrs F, but looks tougher, though she's had a harder life. She wasn't talking about Lally's family this time but about Nick Varley's grand-

father before the Great War when he came to live in Lightholme. I think Grandma would have been a novelist if she'd been given a chance – that must be where I get my story-telling powers from, such as they are. Nellie Varley (that's Arnold's mother), was a 'sour old thing', she said. 'Pity she never lived to see Arnold make his brass – they say clogs to clogs in three generations and that young one'll be riding for a fall for all he went to Oxford!' I pointed out he was in America and doing awfully well and wasn't in business and nobody wears clogs any more. 'They'll come back,' she said, and laughed. Then she got on to the Coopers. (Your description of the dinner party chez Miriam sounds weirdly interesting). She said she'd 'Nowt against them. As you make your bed so you lie on it' she added.

Then she did get on to the Fortescues again but all she said was, 'Miss Virginia wanted to be an actress but all the acting she did was for real.' She's shrewd, my Grandma.

Susan was allowing herself to be a little more unbuttoned these days. Her book had sold well though not outstandingly and I knew there was another in the pipeline. I did wish Gabriel would hurry up and marry her. I was sure Susan would one day want a child. I had an ambivalent attitude to babies and children myself since I knew I wouldn't be able to do anything half-heartedly and was afraid that I'd either be neglectful or too possessive a mother. Perhaps novels would be enough for Susan. I still enjoyed my solitary walks in London. When I told Arthur about them he didn't seem to find my desire for solitude now and then as anything extraordinary. He liked his own company too.

There was a PS to Susan's long letter. *When I said to Lally the other day in York that she was looking much better she said, 'I don't like my body any more. I always used to depend on it.' I suggested she took up tennis again and she said she might. She is a mystery. The more I feel I understand about her the more elusive she is.*

We went to *The Three Musketeers* and I must say it was good fun. The music was easy on the ear and there were two songs that you easily remembered, one sad, the other merry. There was a new sort of syncopation in both – it was some time before I realized that the rhythm was rock and roll! D'Artagnan sang

162

one of them to his mistress, a black girl who was a prisoner in a brothel but had a heart of gold. The brothel was run by the wicked Milady. It didn't seem to have much connection with the Dumas story I vaguely remembered from childhood, but the chorus of the four companions when the mistress died (she was called Cassie), was a really sad tango-like tune, very catchy. It brought back The Holm for some reason. I remembered Tom's playing there and wondered if he remembered how once he'd invented a tango for us to dance to, but none of us, except Lally, knew the steps. I felt sad whenever they played this tune which became a sort of refrain in the opera towards the end. I knew it would be popular. Tom's name if not his fortune would surely be made. Arthur, who accompanied me, noticed that the music affected me. I hadn't expected Tom's music to say much to me since I now found him rather remote, but the simplicity and emotion in the music went directly to my sentimental nature. Arthur said he enjoyed it too. He was a bit preoccupied though, waiting to hear from the many posts he'd applied for. Afterwards, instead of going to a restaurant we went to the Partisan where I hadn't been for ages. The people were all younger than us. I supposed that like most left-wing groups it had been split into factions of lesser or more revolutionary fervour. The people were smarter than four years before. Not so many duffel coats, more eye make-up on the girls' faces.

'Tom Cooper leader of fashion,' I said. 'It *was* good, wasn't it?'

'It will be enormously popular,' agreed Arthur. 'I really enjoyed it.'

'It's amazing how many famous people our little group is producing,' I said. 'There's Susan and her book, and Tom. And Miriam and her political work, though she's a bit too busy to make a splash at the moment. Did you know about her play?' Arthur had never seen it so I had to explain. Sometimes I wished we'd had the same childhood; at other times I was glad he was an outsider; it was not so incestuous. I never said much about Nick to Arthur though he knew I was no virginal lily because I'd told him; but that evening he said, 'And there's that Nick in America waiting for the Democrats to win. And your friend who was a famous model!'

'There's only me and Gabriel who haven't yet done anything,' I said. 'And Gabriel will be a famous psychiatrist, I'm sure.' I felt inferior and untalented.

'Wait till you've written that book about teaching,' he said encouragingly. I was so surprised he'd remembered and wished I hadn't told him about it. It would never be any good. 'Your friend Susan writes well, but I'm sure you might do as well if you wanted. Your friend Lally's still in a mess from what you say. And Gabriel, the doctor, has yet to discover anything world shaking. . . .' said Arthur.

I knew he was trying to cheer me up but I felt cross. Who was he to lower my friends' achievements in my estimation? 'Oh, you don't understand,' I cried. 'They've all done something and all I can do is teach some dreary children in a dreary place and wear myself out.' I was full of self-pity and was ashamed of that too.

'Sorry,' he said.

'I used to be so ambitious,' I said.

'So did I,' said Arthur.

'But you'll be all right. Men always are all right. Miriam would be as famous as Tom if she didn't have to spend her time looking after babies. And Lally was probably let down by some man, and Susan. . . .' I didn't for the moment want to go into what I thought might be wrong with Susan's life, so stopped.

'Depends what you want out of life,' said Arthur in his maddeningly logical way. 'I'd be happy to contribute my mite to history.' (He said this sort of thing without self-consciousness.) 'But I'd like a good personal life too. I've seen so many people who achieve great things but are miserable in their private life. You have to take a long view.'

'Well, I just wish I had Susan's talents,' I said.

'I'd like to meet Susan,' said Arthur. 'She's got a true historian's eye and imagination.'

'I ought to have stayed at home and been a journalist,' I went on, still determined to suffer.

Arthur laughed. 'Think how many little girls you can influence,' he said. He really believed in education did Arthur.

Arthur was finally offered a permanent post at Leeds

University. I was pleased for him but felt he was going to know Yorkshire better than I now did – *my* place and part of the country I'd once known so well. I was a bit jealous.

'Now you can come up and stay with your parents and see me too,' he wrote. It was difficult for him to keep popping down to London and he was very busy.

He always wrote to me regularly and his letters cheered me up when I felt low.

Things went on more or less like this till the summer when Arthur announced that he had to do some more research up north and couldn't afford a holiday. *You go*, he wrote. *And come back refreshed from France. Then what about a little visit to Yorks before term starts again? I'm sorry I haven't the opportunity at the moment to go with you. One day, if you would like, we could go to Paris together. Would you like that?* I knew he was giving me the chance to think about him and me so I replied that I'd go to Brittany with some friends and then would go up north for a few days. But I could not envisage staying at home and seeing him on bus trips to Leeds and was unsure what he really wanted. Did he think I would stay with him? He was going to rent a flat owned by the university. If I took him home Mr Gibson would immediately decide it was serious and I knew it was, in a way, but in what way? Arthur had only kissed me and talked to me and written to me. There might still be other parts of Arthur about which I knew nothing. I had never had a relationship like this before, was a bit at sea. People didn't live with people so much in those days, apart from having love affairs, and in any case Arthur Noble and I didn't even live in the same part of England. I found out later that he had tried for a post in London but hadn't been offered it. Either we should go on having this curious relationship by correspondence or – or what? I wasn't sure. I didn't want to stop knowing him. I kept thinking of things to tell him, often wondered what he was doing – and he asked me to tell him of my daily routine. Was he just shy or did he think I did not care much about him? I was uncomfortably aware that Something Would Have to Be Done. But I put it off and went to enjoy myself in Brittany with Jessica. It had been a busy and tiring summer term and I needed a change. We rented a little stone house almost on the seashore on the northern coast and I rested and went for walks and read and ate enormous meals. From time to time I found myself wishing that Arthur were there to share it all. On returning to grey old London I noticed all the women seemed to be wearing trousers and everything looked damp. I still had a week of holiday, but I'd never before gone up north without letting anyone in Eastcliff know. It seemed a bit unkind. I would go to Leeds though, have a talk with Arthur and then ring home saying I'd just decided to pay a flying visit. It seemed an unnecessary subterfuge, but I did want to see Susan if she were there. I'd like to see Lally in York too but there would not be time.

Once I'd decided I felt better and rang Arthur's number. He came straight to the telephone.

'I thought it might be you,' he said. 'Can you come up tomorrow? I've been slaving away all summer – thanks for your cards by the way. I'll book you a room in the university graduate house, if you like!' If *you* like, I thought, but did not say. 'You can see your parents the next day,' he suggested. 'And all your old friends.'

I took the train north; there were still steam trains from King's Cross – they didn't change to diesel until 1964. Everything looked ugly after France but I always thought that, before I got to the countryside. Then at Doncaster they started to call you love. The train slowed down and we passed through a country of slag heaps and wasteland. Arthur had promised to meet the train. It was odd going home to see someone who did not belong there. But as soon as I saw him standing at the barrier and saw his face break out in smiles when he caught sight of me, I knew.

I won't go into all that except to say that I did not after all stay in the graduate hostel but with Arthur in his not *too* neat little flat.

'I know you don't really want to live in Leeds,' he said after he had made surprisingly passionate love to me. 'But will you marry me one day?'

'Why did you wait so long?' I asked. I meant, to go to bed with me not ask me to marry him, which was a shock.

'I wasn't sure what you wanted. I don't know even now,' he said.

'Well, I like it,' I said. 'You'll have to give me time to think about the other.'

166

'People usually call *sex* "the other",' he said. 'I'll wait – we both have things to do – but will you think about it?' His face was slightly pink. 'I've never asked anyone before,' he added. 'I wanted to get to know you better – not just –' He gestured to the unmade bed. I laughed. He was wonderfully old-fashioned, but not too old-fashioned.

'I'll have to think about it,' I said again. 'I don't believe in engagements. I think they're rather silly, except just private ones.'

I thought – my work and all my life in London! I was twenty-six, not too young to think about marriage, I supposed, even in my father's world.

'But where would we live? What would I do? I'm happy in London,' I said.

'If you want to wait a year or two?' he said. 'But I'd like to know that you aren't thinking of going off with anyone else, that's all.'

'I suppose I could teach French anywhere,' I said. 'Will my parents have to know?'

'If you marry me I expect they will,' he said mildly.

Not yet though. 'I'll go and see them tomorrow. I haven't decided anything yet – I mean about marriage, not about you. I like you Arthur Noble,' I said. And as I said that I realized that Noble was a Yorkshire name. I hadn't thought about it before, but it is.

'And I love you, Gillian Gibson,' he said. 'I'm a romantic too.'

This isn't meant to be a story about me but mainly about my old friends – so I will not dwell upon the logistics of Arthur and my coming together. He met my parents eventually and to please them I became formally engaged. My family, and Mr Gibson in particular, was seen to dust itself down and put on its best face. Engagements are a time for feeling the importance of Family, I suppose. I think my father was pleased. I know Mother was. Rosemary appeared surprised.

We were married at a Registry Office in Calderbrigg over a year later. Mr Gibson had to put up with this. Fortunately he actually liked Arthur. Arthur had already met Susan and Gabriel by then, but not Lally who was still in York. I

167

remained in London till I married and when I moved north I found similar work in Leeds, which pleased my parents. I believe they even thought we might settle in Eastcliff which was not too far away from Leeds, only about twelve miles, but I wanted a new life, did not want to live in childhood haunts. Eastcliff was quite near enough. I was not going to buy a house like Mr Gibson's, though we could have done worse as it turned out. We rented a flat to begin with and Susan and Gabriel came over to see us. Susan told me that Lally was apparently no worse. I invited her to our wedding but she did not come, though Susan and Gabriel did.

Several months later after I'd come to start married life in Leeds, Mrs Fortescue was one morning found dead in her bed. The doctor who was visiting her that day had found the kitchen door unlocked at the back of The Laurels but there had been no answer to his shout. Usually she left the door open in the afternoons and locked up at night. He had gone upstairs to investigate, almost sure of what he would find. She had gone to rest the previous afternoon and not died of any of the manifold things that were wrong with her, but of a sudden stroke. Doctor Robson telephoned Lalage's Uncle Hugh, and Denis Cecil and Clare, and had then rung Gabriel at the hospital. He knew of the problems poor Lally had had in the past and the shock of her grandmother's death might start them off again, so he asked Gabriel to tell her. It was an unenviable task. But Gabriel had not just telephoned, had actually gone to York in the evening to tell Lally in person.

Susan rang me with all this news. 'Should I come to the funeral?' I asked her. 'Lally could stay with us in Leeds afterwards – we have a spare bed. Or are her father and uncle going to sleep at The Laurels?'

'Do come, Gill,' said Susan. '*If* you can get the afternoon off. But Lally's going straight back to York afterwards, she says.'

'All right.'

Mrs Fortescue had always been kind to me. As a child I'd found her fascinating. She was worth losing half a day's pay.

An evening or two later I was looking at the 'hatch match and dispatch' page of the *Yorkshire Gazette*. I thought, they've probably put a notice in and I'd like to know how old she was. Seventy-nine was the answer. I looked idly at the marriage notices and then I saw it. The marriage of *Nicholas Arnold Varley of England and Washington on March 15th last in Washington to Amelia Foster Larue, also of Washington.* I even felt my heart jump from surprise. Nick would not have bothered informing the Yorkshire papers, it would be his parents, full of pride, wanting to tell the part of the world that knew them. It rocked me quite a bit. I was certainly no longer involved with Nick, never had been in love with him and had never felt guilty about our relationship, but I'd known him rather well, when I thought about it, and I simply could not imagine him married or what might have made him decide to wed. I tried to imagine Amelia Foster Larue who sounded like a Southern belle. I saw a tall, glamorous, cool woman, the kind he'd said he would want to capture because she played hard to get. Clever too she'd be, and hard as nails. I was thinking in stereotypes, which is what I find one always does about old friends' new attachments. Nick was nothing to do with me any longer, not that he ever had been for long. As he had once opined, the Democrats had got in at the end of '61 and he was attached to some high research or advisory office, his think tank perhaps. He was doing well, for my mother had heard some time before from Mrs Varley about the wonders of his salary. I thought, power and wealth were what Nick wanted. Mrs Varley was probably having the holiday of her life out there on an extended vacation once they'd seen him married.

I remember thinking at Mrs Fortescue's funeral at Eastcliff Church that she herself *had* probably married money. Lally had never said much about her grandfather, but people remembered The Laurels being run very lavishly before the first war and between the wars. All kinds of people were there from the village, and the church was packed. Both Gabriel and his mother were there since Canon Benson was taking the service. The Bensons hadn't changed at all, still gave off that slightly aristocratic air in spite of their shabby genteel situation. I suppose Canon Benson was rather an incongruous sort of parson for such a place. I preferred Sholey Church myself but I liked Gabriel's father's sort of religion.

I was a bit late, so I sat at the back, and saw Lally with a tall middle-aged man who must be her father and another man of the same age with two young women – Uncle Hugh and two of the actresses I guessed. Lally's hair shone in a ray from a stained glass window; I did hope she would be all right. It seemed ages since I'd last seen her in that hospital. Tom's mother and father were there too and a whole clutch of villagers, a scattering of ancient relations and Susan and her grandmother.

I still felt that if I went out of the church and up the road and turned in left down the drive I'd find Vivien Fortescue waiting in her drawing-room with a glass of sherry. As the service began another figure sneaked in and sat just in front of me. Tom Cooper. No Miriam.

I suddenly had the curious idea that it was Lally's mother not her grandmother who was in that coffin at the front, but pulled myself together. It was an idea that recurred though, that Lally had been haunted by her mother and now that her mother's mother was gone the first ghost might return to keep the second one company.

Only Miriam and Nick were absent from our old band of friends. It was years since we'd all been together in the same place.

Gabriel's father was saying that piece from Corinthians: *The last enemy that shall be destroyed is death . . . if the dead rise not let us eat and drink for tomorrow we die.* I wondered what Lally was thinking. What would it be like to want to kill yourself? I still could not imagine it. I wondered too whether Gabriel Benson had discovered any of the truths he was searching for, that mysterious connection between mind and body. . . . Did the famous Tom ever think about such things?

Lally ought to be able to find solace in religion. What was depression but an intensification of that 'full of misery' the Canon was now repeating from the old prayer book?

After the first half of the committal the family went to the old chantry chapel graveyard for the rest and I saw Tom staring at Lally as she passed up the aisle, but she didn't see any of us. Her father was a handsome man; she must have got her looks from him.

The village people looked both smart and solemn.

When the hearse had gone away down the road, Susan came up to me.

'I think Lally's all right,' she said. 'We are all asked to go to The Laurels in about half an hour for tea – Tom too. Did you see him?'

Gabriel had gone with his parents, and Susan said as we walked along, 'There's just one grave space left, you know, at the old chapel.'

I felt I half belonged to the place and the people. How true it is that as time goes on old friends seem to meet more and more often only at weddings and funerals.

We all met and talked over tea, but it was not the place to chatter about ourselves whilst we balanced cups and ate ham sandwiches. I didn't get a proper chance to say much to Lally except I was sorry. She was very dignified, looked fatter than she had used to be.

It was only afterwards, when Susan and I went off together, that I said, 'Did you know that Nick's got married in the States? It was in the paper.' I'd never told Susan about my former intimacy with Nick and now was not the time. But Susan had news for me. She was going to take a little place of her own, a terraced house in Eastcliff and wanted me to see it. I had an hour or two before I must return to Leeds so went along willingly. On the way past the Stray and down a cobbled road she told me that Gabriel had been offered a post in a new unit in the town for people with mental problems and ex-prisoners, in liaison with the social work department. He'd already had a year helping out the village GP and then some time setting up a hostel for alcoholics. Saint Gabriel I thought. But what was the use of being a saint if he wouldn't make up his mind and marry Susan? It was obvious that the house she showed me that afternoon was to be bought by her alone, though I imagined he'd be a constant visitor. I was never critical about Gabriel to Susan and I knew that once people married they always wanted all their friends to do the same. Perhaps Susan preferred her independence? No, I knew she loved him. Might she not though have loved someone else if she'd left Eastcliff?

'Fancy Miriam having had another baby!' said Susan as we walked along. Tom and his wife now had three small children.

171

I had begun to be quite keen to have a child myself and I knew Arthur wanted children eventually though we both knew it would change our lives. But I didn't want to talk about that with Susan. Instead we talked about Lally who had seemed quite normal that afternoon and indeed very much in charge of herself, able I supposed to put herself on automatic pilot for a social occasion.

'The last time I saw her was three years ago at the Walmsley hospital,' I said to Susan. 'Do you think she ever misses her modelling career?'

'I'm sure she doesn't – she's better off where she is, Gill. I think she'll be able to cope now. Gabriel sees her now and then. I expect she'll be back here in Eastcliff soon to settle the house and everything.'

'I think it's a pity though – she's the sort of person who would be happier married,' I said.

As we walked up the hill Tom's sister Josephine passed us in her car and waved. She was a capable and cheerful woman, totally different from the sulky girl on the Christmas sofa years ago with the steady who had turned out steadier than anyone had imagined for they were now the parents of four sturdy small boys.

Apparently Susan's parents were thinking of emigrating to Australia, she told me, to be with her brother Jim and his family, and this was why Susan had decided to set up by herself. *Tempora mutantur* I thought and wished selfishly that Eastcliff would never change and that people would not change or grow old either. But I supposed that we were all slightly improved upon our original selves if not quite so startlingly as Tom's sister.

'Oh, it's nice having you to myself for an hour or two,' said Susan. 'Though it's a sad occasion.'

I was glad that Arthur had not accompanied me. A husband, even if he appreciates your best friend, makes a subtle difference. I wanted a good long talk with Susan. Arthur liked Susan, but had reservations about Gabriel. I think he found him a bit dreamy and hard to pin down. I was not even sure, strange to say, that the two were actually lovers, though they spent such a lot of time together.

We had arrived at the end house of a little terrace built in

172

stone. It was quiet. The inhabitants of the other houses were most likely having their teas. Neat gardens stretched out at the front of the houses with wallflowers in every one. The backs gave on to a yard with a row of outside privies. Susan opened the back door which led straight into a kitchen parlour with a water heater over a sink and a large black kitchen range. The room had a door into a larger room. 'The parlour,' said Susan opening the inner door. There were rolls of wallpaper and buckets on the floor and another door which opened on to Susan's own garden. 'Two rooms upstairs and a tiny room we could make into a lavatory.' I noticed she said 'we'.

We went back into the kitchen. 'It's so cheap,' she said. 'I couldn't resist it. The water's laid on, and the gas. No electricity though.' I hadn't realized there were still houses in Eastcliff without it.

Susan lit a gas mantle. 'Antique, you see – suits me as an antiquarian.' She made a pot of tea.

'I'm not sleeping here yet but soon will be. Do you like it?'

'Yes I do,' I replied. She looked different somehow. I suppose we all looked a bit older, the bloom of our early twenties having vanished. I had always looked young for my age, younger than Susan, I used to think, and I believe I still did; any ravages of a misspent life, or daily toil, not marked as yet upon my face. But, Susan, who had always been slender, had filled out a little, and though she was still slim, her face was rounder, her arms less skinny. She had a good complexion and the round brown eyes still looked out meditatively at people, but their expression was, I imagined, shrewder. Her hair had been cut into a shoulder-length bob and had a sheen to it. She still favoured browns or navy-blues but the cut of her costume was more professional. I supposed she now had a bit more cash to spend on herself.

I saw her typewriter on the deal table. She must want to be alone to work. 'Tell me about your parents. When are they going? Is it decided?'

'Dad's sixty-four and Mother wants to be near Jim and her grandchild. Jim's doing awfully well in Melbourne. I told them I could always visit. It would be a better climate for her chest too.'

Jim Marriott who had started off in electrical engineering

had then gone into electronics and was said by Susan to be developing something to do with computers. They were a bright pair, the brother and sister.

'Will you mind?'

I thought how she had stayed at home to be near her parents and of use.

'No,' she said. 'Not really.'

Then we talked a bit more about Lally. When women get together they talk about other people half the time.

'Her father's always telling her to get married,' said my friend. 'I suppose he thinks that way she'll be someone else's responsibility.'

'I can't help feeling she was meant to be a happy person,' I said.

'An analyst told her, Gabriel says, that she was punishing herself for some idea she had in childhood that her mother's death was her fault.'

I thought, what an awful responsibility it will be to have children, but *I'm* not going to run away or take to drink or whatever it was Ginny Cecil did.

Soon after that I had to catch a bus back to Leeds and Arthur. I felt guilty not calling on my parents, but they were usually tired after school and I'd see them again soon enough.

I thought, as I waited for the bus in one of those cold gusts of wind that whip round corners in Eastcliff, that The Laurels would soon be sold and Susan would move to her little house on Cobden Terrace and Gabriel would go on being saintly and Canon Benson would take more funerals and Lally would stay on in York like a beautiful ghost of herself even if she did look plumper and even if she did keep sane. And Mr and Mrs Varley would return from America and Tom would return to Miriam and his children. And I would never see Nick again. Not that he ever looked at me the way I thought Tom Cooper had looked at Lally Cecil in church that afternoon at Mrs Fortescue's funeral.

It was to be my last year of full-time work outside the home for many years for by the late summer after Mrs Fortescue's funeral I was pregnant, and pleased to be so. It was a happy time and once I left my job I was less busy than the year before – and certainly less busy than the following year.

We heard that The Laurels was up for sale and that nobody seemed to want to buy it. Large houses were not popular. Then my parents heard a rumour that Tom Cooper was thinking of buying it as a sort of a northern retreat for his family, but if that were true it came to nothing. Tom's second musical was put on. It was called *Hullabaloo* and there was another rumour that the Beatles were going to star in it. Some of the songs became famous: they were catchy, perhaps Beatles-inspired. I took little interest in popular music; only a few songs of those years can I remember with any pleasure. I liked *Eleanor Rigby* and *Yellow Submarine* – but I think they came along a little later. The sixties are confused in my memory. There was *Lily the Pink* and A *Whiter Shade of Pale*, but by that time I was at home with first one, then two, little boys. Not any longer a flat either, but a solid Victorian house we were buying on a mortgage, not far from Arthur's office at the university.

It was around Christmas at the time I left work that Susan published another novel, this time a sort of Gothic romance set in a vague nineteenth century, a departure for her from her well-researched historicals but, I thought, an opportunity for her to write of love. When I read of her heroine clasped in the arms of a 'dark, warm man' I wondered if she were thinking of Gabriel Benson who was still apparently going through some quasi-religious crisis. The heroine, Flora Randal, says at one point: *We were in Eden where lust is not known . . . it was the achievement without the struggle, like a dream when you are visited by a steady, deep joy that can end only when the dream does.* Later in the story when the heroine gets her man they are like *two drops of water mingling and flowing each into the other to become one larger drop.* I thought, this is not Susan's usual way of writing! It was certainly nothing like her *Gazette* pieces which were matter-of-fact, even if occasionally whimsical, or humorous in the manner Susan said her readers liked. I taxed her with it one day when she came for tea. It was a free Saturday for me since Arthur was at some conference over the weekend.

'Your description of love sounds like being eternally enveloped in Schubert's C Major Quintet,' I said.

Susan blushed. She did not like talking about her work.

Nobody yet knew that Susan J Marriott was Jane Sharp, except for a few friends and her family, but I didn't think she would be able to keep the secret for ever. I did not ask her if the dark, warm man was based on Gabriel, the sort of question writers hate to be asked. She was nicely settled now in her own little house and I imagined that Gabriel often stayed there overnight. Her parents had just gone to Australia, both swearing they would return if they didn't like it. I think they'd given up the idea of their Susan getting married. Susan didn't seem to worry about critics or becoming famous, like Tom.

'My *next* book will be quite different, Gillian,' she said. 'I just wanted to see if I could write a romance. I don't feel I've really succeeded.'

'Well, I enjoyed it,' I said.

There was a long silence, then, 'One day last winter I was walking near Sholey,' she began, looking not at me but at a pot plant on the table. 'It was snowing – a dark winter afternoon. You know what it's like up there, the snow falling with a tiny timeless sound. I heard music over the fields coming from the church. I knew it was Gabriel's half day off – not that he usually takes it – anyway, I walked across the fields and then went into the church porch. I often tramp around the village, it gives me ideas for books, just walking – like we used to do. I remember my woolly gloves were wet and my feet cold and the wind on the ridge was making tears come into my eyes. The music stopped as I stood there. I thought he hadn't seen me but he came down the aisle and opened the porch door and – I just felt so happy. Out of time – you know the feeling. I hadn't expected him to be there, had seen him only the Sunday before – but he came home with me that day.'

'Oh,' I said. 'I see.'

'We've known each other so long,' she said. 'Gabriel and I. I shall wait for him. He has the sort of problems that have never worried me.' I thought they must be partly the reason for his not staying in orthodox medicine. I must say I thought he presumed too much on Susan's patience.

'Does he like his new work?' I knew no more than that it was as a kind of liaison between social workers and probation officers and doctors.

'They've refurbished the mental hospital,' she said. 'But

176

they can't refurbish the inhabitants. He's not sorry he left general practice.'

'What exactly *are* his problems?' I asked bluntly, filling a kettle for another cup of tea. I knew I could never have been as patient as Susan, waiting for a man to make up his mind. At least they were now lovers.

'He could spend his life trying to cure physical illnesses – there are quite enough of those, and he'd be a good doctor – *was* one, but he's more concerned with what used to be called the soul, what his father still calls the soul. He thinks that the soul – or the mind if you prefer – might be the seat of physical illness too. He doesn't want to be an orthodox psychiatrist, though he did think of it at one time. He's got to deal with mental illness most of his time though. Lots of social problems are really mental ones, he says. And vice-versa.'

'It sounds as though *everything* is connected.'

'Yes, that's what he believes, but which comes first? He wants a resurrection, a renaissance, something to rise out of what he calls his nihilism. He's frightened of that, says that the seven deadly sins are not only alive and well but cloak the manias of the present day. But if he can't believe in God he can't see the way out of nihilism – and a feeling that evil is in charge sometimes.'

'I suppose it may be when you think of all the violence and misery in the world,' I said.

'And in psychotic people. What the Bible called casting out devils was trying to heal madness.'

'Yes, but Gabriel must believe in the good or there'd be no point fighting evil. What *causes* the soul to be sick? Can you believe in good without believing in God? He must do, or he wouldn't bother trying to help other people, even if he can't believe in God.'

'I think when he lost his father's religion he lost a whole way of looking at the world but kept his belief in – or fear of – evil – in the Devil, if you like.'

I was thinking of Lally and her depressions which though only directed against herself had some power to distress and upset.

'He's interested in the subjective experiences of people labelled mentally ill,' explained Susan, sipping her tea slowly.

'But he says there's an awful lot to be done to improve ordinary lives so that illness can't take a hold, whether mental or physical.'

'What about people who don't have harsh backgrounds and have enough money, yet still get depressed or angry or even violent? I suppose his father would call that sin? Does it make much difference what you *call* it – wickedness, illness? The mad and bad *are* sometimes the same people.'

'Certainly the sad and mad often are,' said Susan. 'But he wouldn't call depressed people mad I don't think.'

'What explanation does Canon Benson's Christianity have for all the casualties of the world – never mind the natural disasters? I suppose I just turned away from trying to understand it all when I left the chapel.'

'Gabriel always has to force himself to try and help people,' said Susan. 'Part of him would like to turn his back on the world.'

'Don't you remember, ages ago, we used to call him Saint Gabriel? At least Nick did,' I offered.

'He says it's probably his parents' Christianity rebounding on him and it's better than doing bad! Then he says, who is *he* to think he can do any good? I think it's the pain of evil he can't bear. He'd really prefer to have been a botanist or an astronomer. He studied medicine just to give himself time to think. Now lack of time stops him agonizing and he just gets on with the job. But he still thinks it isn't enough for him just to heal people's bodies.'

I was thinking that Susan must be a wonderful consolation to him for she seemed to understand him very well. Gabriel had not changed, just become more so. 'He's such a *good* man,' I said at last.

'I wish life were simpler for him,' said my friend. 'I wish his life were more like his father's life ,' she said. 'He has such gifts – he's also taken a cut in salary. Now and again I wonder if I'm a hindrance to him, if he ought not to be in some monastery going out into the world but returning to his cell every evening.'

'I'm sure you keep him sane,' I replied.

I thought later, Gabriel must have put off marriage because he was not sure of his own beliefs. Susan didn't get indignant as I would have done, or give herself over to despair as Lally did. She had never been the sort of person who tried to make a grand synthesis of everything; just got on with her life and her writing. I thought it interesting that she'd finally written a love story and was sure that the hero was Gabriel Benson however much she might deny it. She though more about other people than she did about herself. It was rare for Susan to honour me with such a confidence as the description of her walk in Sholey that snowy afternoon, but she'd known I would understand.

If Gabriel was a sort of saint, I thought, Susan was not far off. She had her *Gazette* column which I supposed strongly attached her to 'real life', and a sense of humour, more of one than she had had as a child when she used to look rather owlish and solemn. Perhaps what Gabriel lacked was a sense of proportion. He was always self-deprecating, but tending to see life through transcendental spectacles. *She* would keep him going, be a refuge for him if things went ill. I had begun to feel a little more certain now about my own point of view . . . I hoped I had grown up at last for I was to become a parent soon enough. In spite of being a pessimist, I always had at the bottom of my heart an expectation of a happy ending to things – naturally within the framework of a final ending for us all. Perhaps I had the idea that happy endings should be provided in marriages, as they were in Susan's last novel, but I knew that life wasn't what the chapel long ago had promised. Wasn't it the Prayer Book that said the wicked flourished like the green bay tree? No, that was the ungodly. The chapel had always posited that we were *all* weak and evil – tainted with Original Sin, and only faith could change us. Perhaps it had been right after all? But Gabriel, even without his faith, was a good man. His father had used to say: 'One just has to plough one's furrow' – 'Well, must go and plough my furrow,' and off he would go, absolutely happy, and absolutely convinced in an eighteenth-century sort of parsonical way that we were all fallen creatures but could alleviate things here and there from time to time. I wondered what he thought of his son's difficulties, was sure that Gabriel was the subject of many prayers. His parents must know what a good man their son was. Why did they think their God tortured Gabriel with lack of faith?

Well, I prepared myself for the birth of my children, Arthur said, as if I had ten vivas for a PhD on the same day. I was aware that nature would be more powerful than I was, but I determined to give nature every opportunity to behave herself. I even found myself now able to put up with Mr Gibson more patiently and it must have been around this time that I stopped thinking about him as Mr Gibson. It surprised me how pleased he was at the idea of becoming a grandfather. I went out of my way to enjoy natural things like moonlight and rainbows and even thunderstorms. When we went to the North Sea coast for a short break I stood watching the tide come in in a way I had not done since childhood. I never had the feeling that *I* had ever controlled anything. Under the world or society was the same old earth. A baby was both natural and made, I thought, would belong both to the earth and the world.

At this time across the Atlantic women began to talk about feminism again, but I still didn't see it as a political thing, though I had never reneged on my feminism. In gloomier moments I would ask myself what it was that bound men and women both but a shared cell in the prison before the executioner rapped on the door, but on the whole pregnancy cheered me up. I felt healthier – and I believed looked better too. The solemn thoughts were a sort of protection against bad things happening, for I was still an anxious person in spite of my comparative youth and good health.

London, everyone said, was changing fast, though I think less than it did a few years after that. All through that time, when Carnaby Street and pop and the pill were in the news, I was living a more conventional life than I'd ever lived before and wasn't even in touch with young people once I left my job. But I didn't feel isolated. I was happy. Prepared for any eventuality, but determined to fulfil my side of the bargain. I could once have loved Gabriel Benson, I thought to myself occasionally – but I don't think I could love him now. I wasn't good enough for Gabriel. I'd got married partly for reasons of security and commitment but my defection didn't worry me as much as it might have done once. Arthur, though often too busy to talk to me or go out with me or to entertain very much, was the soul of integrity, and I thought I'd been lucky.

Sometimes too I thought about Lally. Arthur said that maybe she'd tried on a lot of men for size, but if she had, I said, nobody had fitted, for she was still unmarried, still in York, with her job and her flat in the nursing-home grounds.

Miriam was writing articles about childhood in sociological weeklies and also standing for Camden Council in the Labour cause. The Coopers must be quite well off. Arthur had a friend in London who knew her. I said I just didn't know how she managed to do all she did with three children – the political meetings, the journalism, the occasional lecturing. I supposed that money helped. No more plays for Miriam though – and, I suspected, no time for much play either. She hadn't denied herself ordinary love – as I suspected Gabriel had from a desire to love the whole suffering mass of humanity. But in a different context Miriam was like him in her idealism. I'm afraid my state of impending motherhood stopped me from wanting to die for any good brave causes, or even sacrifice my time for them. I thought my idealism would probably come back when I was over having children. I had given up the idea of writing a book too, apart from my diary. Living one's life was enough.

I settled once more into my North Country where the people are short and stubby and stout with beetling eyebrows and loud voices, and felt more at home there than with the shriller Cockneys. The children were rougher too, but could also be kinder, less sharp. My children will have northern voices, I remember thinking.

Well, I had my first baby in 1964. It was a boy and we called him Dominic. Everything went very well. I suppose I was lucky, though Arthur said I deserved it after all my efforts. Dominic was a quiet baby and once I got things organized I found I even had time to read. I wanted to tell everyone what a wonderful experience childbirth was, but had the sense to keep my mouth shut. Only to Arthur did I exult. I think even my parents were rather surprised that I had come through so happily and they were both absolutely delighted. Naturally there were ups and downs and crises and occasional sleepless nights. I was surprised that I didn't want to go out much, didn't miss whatever social life I'd enjoyed before. We had a roof over our heads, and warmth, and enough food, and I had my routine. Eventually I began to think about fitting some mental work into my day and when Arthur offered to ask if his colleague at the university, Professor Wolman, had any translation work I might undertake, I told him that I'd like to do that. That was how I began translating short historical monographs from the French. Hard work and slow work, but a pleasant change from housekeeping. I did most of the domestic work, since Arthur was out earning our living. I suppose my feminism went into abeyance for a time.

Dominic was about a year old when Susan rang me up one evening. I had seen her a few weeks before when she had come over to see the baby and I was about to ask her to come over again if she had the time, but something in her voice stopped me.

'Gillian – I had to telephone you, I'm sorry. I'm afraid Lally had another breakdown.' *Had,* not *has had.* I waited. I had just been about to give Dominic his mashed banana. 'You'll have to know – I'm afraid she's killed herself.'

I could not speak. When people say their heart is in their mouth that is what I was like.

'Sit down. Are you all right? I thought I ought to tell you,' she went on.

'Oh, Susan!' I clutched the telephone. 'Tell me, Susan.'

Susan's voice was quiet and controlled, but thick, as though she'd been crying.

'Doctor Walker – it's a woman – rang Gabriel up this afternoon. I didn't tell you, didn't want to upset you, so I'm sorry it'll be more of a shock for you than it was for us, but she'd had another breakdown after I came over to see you. She left a note asking for Gabriel to be sent for. Doctor Walker –she's the therapist but she's a medical doctor too – was expecting her to come over to talk because she'd been a bit better, she said, after another short time in the hospital. As you know, she lived in the nursing-home grounds – Doctor Walker was a private therapist attached to it, Lally's father had asked her to help when Lally first went to York – well, Gabriel went there this afternoon straight away – he was at home having a free day – and when he got there the news was

182

broken. Doctor Walker had not said anything over the phone, just asked him to come. He had to ring up her father and tell him. Poor Gabriel, he's blaming himself for not seeing the danger signs – he saw her a fortnight ago.'

'How did she do it?' I asked – as if it mattered.

'Overdose again. They usually locked up the cupboard with the drugs, but some barbiturates had been left there and Lally had found the key – the room was next to where she was staying for the time being. She'd had a few days in hospital and then they'd taken her back to the nursing home – which *was* her home. They didn't think it was any worse a breakdown than before. In fact Doctor Walker thought she was a lot better in general, before she suddenly became depressed again and then just as suddenly became calm. She was distraught, poor woman, saying she was to blame, she should have suspected – even showed Gabriel her notes. Lally left a note to Doctor Walker and her father and everyone and Doctor Walker says there's something else they're going to send on when the Coroner's inquest is over – a diary or something.'

'But why should she do it now?' I asked. I felt breathless. Having had a baby had made me react more physically to other people's griefs. I felt more involved.

'They don't know. She'd got over Mrs Fortescue's death, it's two years ago anyway, and Gabriel says she'd worked out all her problems over her mother.'

'Was there a man involved? I mean –'

'Not as far as we know. She'd no boy-friends in York. It doesn't seem to have to do with anyone new. Just the same as before.'

'Oh, poor Lally.'

'Don't get upset, Gillian. I'm sorry I had to tell you. Go back to Dominic. There's nothing more anyone can do. I'll tell you if I hear anything further. The funeral will be in York, but not till they've had the inquest –'

'I ought to go.'

'No – really not – the baby's more important – it will only be upsetting and there's absolutely nothing we can do now.'

'I thought she'd got over her grandmother's death,' I said.

'Yes, Gabriel thinks it must be some cyclical thing – any little upset and she would go back to the first depression, but

183

worse each time instead of better. Lally's father spoke to Gabriel this evening and it appears that her mother killed herself too.'

'Did Lally know that?'

'They think not, but she may have guessed. It wasn't drink that killed Ginny, though someone smuggled bottles into where she was being dried out and probably gave her the courage to do it. But Lally – they're all blaming themselves now at the home. In the note to Doctor Walker that Lally wrote she said it was nobody's fault – and she *apologized*.'

'Dominic's crying, Susan, I'll have to go. Will you promise to tell me if anything else turns up?' Though what difference would it make – none.

It had upset me so much that I was trembling violently. I told Arthur straight away when he came home. I hadn't seen Lally since Mrs Fortescue's funeral. 'I ought to go to Lally's, shouldn't I?' I said to Arthur.

'I won't stop you, love,' he said. 'But I wouldn't. Can't do any good.'

Just to say Goodbye, I thought. But I decided against it. Afterwards I felt I ought to have gone; I should have gone and was punished, I imagined, for not going by a feeling that it was all a lie, that she was not dead, that she would haunt us who had been able to do nothing for her, as Lally seemed to have been haunted by that mother of hers whose completely unnecessary death had shadowed her daughter's life. I was angry.

'But there must be some other explanation, something to have tipped the balance again – just as I felt before at the Walmsley,' I said to my husband. It had not been her grandmother's death, I was sure. That had been too long before. Maybe Gabriel would be able to shed light on it all, though I felt that we must not pry, that it was none of our business. Would they record 'Suicide whilst the balance of her mind was disturbed'? Attempted suicide, unlike the other matters about which I had felt so strongly, was now no longer a crime. There had used to be something about not being buried in consecrated ground, hadn't there? But Susan told me that Lally was to be cremated so that would not apply. Where had her mother been buried? It was all so awful and cast a pall over

184

us, and more information about her end was to arrive in a week or two. Susan and Gabriel had been handed over the note to them once the Coroner had read it. As the 'mental case' Lally was known to have been off and on for nearly eight years, he had pronounced the words we had expected. Dr Walker herself saw Susan and Gabriel, and Susan wrote to me about it. There had been notes to her father and to Gabriel and to Dr Walker – all planned and written as though she were just about to go on a short holiday and wanted to cancel the milk, Susan said. But also there was that diary which had been sealed with Susan's name and address on the front and in the note a line saying: *Please will Susan take my diary and do what she wants with it.* Susan was a bit horrified, she said. There was the feeling she had that one should not read people's private diaries, added to which was a strong surprise that Lally, who was not known for committing her thoughts to paper, should have kept a diary at all. The Coroner had had to unseal it for evidence before handing it over. I telephoned her and asked her if she had read it. It might hold the key to the mystery.

'Not yet – I only opened it and looked at the last entry,' she replied. 'To see if she had written it just before deciding. There was a clean page with just a few lines, and the date was the date she killed herself.'

'What did it say? Don't tell me if it's confidential.'

'It was rather strange,' she said. 'And it made me feel terrible. Lally was never an unkind person, was she?'

'No, never.'

'That's what makes me feel she might have been rather, well, not herself.'

I waited. What could she have written? Susan hesitated over the telephone. 'Just – *Susan may do with this diary what she wishes. She might even make a story one day out of it.*'

'Well, why should that upset you?' But I knew why.

'It made me feel that she thought all her misery might be seen by us – by me – by all of us perhaps – as just a story.'

'I think she felt that we'd never understand, you know, and wanted us to. Or just you perhaps, since she left you it.'

'Well, I'm not going to read it. Not yet anyway. Maybe I will one day. I asked Doctor Walker if the coroner had found it had anything relevant to her last weeks. She said she didn't

185

think he'd bothered to read it at all. There was enough evidence in her own notes – it wouldn't have added anything. He went by her history. I expect he's a busy man.'

Susan later told me about her further talk with Dr Walker. 'She was a nice woman, showed us all her notes now that Lally's gone. She'd been sure that Lally would cope after Mrs F's death, had actually advised her to write down her feelings and Lally seemed to have got over it quite quickly. She was as surprised as anyone when Lally had another breakdown. But she puts it all down to her childhood. "Sometimes therapy just isn't enough", she said. She's feeling guilty because Lally managed to find the pills. There's to be an internal enquiry about that.'

'Did none of her previous doctors say anything?'

'They lost some of the notes in transit from the Walmsley. Would you believe it! – but Gabriel says it often happens. Doctor Walker had quite a bulging file of her own notes.'

'What does Gabriel say about Lally?'

'It's upset him terribly. He thinks I should burn the diary. Apparently she was on some new pills – he's not against them, they seem to work wonders with some people – but either she didn't swallow them or else they just didn't work for her. He says if someone wants to kill herself there's no foolproof way of stopping them in the end except a straitjacket.'

'But there was so much she had to live for!' When it came to the point my theoretical argument about the right to die sounded feebly in my head. How could anyone as beautiful and nice as Lally Cecil not find life worth living?

'Whatever was wrong with her life or with her,' I said before putting the phone down, 'I can't imagine that it was big enough to lead to her not wanting to go on living.'

'That's because you've always felt you had so much to live for,' Arthur said to me later. 'Your friend didn't. Nobody can feel someone else's feelings or ever understand them completely.' He was quite matter-of-fact about it but he knew I was upset and I cried in bed against his shoulder. Living was the thing Lally had just felt unable to do. I had never seen her dead so that the feeling of her being somewhere in the world went on. But I didn't want her to haunt *me*. She would not have wanted that. The village had been very shocked, Susan reported, and Denis Cecil was inconsolable. Clare was reported to have said: 'Because we have no other children.'

Gradually, since I had not been caught up in the tragedy at first hand, the whole terrible event seemed to become like a dream. Except in my dreams themselves when I would sit across a table, or sometimes a bed, with Lally, who looked just as she had when she was seventeen and she would be trying to tell me something and I was not able to hear her. Her lips moved but no sound came out. It was a peculiarly awful nightmare and when it happened I would creep to Dominic's cot and look at him sleeping there all peaceful and beautiful.

My own life, now bound up with Arthur and Dominic, absorbed me utterly as time went on. I seemed to be living, not in a different world, but in another plane of existence as Dominic grew from a baby into a solemn little boy. When I went into hospital to have my second child all I could think about was whether it would upset Dominic and whether Arthur, who had taken a week's leave, would cope with him and the housework.

For several years my children went on taking up most of my time and pushing away thoughts about the meaning of life. Life was the living of it.

Arthur enjoyed his work though the administrative side of it occasionally got him down and he was promoted to senior lecturer in 1969. We were nicely rooted now in the North. Perhaps one day we might go for a year to the States if there was the chance for Arthur to have an exchange, but he was not dissatisfied to stay for the present in poorer old England where his own students were not 'revolting' in any worrying way.

As time went on I dated things by the children's birthdays. Even if each day sometimes seemed to last an age, what with toddler tantrums or childish ailments, on the whole the years fled by. Let Miriam and Gabriel and their friends deal with social problems, I thought. Sometimes I thought I was getting more and more like my father.

Dominic had just started at school, a nice little primary school near us and therefore full of the offspring of those university staff who believed in State education. Richard attended a nursery group five mornings a week between 9.30 and 12 so I had a little more time for my own work once I'd dashed through the housework. One or two afternoons a week I paid a kind woman to come and play with Richard and went to work in the public library.

Dominic was always asking me questions, some of which I found extremely hard to answer. 'How much does the world weigh?' he asked one day. I had no idea, but answered, 'Oh, millions and billions of tons, I suppose.' 'Does it weigh more when new people are born?' he went on. I was about to try to find some tactful way of telling him that people died too, perhaps it would be a good scientific way of broaching the subject, when he added: 'And what if they make new cars, millions and millions of them – they weigh a lot. Cars weigh more than people.' Wasn't all this something to do with the Second Law of Thermo Dynamics – or was it the Conservation of Mass? I wasn't sure. I knew that 'nothing can be created out of nothing', though perhaps that didn't apply to the first act of creation – and even then I remembered about it all only from a Latin tag, not from any scientific knowledge. I was a prime example of an illiterate arts graduate. I'd already had to brush up on dinosaurs and diesels. How could there be an inconstant amount on a finite earth? I looked it up and tried to explain what I read to a five-year-old, but as I did not quite understand the encyclopaedia myself it wasn't very convincing. Dominic had Arthur's sort of mind whereas I thought – hoped – that Richard would be a bit like me. I ought to have paid more attention in science lessons!

My father had retired the year before and I knew he was looking forward to explaining things to his grandson. I realized he had missed out on something, not having sons himself. I had always wanted a daughter, but however much I had enjoyed maternity and all it entailed, I wasn't sure whether I really wanted to start all over again once the boys were at school. I told myself my indecision was an answer. When I visited Eastcliff I used to see Josephine neé Cooper with her latest baby. She now had six and still worked in her husband's business. Some people were remarkable.

At home my father would grumble about a world that was changing before his eyes. He had not liked the Swinging

Sixties and took a dim view of the future. I now found myself half agreeing with him, a revolution in itself.

It was now common knowledge in the village that Nick Varley had divorced after only five years of marriage. Apparently there had been a child of the marriage, and shortly after his divorce he remarried. I wasn't surprised about the divorce but surprised that he had married once more. But serial monogamy seemed to have caught on in England now as well as in the States and I supposed Nick had enough money for two families. Mr and Mrs Varley did not go to America for the second wedding. They retired not long afterwards and went to live in Morecambe. I'd have thought they'd have gone somewhere more exciting, but times were hard in business and maybe their profits and capital were not enough for Hampshire or Wiltshire.

Sadder news was that Susan's mother died suddenly in Melbourne, never having achieved the little sub-Post Office of her dreams, which I'm sure she'd rather have had than a bungalow in Australia. Susan went out there for three weeks to see if her father could really manage alone. She returned sure that he could, and impressed by her brother's successes. Computers were beginning to be a big thing and Jim had set up his own business which was expanding. But even before this visit half-way across the world Susan had come out of her shell a little more and been to Europe. She liked Scandinavia, Norway especially. Unlike me she wasn't keen on the south of Europe. Arthur and I rented a house in Brittany one summer, but my mother and father politely refused to come out and have a holiday with us. They preferred the Isle of Man. There was then the excitement for them of Rosemary's wedding. She was thirty-two and everyone had assumed she would not marry after the failure of many steadies to remain so. But she met a nice PE teacher and had a big wedding, as unlike mine as it would have been possible to be. Once she was married I found it easier to talk to her. She lived in the same place she had lived in since her first job, a little Lancashire cotton town, so with the building of the new motorway we should be able to pop over now and then to see them if we felt like it.

By 1970 Gabriel and Susan were still not married, though people knew they were a couple I found it hard to understand. Susan no longer worked on the *Calderbrigg Gazette*, but continued to write for the city paper. I gathered that she had made quite a lot of money from her last book and was set to make even more from the next. She was always shy about discussing finances. I sensed that perhaps things were at last about to move in a more orthodox way when Susan telephoned me one day. She didn't mention marriage in those words but began on houses.

'I've made a big decision,' she said. 'I'm going to take out a larger mortgage.'

I waited. She hadn't said 'we'.

'I did quite well on the last book,' she said.

'Oh, good – I thought you had.'

'If I sell the house on Cobden Street,' she went on, 'and put my savings out, guess what I might buy?'

'You're not thinking of buying The Laurels?' I said.

'Certainly not. Somewhere much more beautiful that needs years of work – but it's possible, it's really possible.'

She sounded excited, much more excited than she usually was.

'Tell me,' I said. 'The suspense is too much.' I hoped she wasn't going to tell me she was moving away – or even going to Australia. No, I couldn't imagine that. What would Gabriel do? For a moment I thought could it be The Holm – but no, it was a nursing home now.

'It's Wynteredge!' she said.

'Wynteredge House – but I thought they were going to leave it to moulder away.' The farmer who'd owned the house had died and had not lived in it for some time. I did know that.

'I've had a surveyor and it's still basically sound. Needs a lot of work but as I've saved quite a bit they would let me have a mortgage on it if I repaired it and didn't alter it too much – something to do with historical monuments.' She laughed. I knew the local council was keen to preserve old buildings, but was it liveable in I wanted to know.

'Not all of it at present. Ramsden let the top floor go to pot a bit – but enough to start with. Two rooms downstairs are fine, just need cleaning and painting and repairing. I know an architect who would help with fixing the rest. It might take five years to get it all done but I'm going to do it.'

'Oh, Susan,' I said. 'I'm thrilled. You've always loved it. When did you decide?'

'I've always wanted it,' she said. 'Since I was eighteen. I simply decided I'd buy it if ever I had any money.' She was amazing.

'What does Gabriel think?'

'He's just as keen as I am. You know how badly *he* is paid – he couldn't envisage doing it himself, but he's always loved it too and together we *can* do it.'

I waited. I had to ask. 'Are you and he going to get married then?'

'It's a secret, but yes, we are. Once I get the deeds and sort out the finances. We shan't sell Cobden Terrace or get married until we can move into Wynteredge. He's a lot happier, Gill, you know. We've had a tough time but now he says he knows for sure. I think we'll get wed in spring.'

'I'm so glad for you, Susan,' I said. Susan was the same age as myself, nearly thirty-five, not too old to start a family as people say. They could afford a child, and Susan could always write at home. I wondered how much money she was making now. How independent and strong a person she was, my old friend.

I thought about her quite a lot in the days that followed. It was an unusually long winter that year and we had our share of colds and flu and then both the boys came down with whooping cough.

In the intervals between sick-nursing, which never brought out the best in me, I watched the snow pile up outside. How cold it would be at Wynteredge. I remembered the white fields with the drystone walls black as coal snaking across them, and the wind that was never silent up there. Well, Susan was to have her Wuthering Heights. Rather her than me. I was getting soft.

I listened to Pavarotti singing arias from Donizetti, and to Schubert late piano sonatas as the children lay upstairs and Arthur sat marking termly papers. I thought about Susan at Wynteredge.

Whenever I thought about Susan I found myself thinking about Lally. Susan had never said any more about the diary. I assumed she'd packed it away, or read it and found nothing of interest to communicate. We didn't often mention Lally now; we didn't exactly avoid the subject but it seemed to be an especially painful one for Gabriel who had gone on blaming himself for not realizing the danger signs before it was too late.

Those afternoons in the snowlight from the windows were like the afternoons I'd spent as a child myself ill at home with some childish ailment. How quickly life repeated itself. But I had changed, I hoped for the better. My tastes in music and poetry and painting had changed a little too and I found more sustenance in the classical things I had taken for granted, or not explored enough when I was young. We had had a very short holiday in Italy the Easter before, when my mother had offered to look after the boys – I think she felt safer on home ground than in some Brittany villa – and I saw Michelangelo's *David* in Florence for the first time and fell in love with northern Italy. Mother and I had also begun to visit art galleries together on Saturday afternoons. Many of the British Impressionists and Victorian painters were in Yorkshire galleries and my mother had been full of girlish enthusiasm. Away from home she was rejuvenated. She was still teaching, but had allowed my father to learn the mysteries of the duster.

I had great hopes of my mother.

I remember the Monday the boys went back to school and nursery, the snow had begun to be cleared away and I thought I had just time to go down into the city to buy a new coat. There was even a smell in the air of spring, and grass was showing itself in patches again after the weeks of white icing. I had given up bothering too much about my clothes – one dressed for warmth or comfort in a cold climate and with two small children, but I felt I needed a little perk after the time spent indoors. I took the bus and went down to the Headrow. The sun had come out and for some reason or other I was thinking of Nick Varley. What a bore he'd find me now, I thought, preoccupied with children and new overcoats and looking at Victorian pictures.

I'd managed to find myself something rather nice in Schofields – a cherry-red maxi coat and was considering looking for a red beret. I might even find Susan's latest book in the bookshop in the next street. I'd meant to send it to a

French friend in Bourges with whom, after all these years, I still kept up the semblance of a correspondence. The boy who sold papers at the bottom of the road was shouting about the latest negotiations for Britain to join the Common Market and the ending of the postal strike. I decided on the bookshop rather than the hat shop – I probably had a beret at home that would go with my new coat. I was already wearing that, the old mac in a parcel under my arm. In the bookshop a large stand was devoted to a book written by one of the New Wave feminists. I was wondering how interested most people were in theories of patriarchy as I came out of the shop. Susan's new book was sold out, they had said. I passed the news-stand again. But this time the boy had stopped shouting about the postmen and was shouting about a murder. I bought a paper to read over my lunch. It wasn't the *Gazette* but a rival paper and already the first evening edition.

I was already on the bus when I opened it and saw Gabriel Benson's face looking out at me on the front page.

I read it all again when I got back home and was sitting, cold and sick, in my warm kitchen. But I had to collect Richard from his nursery school. His chatter, his slow putting on of his outdoor clothes, his insistence on returning for a picture he had painted for me distracted me. It was not till I had him seated at the kitchen table with some warmed-up soup, which needed a bit of help with spooning into his mouth that I dared read the front page again. I felt panicky for Susan. My little boy was tired and wanted a rest on his bed so after settling him I went downstairs again and picked up the phone to ring Arthur. I hadn't had any lunch but I forced down a cup of tea. Arthur was not in his office. I'd have to try again at two o'clock. Papers often got things wrong, didn't they, I said aloud and forced myself to look again.

Social worker – well Gabriel was not really that – *knifed in car-park attack. Man held for questioning.*

I was too late for the local radio news bulletin but I put on the television and found I'd just missed that too. I read the front page again.

The dead man is Gabriel Benson who works in the Calderbrigg area as liaison between medical and social worker staff. It is understood he was attacked on his arrival this morning at his office in the centre of town. His assailant who was caught immediately by other staff, alerted by Linda Marsden, (36) office-cleaner, was carrying a knife. It is understood that Mr Benson's injuries are consonant with a blow on the side of the head where he may have fallen against a car bumper. Police are contacting his parents. His father is Canon George Benson, Rector of Sholey near Calderbrigg.

I could not, just could not try to speak to Susan. She might be out of town doing some research, or at home on Cobden Terrace writing. She must know all by now if the police had got hold of the Bensons.

Instead I dialled my father. Mother would be at school. 'You've heard?' was all he said at first. 'I was just going to ring you.'

I could hardly speak. Then, 'Susan?' I whispered.

'They were saying in the shops that she'd gone to the police along with the Bensons,' said my father. Everyone in the village knew that Gabriel and she, in their own quaint language, had been courting for years. 'I'll ring you if there's anything more – it'll be on the local news,' he said. 'But I knew the lad who did it. He's only twenty. I used to teach him about ten years ago – the family moved away but Milfred still lived in Calderbrigg.' He sounded breathless, almost excited.

'Milfred – what a name,' I said stupidly.

'Yes – Milfred Lumb. A bad family. I remember them well.'

'Should I come to Susan?'

'She'll be still with the Bensons. They'll sedate her, I expect,' said my father. 'Write to her in a day or two, that would be best.'

But what on earth could I say? I felt that I too had been bereaved, all of us had. Lally gone, and now Gabriel. . . .

I sat there once the phone was down and then I felt so angry that I went in the kitchen and took the bread knife and stabbed it into a dishcloth imagining this Milfred Lumb was at my mercy. I felt about him as I'd feel about a crow attacking a blackbird. I'd shoot the crow.

Gabriel was dead, *Gabriel*, our angel of light, Gabriel whom we had all loved and admired . . . Gabriel who was going to marry my friend at last. Oh, Susan, what will you do? I burst out crying and cried for a long time till it was time to get Richard up and to go to fetch Dominic from school. I just had time before the last post went to write her a short letter saying I had heard and was too shocked to say more, but to ask if there was anything, anything at all I could do. She would be with the Bensons. They liked her, had always liked her. If it had been their choice I was sure that their son would have married Susan long ago.

Then I managed to get hold of Arthur by telephone in his room at the university and told him. He came home straight away and put the children to bed. We listened to the local news and there was a short item, but no more information than there had been in the paper.

Both Arthur and I went to the funeral, which was taken by a parson who had known Gabriel since boyhood. Canon Benson and his wife were in the front pew looking straight ahead – she had taken his hand in hers. There were several of Gabriel's colleagues and many of his old friends from medical student days. And his sister Christina, who cried. And Susan who did not cry but looked directly at the coffin as though she was puzzling over something she could not quite understand. How different this funeral was from the last I'd attended, it seemed centuries ago, before I had the children. . . .

Another colleague, a lay preacher, gave a short address after the prayers. Sholey church was packed. Everyone looked hushed and grieved. The preacher said Gabriel had been a very good man, a man devoted to the poor, the unhappy, the downtrodden, the sick in mind and body and to men who had served time in prison. I thought, Gabriel was a man of God as much as his father had been. But then the preacher said that Gabriel would not have wanted revenge, that the best thing we could do to remember him would be to go about our lives as he had done.

I had heard by then from my father more about Milfred Lumb, though it was a long time before all the story came out. Milfred was an exceedingly unpleasant character, Father said, a boy with a vicious temper who had been neglected at home. His photograph showed a physically repulsive youth. He had been a petty thief, a work-shy character who had set up house

195

with a woman he abused. That was how he had come to know Gabriel. The woman had often been admitted to hospital herself and the police had been going to charge Lumb with her assault, but she had discharged herself each time and gone back to him. Gabriel had visited her at home and been kind to her. Then Lumb got it into his head that Gabriel had told the girl to leave him, that he was carrying on with her himself. The night before the murder Lumb had been out drinking and had attacked the woman as she was leaving for work in the morning. She'd run out on him and he had taken a bus and gone straight to the office of the Social and Psychiatric Department and hidden till he'd seen Gabriel arriving by car. Gabriel had got out of the car and was standing by it with the car door still open. The cleaner had seen them from an upstairs window; she had just been finishing work. We learned later that the head of the whole outfit had advised Gabriel not to visit Lumb or his common-law wife. Lumb was known to have a nasty temper and harbour imaginary grudges, but Gabriel said he wanted to explain things to him and to offer him help with a job application. Lumb himself had never been a mental patient, though he had been known to the police and to most welfare agencies for a long period of time. The woman he lived with had been pregnant with Lumb's child a few weeks before when she had been taken into the ward again for her own safety. He'd threatened to 'kick her little bastard to death'. He'd got it into his head that the baby was Gabriel's since the woman had been under Gabriel's care. Other psychiatric social workers were to give evidence at Lumb's trial and the woman herself testified that Lumb continually spoke of revenge. He had always been like that, she said. 'Doctor Benson had been right kind' to her. She had been frightened of her boy-friend and that was why she'd left the hospital with a threatened miscarriage because he'd accused her of 'having it off with the doctor' there. He'd told her he'd get his own back that morning but, no, she hadn't known he had a knife with him though, he often threatened her with one.

A pathologist gave evidence that Gabriel's skull was abnormally thin and that his assailant had knocked him down against the edge of the open door of the car and that this blow had caused the death. The cleaner said, 'He didn't try to fight him back.' The knife wounds, though they had bled profusely, were superficial. By the time others came running to the scene the knock on the side of the head had killed him.

Milfred Lumb, slayer of the Angel of Light, got off with a prison sentence for assault to which he pleaded guilty. He was not mad they said, only a prey to irrational and obsessive jealousy. Virtue had been defeated once more by the forces of unreason, said my father. The staff had warned Gabriel too for they had all had an uneasy feeling that the man bore him a peculiar ill will and was immune to reason. I thought, Gabriel *knew* all that, had already been attacked verbally. It was only Gabriel's fateful intervention when he had tried to reason with him the day before that had led in the end to the attack. We never knew what happened to the woman in the case, Joan Sugden, though I suspected that Canon Benson knew. She was most likely already involved with another man, a punch-ball for some other male. I thought of all the children of such unions and of Milfred Lumb's future child. No wonder Gabriel had wondered about good and evil. The office cleaner told her story many times to the papers after the trial. 'He didn't even defend himself, didn't the doctor,' she said over and over again. After the trial and the verdict later in the year, the *Calderbrigg Gazette* had a whole page on its 'Local tragedy'. When I dared to think of those few fateful moments and of a life snuffed out in an instant's madness, I was filled with despair, though it still seemed unbelievable. As with Lally's death, I couldn't believe Gabriel was really dead even though this time I'd seen the coffin. Things like that happened to other people, not to people you knew. They buried him at Sholey where he had kissed Susan in the snow, not far from the house she had planned to buy with such hope and joy.

I didn't see Susan for some time after the funeral. I couldn't speak to her on the telephone; it was too trivial an instrument. Instead I wrote to her again and she replied. She told me that Gabriel had often spoken of Lumb to her, and said how repulsive he found him and *because of this* had determined to help him and Joan Sugden. He had often had problems with jealous men; it was not the first time that staff had been assaulted and would not be the last. I knew my revengeful feelings would not bring Gabriel back and I did not want to

197

upset Susan, so I did not tell her all I felt. Susan, though, was as much a victim of Lumb as Gabriel had been. Had Gabriel taken so long to accept Susan's love because he knew he might one day inadvertently cause her pain? *He* wasn't *a saint*, she wrote. *He* did *have angry feelings. There were people he didn't love and couldn't like, but because of that he tried harder.*

The story of Gabriel and Susan was not yet over for something else was about to transform Susan's life. Only the week before Gabriel died Susan had discovered she might be pregnant and Gabriel had known about it and been overjoyed. The negotiations for Wynteredge had been almost completed and they had spoken to his parents about marrying after Easter. Susan had agreed to marry in Sholey Church because it meant a lot to Canon Benson and his wife. For two months Susan waited to be sure, hardly able to convince herself that it was true. But on the very day they had planned for a quiet wedding she went over to the Bensons and told them that their son's child was on the way. There was still a lot of conventional prejudice in those days about illegitimacy but Gabriel's parents had always loved Susan and were overjoyed. Their grandchild might be fatherless but would have at least two adoring grandparents. She told them the child was to be born in November and she had decided to go ahead with her plans for the purchase of Wynteredge, for Gabriel would have wanted that. The grief all his family and friends felt at his death was softened a little by his leaving a sign of the only immortality most of us ever have.

But Gabriel's death is still something I cannot think about without horror. Those two deaths – of Lally and of Gabriel – have affected me more than anything else in my life, apart from the birth of my children, and made me more aware of life's extreme fragility: two events which might have seemed only peripheral to my own life seem central. I might have lost touch with Tom and Miriam – Tom had been out of the country when Gabriel died so had not been at his funeral – but those two, Lally and Gabriel, whom I would never see again, were two of the people of whom I'd been most fond in earlier years.

What my father called These Terrible Times were changing even more rapidly and now I had another death to date them by. Susan said that from the very day of Gabriel's death the probability of a coming child rescued her from complete despair.

I continued to feel how delicately balanced was any happiness we managed to scrape out of life. I never pressed Susan for more details and because I did not know exactly what had happened that terrible morning, apart from what I read in the papers, and the later reports of the inquest and the trial, I kept dreaming of Gabriel with blood gushing out of him as he lay in that car-park which I always saw under snow. I could not wear the red coat I had bought that morning but gave it to Oxfam and bought a black one later. In other dreams Mrs Fortescue's funeral became Lally's and Gabriel's, and ran together in my mind. But in my dream it was always Sholey Church, where Gabriel's had been.

Susan did not want people to think of her as a victim. She also thought that Gabriel's death, pointless as it was, might have had an element of inevitability in the end. He sought out pain and evil, she said. It was rare for her to dwell on the blighting of all her hopes. The stoicism that had always been part of her character reasserted itself. I think she always believed she was lucky to have had Gabriel for a time, that she might never have known love without him. And she told me also – which to me was a surprise – that in the last Christmas before his death he had decided to be reconverted to Christianity, had taken Communion again, even if she had not felt able to. 'I wished I could have taken it with him,' she said. 'I think it's the only thing the Canon might wish for me. But I shall have the child christened. It means such a lot to him, and to Hannah.'

'Lally was a victim,' she said another time when she had come out to stay with us one weekend at the end of the summer about a month or two before the child was due to be born. 'But Gabriel wasn't. He chose it, you see. Not melo-dramatically –but he was ready for it. That's why he didn't even try to fight back.'

After supper, when she and I were sitting in our garden and the boys were at last in bed, Arthur having tactfully left us together to talk, she seemed to want to broach something.

Finally she said, 'Do you think I could change my name by deed poll? Then the baby would be called Benson. It's quite legal. You can change your name to anything you want.'

'What do his parents think?'

'I think they'd like it. I can't decide.'

'It would be nice for later,' I said. 'When the child grows up – to know he or she had a father with the same name. The baby could have *both* your names.'

'Sometimes, Gillian, I still think that Gabriel, if he'd lived hundreds of years ago or even in the last century, would have been a monk, a celibate man. We *were* going to be married, but I wonder whether I was right to want him for ever.'

'I suppose some priests still don't marry – Catholic ones anyway – but even Canon Benson married! Wasn't he an Anglo-Catholic in his youth?'

'Yes, he had a great struggle, Gabriel once told me, to know where his duty lay. Gabriel used to say that there were some professions where not being involved in loving one special person perhaps gave more time to some men – and women – to love humanity.' I had often thought the same thing myself – the idea of celibacy was not a perverted one to me. 'Nowadays you are not supposed to understand anything unless you have experience of it,' she went on. 'But in that case what are we given our imaginations for? I can quite see that carers are sometimes people who are better at loving humanity – no, not humanity – that's too abstract, but loving other people, children, old people, imbeciles, ill people, if they are un-attached themselves.'

Perhaps Gabriel found that easier than loving just one person, I thought, but did not say so.

'I often think that I was selfish wanting him just for myself.'

You selfish! I wanted to say. You loved that man ever since you were seventeen, and waited for him. Wasn't Gabriel just a little selfish to make you wait? But of course I didn't say that either.

'I think I *will* change my name,' she said. 'Gabriel's baby will have both our names then. Sometimes, you know, years ago, I even used to think that I could go away and have his child and not marry, that I could have a child and bring it up and not demand married life from Gabriel. And now I have no choice.'

Well, shortly after this conversation, Susan purchased Wynteredge, though she didn't move into it till after little Sarah Gabrielle Benson was born. By that time the news had broken that S J Marriott of the Yorkshire *Gazette* was one and the same as the Jane Sharp whose next book – finished just before Gabriel's death – was a best-seller. That she was also the mother of the child of a murder victim and lived alone in a seventeenth-century house made a good story for a few weeks around the time of that novel's publication. But it blew over. Eastcliff folk were proud of her and resisted attempts by reporters or writers of features to pry, and her own colleagues on the *Gazette* headed off many other nosey parkers. As Susan said, success had its compensations, and if she was able to go on writing after the upheavals of the move to Wynteredge and the early months of baby care, she hoped that the financial rewards would be commensurate with her 'fame'. I think that novel in fact paid a hefty part of the mortgage, and with the sale of the little terraced house, and the income from the now fortnightly column she had returned to producing, she could afford to live independently. Jim and her father came over for the child's first Christmas, Jim, Susan told me, looking every inch a middle-aged, successful businessman with a nice Australian wife and two tall, sunburnt adolescent children.

Susan kept her own maiden name for her column, and Jane Sharp for her novels, but at Wynteredge became known, not because she asked, as Young Mrs Benson, as though she were a widow.

The house was one of those old mullioned-windowed seventeenth-century Halifax houses with three gables and the date over the door and Susan altered little of its structure. From the outside it looked just as it had during our child-hoods, though the tiles on the roof had been replaced and the stonework repointed. Inside it was comfortable with a big sitting-room fireplace where she burned logs. You went straight into a room from the porch where Susan had placed an old oak chest with pewter mugs standing on it, and there was a room on each side of this one, each with a door leading into the central room. The kitchen at the back she did eventually modernize, and bought an old Aga. One room on the ground floor she used as a study and it was lined with books from top to bottom on three sides, and with a big oak table in the middle where she worked. The other end room was a dining-room and from it there rose a staircase to the floor above . One of the bedrooms – there were only three – was Sarah's bedroom and playroom, and one was Susan's and the other was the guest room where she said I must come to stay when I needed a rest. All the furniture was either from Cobden Terrace or junk and secondhand shops. You could get lovely things locally then for a song, before they opened antique shops in Lightholme and the dealers descended in droves upon every house in the two villages when an old occupant died. But Susan lived simply in her new old house. Her domestic tasks were similar to mine. I wished that I could earn more myself, without wanting to be rich.

A new factory was opened on the outskirts of Eastcliff, a clean place where electrical instruments were made, and the villagers with skills became more affluent. I began to feel around this time that there was too much in the shops. Being a child of austerity I didn't want my children to become consumers – dreadful word – beyond what was necessary for a reasonably pleasant life. I often wondered whether Miriam and Tom were now more materialistic, with all the money he'd made from his musicals. I supposed they would have dishwashers and hi-fis and cars galore, and Tom would have a giant computer for his composing. I sympathized with the poor in the North for there were many people who were debarred from a share in the goodies in the shops. But I had little sympathy for the people who spent their brass on getting drunk; I was getting more like Mr Gibson year by year! As I did not contribute to the bulk of my own housekeeping money I felt I had better not criticize those who worked hard to acquire their things. I wondered if Nicholas Varley had become more American in his tastes. I was sure *he* would be a consumer.

We were soon to see Tom and Miriam in the flesh. They had bought a place in the Dales, some old barn they were converting. My mother heard from Mrs Cooper that they wanted to see us and Susan on their way further north. Susan then had a letter from them and the upshot was that Arthur and I and the children were invited over to Wynteredge one

202

Saturday in the spring of Sarah's first year. Miriam and Tom and their three children were to take tea and then stay with the Jacobs overnight and motor on to Upper Wharfedale on the Sunday.

Susan was having some help with washing and cleaning and cooking, and some baby-sitting, from a woman we had been at school with who had actually approached her for work. She was a widow – I was going to say like Susan, for this was how I felt about it too – and allowed her to get on with her writing.

On that Saturday little Sarah was about seven months old and already sitting up. Richard and Dominic were fascinated by her. When we arrived there were other children already in the garden. Two tall, dark boys in jeans and T-shirts and a girl in a mini skirt. It was eight years since I'd seen Tom, and longer since I'd seen Miriam, and not surprisingly they looked older. So did I, I suppose, but one never thinks of it that way round. I was curious to know what Arthur would think of Miriam now. Would her Socialist fundamentals be lost? I need not have speculated. Miriam was a hard worker on the Council and also, we learned, active in anti-apartheid and CND. But her main concern now seemed to be community politics. We sat in the garden with its high wall. Sarah observed us from her pram as we discussed high-rise buildings and student revolutions, the erosion of a working-class base in the Party, technological innovations, the war in Vietnam and other topics that one cannot avoid when a politician is present, unless he or she is heartily sick of them and prefers to discuss fashions and fripperies. It was clear that Miriam clung on to her old certainties: was now, she said a 'new feminist'. I knew all about that long before the new wave arrived in Britain. 'I ally myself with younger women,' said Miriam, portentously.

'Oh, I've always been a feminist,' I said.

Arthur was talking about unilateralism with Tom who didn't seem very interested in the subject, unlike his wife. Pressure groups and protest movements were still not Tom's style and I wondered if this annoyed his high-powered wife. Tom was not an intellectual. His children were nice, if informal in manner. Jake and Naomi and Joshua – twelve, ten and nine I guessed. They told me that they liked America where they had been taken the summer before and they mentioned certain pop groups whose names I've forgotten. They climbed the wall at the bottom of the garden and sat swinging their legs over into the field. I thought Miriam would be one of those mothers who treat their offspring with what they call healthy neglect.

'Did you know we saw Nicholas Varley in the States?' said Tom.

'No! How is he?' I asked. 'I saw he'd married again.'

'Yes, we saw *her* too,' said Miriam. 'Very lovely and smooth. The first wife left him, you know.'

'I can't imagine anyone *leaving* Nick,' I said levelly.

'Oh, but she did. She became a Republican when Lyndon Johnson was replaced by Nixon. That was one in the eye for Nick since he was working for the Democrats.'

'What exactly is he doing now?' asked Susan.

'Still hoping Camelot will come back – he's an adviser with the World Bank,' replied Miriam. 'He was always so arrogant,' she said. 'The sort of person who gives a bad name to progressive politics.'

I could see that Miriam's progressive politics were still pretty solid.

Nobody had yet mentioned Gabriel and I didn't think anyone would, but Tom said to Susan as we were going into the sitting-room, afterwards, 'The little girl looks just like him,' and squeezed her hand.

I thought about Nick all through Susan's tea and scones. He would be anti the war in Vietnam, I was sure. His politics had always been pragmatic. But he wouldn't have sympathized with the student revolutionaries Miriam was interrogating my husband about. She seemed disappointed that nothing much had happened in the northern universities in comparison with London.

It was Tom of course who mentioned Lally as he and I were watching the children in the garden from the back door. Dominic had found a picture book and Richard was almost asleep. I was thinking, one day perhaps all our children will get to know each other – but Nick's are missing. Tom said Nick had a daughter, Victoria, now living with the wife who had left him for the Republicans.

Susan was drying something at the sink. Sarah had been put down in her cot upstairs.

'I often think about Lally,' Tom said to me, a frown puckering his still handsome face. 'I'd like to write a song that would remind us of her. Dad was telling me just at lunchtime about her mother.'

'What did he say?'

'Oh, that Ginny was a real good-looker and danced the Charleston better than anyone else in town. She was a raver he said – a really lively girl. Everyone thought she wanted to be an actress, but he said – and I quote – "her life was one long act". Not like Lally, I don't think.'

'He knew her before she was married then?'

'Oh yes, she met Denis Cecil – who was managing some export business and was here doing some negotiating – in the Great Northern Bar and he married her within the month.'

'Talking about Lally?' said Miriam coming into the kitchen. Susan had now gone back into the sitting-room and was telling Arthur about dry rot.

'She threw her life away,' said Miriam grimly. 'If only she could have given it to Gabriel,' she added in a low tone, in case Susan could hear through the door.

'Her mother wasn't *her* fault,' said Tom. 'Lally was a lovely creature.'

Miriam frowned.

We were all silent thinking about Lally and Gabriel and then Miriam said, and jerked her head in the direction of the sitting-room 'Is she over it? She looks all right.'

How could I say to Miriam in the midst of the washing-up that you hardly get over the murder of the man you love? It was only just over a year ago after all. But Miriam went on, 'I think the baby looks like both of them, don't you?'

'Everyone always sees both parents in babies,' I said. 'Mine were said to look both like me and Arthur's father.'

'Ours are all like Miriam,' said Tom at the door.

'Yes, yours *are* like you,' I said, as Tom strolled off into the garden.

'Tell me more about Nick,' I went on to Miriam. 'Has he changed?'

'You mean in looks? No, not at all. I didn't think so. Not

205

even fatter, like us.' She was always frank. But she didn't seem to want to pursue the subject so I tried to get her on to her children's schooling. Here she was evasive.

'Nick and I were the only two who "married out",' I then ventured.

'Yes, that's true – I like your husband,' said Miriam. 'Of course Lally never married, did she? Amazing for such a sought-after girl.'

But now Naomi was crying and Miriam strode out to settle whatever argument had blown up. I could see that Tom was taking his daughter's side. I was thinking of that sought-after girl as I went into Susan and Arthur. I still saw her the way she had been when we were at school and sometimes the way she had been that time I visited the Walmsley after her first overdose, all blotchy and lethargic and thin. Susan had told me she'd got quite fat the year she died, and she had already looked different at Mrs Fortescue's funeral.

Just before the Coopers left, Canon and Mrs Benson turned up to say hello to us all. Susan sent Canon Benson up to his granddaughter. 'I don't want to wake her,' he said.

'You can bring her down,' said Susan. 'She usually has a drink and rusk at six o'clock.'

The tall, white-haired man came down shortly afterwards, the child in his arms. Sarah's eyes *were* like Gabriel's. Mrs Benson took her on her knee, and the Canon continued to gaze at her with adoration. They were such good, kind people; no wonder their son had been as he was. Susan had told me that they respected her independence, so long as they could involve themselves in Sarah's life. 'They think I might marry,' she had told me. 'But I don't think I ever shall.'

Miriam seemed to be reviewing some mental job list for she said suddenly after a silence, 'We must be off – there's the petrol to get for the car and the dinner treat that Mother's been preparing all day. Ruth's bringing some documents to sign too – I'm afraid we'll have to go. Thank you so much, Susan.' Tom rose, rather reluctantly, I thought. Their children were crowded into the enormous car which Miriam was driving. Arthur was shown the automatic transmission and made suitable sounds of approbation to Tom and off they went. It was quiet afterwards. The Bensons soon took

206

their leave. They were on their way to some meeting at the church.

Susan let me bathe Sarah, and the boys watched. Having no sisters they knew only theoretically about girls, except when on hot days they played naked with their small friends, both boys and girls. I wanted them to like babies, hoping that they would grow up to be the sort of men who bathed their children and cooked and shared chores. 'Isn't she neat?' said Dominic observing the small Sarah. She was a lovely baby, happy and solemn by turns and she certainly did look like her father. I had explained that Sarah's Daddy was dead, but I'm not sure if Richard understood. But on the way back home he said, 'Sarah's Daddy *did* come. You said he was dead. But he came with his mother.' Canon Benson had obviously made an impression, even if his wife had been reduced to maternal status.

I often compared Arthur with my father. Both had temperaments very unlike mine, alike in their scrupulous habits and rather old-fashioned sense of honour. Dominic had inherited these qualities, but Richard had my quick temper and impetuosity. The only man I'd ever been involved with who was like myself was Nick Varley, I thought. But as I was a woman, my monogamous nature had so far saved me from marital disaster. I had always been faithful to whoever I was in love with at the time, even for a few weeks! I wondered if Tom ever tired of Miriam. Miriam was even more impressive than she had been as a young woman, but she was rather intimidating. Arthur quite liked her since she liked to talk 'man to man' or person to person I suppose one must now say, and he was excused the sort of small talk that bored him.

Those years all seem to be elided now in my memory – when the children were small, and Sarah was still a baby. I was always too busy to wonder whether I was leading the life I wanted and I suppose that shows that I was reasonably content. I did wonder whether Miriam and Tom were living the sort of lives *they* preferred. In Miriam's case I think she was. About Tom I wasn't sure. He had occasionally looked cynical, except when he talked of Lally. Miriam clearly didn't relish Tom's dwelling on the past. She was still the same

brusque, brisk, competent woman she always had been and I
don't believe Susan's suffering had essentially changed Susan
either. It had been an interesting afternoon, I thought then,
even if the lost presences of Lally and Gabriel, and even Nick
– two gone for ever, one far away – had never been far from our
minds.

2   Revelations

The inseparable propriety of time,
which is ever more and more to disclose truth.
   Bacon: *Advancement of Learning* xxiv

We had eventually decided that two children were enough. I
adored my boys but quailed before three possible male
children and there was no way of making sure the next was a
daughter. I had always felt that women were made to feel that
giving birth was a hurdle they had to jump, equivalent to a
man's going into battle and I had already jumped it twice.
Susan laughed at this. She had not felt any need to prove
herself, I suppose. Sarah grew from a baby into a toddler and
then an independent-minded little girl and her mother and I
saw each other quite often, but more often telephoned.

My mother retired from her teaching post and received
many affecting tributes from pupils and staff and ex-pupils,
more than my father had received if truth be told, in quantity
anyway. Then my parents decided it was time for them to
leave Eastcliff and move to a village in the 'real' country
between Leeds and Harrogate. I was surprised at their
wanting to leave, for I thought Eastcliff was a fixture in their
lives, if not in mine, and I was rather aggrieved. That surprised
me. Once I would have no home base in the village I hoped
Susan would not mind if I visited her more frequently. I felt
real grief when my parents left their neat house and garden for

the last time, for I liked the place, the smell of my father's roses and the feel of the rooms in which I had grown up. I must be turning into a true conservative.

Eastcliff was connected with those childhood memories which begin to return once you are middle-aged. By the time Mother and Dad left the place I was over forty, and tastes and sounds as well as sights and scents were all mingled into my memories of it – the taste of the sherbet we used to call Kali from Susan's old shop, and the sound of the bell tolling every quarter hour from the church. Now that the responsibility of earning a living had gone away, my father, who looked older since his retirement, had become a little more mellow, in spite of bewailing the modern world. It was my father whom I must always have resembled, I began to feel, though I'd loved my mother best, and admired her as well. Mother had put her eggs in two baskets, home and work, at a time when not many women, in Eastcliff at any rate, did. My father however still used the terms to describe others that he had always used, and in bad moods he could still annoy me, especially when he did not consider my mother's feelings. He had always underrated other people's sensitivities. But with his grandchildren he was more benevolent than he had ever been with Rosemary or me. They got less of the 'Don't get above yourself', and the 'He needs to be taken down a peg', and he taxed them less with showing off than he had taxed me; maybe they were just nicer children. They were both bright, but he never said they were 'too clever by half'. My father hated to be criticized and now I knew it was because he was not sure of himself, never had been, and that that was the reason for his constant need for admiration and reassurance. He had been a hard-working man all his life and I realized that he had never really enjoyed responsibility. He had been brought up, as he had brought us up, to believe in authority and his teachings had been too powerful for me to entirely abandon. Miriam would say that I had the moral attitudes of the meritocracy and that I cared about appearances, and it was true to some extent – I'd rather have a fairly tidy house with untidy drawers and cupboards than a place that looks a mess on the surface but is all tidied away elsewhere, though my 'tidy house' was not itself very tidy. I liked to see Dominic and Richard well fed and reasonably clean although I believed that giving them kisses and reading them stories was more important. I had taken them to clinics, to pantomimes, to fairs; visited museums, taken them on long walks and out to tea to other children; and I had been gardener, cook, cleaner, house-painter and nurse during all these years. Whilst the world was in revolt I had been just a housewife, though I had also toiled over my translations in the university library, enjoying the freedom of a few hours away from domestic responsibilities. I still had a few ambitions locked away, I suppose, and looked forward to the children's growing up, yet hoped it would not arrive too quickly.

Susan published another book in 1976, called *Surviving*, which was so successful that she was able to pay off the mortgage and invest the rest to live on, and for Sarah one day. 'I wrote it for Wynteredge and for Sarah,' she said. Although it was set in a past Eastcliff and ranged wider and further from there than her other books had done, I felt it was imbued, whether she had intended it or not, with the spirit of Gabriel. She and the Bensons kept Gabriel's grave tidy and had planted crocuses there, and daffodils. They had also planted a rambler rose that was eventually to cover the tombstone. I do not know why he had not been cremated, but he had not. In *Surviving* she wrote of a man like him. It was an intricately rich tapestry with the central figure of the man seen against the activities of a village at the time of the Luddites. 'I was made to realize how many human tragedies there were then, it helped to put my own into perspective,' Susan said. Long, long ago a person like Susan would have been the village recorder, the one who kept alive the past for the Britons when the Anglians came and for the Anglians when the Normans arrived. Miss Dalby, now retired, wrote to her saying she had made something out of the shards of history that was more than a historical novel.

But Susan was not invulnerable, often woke at dawn with thoughts about the meaninglessness of life, the kind of thoughts that had pursued Gabriel. In her newspaper column she never wrote of serious matters, preferring to keep a light touch, which was another way, she said, to keep sane. On the City *Gazette* she was still known for her humour – there was a whiff of whimsicality in her sometimes consciously old-fashioned style which pleased her readers who were our age or older. 'People don't change,' she would say. She had a popular touch, but did not write down, rather lifted her readers up. Her descriptions had the magic of a large-scale map for readers, and there was an additional spice for those actually living in Eastcliff. The truth that came out of it all was a poetic truth, not a political one or even a historical one. Wynteredge House came into her books too, not as a distant speck on the landscape but as the home of her characters.

She had to give interviews to publicize her books on the radio and to newspapers – not yet on television, though that was to come later. Her interviewers seemed often to be puzzled by Susan. They did not quite dare to ask about the fact that she had never married, yet had a child, and they had been told not to question her about Gabriel, so the questions seemed odd till you realized that they were concentrating on only one aspect of her. 'Have we outgrown marriage as an ideal? Are you a religious woman? Do you believe in fate? Are you a "women's libber"?'

She preferred to talk about sheep and water-wheels and the old Roman road that became the packhorse route. 'I think people in the past were in all essentials much as we are. Their bones did not make different shapes when they arrived in the graveyard,' she said.

The interviewers said 'Oh!' – seemed startled.

I did wish I could one day see Nick again. I had begun to think of him as something rather pleasant that had happened to me long ago. I thought it would have been better for me if I'd been a bit more like him myself, might have gone further if I had been. But I wasn't discontented, just wished sometimes that I was young again. My little adventures with him – how long ago were they? Nineteen years? It wasn't possible.

On one of my visits to Susan when there was snow outside and a glowing fire in the hearth she talked about Canon Benson and his Christian consolation that he said came from grace, not from trying to believe. Susan had benefit of clergy with a vengeance now, I thought, for the Bensons continued to adore Sarah, who was five and still with her father's looks but quite different from him in temperament, very poised and sociable.

'They pray for me and for Sarah,' she said. I wondered if Susan was thinking of joining the church. I saw her more as a Quaker than a member of any more orthodox sect.

'I just loved being with Gabriel, you know,' she said to me once. 'It's the companionship I miss. I don't want Sarah to feel cramped by me.' I didn't think she would.

Sometimes we visited my parents in their new bungalow, and, less often, they came to us. Mother seemed to have taken on a new lease of life, though my father often looked tired now.

'Do you ever hear from that good-looking boy, not Tom, the other one you used to play tennis with?' my mother asked me one day.

'Oh, you mean Nick Varley?' I answered innocently. 'Still in America waiting for the next presidential election I expect – he's advising the World Bank or the International Monetary Fund or something.'

But by the time President Carter had been a year in office, my father, Mr Gibson, was dead. His not feeling quite up to the mark had turned out to be cancer. If I had felt grief at leaving my father's roses behind in their garden in Eastcliff it was a similar grief, compounded of nostalgia for my own past and the loss of one of the familiar landmarks of my life that his death raised in me. I tried to be sorry for *him*, not for myself and for a long time afterwards I felt there was nothing to rebel against. I must at last have grown up. It was strange to be without the father I had once disliked and now begun to love.

In the spring after Dad's death something happened to change my life – my inner life and my estimate of myself, making me reconsider the whole of my youth, like one of those snow scenes imprisoned in crystal which when you turn it upside down transforms the whole. Snow settles on houses and people and trees and makes them look different and also different in relation to each other. I have tried so far to speak honestly about myself and the others, though now I see everything so differently. The truth is either something that is continually being revealed and slowly nudges itself into your consciousness, or else it bursts into it only when you are ready.

212

When I was young, people saw me as a romantic, but I think that description, if it ever were true, had been wiped away by the steadiness and the settled nature of my married life. If Arthur had never existed I should, I now believe, have found someone very like him. But whom might Arthur have found? I put this to him once in a half-joking way, but he laughed and said, 'Marriages are made in Heaven, didn't you know?'

I went on thinking about Nick Varley, not obsessively but rather gratefully and the memories were pleasant and good, except for that last time in London. I could never remember exactly why I had been annoyed with him or displeased. The memory of love-making in that high-ceilinged flat in Barcelona I had kept in isolation from the rest of my life, but one never can isolate such experiences in the end. The most satisfactory sexual experience of my life! Yet I had not been 'in love' with him, was sure I had not. Maybe I ought to have been? I had been young and unattached, with no real anxieties except those common to youth, never having enough – or any – money and without anything permanent in my life. I had been happy with Nick – intrigued, contented, not yearning or besotted. Had I thought it would be the beginning of a life of affairs spent under sunny southern skies? I really could not remember. We forget so easily parts of our lives.

I think Susan whom I admired more and more, was always pleased to see me. I didn't see her as often as I'd have liked, but when I did I found her very restful. In the weeks when she was writing the first draft of a story I left her alone, but always told her to telephone or come over if she wanted a little change. Sarah liked playing with the boys and they were sweet to her, finding her extremely amusing. Just now and again I'd go over to Wynteredge and combine a trip with a visit to an old aunt who still lived in Eastcliff. This was more in the nature of a duty but pleased my mother who sometimes accompanied me, leaving me to walk up the lane that led to Sholey where I visited Gabriel's grave. There were not only crocuses and daffodils and roses now; his mother had planted primroses, and although it was rather a cold place for them, some survived, and later there were even bluebells that had crept over from the woods.

One of those afternoons I'd left the car and Mother at Aunt

Elsie's and had passed by the churchyard before going any further. Sarah was at Eastcliff school now and I was going to offer to collect her for Susan if she were busy. Then I had to get back to relieve our au pair. We had been lucky to find a motherly girl from Switzerland called Rosina who thought I was a hopeless housekeeper. Her favourite occupation when I was working in the library was the scrubbing and rearranging of my kitchen shelves.

Susan was in her garden expecting me. 'Mrs Harrison is to collect Sarah,' she said. 'Let's go in for a cup of coffee whilst we can. Sarah usually brings Amanda Harrison back with her to play.'

We sat in her kitchen and I told her how beautiful Gabriel's grave was looking. Then idly, not knowing why I said it, but as though something that I couldn't quite remember had re-surfaced in my head and spoke to me, I said, 'Did you ever read that diary of Lally's?'

She was pouring the coffee into two pretty Victorian cups she'd bought from one of her forays into a new antique shop that had opened in the town.

'Yes – I did in the end. It was some time after Gabriel died – but I haven't looked at it since.'

'For ages I just couldn't bear thinking about Lally's life,' I said. 'What did she say? Did it cast any further light on why she did it?'

'I don't expect she would mind your reading it now after all this time ,' said Susan. 'Actually she wrote it all as though it were a letter to me.'

'I remember – she asked that doctor to give it to you. The coroner couldn't have found anything in it, did he, or he'd have said?'

'Oh, there was plenty in it,' said Susan. 'Do you want to read it? I think I put it with my old school books and things when I moved here.'

'It doesn't really matter, I was just curious,' I said.

We drank our coffee and then I looked at some of her books on local history and Susan went rummaging upstairs.

'It was in my old wooden trunk. There you are, have it – you ought to read it,' she said. The diary was a thick ledger-like book, the sort of book people used to use for accounts, with a leather spine and black cover.

'Gosh, is it full? She must have written a lot!' I said.

'Doctor Walker told her to write for therapy, I think,' said Susan. 'I suppose you'd better give it me back when you've read it.'

'Is it all about men? – or her mother?' I asked.

'I think she told the doctors and psychiatrists about her mother – she didn't tell them all she wrote in the diary, I'm sure. Doctor Walker knew she'd been knocked over by some love affair, but Lally was very secretive, you know.'

'I wonder why she wrote it for *you*,' I said.

'Well, you know what she said – "perhaps Susan will make a story out of it". Actually, I haven't, and don't intend to. Take it home and tell me what you think about it afterwards. I was surprised, though I think Gabriel had always known.'

'Gabriel?'

'He understood most things about Lally,' said Susan. 'He visited her quite a lot you know. About a fortnight before she died she told him she'd written something for me.'

'Did Gabriel read it afterwards then?'

'I think so – he must have done. Here you are.' She handed it over to me. It had L. M. Cecil on a stuck-on label on the front.

Sarah came home then and I had to go and fetch Mother. She always stayed with us for the night in Leeds when I took her over to Eastcliff so she wouldn't have the bother of a further journey but could make her way back to her bungalow in Wharfedale in the morning when I was working in the library. She didn't really trust my driving and even now as we went back I saw her look nervously at the heavy traffic which passed us as people went home from work. I put the diary on the back seat in the big bag I always carried round with me. I didn't think I'd mention it to Mother.

Rosina kindly put the boys to bed and then went for her evening English classes. I made a pot of coffee and sat at the table with the diary. Arthur was out at a meeting, poor man. He spent more and more time on committees but was thinking of applying for promotion – which might unfortunately mean even more of the same.

215

As I started to read Lally's tall, backward-sloping hand which was not hard to decipher, though towards the end it was a bit illegible, new truths began to dawn upon me, and a pattern began to emerge from the very beginning. Why had Susan never told me to read this before? I suppose because she thought it was none of my business.

I lit cigarette after cigarette and my coffee went cold. I read her account – written thirteen years later – of a story which went back to 1952 when events which started one summer led to a long story of betrayal and unhappiness, and eventually to her suicide. When Arthur came home I told him what I had been reading. My heart was thumping and I was dry-mouthed.

'Oh, I always thought that would be what had happened,' he said.

'You just guessed?'

'No,' he said, making us another pot of coffee. 'I just used my historian's imagination.'

Lally's Diary

I still see Dr Walker every week. She says it might make me feel better if I wrote down what troubles me. I didn't tell her that I was frightened it might make me feel worse. She is very kind to me and she must know best. She says she won't read it, it is just for myself to sort things out in my head. I have never been any good at writing things down so I am going to imagine I am writing for Susan and one day I might show it to her and she will read it. It is very tiring, writing, so I will only do a bit every day. The new pills have made me sleep better. . . .

. . . I don't really know a lot about Mummy – like I told the other doctor in London, the one who gave me electric shock treatment. After that treatment I forgot more recent things for a time but they came back and I did not forget the important things, just dates and things like that. I talk to Gabriel about Mummy when he comes to see me and I tell him more than I tell anyone else, but I don't think even Gabriel understands what I feel.

Dr Walker writes down things I tell her about my mother and about when I was small. Little by little as I talk to her I remember more and more, things I'd pushed down and tried not to think about even when I was only six years old. The time when my mother took all her clothes off and my father threw her medicine on the fire, for example. Dr Walker suggested that I must have felt I was responsible for sending her away. I told her about Dad and Gran talking about me when I'd been hidden behind the curtains. I knew my mother loved me so she would not have gone away if she had believed I loved her. That was my childish reasoning, I suppose. But she had not wanted to go away and so if it were not my fault it was my father's, for it was after he came on leave that they fetched the doctor and she went away with him. But Daddy was sad – it could not be his fault. I don't suppose I'll ever remember exactly what I thought. I know Gran used to tell me that it was not my fault, but I didn't believe her. As I grew up I knew with my mind that a child is not responsible for a grown-up's actions, but although I KNEW it I still didn't FEEL it. When I dream that I am a child again I still feel that she has not come back because of me. When I knew she couldn't come back I sort of closed it off in my memory and it came back in that way when I had my first depression. Lots of children have a parent who dies when they are small, but do any of them recover? I know I was close to my mother – and I loved her so much. When I went to Gran's I used to think about her playing at The Laurels when she was my age and I found things that had belonged to her – a doll in a drawer and some suitcases in the attics that she'd used when she went away to school. I wasn't homesick for Edinburgh, and anyway Daddy'd gone back to London with Clare. They'd got married and then they went abroad and that was why it was better for me not to be with them.

I often felt sad when the others talked of their mothers. I'd never belonged to a proper family. If Dad and Clare had a baby I supposed I might go back and be part of a new family but I didn't feel it would happen.

I had confidence in my body in those days – running and playing games and swimming and riding. When I was doing something like athletics at school or cantering round Hyde Park on holidays with Dad and Clare later, I'd always feel better. The rhythm somehow made my thoughts pleasanter, though I could never remember what was unpleasant about them before. Remembering was like scratching a scab. I decided most likely I'd misunderstood things that I'd over-heard when I was six and before. But I realized Mummy's medicine must have been the gin bottle which I fetched from the off licence in Bath when we were living there.

Privately I thought that my mother might not be dead. I thought that till I was about thirteen. I thought she'd gone mad and they didn't want to tell me. Much later, I guessed that she had killed herself, partly as a result of drink, partly from some depressive illness. After I'd been born she'd never been right – Dad said she'd gone a bit 'mad'. But he never said in so many words that she had done away with herself and as he didn't seem to want me to know I didn't pursue it at the time. Later I looked up her death certificate when I was in London.

. . . 'You are just depressed,' they always say to me and I try to believe them. But what if I have inherited something bad from my mother?

. . . When I first came to York I felt much better. Numb, but not wanting to end it all. I used to listen to music a lot. I heard Tom's opera here on my radio. I like working in the hospital doing the secretarial things, and I thought, two years ago, that soon I would be able to go back and find a job in London – or go to Gran's to live. But then Gran died and that was awful, though everyone was kind to me, and I realized I just couldn't bear to go back to London again. . . .

I am writing in my room at the nursing home next to the office – if ever I get depressed again I shall have the hospital nice and handy.

It doesn't begin in London but in Eastcliff, what I want to write about. I don't really want to, but I will try – not the bits about Mummy because I have told them all I can remember. They said that was the beginning, 'predisposing my depression', but they don't know why I had the breakdowns!

Feb 15. It all began at The Holm. It was the year before I left school. I was seventeen, I do remember that, because someone asked me how old I was and I told them and someone said something silly. We used to go around with those three – boys – I suppose they were. Susan and Miriam and Gillian and me. Tom was sweet on me – it was obvious. He used to compliment me on things like my hair and my tennis. I wasn't clever like the others at school, though I wasn't actually thick, I don't think. I passed my exams in everything but Latin and maths. I thought I was fairly happy, and I was really, because I'd stopped dreaming about Mummy, but I was sort of empty.

I knew that I was quite good-looking and it embarrassed me rather. My mother had been pretty Gran said. I liked sports and swimming and listening to the others. I didn't really know what I wanted to do, except get married one day. I used to hear funny voices when I had first come to Eastcliff and a bit after that, but they went away. I mean I really did hear them, two girls talking and I just knew that one was Mummy when she was young. But a part of me knew that was not possible. I only mentioned it once, to Susan and Gillian, and they were very comforting. At first when I'd come to Gran's I had had nightmares and shouted in my sleep and worried her, but it got better as time went on. I can't seem to get to the point, but I will try. I just don't want it to make me cry. I hate crying, but I can't help it whenever I think of him.

I've never told anyone directly about it at all.

Feb 17. This morning I told Dr Walker I was still writing my diary, but it's not really a diary because a diary is what you do every day and I do nothing but think and write down what I can remember.

I am not writing this at all well. I will try again.

I want to write down about all that happened and I shall not tell Dr W if she goes on about it. Perhaps if I can get it all on paper I SHALL feel better. It is just not being able to say his name, not being able to talk about when it began that has depressed me. But now I will say it and that will make me be able to remember.

Nick, Nick, I love you Nick like I did in the attic at The Holm and everywhere afterwards for years and years till you left me and went away and I was so unhappy because it was like being left when I was little after I'd been so happy.

219

Then a long time after, when I had been ill because you had left me, you came back. But then you went away again and that was worse. Nobody knew, nobody at all, not even Susan.

Feb 28. Now I have written that, I will try to remember it all. I don't know why I've never told anyone about Nick and me. We promised each other we'd keep it secret right from the beginning and I've always been good at hiding my feelings. It was all quite simple really. I had a private life and that's what I wanted. Away from Gran and Dad and the others. There was nothing dreadful or awful about it, it was what I wanted. It was just natural, what we did.

Gillian was always going on about fancying people and having lovers, but it was all talk for her then. Nick said she had 'sex in the head' which I thought was funny. But that was before we used to meet at The Holm. I remember saying that Nick looked at people a lot, I meant stared rather, but I didn't know he stared more at me than the others. Right from the beginning I knew I would have to be chosen by whoever it was who would want me. I didn't do anything to attract men, or even Nick – except that after we had played that game of tennis which I'd won he did look at me in a special sort of way. I thought he was angry that I'd beaten him, and I suppose he was really. He didn't like anyone to beat him in anything. I didn't think he was pretending when he sometimes walked me home and kissed me goodbye in the shrubbery. He was the first boy I'd ever kissed and it made me feel strange. I didn't feel we were too young or anything like that. I was seventeen and he was a bit older and I'd often thought of a strong man who would love me and make everything right. I can remember thinking those words 'make everything right'. I knew he found me attractive and I found him attractive right from the start. After a few kisses I was in love with him as though I'd drunk a magic potion like in that story they told us at school. I remember I laughed because I was happy when I saw him. Not when the others were there, but whenever we could snatch a minute alone. I was ready to love someone, you see, and I was not surprised or ashamed of how I felt. I wasn't the sort of person who ever went around telling friends what I got up to and Nick insisted on what he called 'discretion'. That was right from the beginning. I don't remember wondering why he should not want anyone to know, but it made it more exciting. But I'm surprised that nobody guessed what our feelings were. It wasn't long before he said: 'I want you Lally – oh, I want you so much.' It makes tears come in my eyes now when I remember how he said it. As though he would die. I knew what he meant. I had always known about sex; I can't remember who told me but I did know and I was glad. It was what I wanted too, though I hadn't any idea how it would make me feel.

Afterwards we went up to the top floor. Nick had explored it before – he said there were a few sticks of furniture, a sofa and a bed and things and that first time we just looked at the rooms and stood by the window. It was like having a secret house all to ourselves. He undid my dress and kissed my breasts and I could feel him against me. He kept saying, 'You are so beautiful, so beautiful.' He said we could stay on afterwards or creep back one evening and be together, as there was a bed. I didn't even think about getting pregnant or anything like that. I wouldn't have cared, though *he* would. He said, 'You are like someone out of a story-book with your golden hair,' and I laughed. I can't remember the feeling of being so happy. I mean I can remember feeling happy but now it all seems as though it was happening to someone else, though at the time I did not feel that.

It was one evening when it had thundered and we had sung songs round the piano and the others had mostly gone and only Tom and Miriam were left downstairs and he was playing the piano. Nick said, 'We'll shout goodbye and then we'll creep back by the kitchen door – I've left it open.' I thought he meant, stay the whole night, and I said, 'Gran will worry' – and he said, 'Well, we both have to go home – afterwards,' and we stood behind the door of that big room where the piano was and Miriam was too busy talking to Tom to notice. Nick had his hand inside my dress and I felt all swoony and melty. We went upstairs and we could hear the piano from downstairs in the distance but then it stopped and they went out and we saw from the window, that was all smeary with dust, that they were going away. 'Now we're alone,' he said and he began kissing me and then we fell on that narrow little iron bedstead that someone had left for the evacuees. The wallpaper was pink roses in twirls and columns and whilst he was beginning to make love to me I was thinking in a funny way that it was like the wallpaper in Mummy's room when I was very small.

I can't describe what we did. I don't like going into details. I've never liked talking about those things but I do know that it was a surprise. It was a revelation to me. It was like suddenly knowing that this was what you had been waiting for all your life. Nick had made love to a woman before when he was in France – he told me that he had, and he was always a person who knew what he was doing. It wasn't difficult for me, more like doing something well, like swimming or riding. I think he was surprised because afterwards he said, 'You came like a bird.' As soon as he was moving inside me I felt that delicious feeling and it went on and on like flying higher and higher. I loved him for making it happen and he said I love you, I love you and he was happy too.

Afterwards I said, 'Now I know what it must feel like to be always happy!' You see I hadn't realized that I had not been feeling anything much for years and years. I had felt sort of neutral for a long time so that I just hadn't felt that light feeling of joy for years. It *was* joy I felt. Nick said, 'You are very lucky I think,' and I said, 'It is because I love you,' and we lay there and felt so comfortable and blissful, but he said 'We'll have to go. I'd like to make love to you all night but we can't.' I thought, this feeling of being like a bird or like having a bird swoop down inside you and then up and up is because of Nick. I would just like to keep him there for ever.

He said he loved me then and he went on saying that for a long time. He said, 'You can wear your mother's ring on your wedding finger and we'll contrive to go away together when you go to London – or you can get a flat of your own and we can be together.' He knew I was going to live there, and he had to do his exams, but he had an allowance from his father and they didn't mind if he went to London and found some job after he'd got his exams done with. But that was a bit after.

Mar 4. Writing all that made me happy when I was writing it but now I feel that it has made me remember him and he has gone and will never come back and I can't believe it. We went

222

on seeing each other and being lovers all the time the others were meeting at The Holm. Once we didn't do it there but in the woods where we'd gone for a walk one Sunday, but that was more risky. Nick always wanted me. It was like a drug for me and I think it was for him. He said, 'The more I have the more I want,' and I felt the same. 'But we need never stop,' I said. 'After you've done your degree and I've found a job we might be parted from time to time but if we want to be together there's nothing to stop us,' and he agreed. When I was with him I really did think we were married. I *felt* married. I knew there would never be anyone else I'd love. Sometimes he would say, 'Oh, there'll be heaps of men who'll fall in love with you,' but I stopped his mouth. I couldn't bear to think of that and I knew nobody but Nick would do for me even if we had to wait ages before we got really married. 'I won't ever want anyone but you,' I said. 'Why should I when I am so happy with you?' 'You are a very physical person, Lally,' he once said. But people are all physical, aren't they? I was my body and it was both my body and myself that loved Nick because they were the same. Just once there was a time when we went upstairs and Gabriel had come back for something he'd forgotten. We must have made some noise because we heard his footsteps on the stair. Of course we didn't know it was Gabriel till he called, 'Is anyone there?' We just lay frozen not moving or daring to breathe and then he went away. I said it wouldn't matter if the Angel Gabriel found us. He wouldn't tell. But Nick was quite upset. 'I don't want anyone moralizing at me,' he said.

The first time was so good that I couldn't think of it getting better but it did. Often I felt like the Babes in the Wood. Once we went to sleep and it was dark when we woke up and we had to dash out and run back home. One day I said to him, 'We could get married now – we could live in London during your holidays from Oxford and I could work.' But he said, 'They don't allow married undergraduates and what would we have that we don't have now?' I knew that was true.

Mar 5. Nick never made compliments like Tom did except when we were making love. He didn't need to. We were always absolutely honest to each other and all that summer and afterwards when we met in London – and sometimes in Oxford, we never quarrelled. He never needed to ask me what I wanted because what he wanted I wanted. Once though, after I'd fallen asleep for a minute or two he said I was shuddering in my sleep and asked me what I'd been dreaming about. It had been something to do with my mother, a hazy sort of feeling but to make it go away I asked him to make love to me again. 'You are incredible,' he said. 'You came to me like a dream and you are insatiable like a dream.' 'Should I be different?' I asked and he said 'No Lally, stay the same however much other people change, just stay the same.'

I did stay the same. It seems unbelievable that our love went on like this for almost five years, but it did. All through his time at university and whenever we could get together – in punts, in little hotels near Paddington and then in the little flat I rented when he came down from Oxford and stayed with me whilst he was beginning some research in London. In London Tom sometimes used to ring me and ask to take me out and once or twice I went with him. Once Tom kissed me and I knew that Miriam would not like that. Tom just said, 'There's someone else, isn't there Lally?' And I said yes there was. 'So I'm too late?' he said. I was shocked because I knew that he and Miriam were going out together. 'Never mind,' he said, 'you've never given me any encouragement.' After that I didn't go out with him again. Once I was with Nick at a concert and he and Miriam saw us. I'd begun to model by then and lots of men wanted to take me out. I always said no, I didn't want to go out with them; they didn't interest me at all. If it had been Tom who had made love to me at The Holm I wonder what would have happened. But Tom was like a little boy compared with Nick. Nick wasn't 'sweet' on me or anything like that. It was more like I was a necessity to him that he took for granted and as I grew older I wanted him to take me for granted. I'd always be there for him. I liked to go along with whatever he wanted because then I wanted it too. 'You are all female,' he once said. I explained I liked him to be in charge. It was such a relief you see. All the time we were together I never had to decide anything and we could laugh at all the others, the silly men who wanted to take out a 'Model' and the ones who made passes. Apart from Nick, sex didn't make any sense to me. I never got pregnant. In fact that worried me a bit because I wanted to have children with Nick. But Nick was pleased. 'I can't see myself as a father figure,' he said. He would tell me how he disliked his own father who was a bully, he said, and a womaniser.

Mar 6. I've been having strange dreams since I began to write all this down. I don't think Dr Walker agrees with the other psychiatrist Mr Robson about the treatment. He's just gone off on holiday. He thinks I just have to finish solving any problems I have at present and not worry about why I have them. He said, 'We know why you have had severe depression but knowing doesn't cure unless we can find something to fill up the void in your life left by your mother's defection.'

I said, 'But my mother died, not defected.'

'The child saw it as an abandonment – but you are no longer a child.'

I knew he wanted me to find another person to love. But he doesn't know anything about Nick and neither does Dr Walker. They don't know anything about it or that Nick promised he would love me for ever. But he didn't. Yet the thing I clung on to after my first breakdown when I came to Gran's for a time was that he *would* come back. And he did. But I'm getting ahead of this account of my life. It was after Nick had started his post-graduate work, in London one day, that he said to me, 'I have something to say, Lally.' I waited. I thought now he is going to fix a date for our marriage. But he said, 'You are too dependent on me darling – it is very flattering for me but you must have other people in your life. Five years is a long time. It's all my fault – we were too young.' I stared at him. I felt cold. I couldn't speak.

'Don't look at me like that!' he said and *he* looked strange.

I gasped, 'I don't want anyone else Nick! I love you. You love me. If you want a fling now and then – I know some men do – I shan't mind – I mean I *wiil* but I will put up with it so long as you come back home to me.' I hadn't meant to say 'back home'.

'This isn't our home – we aren't married – I think we ought to give each other a breathing space.'

I couldn't believe it. He was going to leave me!

225

I went all funny as though my limbs were weak and I didn't know who I was but I think I tried to shout – Don't go away, don't leave me, but it came out as a whisper. You see I have not had time to describe to you all the years we were together, not every day I know, but we were together whenever we could manage it and I'd been able to get a good job with the agency and do everything else just because I knew he was always there.

'Lally, we are still young – I am very fond of you, but –'

'You love me,' I said. 'You always said that, and *I* love *you*. Why should we have a breathing space? I can't breathe when you are not there. I don't want space. I thought you felt the same. You did! You told me that. You told me.' And all the time it was just like I was six years old and Mummy was going away and it was my fault. 'What have I done?' I cried. 'Tell me and I'll do what you want!'

He made me sit down. I felt I was on a high mountain looking over the edge. 'I just think we should have a little time apart so that we are sure what we want to do,' he said. 'I never meant to hurt you.'

It was all so sudden. I mean we'd never quarrelled, never. It had been just perfect. I said so when I could get my breath again.

'I just don't want you to be all passive – it was fine when we were eighteen – I confess it was amazing. But people change, Lally, I know I was a randy bastard and you were wonderful, so sweet . . . and I still can want you. (We had made love only the night before.) Anyone but you would have seen the danger signals,' he said. 'I have to be cruel to be kind. I just want you to have a summer away to enjoy yourself in other ways – then perhaps –'

I lost my head and I said, 'But I am special to you. You are special to me. It's for always, Nick, it can't be anything else. I know you love me.' Then I thought, but has he said that recently? How long is it since he said it? I'd taken it for granted, you see, in my stupid way.

But I'd never been close to anyone else. What more could anyone want? I had taken him for granted because I wanted him to take me for granted and he had. 'Men and women are different,' he said. 'I can't bear being made to feel guilty,' he said.

'It isn't your fault – I've been stupid – it's my fault,' I said.

'Don't be so bloody acquiescent,' he said.

'I'll try to be whatever you want me to be,' I said.

'That's the trouble,' he said. Then he sat down and took my hand. 'We mustn't hold each other back, Lally,' he said.

I didn't know what he meant.

'You're starting a brilliant career, you'll be going abroad, meeting new people,' he went on.

'Oh, darling Nick, I don't care a bit about all that,' I said. 'It's nice to have money just for looking at a camera but you know all I've ever wanted was for us to get married and then I can help to keep us with my little job.'

He looked stunned. The words just popped out of my mouth quite naturally and I didn't see what I'd done to offend him. After all we had pretended to be married – I'd worn Mummy's ring for him.

'We've never talked about getting married exactly,' he said and he looked away.

'I know, darling, it's such a bore, but we can, can't we? I mean if you have this little breathing space? I know you've got your military service thing to do, but I'd be able to stay near Cambridge and just go up to London when there was work for me –'

'People don't always have to marry, Lally,' he said. 'We've known each other so long that marriage wouldn't make any difference to us!'

'Of course it would,' I said quite gaily, thinking that he meant that we loved each other – I still believed he loved me – so much that marriage would only be a formality, which of course it would have been in a sense, but then also it was our commitment to each other.

'Lally, have you been listening to anything I've been saying?' he said. 'We should have had a serious talk long ago.'

I will say that for a man who is about to break your heart and send you round the bend for the rest of your life he did it with style. He explained that we'd had the most terrific affair, better than he would have believed possible, that because we hadn't always been able to be together we'd gone on wanting each other but that now we were grown up he was sure that one day both of us would want to love other people. That it

227

had been fantastic and he wasn't saying it was completely over yet but it might be. That he'd never forget me, that we'd always be friends – all that. I just couldn't take it in. He'd never mentioned anything like that before. I was shattered.

Mar 7. I think I blacked out because my mind is a blank. I remember coming to and he was bending over me and I must say he looked scared. It took me a few seconds to remember why I had this terrible pain in my brain and when I did I seemed to go all icy. My hands were freezing and then I felt numb everywhere else. I expect it was the shock. Anyway Nick stayed with me that night and over the next few days he rang me and told me I must start seeing other people, that I deserved someone better than him. Then I guessed he must be seeing other women. I still couldn't quite believe it for we'd *never* quarrelled, never even disagreed, and I thought sex had always been marvellous between us. I thought, he must be bored with me so why didn't he say so? I told him again I didn't mind if he wanted other girls as well. I knew I wasn't an intellectual, and he said, 'That's nothing to do with it, Lally,' and he sounded quite ashamed and said, 'You mustn't be so humble. I told you about my feelings on marriage because I wouldn't want it to sneak up on you or for me to leave you with no explanation.' Apparently he'd been trying to tell me for months that it was over and I'd been too stupid to realize. He wouldn't tell me why, just said, 'If I want to make love to other girls I don't want to feel I'm betraying you. I'm too young to have to feel that. . . .'

Oh, I can't go into it all. In the end he went away and I tried to carry on. But the strange thing was that my periods stopped. At first I thought I was pregnant and couldn't help feeling pleased – it might change his mind for him, I thought. But as time went on and I lost my appetite as well and yet managed to carry on at work – I believe they liked me looking a little pale and thin – I realized he might not be coming back and it was like a mine he'd laid on the path before me. It didn't get better with time; it got worse. Everything reminded me of Nick and yet there was no one else. So in the end I went home up to Gran's and Susan came over and talked to me, but I couldn't tell her the truth. I felt so stupid, so silly, that I'd thought Nick and I were a fixture for life. And I began to think there was something wrong with me because all the people I loved went away and left me.

Mar 8. After that it's all muddled in my head because after I'd recovered a bit at Gran's and gone back to London for about six months I just carried on automatically. I made myself believe that he would come back. And then for a time you see, he did! He was in Cambridge and he came to see me one weekend in London and he said that so long as we had no claims on each other we might just enjoy going to bed together and for a time I managed to convince myself that it would work. I thought perhaps there was someone else that he wanted to make love to but that he knew me better and had decided to give himself time to make up his mind. I wasn't really *better*, but I kidded myself it would all work out. By now I'd seen how some men treated women and Nick had always been nice to me. I knew there was something he still felt for me; he wasn't just being sorry for me. He told me then that he'd slept with other women and this didn't shock me because by then too I'd seen that many men did that, even if they loved one special woman. He wrote me a long letter, a strange letter. He said he couldn't help himself, that I was right to think he ought to marry me but that he was a 'shit', wanted lots of sex and lots of women. But he said, 'If I were capable of love it would be you I loved.' He tried to explain that he didn't regret the years we'd had together but he wasn't yet ready to settle down. He said I'd been addictive, that the way he felt about me was not the way people felt when they were going to settle down for the rest of their lives. He said I was 'dangerous'.

I thought that marriage would grow naturally out of love but Nick never talked about love now, only about passion. Perhaps I was wrong and what I'd felt for him was not love, but just desire . . . . I tried to convince myself it had been just that. But it hadn't. It had been that too, but I had truly loved him.

Mar 9. I got some of my hope back and realized I'd been foolish to think that things didn't ever change between people who loved each other. And why should I be special? Yet it was Nick who had *made* me special! I still didn't feel hungry and I never got the curse, but I managed. But then two things happened that changed things again. We had been jogging along for some time, him coming to see me when he could and me busy at work trying to forget what it had once been like. I still thought all this time that he was making up his mind and the best thing was to leave him to it. But he kept wanting me to let myself be taken out by other men. 'You have no standard of comparison' he said. 'How do you know that someone else wouldn't make you just as happy?' But I did know. Nobody could have made me happier than he already had. 'It's changed Lally, now – I don't always make you happy now, so someone else might.' He kept saying, when now and then he did come to see me, 'Try, Lally, just to please me. Will you?' And I did. But not till a bit later. I think it was when one day he told me about meeting Gillian in Spain and how she was all I was not and she didn't talk about marriage and liked to be free like a man. That shocked me. Gillian had always been my friend. But she didn't know about me and him, he said. Nobody did, so she hadn't done anything wrong. And even if she *had* known, he said, she might have done just the same. She came to see me at Dad's flat and she didn't act any differently towards me. In fact she was nice to me so I knew she didn't know, unless she were a very good actress. It was around the time Nick and I were just seeing each other, waiting, me hoping he would tire of other women, though I didn't know about them, only imagined them. He kept telling me to experiment, to enjoy life. I did try. But then he told me one day around Christmas, it must have been 1959 I think, that he was going to America for good. I didn't believe him. Or I was sure he would take me with him. He came to see me again whilst he was getting all his visas and things ready and he said he'd seen Gillian again and she'd stayed with him in London. And that he was doing the right thing going away and that it was finished. For a time I went mad. I slept with some men to try to make it stop hurting. But it did not. It made it worse. With the men I felt nothing, nothing at all, but I acted as if I did and one of them did ask me to marry him. In the end I just stopped going out at all. If I did I would destroy myself.

Mar 9. I began to wonder if there was a jinx upon me that I could not have the only person I wanted in the world. I knew that people can't always get what they want, but you see Nick had really loved me, I'm sure he had. I began to feel again all those terrible things I'd felt when I was little. I felt I was a worm, nothing, unworthy of being alive. I began to hear things in my head again. I used to see my mother and she was being made love to at The Holm as though I were her and she were me. I can't explain it better than that. The next breakdown that developed out of all this was much worse than before. Nick had just gone away to Washington and there was nobody I wanted to see, nothing I wanted to do, and I felt there was no hope. I took an overdose but at the last minute I phoned Dad. I can't remember why I did that. I'd never wanted to be a nuisance to him. I suppose I thought someone ought to know in case they didn't find my body for ages. I wasn't thinking clearly by then. I just wanted out. My stepmother got me to hospital in an ambulance having made me walk up and down, up and down, and be sick, and the minute I came round properly – it was the next day and they'd lined up psychiatrists and doctors at a hospital – my father was in a towering rage. It was not just Nick, but not being able to sleep at all and lying there with this longing to be annihilated. After they sent me to the hospital to have my stomach pumped they tried ECT and then they sent me to the Walmsley. I think all this happened in the spring of 1960. The minute I could walk and see properly I thought I would ask Gillian to come to see me. It was crazy. I felt that she knew Nick and it would make him feel nearer. I didn't feel any jealousy of her when she came to see me. I talked about Mummy and other things when I could talk at all. She was kind.

For weeks after that they sent me to a doctor with a private psychiatric practice and they stuffed me up with pills so that I felt like a zombie. I don't want to feel like that again. Then they found me this place here in York with a little job to go with it. It was a friend of my stepmother's who knew the matron. The main thing was to get me to want to go on with my life. All I wanted was to stop being a nuisance. The nursing home takes people with depressions and mania and other chronic conditions. Since then I've been up and down. But I can't believe that it is over with Nick. I've never been able to

231

believe that. I just *know* he will come for me in the end and that keeps me going. And in another part of my head I don't believe he will.

Mar 10. Writing has made me remember things I'd forgotten, but I'm glad I have written down about Nick. After he left me that first time and went to Spain he never knew really how low I'd been. I told him I had had a virus. The second time in London, after he went to the States, I never let on I'd been ill. I had letters from him just now and then and in one of them he said a clean break was better, but he would tell me if he came back. This kept me going after my illness. It wasn't Nick's fault, I see now. It was my own stupidity and knowing him so young when maybe I hadn't really recovered from Mummy's death. So long as I know I might see him again I think I shall be able to bear it. Gabriel says, like the others, that I have a 'predisposition to depress' and there was a 'trigger' in early childhood. I told him about my mother and also told him I'd had a wonderful love that had been taken away from me, but I never told him who. Gabriel said I had been so sad that I thought I'd let Mummy down and then she had died, but that I was also angry she'd gone away and turned it against myself and that's why I didn't want to live. What I ask myself now is, am I angry for expecting too much and then being disappointed? Gabriel said I could be happy again if I could forgive myself and let myself love again. He is such a sweet man. Susan and he will be so happy together, I'm sure, and will grow old together in Eastcliff.

Mar 14. Now I am beginning to have the feeling that Nick *will* come back for me. I never wanted to have any other men before and not since I came to York four years ago either. I can imagine now that Nick will one day be with me again and we shall be together as we used to be and do the things we used to do. I believe in him. He is my destiny. I think it is beyond sex and everything. I think of those first weeks when we were young and I can remember that it was as if a terrible burden I'd been carrying slid off me the minute he took me in his arms. He was amazing and he did it out of love, I know he did. And now I'm crying, but only out of remembered joy. Gabriel is wrong if he thinks I shall ever feel that with anyone else but Nick.

Mar 20. Things haven't been going too well since I last wrote. I felt I had not explained it all properly for myself and if anyone ever reads this diary they will get the wrong impression. I've made Nick seem hard-hearted. I remember that letter of his word for word, but I see now he was being hard on himself. I see now that I was too much of a responsibility and that he felt he had to grow stronger to be able to take me on for ever. He could have gone right after he left for his first term at Oxford, and later when he had that fling with Gillian. But he came back because he felt guilty. I have made him feel guilty and have probably ruined his life. I asked too much of a young man. I am going to write to him in Washington – I expect if he has moved they will forward my letter and I shall say I am sorry but I am stronger now and am still here for him. It all came to me last night when I was thinking it over . . . what I should do.

Mar 21. He must have told me to sleep with other men because he wanted to even things up between us. He must have thought they would give me something he could not and would cheer me up. Usually as it turned out they were quite happy just to have my body, not me, and it was then that I started to see my body as separate from myself. With my darling Nick they were the same thing. Nick didn't just want me for that, he was a true lover; how lucky I was. . . .

Apr 11. I have written to him to ask if he will come back! . . . I believe he *will* come back and then we shall be married as we were meant to be. I keep remembering other things. Now that I have begun I haven't dared think of them for so long. Now I remember that first time again and how we took off all our clothes in a sort of slow motion and he was smiling all the time. I was never ashamed before him, never. And he stood there smiling and he said, 'You are the most beautiful girl in the world and I am going to love you.' And he did. And it was like coming home . . . and it was odd because I've just remembered that after he'd made love to me that time, I began to remember things I hadn't thought about for ages like what

Mummy had used to say when she bent to kiss me goodnight when I was very small from the time she and Daddy and I lived all together in that house in the meadow. 'Good Night, rabbit,' she'd say, 'and don't eat all the lettuce up.' It was just a silly joke for going to sleep and I'd forgotten it for years till Nick and I lay together in that old house. Although we were doing a grown-up thing he made me feel a little girl again.

Last night I was thinking how I'd never been so close to anyone since Mummy went away till Nick cuddled me. I suppose that Gran must have cuddled me sometimes, but I was a bit shy of her and before that Nanny Partington had rather rationed her hugs. With Nick I could just be affectionate as well as the other things. It was a great relief. And it was fun too when we were with the others knowing what we were doing with each other. I remember one Christmas when we'd been together in London just before and then we saw each other again in Eastcliff. He hadn't decided whether to come home for that holiday when we'd said goodbye in London and when I saw him in his father's car with Susan and Gillian and I couldn't resist saying to him, 'So you decided to come then?' in a cool way. I suppose it was silly. I'd have been quite happy to tell everyone about us but he didn't want that. He said it was just a secret between us. Now I can only wait for him to reply and I must be patient. He may have changed his address. . . .

Apr 18. Gabriel came this afternoon to see me and he always gives me a hug when he goes. I thought, I really like him – it would be nice to snuggle up to him, but the minute I thought that, I knew I never would, could not. Nick is the only man I want to be close to. I wonder if he's got my letter yet. If Nick loved me once, I must have been worth something, mustn't I? Gabriel said yesterday that everyone has to stand on their own feet but that most people tread on each other's toes as they do so. He is very sweet and funny. I think Nick always respected him even when he thought he was too saint-like. 'We used to call you The Angel Gabriel,' I said to him. He looked quite upset. . . .

Apr 20. Nothing yet from USA. Susan came over – she was

234

researching something about the York Mystery plays and called in when I'd finished my clerking in the office. We had a cup of tea. I explained to her that Dr Walker said the other day that I had a weak ego. 'Lally,' Susan said. 'You had in some ways the strongest ego of all of us. At school you always seemed so sure in your private world, especially in our last year.' That was The Holm summer she was remembering. I almost told her. But I did not. Even Susan doesn't know I am writing this.

Instead I said, 'Because I didn't talk much everyone thought I was well balanced.' 'You never grumbled,' she said. 'I suppose if you had grumbled more, like Gillian used to, you would have been happier in the end. You were too little when you *could* have grumbled.' She is a great comfort. One day I'll tell her – but by then we'll be together again, Nick and I. She's never once mentioned him to me. Neither has Gabriel.

Apr 21. I never modelled again after that suicide attempt of mine. The papers made a fuss about me being overworked and I think they were scared to ask me to go back. Not that I would have done. I only did it whilst I was waiting for Nick, to save money to help us get married. But then I helped Dad pay for some of my treatment with it instead. I think the agency thought I was a druggie or something. So much for the face of the New Decade, the decade in which my breakdown was waiting for me. They wouldn't want me now. I don't get enough exercise. I ought to start to look for a little place of my own again. I've been long enough here. It's convenient for my work and for the sessions with Dr W and Mr Robson, but I must start getting ready for Nick's return. I'm sure he is coming back. Last night I had a dream and Mummy and Nick were both there and Nick said, 'I shall look after your mother, Lally, now, so you need not worry.' And Mummy laughed and said, 'I give you both my blessing.' I was so happy.

Apr 22. I never saw the difference between making love and loving and being in love the way Gillian used to talk about it. I knew when I was seventeen that people frowned on that sort of thing, but I just took it for granted that in these things you did what you wanted because it was a good thing and gave people happiness. I never did see that I did wrong or that Nick did. That part of it was always sweet and good. I remember finding secret places in the meadows in Oxford where we could make love. I never introduced him to Dad, I thought there'll be plenty of time for that when we've settled where we live when he's finished his studies. Once or twice I even went to his rooms in college and hid there overnight. It was all bliss. To me it was the love that was addictive. I think of those times and I haven't changed. There is nobody and nothing else in the world I want and I can't believe he does either. He's been five years away. Haven't I waited long enough? When we met at first we could hardly keep our hands off each other – I was as bad as he was. I wonder how many other women he made love to – it cannot just have been Gillian. I must not think these things.

May 5. I have been to church today and prayed he will answer my letter soon. Then I shall get out of here and rent a flat and prepare for his return.

May 10. It is over. He is married. I never knew. I have been in hospital for a few days. I crashed, couldn't speak. But I feel quite clear-headed now and know what to do. Nobody ever told me – I have his letter here – He was married just about when Gran died. I must believe it. I cannot. I feel strange again. I dare not go to sleep for I know I shall have the nightmare again about Mummy and the poison that must have been in the bottle I gave her. I am back now in the nursing home. Darling Nick. Be happy.

This was the end of the diary, but these notes were on a separate piece of paper and crossed out. She obviously made fair copies of them.

May 22. Dear Dr Walker,
    Please forgive me and thank you for all you have tried to do for me. But it is no good. I keep thinking of my mother and that she will be waiting for me. It is not anyone's fault. Please inform Gabriel Benson and thank him too. Ask him to give the enclosed diary to Susan Marriott. Give my father the note.

None of it is his fault, and give my love to him and to my stepmother. I am perfectly sane. I leave all my clothes and things to the hospital. I send my love to everybody. You were right about my mother. I was just not strong enough to bear it all happening again and worse this time I know. Please do not blame the nurses. I knew where the key was to the cupboard. I am sorry.

Lalage Mary Cecil

Dear Dad,
    Forgive me because I am going away. Be happy with Clare. I know I am doing the right thing. I cannot bear to have another breakdown.
Love from
Lally.

Dear Gabriel and Susan,
    There was *nothing else to do*. I know I shall never get better. You have been so kind to me. I remember all our happy days.
Love from
Lally
P.S. Susan may do with the diary what she wishes. She might even make a story one day out of it.

The writing at the end was wobbly. The note had been given to Susan, I supposed, after the inquest. Had the Coroner not bothered to read all that painful story? Or had he just thought it was the usual disappointed love story? I suppose if she hadn't seen the man in question for five years he might have thought it was all a fantasy.
    'She was not mad,' I said to Arthur.
    'No – a bit unbalanced though,' he said looking at me over his coffee.
    'I told you about me and Nick before,' I said.
    'I know.'
    'What do you think happened? She doesn't say much at the end, does she? What do you think he wrote to her? And now he's divorced and remarried – what an irony!' How could he bear it? I thought. Yet he had done only what many men do;

just chosen the wrong girl for a youthful passion. And not one of us had guessed. Or perhaps Gabriel had. I would have to talk to Susan. I'd never told her about Barcelona – or afterwards. And all these years since Lally's death she'd known and kept it to herself waiting for me to ask to read that diary. Did Nick know what had happened? He must do by now.

In bed that night I tossed and turned.

Lucky Lally, I was thinking. *Lucky* Lally to 'come like a bird', to have a 'perfect love'. Too perfect. *Unlucky* Lally to have it all shattered.

What has sex to do with anything? I thought. She loved him. It was her way of showing love, wanting love, the way young people try to express love. It had been Lally who was the romantic, not I, Lally who, if her wretched mother had not shown her the way, would be here now happily married to someone else, at least as happily as anyone ever is. . . . No wonder he'd been glad to dally with me in Spain. . . .

And my precious memory, my memory of happy love-making, of a time snatched out of the jaws of time, a time that had grown more romantic and alluring in retrospect was built on the ruins of his love for Lally Cecil. I dared not telephone Susan. After a few days I wrote to her: I *thought it might have been Tom whom she loved, who married someone else. I never, never guessed. I feel as guilty as hell, but is that stupid when I knew nothing of their love? It'll take me a long time to assimilate all this. I'd like to know if she ever told him what she was going to do. Do you think he even* knows *she is dead? His parents must surely have mentioned it to him?*

Then I told her briefly and baldly about Nick and me in Barcelona. There had been no compulsion on me to tell her before; Arthur had always known about it as he knew about others of my escapades. But it all left me feeling, in the end, soiled as well as sad.

I waited in some trepidation for a reply to my letter to Susan. I valued my old friend and hated that she might think I had deliberately withheld something from her. But she had never offered to tell me what was in Lally's diary and I'd been too preoccupied with domestic life and children and work. I suppose she may have imagined that since Lally knew about me, I must know about her. But she must have known it would have been against my nature not to say anything after Lally's death if I had.

After a few days I posted the diary back to Susan. The thought of those short 'Goodbye' notes practised in it as though they were some monstrous homework disturbed me and sickened me. Lally had never properly finished the diary either, not given any idea of her state of mind except to say she had heard from Nick and that he was married. Any of us could have told her that, for I remember telling Susan – or was it Tom? – at Mrs F's funeral. But Susan was not interested in Nick, and perhaps Gabriel, if he had known, might have preferred to say nothing? Had *he* ever guessed about Lally's past? If he had, I'd heard nothing of it. If only we had known what was going through her mind in that last week or two. But we never would. I could imagine it, and that was bad enough. Towards the end of her life, before she heard from Nick, she was clearly building up a fantasy to comfort herself, a fantasy that had arisen out of her memories. Remembering was not always a healthy activity, I thought.

It was to Lally that I owed an apology, though that was hardly the right word. But as I thought back on my own time with Nick Varley I began to wonder whether myself of twenty years before would have refused him, even if I had known of his long liaison with her. He would have told me it was all over, I felt sure – and it should have been. He should have ended it cleanly, but perhaps he was as much a coward as all of us, and guilty that she could not bear to live without him. It was thirteen years too late to apologize to Lally. Nick was the person I wished I could talk to. Did he ever guess why she had killed herself? He had not communicated with any of us for years, and his parents were as far as I knew still enjoying their retirement at Morecambe. Not that they had ever known much about their son.

I tried to apportion the blame for Lally's wretchedness on her mother – on Nick – on herself. Whatever part I had played in it was a minor one. But I had been the catalyst for his returning to her and then perhaps leaving her once more. As I turned these thoughts over and over in my mind I could not help reflecting that Lally had shown to an extreme degree only what many young women show when they give their hearts away. Love began to seem to me something catastrophic rather than the imperious hunger of youth or the comfortable pleasures of married life.

The parcel the diary made seemed a pathetic little reminder of Lally's short life. She had expressed herself so well in it, too well for my comfort. Now that I was older by thirteen years than the young woman who had written it I began to feel an almost maternal solicitude for her. She had needed a mother to love her and help her, I could not help thinking. Her father appeared in it as rather an unsatisfactory character. We would never know what part *he* played in his first wife's death, even if everyone who had known her had considered Ginny an unstable woman.

If only someone had said to Lally – 'Wait and see, life has other things to offer.' Gabriel must have told her that. I was thankful that she had never known what had happened to *him*. And even if she'd discovered earlier about Nick's marriage – if I'd told her the day of her grandmother's funeral – the outcome might have been the same, just might have happened earlier.

Thinking about Lally, which I did obsessively for a week or two, led me to think about us all again, all the old band of friends. Just as Lally had been her mother's daughter, so had Gabriel been his father's son. I was Mr Gibson's child. And Miriam had inherited many of her opinions and attitudes from her own father. Nick was probably the thrusting, ambitious manager of ideas as his father had been the thrusting, business man. The two of us who had achieved the most fame in the public eyes, Tom and Susan, were different from their own parents. Tom and Susan were the most talented, I thought, the two who had said the least when we were young, confronting life and ourselves. I found myself hoping that Miriam would never know about Lally and Nick, I don't know why.

Only a week or two after all this and when I was still reeling from the shock, I heard news about Miriam and Tom. From Jessica Coleman of all people. I had always kept up a desultory correspondence with my old friend who most surprisingly had never married and now ran a successful business to do with this new thing called The Media.

I've had the most extraordinary conversation with your old friend Miriam Cooper, she began in a letter that was as neatly typed as her style was gushing. *She is to stand in the Labour cause in the next election! Did you know? I was at a party at her house as the man I am living with (since last Christmas!) has connections with the college of which she is a governor. I don't suppose you know that she and her husband split up this year? She is rather impressive, but I felt a bit sorry for her.*

I put the letter down. Miriam and Tom? I read on.

Well – she's writing a book about the Third World and the new climatic and demographic problems (don't ask me what they are!) – and asked if I might talk about a contract for it with my boss. Her children were around – two great big boys with the most extraordinary pink hair, and a sulky looking girl – but quite pretty.

I heard later on the grapevine that her husband, the one you knew, fell in love with the lead singer in his last opera, a beautiful little waif, but, they say, tougher than she looks. Miriam has magnanimously consented to give him a divorce. Apparently it had been going on for ages but the child is only about twenty-two now, a blonde with the most ravishing green eyes. Your friend Miriam is left with house and kids and I expect there's a lot of bread coming in from his royalties etc, etc. I can't imagine how a man can first of all fall in love with a dedicated committee lady of undoubted brains and then fall for a little singer who you might say was the exact opposite. But such is human nature. Miriam told me she's also written a play – about the disillusionments of the Seventies, I think – but as we're not yet through with the Seventies perhaps she'll cheer up later. She looks to me like a monogamous woman who's making the best of it. This girl – Belinda Matheson is her name – is tipped for the Big Time. Began as a pop singer, apparently – I don't keep up with all that and I've no offspring to help me be 'with it'. They say in my circle that everyone calls her Fancy Boots and that she's had her eye on Tom Cooper ever since he first chose her to play his heroine – but maybe he's had his on her too. It's always a shame for the children. I begin to think I've been quite lucky never to have got hitched, the way things

241

are going nowadays with marriages breaking up right left and centre. But your Miriam is one of the Great and the Good. I don't think she'll want to marry again.

Well, the point of all this is to say that Miriam said: 'You're a friend of Gillian up in Yorkshire? – tell her about us. My parents are not broadcasting it round the village. And send her my love.' If you come to London you are invited chez Miriam and her tribe. Are you surprised? I mean about the split up?

To say I was surprised would be like saying I was surprised that Big Ben had started walking down Whitehall. More surprised though that Miriam wanted me to know. I was astonished. Not surprised, if Jessica's description were accurate, at the sort of girl Tom had fallen for. I was really and truly sorry for Miriam with her perfect marriage shattered. I admired – and admire – her. If Tom hadn't married her he'd have courted Lally Cecil, I felt sure. Or if he'd got his oar in early enough, and if Miriam hadn't urged him on, he'd have ended up a contented mill-owner, practising with a choir in his free time – and nobody would have known what he could have done with his musical talents. Tom Cooper would never have divorced if he'd married Lally Cecil. Stop it, I said to myself. Life's not like that. Lally loved *Nick*.

I heard more later about it all, and I imagined the rest. Belinda Matheson, singer or no, sounded like a dead ringer for Lally – blonde hair and green eyes. Not much older than the Cooper children either. How old would Jake be? He must be nineteen! I tried to imagine him with pink hair and padlocks – punks hadn't quite arrived amongst us backward tribes in the North.

I found myself thinking about Miriam and Tom quite a lot when I should have been working on *Jacobina*, a historical novel which I was translating from the French, a change from history proper. I kept seeing Miriam neé Jacobs as the eponymous heroine, with her fierce beliefs and managing sort of personality. I thought, they will take away Tom's piano and then she will know he isn't coming back. I imagined the look of the Belinda girl with the silvery-blonde hair. Lally once had a pure singing voice too – but not a loud one. This girl would belt it out. How did Miriam really feel, apart from hurt pride? I thought, she won't let him go so easily, he's relied on her for so

242

long. Tom though might want to have somebody rely on *him* for once. What a ruination love is for women, I thought, even for Miriam, who I had imagined immune. She'd loved Tom – probably still did. She'd miss having him around if nothing else. I tried to think how I'd feel if Arthur fell in love with some slim, sexy, bejeaned student, and upped and left me and the boys. I couldn't imagine that. I know all things are possible, but this did not seem likely. One never knew though and I'd survive if he did, missing the domestic part of it all most, I realized – and so would he. He *loved* being at home. Arthur fortunately had got over his adolescence before he met me. Tom hadn't, before he met Miriam. Still, he'd needed Miriam and she'd 'made' him. Sexual thrall was something different. I couldn't imagine he had ever felt for Miriam in that way. And this made me feel obscurely guilty to think such a thing of my old friend Miriam. Should I write to her? What was the etiquette in such matters? She'd wanted me to know, so I ought to acknowledge the fact that now I did.

Susan didn't seem as surprised as I was. We had talked over the Lally story a little by now – and I'd told her about Barcelona and how I'd never known about Nick and Lally. 'I don't think her diary was a surprise to Gabriel,' she had said. 'Not about you I mean – but Lally and Nick.'

The Jacobs were still based in Eastcliff in that Georgian gem of a house, though Mr Jacobs liked to travel a good deal in his retirement and the shop was now sold to someone else. Aunt Elsie said she saw them occasionally when they were not in the Himalayas or Hawaii or Houston.

As for the senior Coopers, I'd lost touch rather. Susan said they had bought a house to be near Josephine and her numerous family. I think they must have got more pleasure from their daughter than from Tom who had never visited Eastcliff as often as he might. I wondered what would happen to the barn in the Dales which I believed Tom and Miriam still used as a holiday house.

I told Mother about them. 'Marriage is such a refuge,' she said. 'We used to think, your father and I, that you might marry Tom – but that Miriam Jacobs had her eye on him from the time they were at school, didn't she?'

'I never liked Tom in that way, Mother!' I said. 'Or even as much as I liked Gabriel Benson.'

'Poor man,' she said, which was her usual remark if Gabriel's name ever came into our conversation. 'I expect Tom will start another family,' she mused. 'It's easier for men to do that.'

That had not occurred to me. It seemed strange that twenty years later a man could start over again in a way a woman never could. Not if she were forty-four anyway. I certainly would not wish to do so myself.

'Well, Miriam won't want people feeling sorry for her,' I said. 'I'm surprised it hasn't been in the papers. He's quite famous.'

'You don't read that sort of paper, dear,' said my mother.

Obviously a pending divorce was not going to stop Miriam from political activity. I told Mother she was going to stand for Parliament. There'd be an election in a year.

'Fancy that,' said my mother. 'But perhaps it'll take her mind off things!'

'I believe Miriam managed a lot of Tom's business for him,' I went on. 'She entertained for him too – kept people sweet. He was always absentminded, you know, and I bet Miriam organized his appointments and his correspondence, though she'd never be called his secretary. I don't know how she ever found time with the children and her own work. I thought she was a paragon of a wife – good cook, good gardener – all the things I'm not.'

'Oh, you do very well, Gillian,' said my mother.

'I think I can guess what will happen,' I said, unwilling to leave the subject of Tom and Miriam alone. 'She'll end up making herself indispensable to Tom and his new wife – you wait and see.'

Divorce was not so common among the middle class in our neck of the woods as it had begun to be in London, but gradually we were to see many marriages around us crumble. When we were children we'd seen married couples as rock-like and immovable, even if we knew that parents did not always agree. How many women, even in Eastcliff, might have left their unsatisfactory husbands if they'd had the money to do so? I think the men were more likely to have had a bit on the side, not to leave the security of home and 'Mother'. Did love sometimes ruin men too? They always seemed to be able to fall in it again quite easily, though the pursuit of it unsettled them. But then they always had their work. Perhaps men and women alike were not all made for a lifetime's sexual bliss together. All our old moralities had insisted that marriage was for the taming of such passions and for the upbringing of children. I still had quite a lot of the latter to get through before Dominic, who was now fourteen, and Richard who was eleven, advanced upon the world. My younger son was more of a rebel than his brother and the star of the primary school stage. One day I might know as little of their real lives as I did now of Tom's or Nick's, I thought.

That past world I had constructed and placed my friend in seemed to have been built on false foundations, needing only a push – Lally's pathetic diary – to bring it all down. I had so misjudged her, and Nick too. Probably, I felt sadly, I had never understood anyone, least of all myself – and perhaps not even Arthur. My relationship with my husband was pleasant and friendly and we gave each other private space. Without that I wouldn't have wanted to be married to anyone, would have been stifled. Arthur had been the right sort of husband for me, though it was not the sort of exciting marriage I might have dreamed of at twenty. Yet I'd seen many of those dissolve after a few years into bickering or boredom. Arthur and I were, in any case, both far too busy to sit contemplating our navels or each other's. Arthur had his own professional life and I'd never felt my smaller one swallowed up in his. I enjoyed my work, and my occasional periods of solitude, and I liked talking to and being with our children. I supposed I must have finally grown up. My husband could be irritable, and was sometimes lost in a brown study, but he had times of bursting out of it all and getting close to me, either through love-making or, as often, through midnight parleys, comfortable embraces. We got on well.

Those dozen years or so between my adolescence and youth – and our marriage – and especially before the children came into my life and I was forced to think about others before I thought about myself – seemed to have happened a hundred years before! I had been an awfully silly young woman. Now I did seem to be able to live in the present. Sometimes I thought I'd just been very lucky, but I didn't want to become smug.

My new knowledge of the past did however begin to influence my estimate of myself. I was still the same person who had mistaken for a shared and friendly idyll what had been, for some, a traumatic summer. Those of us who had grown up together – Susan and Miriam and Lally, and Tom and Nick and Gabriel – I also began to see from another perspective. If I had known then that two of us would be dead by the early Seventies I would have imagined that *I* was to be one of them, immolated on some romantic altar, for I had had strong feelings in those days even if they were misplaced. Distant events had certainly cast their shadows forward, but too late for any of us to do anything about them. Gabriel should have stuck to his butterflies. But what could any of us have done to help Lally? Maybe Tom had never envisaged an early marriage and the responsibilities of parenthood, but like Nick he had done what he wanted and received recognition from his peers, which must matter to him. It seemed to matter to most men, even to Arthur.

Once again, as I used to feel when I was an adolescent, I saw myself as the outsider, the one who observed the others. I suppose each of us sees herself or himself as the one looking on, not quite belonging. . . .

If only Lally could have had a bit more of my egoism and enjoyed her love affairs, even if they had been unrequited. But something about Lally had been determined long before any of us even knew her. Lally and Gabriel were out of the running now; Susan and Nick and Tom and, I suppose, Miriam, were successful, and *I* could laugh at myself – the refuge I suppose of those who had never quite made it, but a more comfortable position!

It must have been about six months after I had received a short note from Miriam Cooper, thanking me for my letter and saying she was *fine and busy, though it has been a blow, I can't deny it*, that I had an unexpected telephone call.

'I'd like to speak to Gillian Noble,' said a faintly trans-atlantic voice.

246

'Speaking,' I said, cross because I had been in the middle of washing my hair. We were going to the university to one of their infrequent faculty parties that evening.

'Is that you, Gillian? It's Nick Varley here.'

'Nick! Here in England?' I stammered, completely thrown.

'Not only in GB but here in Yorkshire,' he said. 'My mother died – I've been over for the funeral – I thought I'd look a few people up.'

'Oh, I'm sorry – about your mother,' I said. 'Is your father still alive?'

'Oh yes, Dad is still functioning, more or less. I've left him with his sister who's going to look after him. But I'd like to see you if you can spare the time – what about a drink in the Great Northern in Woolsford? I'm staying there till the day after tomorrow. Thought I'd better catch up on everything.'

He sounded very cool, just as he always had, and except for the slight American accent, just the same.

'All right,' I replied rather ungraciously. 'Tomorrow – I expect I can get away for an hour or two. Where shall I meet you?'

'I'll be in the hotel foyer – about six? I can drive you back. I've rented a car. You live near the university?'

'Yes. Thank you. All right. I'll be there. I can take a taxi back home though.'

'I think we have a lot to talk about,' he said. 'I'm glad you can come. See you then.' He put the phone down and I sat down myself feeling weak at the knees. Why hadn't I thought to ask him home for a meal? No, Nick didn't belong in Arthur's house. Stupid, I admonished myself, it's your house too!

I spent the next day, apart from the usual chores, trying to decide what to wear. But why should I bother?

Yes, he did look older was my first thought. And a little tired. The bar was almost deserted and we had a corner table to ourselves. He was dressed in a linen jacket and a shirt with a button-down collar and he had that tidy look academic Americans have. I noticed his teeth were capped and his hair was shorter than I remembered it, but still blond. We sat down and he went to the bar and after enquiry brought me my usual vermouth and soda with a slice of lemon and ice. I love The

247

Great Northern. Built in the 1860s it is still the best hotel in the city, and all its rooms are spacious and comfortable. I felt immediately at ease with Nick there, in spite of everything and all the years that had gone by – and Lally.

He took a sip and then put his glass down and looked at me without saying anything for a time. Then: 'You haven't changed,' he said.

I knew I had – for one thing I was a stone heavier than the last time he'd seen me. I didn't know whether he really thought I had not changed in appearance or was just being polite. Perhaps he looked beyond my now less prominent cheekbones and thickened waist to some essence of Gillian. But that might be giving him too much percipience or even interest in me. I had never worried how he might have looked at me as an individual, even thought I had been a pleasant bed-companion, and even friend. Once in Spain when I was plastering my face in Max Factor pancake in the way we used to, he had said, 'You don't need that – the sun makes your face brown.' Little did he realize that my skin without it looked rather greasy. He had liked my bright lipsticks though. I stifled a sigh, remembering days when I could have dispensed with additional adornments. I still wore make-up and I suppose that for my age I was reasonably unwrinkled. Nick must be a connoisseur of women's faces and persons by now. In the old days he'd been more concerned with my legs and ankles, having the habit of encircling the latter with his thumb and forefinger and then grinning up at me. . . . What silly things one remembered – even that he had once said he liked my rather boyish thighs. Well, he wouldn't like them so well now. I should be thinking about *him*, not about me, yet little memories still stirred somewhere in my brain, the sort of memories it would only embarrass Nick to remember, I felt.

'More than twenty years,' I said aloud, thinking about Spain.

'It's a long time,' he said.

I watched him and compared his face with the younger Nick's. He was just as good-looking, perhaps even more so, but there was less of the nervous energy I remembered and the eyes were more hooded; the blond hair had grey in it.

'Do I pass muster?' he enquired.

'You look rather American,' I said, for want of anything less personal to say. Here before me was the cause of all Lally's misery. I had to mention her name soon.

'Tell me all about you,' he said.

'There's nothing to say about me – I've two boys and am Happily Married.' I essayed quotation marks in the air. There was a long silence between us.

I was just going to say – I know about Lally and you all those years ago – when he said, 'I went to see them in London, you know – Lally's father and her stepmother.' My heart seemed to miss a beat. He put his glass down and waited for me to say something, but he also had the look of a man back in some dream trying to remember what it was he must not forget. His forehead puckered with the effort.

'I only knew about you and her when I read her diary – last year,' I said.

'Do you blame *me* then? You do, don't you? For what she did? What diary?'

'I blame myself for not guessing, and you for not telling me –'

'I never lied,' he said.

'It was because she was a friend of mine – if it had been anyone else – but when we were in Spain – *and* after. . . .' I didn't feel coy talking about Spain, hoped I looked sufficiently changed for him to realize I regarded it (did I?) as past history.

'I'm sorry,' he said. 'But I was attracted to you, Juliana, you know. And it was good, wasn't it?' He was blatant, smiled at me.

'I thought it had been, till I knew about Lally. But even when you were in London, that Sunday when I had to leave you, perhaps I wasn't so sure.'

'I went to see her before I left the UK, you know. I didn't promise anything, I shouldn't have gone. You can't marry someone because she'll go mad if you don't.'

'Lally wasn't mad, Nick. She was just depressed.'

'Not when I first saw her! I had loved her – been in love with her. I didn't know about what had happened later when I'd cast adrift. She'd seemed OK when I left her that January. She wasn't even a worrier. I knew she'd been unhappy in '57 when I'd parted from her – we went back together for a bit afterwards. But it just became impossible.'

249

I thought of all the miseries, the depressions, the break-downs, Lally had endured, the whole failure of her life. For him all summed up in one word: impossible.

'You think I should be brought to account?' he said. 'In the old days her father would have horsewhipped me – taking a girl's virginity and making love to her for five years – on and off – then, knowing it couldn't go on for ever, leaving her because it *was* over. It was over. She couldn't see that.'

'What good are we to each other, men and women?' I said. 'It isn't only women who can be the victims of emotional havoc.'

'No, I know. What about you afterwards? I know you married and had a child –'

'I've been married twice, and I have *two* children. I divorced again last year.'

'*You've* been in love again then?'

'You might call it that.' He paused, lit a thin cigar. 'We took advantage of each other, Lally and I,' he said. 'She wasn't averse to being made love to – she was a lovely girl though. I couldn't believe it when Mother wrote to me about the suicide. I'd had an odd letter from her – I just wrote back to say I was married.'

'You were the love of her life,' I said. 'To make up for the derelictions of her mother. If she'd married you, wouldn't she have been quite normal? Nick, she did *kill* herself you know. Lally would have stayed married for ever with you.'

'Do you think I haven't thought about it, wondered if it were my fault?'

I didn't quite trust him. I'd always considered him a strong man but now there seemed to be a slight air of self-pity about him.

'I thought you were both cynical and romantic – always looking for excitement.'

'I've had plenty of that. I know I was selfish with Lally, but we were kind to each other too. It wasn't my fault. That's easy to say, I know, but I truly don't believe it was my fault that she reacted as she did. Weren't we lucky to have had each other for so long?' He looked at his drink, then back at me. 'Now it seems bathed in a golden haze – those years. Do you remember that Christmas when we all sang carols at Tom's? Lally could hide things too. She never told a soul and in those days girls didn't leap into bed with young men quite so easily.'

'I wish she *had* confided in someone – Gabriel guessed, I think. He was awfully kind to her.'

'God, wasn't that a terrible thing; my mother sent me the report of the trial –'

'I think Gabriel chose his death as much as Lally did.'

We were both silent. There was nothing to say about that and perhaps there was nothing to say about Lally either, except, what a waste.

'I wanted to see *you* as well, not just to talk about *her*,' he said.

'We had to talk about her. Ever since I read what she said about you – I wasn't sure if any of us would see you again – I wanted to talk about her.'

'She could have taken her pick you know – later,' he said. 'They were all after her. Being loved by someone like that – I wasn't old enough to realize what I was letting myself in for.'

'But she was brave, I think, to take you as she did – she was so young – she just followed it through and it didn't lead where she thought it would or ought to have done. She wasn't "ordinary", Nick. In many ways she was – and simple and kind, but her looks were not, and I suppose once she'd got you under her skin –'

'Tom ought to have got her,' he said. 'I used to think that –'

'And now he's left Miriam and is living with a girl of twenty-two with blonde hair and green eyes,' I said. Nick lifted his eyebrows.

'I didn't know that.'

'So everything changes: *tout passe, tout casse, tout lasse*,' I said.

'A quotation for everything, Juliana,' said Nick and went on, 'I never wanted to marry *anyone* till I went to the States – my first wife was a beauty too. I thought then I could forget all other women. But you don't. Or at least I don't. Not till afterwards when that one's finished – then you find another and then in the end she becomes just one of the women you've loved or thought you did.' It all sounded depressing.

'I think I must have decided romantic passion wasn't worth it but there are different sorts of men too,' I said.

251

'Yes, the happily married sort – all part of life's rich pageant, I suppose – or, more like a kaleidoscope that shifts every time you move.'

'You never used to be so reflective.'

'I'm not usually. Or not to other people. Sex and friendship are better answers than love I think now, but I know I'll want more, one day again.'

'I think that, whatever we do, things are in the saddle – and ride us.'

'You're a fatalist then – doesn't sound like you.'

'About some things I suppose. People's characters and the way they were brought up, making them act in a certain way.'

'I didn't even know, wasn't sure whether I even dare mention her name to you when I rang you on Wednesday, then as soon as I saw you I knew I would be able to . . . she was so serious, Gillian, and so naïve. What did she say in this letter she wrote? Who has it now?'

'Not a letter, a sort of diary she began, to cure herself. Susan has it – she left it to Susan. Lally said it was nobody's fault.'

'I suppose it *was* my reply that tipped her over? Did she keep my letter?'

'No, there was nothing there from you except she said that she had heard from you and you were married – it was almost the last thing she wrote.'

'And I was divorced a few years later! But I couldn't have made her happy.'

I wasn't sure if he meant his first wife or Lally Cecil.

'When she was not ill Lally enjoyed life,' I said. 'She didn't bother what other people thought, did she? Like her mother, I suppose. She always wore her mother's ring,' I added. 'She always looked so virginal too. I remember at a party at Tom's how she looked, shining and happy; it must have been one of the times you went back to her.'

'It was so easy to make her happy,' he said. 'Shall I fetch you another drink?'

When he went up to the bar I looked at his slim back and purposeful movements and thought, once I had that man in my arms. He was happy then with me – a pleasant sexual romp I suppose he thinks it was. . . . Talking about the past, thinking about how I had once been . . . was I going to indulge in some retrospective jealousy? He had Lally for five years and I'd slotted in for a few weeks and a few days with all the other women he'd doubtless been to bed with by then and made rather happy, and then miserable. I'd never made any demands on Nick and so I could now be his friend. Was that how it worked? No wonder he'd enjoyed it with me after escaping from Lally's miseries.

Yet twenty years had made our little time together stand out from other experiences for me. How he saw it I did not want to ask. I hadn't waited for Nick Varley, had passed long years thinking about other things, doing other things. Now here he was again. I thought, he's paid for whatever he's done – he's not happy himself. But my time with Nick was something I'd never ever felt guilty about until Lally's revelation. What had he once said? 'I don't think I can love anybody,' and had gone on to 'love' many women.

'Off you went,' I said, when he had handed me another vermouth, saying 'Sure you don't want something stronger?' 'Off you went, to be ruthless I expect, and successful, and off I went, and off Miriam went to have babies. Susan too – she's got a lovely little girl, though she never married. Sarah is nearly eight.'

'Gabriel's child?'

'Of course.'

'Poor Old Mystic,' he said. 'But Susan's all right, isn't she?'

'Susan is very all right as far as a woman can be whose lifelong love has been murdered. Have you read her novels?'

'Not much time for novel reading – I've seen them at home though.'

I realized he meant America.

'I wish we could all be reincarnated for a second go,' I said, 'knowing all we do now, so that we could act better next time.'

'But where should we start from? Not very logical. How would you act differently?'

'I always felt guilty about things – towards my father, you know, for not having his religious beliefs and his code of conduct. Towards Miriam for not believing in her political ideas. No God, and no political creed. But till recently I'd never felt guilty about the way I'd behaved with people. *You* never made me feel guilty when we were together. When

I knew about Lally and you it changed that little bit of the past.'

'We were well suited you and I,' he said.

I knew that if I ever let myself be attracted to Nick Varley again I'd feel guilty towards Arthur and that was something I was not prepared to feel. Yet I *was* attracted, in spite of myself.

'You always said I was a bourgeoise – I suppose you were right.'

'Did I? What an insufferable little twerp I was.'

'Very sure of yourself though.'

'And now you know the ghastly truth. Do you know, I can't even feel really sorry about my mother. Father led her a dog's life, but he's mellowed in his old age. My little brother is a successful businessman and that pleases him no end. He's always saying I should come back to England, but I shan't, you know.'

'Will you marry again?' I asked him. 'Are your children ever with you?'

A cloud came over his face. 'I have access and I pay maintenance and alimony. The girl, Victoria, is twelve and the boy, Alexander, is only four. I'm afraid I've mucked up both their lives, like I did Lally's.' He paused. 'You know, with Lally it was true grief I felt when I knew she was dead. I'd tried to be kind in my letter. I said I'd married, and hoped she would, and that I'd always remember her and that she shouldn't regret us either. We'd been too young; it was my fault how it had turned out – all those things you say when you can't say the truth. The grief, though, I hadn't expected. As though something had been working away in a subterranean fashion for years, then the shock jolted it up and took me over. It had something to do with the failure of my first marriage. My wife was even jealous of my past.'

'Was she a Southern belle?'

'Yes, how did you know?'

'I read the announcement in the Yorkshire *Gazette*. None of us thought to tell Lally. It was just about the time her grandmother died. We were worried Mrs Fortescue's death might tip her over again.'

'Lally's dying made me *feel* again,' he went on. 'Really feel.

Do you think we only feel things years after they've happened, or is it just me? I envy people who can cry at funerals.'

'I understand,' I said.

'I haven't had such a conversation with anyone for a long time, Juliana,' he said. For some reason his saying that name again made me feel like crying myself. I wished I were young again.

'I cried for Lally, Nick, more even than I cried for Gabriel. You did love her,' I said, 'even if in the end you weren't right for each other. You *did* love Lally.'

'For two or three years. You know young men – lusts growing hot and damp like orchids, most unhealthy. It was better to love Lally than that, wasn't it? She was so fresh and open – and seemed free. Not cool and dry and frightened like so many young girls are. I didn't deserve her. At the time I thought I was God's gift to girls.'

'You were her first man, I suppose that's always important for a girl like her.'

'Her skin tasted like lemons,' he said. 'God, I *can* remember. It was so smooth. She was a dream of a girl, always willing, always welcoming. I even used to wish later you know – and this sounds wrong – that sex didn't get in the way of just being happy with her. Other times I was glad when it did. I'm sorry, Gillian, do you mind my talking like this about her? There's no one else I could talk to about it.'

I swallowed hard. 'She said she felt like a bird with you – in her diary – that with nobody else did she feel like that. She was lucky.'

'It was unnerving,' he said.

'I keep seeing you and her together at The Holm. I wonder how I would have reacted if I'd known about her and you – been envious I suppose – not, not because it was you, but because there was a girl who went straight as an arrow for what she wanted. So did you.'

'Yet Lally was a passive sort of person – it sounds as though she was a go-getter when you put it like that. If you'd known about her and me I don't think it would have made any difference in Spain. We didn't know then she was going to have breakdowns, did we? Anyway, you're a survivor, Juliana.'

255

'That's what Susan called her best book, *Surviving*.'

'Well, you wouldn't think there was something wrong with *you* if a man didn't want to go on with you or if he didn't love you, would you?'

'No! I'd be surprised if he did. I was surprised when my husband declared himself.'

'I don't know if staying married is a matter for commiseration or congratulation. But you look contented – settled.'

'Settled, oh dear, I suppose I am. What more has life to offer?'

'I should have married *you*,' he said and cast a long meditative look at me and then smiled, and I smiled.

I wasn't going to upbraid him any more about Lally. Her ghost had been laid. 'She just needed loving,' was all I said.

'I know,' he said.

'And you were too young. She wasn't.'

I knew it had been in his head as sure as I knew anything that for one moment he'd had the notion that he might invite me up to his room. In spite of everything. For old times' sake. Because we had colluded, if unconsciously. He was not a wicked man. I was sure that women had often loved him, that there might be other Lallys in his life even now, but not as important in the end because she was the first, and inimitable.

I could see also that he had at least one more marriage in him.

Perhaps next time it would work.

'Love!' he said. 'She was a simple girl and simple girls are dangerous.'

After that I tried to lighten the conversation.

I told him that there was a possibility Arthur might have a Sabbatical in the States. If he did we might both see him. It would have to be *both* now. This was to be the last conversation of this kind we were ever to have. I was determined about that. I knew danger when I saw it. Yet I did like him. I didn't ask him home. Home was not the place to go after such a talk.

'You must look me up, both of you,' he said. 'Whenever your husband and you come over.'

I showed him the photos of Dominic and Richard and he showed me one of his daughter and he had one more drink. It was getting dark as we came out of the bar and he took my arm, then put his arm around me. He kissed me quite gently when we said goodbye.

I told Arthur quite a lot of our conversation, and Susan later. 'He doesn't sound to have changed much,' she said.

People often say they don't want to be young again, that it was a miserable time for them. I don't agree. I would like to be eleven years old once more, though perhaps not fifteen. I enjoyed being eleven, with that feeling of all the world before me. Even if I had to live all my life again and make the same mistakes, I think I would do it.

I often wondered about Tom and Miriam's children, and Nick's too. Sarah Benson was growing into a beautiful child with Gabriel's thick, dark brown hair. She was going to be tall; you could tell that even at nine years old. I loved both my own children. Love for your children is quite different from other sorts of love – I sometimes think we should have another word for it. People call it a possessive love and there is always a little of that till they grow up, however hard you try to avoid it. But it is also an unselfish love, not wanting anything for yourself, but for them – and then you will be happy for them and with them.

Arthur and I and the boys went over to Wynteredge sometimes on a Sunday for Arthur vowed he must spend Sundays with his family. The administrative work was getting too much, taking up all his weekends. So we went to see Mother, or to Eastcliff, and Arthur did more work on weekday evenings. Sometimes I saw the children of people I was at school with, people whose names and faces I'll always remember. Josephine Cooper's six of course, and now Miriam's sister Rachel's offspring for Rachel had come back to the place. The other twin, Ruth, emigrated to Israel. Sometimes if it were fine Arthur took the boys for a walk in our old woods and left Susan with me to talk. Sarah went with Arthur. She was a very sociable girl and always pleased to see us. Susan still worried lest she had too lonely a life and no fun, since her mother was always busy. But I told her this was nonsense. Sarah had heaps of friends – and her grandparents – to talk to and always seemed to me most well-balanced and quite accepting her mother's story-writing. The years go by so quickly. Soon Sarah would be at the old grammar school in Lightholme where her father had been. It was now open to girls as well as boys though it had become a fee-paying independent school. The sixthformers didn't have to meet on the Stray any more since they were in classes together. Often the older ones went to school in their own cars. *Tempora mutantur* again.

We were in Eastcliff last spring when warm weather suddenly arrived in a rush of green, bringing with it the sound of water from the brook that still feeds the Wynteredge pastures. Scattered armies of crocuses, white and gold, mauve and purple stood in the grass by the side of the long winding drive at Priestley, but now the Lent lilies were displacing them: small, slender white-trumpeted daffodils that came every year with their faint waxy scent. I had seen Gabriel's grave in all seasons. In summer the Zéphyrine Drouhins, and the three Cornelia roses they planted from the Canon's own stock wafted the buttery smell from their pink blossomings across the grass. In the autumn a few Michaelmas daisies crept over from some garden and their colour was smoky blue against the headstone. Susan did not often talk of Gabriel; she spoke more often to me of her latest book. Her next was to be called *Spring at Wynteredge*, a non-fiction book for a change, which gathered together some of her occasional pieces that had now appeared in the *Gazette* for over twenty years. Times were changing, *she* said, and she thought she should bow out gracefully from her journalism now that her books had all been reprinted in paperback and were bringing more royalties. There was even talk of a film of one of her books. She talked to me of the actual difficulty of writing and all the cutting and clipping and darning and smoothing down that was necessary to produce the tapestry she wanted. 'It is like making a garment,' she said.

Susan and I were sitting on the wall at Wynteredge the year after Nick's visit to England when she suddenly began to speak to me of Gabriel. I was glad she was talking about him again.

'Sometimes the need to see him again overwhelms me,' she said. 'I feel like a child who is crying and crying for someone to come and comfort it after a nightmare, but they don't hear, and nobody comes.'

'Oh, Susan,' I said. 'I am sorry – I expect you will always feel it – it's dreadful.'

The sky was blue that day though there was still a nip in the breeze up there. I looked across to the church and the graveyard where trees were just beginning to veil the building with a soft green.

'And yet he was never in love with me,' she said. I waited, staring at her. Her face was in profile, her coat collar up and she looked into some far distance, not at me.

'He was always hopelessly in love with *her*,' she said. 'Not with me. He liked me, loved me even, but he was never in love with me. Not like he was, always had been – with *her*.'

'Who?' I asked stupidly and she turned her face towards me.

'Why, Lally of course,' she said.

I caught my breath, stared at her. She looked quite calm, rather sorrowful.

'Ever since we used to meet on the Stray. He worshipped her, never told her. It was hopeless. She only wanted Nick. I've always known. I knew I could wait for him.'

'But – if that's true, why didn't he ever tell her?'

'Gabriel wasn't like that,' she said and jumped down from the wall and took my arm. I squeezed hers and we walked across the field to the lane that curved up back towards her own front porch. She seemed to want to go on talking.

'He idolized her after she died. When I had read what she had written, he told me he'd always known about her and Nick.'

'Why didn't he rescue her then? He could have done later, couldn't he?'

'Oh, no. He was a fatalist. He thought one day she might love him. She never did, thought of him just as that sweet man, so kind, who went to visit her when he could to cheer her up.'

'But you *were* going to marry in the end, you and he?'

'Oh yes. But it took him a long time to decide. The memory of her was always with him. I think he knew I'd always known. Then you see there were all those years before, when he was studying – and after that. He knew I loved him and he did accept it. But I knew I'd have to wait till he got her out of his system. And, too, there was the struggle he was having against that nihilism of his – it was a noble struggle. He never resolved it – Milfred Lumb resolved it for him.'

She didn't say it bitterly.

I thought again, the virtuous man at the hands of unreason. Father's words.

'He was always saying one should not judge others. He had not had to suffer as the victims he knew had suffered. Even Lally. Often suffering inflicted upon the next generation, like Lally's mother. And I often wonder what Lumb's child is like now. . . .'

'Gabriel was a good man,' I said.

'Yes, he was a good man. But he hated Nick and was ashamed of his hatred. He wanted Lally to come to him when she came to York, but he never asked her to, just waited. I knew she never would. When she died, Gillian, I couldn't help thinking – How long will it take for him to exorcize her and come to me properly? I'd waited a long time. I understood his despair too. He never talked to Lally about things like that. She wouldn't have understood. To her, despair was a personal thing, something wrong with your life, not with the world. Gabriel said that he despaired that a world had been created where no Christ – no God – existed to redeem the misery and the suffering; no life after death where sinners could be punished; no meaning in any of it. So he tried to do his best with the sinners, you see. Then, that last Christmas, I think he had been dreaming of her, I don't know, but he said he was going to gamble with faith, go back to the Church. It was necessary that God existed, or nothing else made sense to him. He always thought of himself as a sinner although he was the least sinful man you could imagine. I think he'd decided to give up Lally in his heart, Gillian, to make the biggest sacrifice he could . . .'

'But she was dead ! She'd been dead – how many years?'

'Six years, and he was still thinking about her, that he'd failed her . . . I think. But I knew the time had come for me at last. He'd made love to me before, though sometimes he said he felt it was wrong. I could bear that. Then we made love the day he went back to take Communion. He saw it as something sacred.' She stopped and looked at me. 'I suppose I was wicked to do it, but I wanted to be sure . . .'

'So you got yourself pregnant! Clever Susan,' I said, and laughed.

'I know, but he asked me on Boxing Day to marry him and we talked about a wedding. He was very quiet, rather exalted. I knew he'd finally stopped thinking about her. And Sarah was conceived. You know the rest. It was Gabriel who was punished, not me.'

'You don't really believe that! Punished for what?'

'*I* don't believe it, but *he* would. When that man – attacked him – he put up no defence. I do believe he thought it was a sign from the Lord.'

'But that sounds as though he were mad. Gabriel wasn't mad.' I was shaken.

'No, but everything had to *mean* something for him. Even when we were still seventeen or so and he heard her and Nick at The Holm he thought it meant that if she loved someone else and could not be his at that time, if he waited she would turn to him. By a sort of magic, I think. He never told her how he felt about her, and she never did know.'

'It seems scarcely credible to me.'

'He heard them at The Holm,' she repeated. 'When he went back for a book. They were upstairs. He was not surprised, not shocked even, but he was worried about Lally in an ordinary sort of way. He always said she was vulnerable, didn't he? That she craved love?'

'Why did he never speak to Nick?'

'It wasn't his business on that level. He should have told him that taking on a girl like Lally was a terrible responsibility, but you can imagine how Nick would have reacted if he'd said anything of the sort to him.'

'Lally surrendered herself completely,' I said. 'Like Gabriel would have done, I suppose, but he did love you, Susan. I've seen you together so many times. You were the right person for him.'

'And he for me so long as I was strong. But that's the reason why we waited so long – too long – he didn't want to commit himself till he was absolutely sure of himself. He wanted things to be for ever, you see,' she said after a pause. 'In the end he would rely on me to make them so.'

'Did the having to wait make you a writer do you think?'

'It certainly took my mind off it,' she answered with a smile.

I was thinking how admirable a person Susan was, how I would not have waited all those years for marriage to a man who could not make up his mind or get the idea of another woman out of his system. Or was it that I had never loved anyone enough to do that? Susan had had a bit of sense though, I thought, making finally sure of her man by conceiving his child, except the man had died.

'If Gabriel had lived,' I said, 'he would have loved Sarah so much. All the past would have melted away once you were married and had children.'

'I always hoped that would have happened,' she said, 'but I can't be sure. I ask him sometimes in my head, tell him things, talk to him about Sarah.' I thought, love has not ruined or diminished my friend. I would like to have asked her if she had had to choose between having Gabriel marry her in her twenties and not achieving success as a writer, which she would have chosen. But that is the sort of question nobody, not even an inquisitive old friend, is allowed to ask.

We walked up the lane and back to the house in silence and we did not ever speak of the matter of Gabriel and Lally again.

Later that year Arthur applied again for another promotion. He was both pleased and a little fearful when he succeeded in being appointed to a professorship in London. It would mean leaving all our northern life and he was more worried about how I would feel about it than on his own account. But it was a wonderful opportunity, I said. I'd like now to return to London in my sober middle age, provided we could find decent schools for the boys without completely draining our financial resources. We'd be mortgaged up to the hilt in any case as the price difference then between our rather large house in Leeds and the smaller house we wanted in Hampstead Garden Suburb, was in the early Eighties, immense. But things were sorted out and soon it was almost time to leave. We had been anxious about my mother for she did not wish to live in London. Fortuitously, Rosemary's husband who was now a primary school head put in for transfer to a village school in the Dales. It was not far from Mother – and not too near – so that was satisfactory to all.

But before our move in the August, we decided to leave the boys with Rosemary for a week in the country, and go abroad for a few days – all the time we could spare, for this summer there'd be no Brittany holiday for us. Arthur asked me to choose where I should like to go and so I went with my husband, finally, to that Catalan city where I had been a quarter of a century earlier. And the names were now in Catalan; and we walked across the Placa de Catalunya and the Avinguda del Paralell – and also made many sorties down the familiar Ramblas. It had changed a lot but still to me preserved its charm, though its noise and its heat seemed even more in evidence. A great cosmopolitan city, new buildings going up everywhere and everything costing about a hundred times as much as formerly. But there were still the flower stalls and the birds and the great old buildings in the Gothic quarter. Arthur had some business for a colleague in the Archives of the Crown of Aragon, so I walked alone one afternoon to what had once been called the Calle de Paris and was now the Carrer de Paris and stood outside the pavement of the apartment block where I had stayed with Nick. The sun beat down on me as I looked up at the balcony from which we had looked out over the streets of the city, and there I said my farewells to my memories of that past. One day Arthur and I would visit America and might even see Nick there, but that would be after I'd started a new life in London.

When I got back to Yorkshire I went one last afternoon to Eastcliff to say goodbye to Susan and to the village. Leeds had never quite seemed home in the way that Eastcliff always had. The village will always be 'home' to me if home is the place that comes before your eyes when you fall asleep. To my children Leeds would be replaced now by something very different, and one day perhaps they would return north. But for the present there was a new life waiting for all of us. Once we were settled in London I had plans for taking another degree – and writing that book on culture and anarchy and what schools should be for, a nice reactionary tract.

I walked round the village before I went over to Susan's,

thinking of something Miriam used to say, 'It'll all be the same in a hundred years.' I hoped that she had been able to live up to her own philosophical outlook. It wouldn't 'all be the same'. Nothing ever was. In one hundred years we shouldn't be there. Nor even Dominic, or Richard, or Sarah. Wynteredge would be there, I thought. I believed the house would stay standing if nothing else did. And I hoped too that Susan's books would still be in the world.

'We are going to live in London,' I told the inhabitants I met who still knew me, and they expressed mild interest, but obviously did not envy me. Saying goodbye to Eastcliff was easier said than done. I walked down by The Holm, still a nursing home for the widows of businessmen. The lawn was mown close; the tennis courts had long ago disappeared.

I passed by the much enlarged school, empty that afternoon as the children and teachers were still on their summer holidays. There Susan and I and the others had begun our apprenticeship in both love and words, copying those magic signs that were letters, that made words, and made stories. . . .

In term-time now the children were ferried to and from it by mothers who seemed to spend their whole day coming and going. I went down by The Laurels too that afternoon. It had finally been bought by the owner of another micro-electronics firm that now stood where the old stoneworks had been.

The Snicket was much the same, but the old 'haunted house' of our childhood had been pulled down now, and there were plans afoot for new buildings. The handsome pillars that had guarded the old Coach Road that wound round near The Nest had disappeared and the paving stones been vandalized. I passed Braemar Road where the Coopers no longer lived and where The Angel Gabriel and Tom-Tom and Old Nick had sung along with us. Little children were playing on the Stray accompanied by mothers who did not look much older than I had been when I left the village. Some children were on the new swings. The old 'rant' had been taken away as being too dangerous for modern children.

As I walked over to Wynteredge I felt I *was* finally the Outsider now, and the only one of us all who was still married to a first spouse. All the old alliances had split up or been forced apart. We knew the cost of love and the cost of marriage: solitude or solid mortgages, dreams displaced by marriage or children or death or time. Lally and Nick, Gabriel and Susan, Tom and Miriam . . . Nick by now with – I was sure – yet another love; Tom with his new Lally-like wife; myself with Arthur, who had never belonged to Eastcliff.

I wondered, as I walked up the hill in the direction of the grammar school, towards Susan, what was left to me and to her and to Miriam as we became middle-aged. A great deal, I hoped, surrounded as we all were by the rising generation. Our desires might have grown less imperative, less unruly, and perhaps we had toppled one sort of love from its high pedestal. Tell that to the girls who wait even now in this village, in every village, I thought. They will not believe you. You did not believe it till life forced its lessons upon you as though you were a character in some early Victorian improving morality tale, in which Lally, the beautiful princess, lost her Prince Charming too young and was destroyed, and in which the hero succumbed to bad magic.

I stood by Gabriel's grave again. The pink roses were in bloom, climbing once more the upright slab with his name and 1933–1971 incised on the plain stone. I noticed that the roses had no thorns, and it seemed to me as I stood there that Lally and Gabriel might return, with the ghost of a younger Susan and of my young self too, not as our actual selves but as wraiths of feelings hovering over the fields and the village below, mysterious clusters, meeting, mingling, exchanging ideal selves.

But I made my way to Wynteredge to say goodbye to the real Susan, knowing that I should find another of her stories on the typewriter, this time perhaps one that took something from us all and from our old loves.

Also available from Woman's Weekly Fiction

Jan Webster
Tallie's War

Tallie Candlish is put upon by her clever sister Kate, a pupil teacher and suffragette, and by spoiled Belle, the family beauty. Wilfred Chappell, a young English schoolteacher lodging in their Lanarkshire home, is attracted by Tallie's diffident manner and quiet beauty. He encourages her to put herself first for once and follow her ambition to train as a nurse – and promptly finds himself wishing he hadn't.

While suffragette Kate discloses a vulnerability that takes him by surprise, Tallie reveals a strength and single-mindedness he has never suspected. But when war breaks out she needs every ounce of that strength to bring her through the horrors of nursing the war-wounded and the devastating news that Wilfred is missing, presumed dead . . .

Further titles available from Woman's Weekly Fiction

While every effort is made to keep prices low, it is sometimes necessary to increase prices at short notice. Mandarin Paperbacks reserves the right to show new retail prices on covers which may differ from those previously advertised in the text or elsewhere.

The prices shown below were correct at the time of going to press.

☐ 1 86056 000 8	**A Place in the Sun**	Nina Lambert	£1.99
☐ 1 86056 005 9	**The Bellmakers**	Jean Chapman	£1.99
☐ 1 86056 010 5	**The Bridge Between**	Mary Williams	£1.99
☐ 1 86056 015 6	**Promise of Summer**	Rose Boucheron	£1.99
☐ 1 86056 020 2	**Tallie's War**	Jan Webster	£1.99
☐ 1 86056 025 3	**Time Will Tell**	June Barraclough	£1.99
☐ 1 86056 021 0	**Lucky Star**	Betty Paul	£1.99
☐ 1 86056 055 5	**With This Ring**	Jean Saunders	£1.99
☐ 1 86056 065 2	**A Captain's Lady**	Jennifer Wray Bowie	£1.99
☐ 1 86056 060 1	**Lily's Daughter**	Diana Raymond	£1.99

All these books are available at your bookshop or newsagent, or can be ordered direct from the address below. Just tick the titles you want and fill in the form below.

Cash Sales Department, PO Box 5, Rushden, Northants NN10 6YX.
Fax: 0933 414000 : Phone 0933 414047.

Please send cheque, payable to 'Reed Book Services Ltd', or postal order for purchase price quoted and allow the following for postage and packing:

£1.00 for the first book: £1.50 for two books or more per order.

NAME (Block letters) ....

ADDRESS ....

.... Postcode................................

☐ I enclose my remittance for £........................

☐ I wish to pay by Access/Visa Card Number

Expiry Date

☐ If you do not wish your name to be used by other carefully selected organisations for promotional purposes please tick this box.

Signature ....
Please quote our reference: 3 503 500 C

Orders are normally dispatched within five working days, but please allow up to twenty days for delivery.

Registered office: Michelin House, 81 Fulham Road, London SW3 6RB

Registered in England. No. 1974080